"I'm S⋯⋯⋯ he came near enough to extend his hand.

"Becky Dennison." She drew a shuddering breath. "Thank you for coming."

Scott nodded toward the house. "Is Haldeman…"

"He's in the barn. I didn't touch anything." Fresh tears sparkled in her eyes. "Maybe you can figure it out. He's right outside the back door."

Scott glanced down at Becky, whose eyes locked on his, wide with panic. Steeling himself, he gave her a brief smile. At the doorway, he took a deep breath before stepping inside. When he caught sight of the body, it blew out in a rush.

Gashes punctuated Haldeman's bare chest. A sharp instrument had inflicted those many wounds. No matter what that woman out there said, this was no accident. Haldeman had been murdered.

Books by Virginia Smith

Love Inspired Suspense

Murder by Mushroom #63
Bluegrass Peril #82

VIRGINIA SMITH

A lifelong lover of books, Virginia Smith has always enjoyed immersing herself in fiction. In her midtwenties she wrote her first story and discovered that writing well is harder than it looks; it took many years to produce a book worthy of publication. During the daylight hours she steadily climbed the corporate ladder and stole time late at night after the kids were in bed to write. With the publication of her first novel, she left her twenty-year corporate profession to devote her energy to her passion—writing stories that honor God and bring a smile to the faces of her readers. When she isn't writing, Ginny and her husband, Ted, enjoy exploring the extremes of nature—skiing in the mountains of Utah, motorcycle riding on the curvy roads of central Kentucky and scuba diving in the warm waters of the Caribbean. For more information visit www.VirginiaSmith.org.

Bluegrass
Peril

VIRGINIA
SMITH

Steeple
Hill®

Published by Steeple Hill Books™

STEEPLE HILL BOOKS

Steeple
Hill®

ISBN-13: 978-0-373-44272-0
ISBN-10:   0-373-44272-6

BLUEGRASS PERIL

www.SteepleHill.com

Printed in U.S.A.

I will put my law in their minds and write it
on their hearts. I will be their God,
and they will be my people.
                          —*Jeremiah* 31:33b

Acknowledgments

I'm thankful for the patience and expertise
of those who helped as I researched this book:
Mary Leigh Patrick, Michael Blowen, Paul Carter,
Trooper Ronald Turley, Anne Banks and
Phyllis Rogers at the Keeneland Library.
If I goofed on anything related to their areas
of expertise, it's not their fault.

I'm grateful to several people who have provided
invaluable feedback on this book. Thanks to
Susan Kroupa, Jill Elizabeth Nelson and the CWFI
Critique Group: Amy Barkman, Corinne Eldred,
Richard Leonard, Tracy Ruckman, Mary Yerkes
and Lani Zielsdorf.

Thanks to my agent, Wendy Lawton, and my editor,
Krista Stroever, who help me in more ways
than I can name.

Special thanks to my supportive family for loving
this book, especially: Christy Delliskave,
Susie Smith and my husband, Ted Smith.

And especially, thank You, Jesus. You know why.

Dedication

For my aunt, Mary Leigh Patrick, whose love for
her horses is an inspiration.

ONE

"Mommy, can we go to work with you and see the horses today?"

Becky Dennison licked a finger and smoothed an errant strand of Tyler's hair. "No, sweetheart. You have kindergarten today."

"Aw, man!" Tyler twisted in the high-backed chair and jerked away from her hand. "Do I hafta go? I got the meanest teacher in the whole world."

Becky carried her cereal bowl to the sink. She rinsed it and set it in the dishwasher, then returned to the small kitchen table where the twins sat finishing their breakfast.

"Miss Mallory is not mean." She gave Tyler a stern look. "You hurt her feelings when you told her she looked fat in those pants."

"But she did!"

Becky put her hands on her hips. "You don't say that to a lady. It's rude."

Across the table, Jamie's dark eyes, full of questions, looked up into hers. "You ask me and Tyler if you look fat all the time."

He looked so serious Becky worked hard to hide her smile. "That's different. I'm your mom. And Miss Mallory didn't ask." She turned back to Tyler. "She's a nice lady and a good teacher. If you would behave yourself like the gentleman I know you can be, you wouldn't get into trouble so often."

Tyler slumped in his chair, pouting. "Why can't I have Miss Peters? Jamie never gets yelled at."

Becky's gaze shifted toward the other twin. One of Jamie's hands busily played with a colorful action figure in a cape, the latest addition to his enormous collection of "men," as he called them. He fished the last bite of floating cereal out of his bowl with the spoon clutched in the other hand, and swallowed it with a loud gulp.

"Jamie, chew your food," she said automatically.

Tyler was right. Jamie never got into trouble at school. In fact, Miss Peters regularly sent home notes full of praise for his polite manners and excellent study habits. Notes from Miss Mallory set her teeth on edge. How could two boys who looked so much alike have such different personalities? Because they each took after a different parent.

Becky picked up Jamie's empty bowl and turned toward the sink, her back to the boys so they wouldn't see her grimace. Jamie was like her, quiet and introspective, except when his brother involved him in mischief. On the other hand, from birth Tyler had proven himself to be so much like his father it was almost frightening. He came into the world yelling and fighting, as though angry at his brother for being born first. From that moment, he seemed determined not to settle for second place ever again, and greedily demanded more than his fair share of everything—attention, milk, even space in the bassinet.

Becky set Jamie's bowl in the top rack beside her own and blew out a deep breath. She would not ruin this beautiful April day with thoughts of her ex-husband.

"You can't have Miss Peters because you have Miss Mallory," she told her youngest son. "Make the best of it."

Tyler folded his arms across his chest and slid farther down in the chair, his dark eyebrows drawn into a scowl. A typical Christopher expression. The resemblance between father and son struck her anew. In fact, both boys looked like their father, with his dark hair and eyes, his strong chin and chiseled nose. They were both good athletes, too, with tall, slender bodies that shed all traces of baby fat by their third year. Taking after Christopher in that respect was probably a good thing. She wouldn't wish her short, plump body and heart-shaped face on anyone.

Across the table, Jamie lifted his chin and smirked at his brother. "My teacher rocks."

"Jamie, don't be annoying," she scolded. He might be quiet at school, but Jamie wasn't a wimp. He could hold his own with his rowdy twin. "All right, boys, brush your teeth and get your backpacks. It's almost time to leave. Jamie, leave the men at home."

"Aw, Mom!"

Chairs scraped across the floor as the boys tumbled out of them. They ran from the room, and Becky swiped the table with a dishcloth, mentally planning her route to work. She had a couple of errands to do on the way this morning. She needed to stop for gasoline, and yesterday her boss, Neal, asked her to pick up some carrots. They had a tour scheduled at eleven o'clock, and the horses expected lots of carrots while the tourists gawked at them.

* * *

Forty minutes later, Becky turned from a two-lane country road onto the paved driveway of the old converted farmhouse where she worked. She noted with satisfaction the freshly painted letters of the wooden sign in the front yard: Out to Pasture, A Thoroughbred Retirement Farm. That faded sign had bugged her for the two months since she came to work here, and she finally took matters into her own hands and re-painted it a few days ago. It looked much better, nice, even. At the rear of the house she parked beside the boss's pickup, in front of the small barn where they stored supplies for their fifteen retired Thoroughbred champions.

She got out of the car and leaned against the open door to let her gaze sweep over the deep green Kentucky horse farm. Double rows of black plank fencing divided gently rolling swells of pasture. Heavy dew clung to the grass, sparkling in the sunlight on this crisp spring morning. She turned and looked across the road, where the mares with their foals were pastured. The babies hung close to their mothers today. Sometimes they ran and frolicked, and Becky loved to watch their graceful movements as they stretched their limbs and tested their limits. They seemed to know they were a special breed among horses. Thoroughbreds. Born to run, to train as elite equine athletes, and perhaps even to win that coveted Kentucky prize, a blanket of roses.

Becky leaned into the car and snatched the bag of carrots from the passenger seat. A muted bark reached her ears, and she glanced toward the back door of the farm-house that served as the retirement farm's office and founder Neal Haldeman's home. The wooden door stood open, indicating the boss was already out and about, as usual. But Neal's yellow Labrador retriever stood on hind legs inside the house, his front paws pressed against the glass storm door, barking. Odd. Neal always let Sam out first thing in the morning. Why was the dog still inside? Becky scanned the paddocks, but saw no sign of her boss. He must be in the barn. She slammed the car door and headed toward the house.

Galloping hooves thundered behind her, accompanied by a loud whinny. She turned to see Alidor racing across the turf toward her. Her pulse picked up speed, pounding in rhythm with the sound of his hooves. He arrived at the black plank fence, turned sideways and came to a quick stop.

Alidor frightened her. He was the biggest of the champions at the Pasture, and the meanest. No stallion was nice, according to Neal, but Alidor's fiery personality and aggressive behavior had scared even him when the horse first arrived. Becky stayed as far away from Alidor as she could, and he ignored her completely.

But not this morning. Alidor continued to whinny, his ears pinned almost flat to his head, his lips pulled back to show his teeth and gums. She had never heard that loud, high-pitched sound from any of the horses. Her stomach tightened at the urgency in the stallion's tone.

Surely Neal would hear and come to investigate. She glanced at the barn. Seeing no movement, she took a hesitant step toward the agitated horse.

"What's wrong, Alidor?"

Alidor tossed his head and pawed the ground with a front hoof. Becky took a few more steps. Maybe he smelled the carrots. Should she offer him one? Her heart thudded with fear. He had been known to bite, and was one of the stallions Neal would not let visitors feed.

Besides, he didn't look hungry or as if he was demanding a treat. He looked distressed.

Swallowing against a dry throat, Becky drew closer to the disturbed animal. She kept her voice low, the way Neal did when he talked to the stallions.

"It's okay, Alidor. Whatever it is, I'll find Neal and he'll take care of it."

As she neared the fence, she could see the rear of the barn. The back door stood open.

"Neal?" she called in that direction. "Something's wrong with Alidor. Are you in there?"

Nothing.

In the next paddock, Rusty Racer ran to the nearest corner and took up Alidor's cry. And behind Alidor's paddock, Founder's Fortune also began to call out in a loud whinny. Ten feet in front of her Alidor tossed his head repeatedly, white showing all around the intense dark depths of his eye.

The skin on her neck prickled at the sound in stereo. She'd only worked at the Pasture for two months, and she had never seen the horses act this way. Whatever was wrong with Alidor was getting to the others, as well, and she didn't have a clue what to do. Where was Neal?

"Neal!" Her voice, sharp with worry, sliced through the cool morning air like a blade.

His cell phone. Yes, that's what she'd do, she'd call his cell phone. She ran toward the barn. That extension was closer than the phone in the office. Alidor trotted along the fence, keeping pace with her, whinnying as he ran.

Rounding the corner, she shot through the open barn door. Inside, she tripped over something and landed facedown on the dirt floor with a hard thud. The bag of carrots flew out of her hand.

"What in the world?" She rolled over to see what had tripped her.

And screamed.

Neal lay in the dust, a pool of dark liquid beneath his head.

Outside the barn, Alidor and the other horses fell silent.

TWO

Scott Lewis paused, his pitchfork full of manure-laden straw. What was that noise? It sounded like a scream in the distance, coming from the direction of the Pasture. He strained his ears to filter through the normal morning sounds of the farm. One of the stallions over there had been agitated all morning, but Scott knew Neal Haldeman could handle it.

The horse was quiet now, and he didn't hear anything else. The scream probably came from one of the peacocks over at the Hart place down the road. Pesky nuisances.

Scott went back to his chore. Mucking stalls wasn't part of his job description as assistant manager at Shady Acres farm, but he took pleasure in the mundane task and gave the boys a hand every so often. He enjoyed the chance to stretch his muscles, and the earthy smell of the barn brought back vivid memories of performing this same task as a boy alongside his father. Horse manure did not stink, not like cattle or pigs. Instead, the rich odor, reminiscent of sweet grasses, fertile soil and horse sweat, tickled his nostrils and settled a sense of contentment deep inside.

The phone on the far wall, an extension of Shady Acres' private line, dinged once. In the next instant, the cell phone on Scott's belt vibrated. Scott sighed. Marion over in the office must have forgotten to take it off forward when she came to work this morning.

He unclipped the phone and looked at the caller ID display. Uh-oh. Out to Pasture. His gaze went automatically through the wide-open barn doors and across the acres of fencing in the direction of the retirement farm. He flipped the cover open.

"Lewis here."

"H-hello? Is this M-Mr. Courtney?"

The voice on the other end was female, and tearful. Scott's grip on the phone tightened. Maybe that wasn't a peacock's scream after all.

"No, this is Scott Lewis, Lee Courtney's assistant manager. Can I help you with something?"

"I d-don't know. It's Neal. He's…he's dead!"

Her voice rose into a high-pitched sob. Scott's jaw went slack. Haldeman dead?

"How?"

The woman gasped a few shuddering breaths. "Some kind of accident, I think. There's a lot of blood. I called 9-1-1, but the horses…I don't know what to do."

Scott remembered now. Haldeman had hired a woman over at the Pasture not long ago, someone to answer the phone and schedule appointments, things like that. Zach Garrett, Scott's boss, made a sly comment at the time that she must be one fantastic secretary, because she didn't know a thing about Thoroughbreds. Knowing Haldeman's reputation with the ladies, Scott figured the woman's qualifications probably had nothing to do with horses.

"I'll be right over," he said into the phone.

"But Mr. Courtney should be told."

"I'll call him."

* * *

Minutes later, Scott turned the farm truck into the driveway of the Pasture. Sirens wailed in the distance. You had to hand it to Davidson County EMS. They were certainly on the ball.

He pulled the truck onto the grass in front of the house. A parade of official vehicles was sure to crowd the driveway soon. He closed his eyes and spoke in a low voice. "Lord, this is gonna be a zoo. Help me see what needs to be done, and give me strength to do it. Amen."

He slammed the door and jogged through the damp grass toward the rear of the house. The stallions in the nearby paddocks were all in distant corners, as far from the house as they could get. They stood still, heads and ears lowered. Horses were smarter than most humans, in Scott's opinion, and definitely more astute. No doubt they sensed the tragedy.

When he rounded the corner, the door of an old red Chevy opened and a woman climbed out. She wasn't tall, probably wouldn't come up higher than his chin. Her light brown hair formed a widow's peak in the center of her forehead and hung in soft curls around her shoulders, giving her round face a heart-shaped look. Dirt stained her elbows and smeared the front of her white blouse, along with a few spots of what looked like dried blood.

She stared at him with wide eyes, and as he drew closer he saw dark smears of mascara beneath them. He steeled himself. Crying females always got to him.

"I'm Scott Lewis," he said when he came near enough to extend his hand.

Hers felt soft and warm, and his calloused mitt engulfed her dainty fingers. Tears marked the face she tilted up toward his. She sure didn't look the way he expected. Haldeman normally went for the flashier type.

"Becky Dennison." She drew a shuddering breath. "Thank you for coming."

"Lee will be here soon." Scott nodded toward the house. "Is Haldeman…?"

Becky's shoulders quaked. "He's in the barn. I decided to wait in my car. I didn't want to disturb anything."

"That's good. I'm sure the police will want to look around. Any idea what happened?"

She shook her head, swallowing. Fresh tears sparkled in her eyes, highlighting green flecks among the brown. She had eyes like Megan. Scott looked away, his throat suddenly tight.

"Maybe you can figure it out." Her voice trembled. "He's right inside the back door."

The last thing Scott wanted to do was look at Haldeman's dead body. "Let's wait for the experts."

The scream of sirens grew louder as a fire truck and an ambulance topped a hill and rounded a curve down the road, just beyond neighbor Justin Hart's farm. Within seconds the driveway was full, and Scott fought the urge to imitate Becky and cover his ears from the piercing noise. Behind them, the horses whinnied at the unfamiliar sound. Uniformed men leaped from the vehicles, and thankfully, the sirens stopped. Red lights, dimmed by the brilliance of the morning sun, flashed rhythmically against the white house.

Emergency bags in hand, the EMTs headed toward the two of them. Scott glanced down at Becky, whose eyes locked onto his, wide with panic. Apparently, she didn't want to see Haldeman's body again, either.

Steeling himself, he gave her a brief smile and spoke to the men. "He's out here, guys. Follow me."

He led the troop around the barn. At the doorway, he took a deep breath before stepping inside. When he caught sight of Haldeman, it blew out in a rush.

The man lay faceup on the floor wearing a pair of jeans, an open flannel work shirt and moccasin-style bedroom slippers. His body bore evidence of a struggle—bloody gashes punctuated his bare chest. Thick, dark blood covered one side of his neck and matted the hair above one ear. A sharp instrument inflicted those wounds. A knife?

The group of officials stopped beside Scott, all of them staring. One EMT approached the body and knelt to press a finger against Haldeman's neck, taking care not to disturb the pooled blood beneath him. A shake of the man's head provided the unnecessary verification of Haldeman's death.

A bitter taste assaulted Scott's mouth. No matter what that woman out there said, this was no accident. Haldeman had been murdered.

THREE

It was a bad dream, a nightmare. Becky leaned against her car, trying to stay out of the way of the army of officials swarming toward the barn. After the ambulance and fire truck, three sheriff's vehicles arrived along with two more fire trucks, and then the sheriff himself.

"Ridiculous, isn't it?"

She tilted her head to look up at Scott Lewis. He stood, arms folded across his chest, watching the deputies wrap yellow tape all around the barn.

"What?"

He shook his head. "I was just thinking of the cost of sending all these people out here. How much do you suppose the accumulated salaries would come to?"

Becky shook her head. Strange man. What in the world would make him think of salaries at a time like this? "I really don't know."

"And most of them aren't doing a thing. Just standing around, waiting, like us."

"What are we waiting for, anyway?" Becky rubbed her hands on her arms, cold despite her sweater. "Why don't they question me?"

"Sheriff said we're waiting for the state police." Scott

must have noticed her shiver, because he said, "Here, stand over here in the sun. It'll warm you up in no time."

She stood where he indicated, and warm rays penetrated the chill. Smiling her thanks, she studied him. His skin was permanently tanned, the color of a man who worked in the sun every day of his life. Dark hair, combed straight back from his forehead, brushed at the tips of his ears and flipped out just above his collar. And muscles! Here was a man who wasn't afraid of hard work, and proved it every day. The merest hint of a cleft divided his narrow chin. She'd always been a sucker for men with cleft chins.

Get a grip, woman! Your boss's dead body is no more than fifty feet away and you're checking out the guy next door. How gruesome is that?

Inappropriate or not, her breath came shallow as she looked into dark brown eyes framed by lines that deepened into creases when he returned her smile.

He could use a shave, though.

"Here's Lee." Scott's voice cut into her thoughts and she looked quickly away, face warming. Had she been staring?

A silver Lexus slowed in front of the overcrowded driveway and then rolled into the grass along the front fence. Mr. Courtney emerged and walked with a confident step toward her. Zach Garrett, the manager of Shady Acres horse farm, got out of the passenger seat and followed the older man.

Thank goodness Mr. Courtney was finally here. He held both hands out toward Becky, and she restrained herself from running into them. Besides being a familiar face, his distinguished gray hair and easy confidence made him seem at the moment like a long lost friend. But he was a rich horse breeder, and the owner of the land leased by Out to Pasture to house the retired champions. He was also on the Pasture's board. He might be familiar, but he was definitely not the kind of man she should hug.

Instead, Becky stepped forward, grasped both of his hands in hers and squeezed. "Thank you so much for coming, Mr. Courtney. It's terrible."

"My dear, I know it is. You're in shock, as we all are." He looked past her shoulder at Scott. "Have you seen him?"

"Yes, sir. Looks like there was a fight, and he put up quite a struggle."

The sheriff approached the group and dipped his forehead toward Mr. Courtney. "Morning, Lee."

The two men shook hands. "Frank, I'm glad you're here. You can tell us what's happening."

Sheriff Holmes shook his head. "Haldeman's dead. That's about all I know at this point."

Zach gave a snort. "Betcha somebody's husband finally caught up with him."

Beside her, Scott grunted. "The man's dead, Zach. Show a little respect."

Zach cocked his head to one side. "Just statin' the facts as I know 'em."

Becky's gaze flew toward him. She had met the Shady Acres manager once or twice. He reminded her of Daddy, with his salt-and-pepper hair and no-nonsense manner.

Color rose up Zach's neck, and he pushed the cowboy hat to the back of his head with a finger. "Sorry, ma'am," he mumbled.

"That dog's going nuts." Scott looked toward the house, and Becky flushed with guilt. She had forgotten all about Sam.

"I'm sure he needs to go out," she said. "I was afraid he would disturb, uh, Neal, so I didn't release him when I got here."

"Put him on a leash," advised the sheriff. "He might get in the way of the investigators when they arrive."

Scott shook his head. "He doesn't need a leash. I'll watch him. Sam and I are buddies."

With a nod toward Becky and the men, he walked off in the direction of the house where poor Sam, trapped behind the storm door, had lifted his head and begun to howl.

"Investigators?" Mr. Courtney looked at the sheriff.

Sheriff Holmes nodded. "Soon as we ruled it a homicide, we called in the state boys. They ought to be here soon."

"That's probably them now," said Zach.

Becky followed his gaze. A dark blue sedan rolled to a stop behind the Lexus. A man in a gray suit got out of the driver's side, and a tall man in a state police uniform stood on the other side.

Becky recognized the state trooper. Jeff Whitley. He attended Grace Community Church and dated Becky's friend Amber. If Jeff had been called, that meant the other guy must be the police detective she'd heard him mention so often. She switched her gaze to the suited man and watched him side step between the cars in the driveway as he approached. Her mouth went dry. Jeff had talked about the tough detective, said he was one of the most thorough interrogators on the force. Looked as though she was about to see him in action—firsthand.

When the door opened, Sam exploded outward and leaped up to plant his paws on Scott's chest.

"It's okay, boy." Scott rubbed the velvety ears with

vigor and tilted his head backward to avoid a wet tongue on the mouth. "You can come out, but you've got to stay with me, okay?"

He gave the dog's neck a final brisk rub and pushed him gently away. As soon as his front paws hit the ground Sam started toward the barn, but stopped when Scott said in a low, firm voice, "This way, Sam."

He led the yellow lab to the grass beside the house and waited while Sam sniffed around the bushes to find a suitable place to relieve himself. That done, the dog tried to make another dash for the barn, but again obeyed Scott's command to "Come!" They returned together to the small knot of people standing around Becky's car and arrived in time to hear the newcomers' introduction.

The man in the suit nodded at the sheriff. "'Morning, Holmes." He then extended a hand toward Lee. "Detective Glenn Foster, with the Kentucky State Police. This is Trooper Jeff Whitley."

Lee shook both policemen's hands. "Detective, I'm Leland Courtney, owner of Shady Acres next door." He dipped his head toward the others who clustered around him. "This is Zachary Garrett, my general manager, and Scott Lewis, my assistant manager. And this is Becky Dennison, who works, ah, worked for Neal Haldeman."

The detective, a fiftyish man with a mustache, shook Garrett's hand first, then turned to Scott. He had a firm grip, the kind that made Scott want to look him straight in the eye. Scott nodded toward the uniformed trooper, who stood slightly behind Foster.

Becky shook the detective's hand. Her throat convulsed as she glanced over the detective's shoulder at Whitley. The cop gave her a reassuring smile. Scott thought he could like this guy. Not so sure about the detective. With that direct stare of his, Scott wouldn't be surprised if he whipped out a magnifying glass.

"Mrs. Dennison and I know each other," Whitley said. When Foster raised an eyebrow in his direction, Whitley lifted a shoulder. "We go to the same church."

Scott glanced at Becky with new interest. She attended church? For the first time, he noticed a glimpse of gold at her neck, almost hidden by the collar of her dirt-covered blouse. A cross. Definitely not Haldeman's type then.

Foster caught and held her gaze. "I understand you found the body?" Two bright spots of color appeared on her cheeks as she nodded. The detective turned to the trooper. "Whitley, check out the crime scene. Make sure nobody has touched anything, and keep everyone out of the way until the lab boys arrive."

Whitley nodded, and Sheriff Holmes volunteered to take him to the body. Beside Scott, Sam whimpered as he watched the two men walk toward the barn. Scott rested a hand on the dog's back.

Foster turned back to Becky. "Tell me what happened, Mrs. Dennison."

Becky began to recount her morning, but Scott's thoughts snagged for a moment on the detective's words. He called her *Mrs.* Dennison. She was married, then.

Yep, she definitely reminded him more and more of Megan.

Becky described her morning, beginning from the time she arrived at the Pasture for work. She had pathetically little to say. Why did Detective Foster's eyelids narrow? Did he suspect her of holding something back?

"That's all I know, Detective." She looked him in the eye. "As soon as I realized Neal was dead, I called 9-1-1, and then Mr. Courtney. But I got Mr. Lewis instead."

"Why did you call Mr. Courtney?"

"Because he owns this land, and he's on the Pasture's board of directors. I thought he would want to know."

He held her gaze for a long moment, then jerked a nod. Becky relaxed when the detective's focus shifted toward Mr. Courtney.

"What exactly is your relationship with the deceased?"

"I've known Haldeman for years. He used to sell equipment and supplies to breeders all over the country. Then a few years ago he approached me with an idea for a farm for retired champions. That was right after we found out about Ferdinand."

The detective's eyebrows rose. "Ferdinand?"

The older gentleman dipped his head to level a disbelieving stare at Foster through piercing blue eyes. "You don't know Ferdinand?"

Scott's head turned toward her to hide the grin twitching at his mouth. Mr. Courtney's disapproval radiated as he glared, incredulous, at Detective Foster. Becky had to bite back a grin of her own. When she applied for this job just a few months ago, she'd never heard of Ferdinand, either.

Zach spoke up. "Ferdinand was a champion, one of the finest Thoroughbreds ever bred. He won the Derby in '86 and went on to take the Breeder's Cup Classic the next year. He stood stud at Claiborne Farm for a while, then went to Japan." Zach's voice suddenly trembled and his eyes blazed. "Back in 2002 he stopped producing, and they sent him to the slaughterhouse."

Both Scott's and Mr. Courtney's faces reflected Zach's

outrage. Becky had heard Neal tell the story dozens of times with the same indignation until she'd caught a little of their righteous anger herself.

Detective Foster's expression remained impassive. He looked toward Mr. Courtney. "And then?"

The older man sighed. "The problem with stallions is they're difficult, hard to deal with. They can't paddock with other horses, so they require a lot of space. Haldeman's idea was to start Out to Pasture, one of the only retirement farms for stallions in the world. He and I worked together to set it up legally, get tax exemption status, sponsors, everything. We arranged a lease agreement for the land, set up the paddocks, and a few months later we rescued our first champion, Rusty Racer, from the same farm in Asia where Ferdinand stood."

Becky looked toward Rusty's paddock. The chestnut stallion had positioned himself in the far corner, his tail turned toward all the excitement by the house and barn as though to protest the disturbance of his peaceful day.

"So Out to Pasture leases this land from you?"

"That's right." Mr. Courtney's arm made a wide arc. "My farm, Shady Acres, is all around this place."

Foster looked first at Zach and then at Scott. "And you two work for Mr. Courtney?"

Zach nodded, and Scott said, "That's right."

Another car arrived and four men got out. The detective pursed his lips.

"Those are the lab boys from Frankfort. I need to spend some time with them, but I'll want to talk to each of you later."

His gaze slid around the small circle, coming to rest at last on Becky. She forced herself to return his look calmly, though her pulse pounded in her ears at the thought of being questioned again. She managed a nod, and he seemed satisfied.

"Interesting man," said Mr. Courtney as they watched Foster's retreating back. "Hope he's good."

Becky had heard Jeff Whitley sing the detective's praises at church often enough. "They say he's the best in the state."

"Can't say I like his attitude much," said Scott. "Seems a bit arrogant."

Mr. Courtney shrugged a shoulder. "Arrogance is permissible, as long as you have something to back it up."

Zach inclined his head toward the road. "We've got more company."

Mr. Courtney's gaze followed Zach's gesture, and his eyelids narrowed. "What's he doing here?

Nicholas Stevens's BMW pulled up and parked on the other side of the road. Becky had met him several times. He and his wife made sizable donations to the Pasture and visited frequently. Nick was a Thoroughbred breeder, though a lot younger and newer to the business than Mr. Courtney. He owned a farm up the road.

"Got half the county out here, Courtney," Nick called out as he approached, stepping high across the drying grass. "Hope nothing's wrong."

Mr. Courtney's shoulders squared. He turned a smile on his neighbor, but it looked a little pasted-on to Becky. Well, that was to be expected. They were not only neighbors, they were competitors. They both had horses running at the Keeneland race track this month. In fact, she'd heard Neal talk about the rivalry between the two men.

"Bad news, I'm afraid." Mr. Courtney grasped Nick's hand, shaking his head. "Haldeman's been killed."

Nick's smile melted. "Killed? Like an accident or something?"

"Not likely," Scott answered. "Not from the look of him."

"But…" Nick looked at each of them in turn, face pale. "But I just saw him yesterday. He was fine."

Becky felt a flash of sympathy for the man. She saw Neal yesterday, too. Seemed impossible that he could be dead now.

Mr. Courtney softened. "You might tell the detective that. He'll probably want to know what time you saw him."

Nick nodded and looked toward the barn. "I was just on my way into town for an appointment and stopped when I saw all the cars. Let me make a call to cancel."

He walked toward his BMW, shaking his head.

Behind them, Alidor gave a loud whinny. Becky whirled to find the stallion watching them. He tossed his head and issued another insistent call, but his tone didn't sound as anxious as it had this morning. He was probably hungry. In all the excitement, none of the horses had been fed.

"What are we going to do about the Pasture?" she asked Mr. Courtney. "I'll help, but I don't know anything about caring for horses."

The distinguished gentleman looked at Scott. "Feel up to taking over for a while?"

Zach's spine stiffened. "No offense to Scott, but I think I'd be a better choice." He gave Scott a brief smile of apology.

Mr. Courtney raised an eyebrow. "Why is that?"

"I have more experience with stallions." Zach's answer came instantly.

Beside Becky, Scott's jaw clenched. He obviously didn't like the insinuation that he didn't know as much as his boss, but he held his tongue.

"That's why I want you to handle things back home." Mr.

Courtney slapped Zach on the back. "I need my most experienced manager in charge during breeding season. I know I won't have to worry about a thing with you running the show."

Zach considered that compliment for a fraction of a second before he gave a single nod of acceptance. He clapped Scott on the back. "If you need a hand, son, just holler. I'll help any way I can."

"Think you can handle it?" Mr. Courtney asked Scott.

Scott straightened. "Yes, sir. I'd like that."

"Good." Mr. Courtney stepped forward to place one arm around Scott's shoulders and the other around Becky. "Zach will handle Shady Acres, and you two can manage things here. I'll call an emergency meeting of the board within the next week or so, and we'll figure out what to do from there."

Becky felt a burden settle on her shoulders along with the weight of his arm. Neal had loved this place, these horses. What would happen to the Pasture without him? Would it shut down? Could her job be in jeopardy?

She glanced sideways to study Scott's profile as his gaze swept the paddocks of Out to Pasture. The muscles in his jaw bunched, and deep lines creased his forehead. Was he worried about stepping into Neal's shoes?

A chill crept down Becky's spine. He had a right to be worried, and she should be, too.

Whoever killed Neal was still out there.

FOUR

Becky, leaning against her car, hefted herself upright at Detective Foster's approach. Jeff strode beside him carrying a black bag. Though she'd seen him in uniform a time or two, she'd had to readjust her thinking about him today. Here, he wasn't simply Amber's boyfriend or even just a guy at church. He was all business, his face almost as closed as Detective Foster's while he went about his murder investigation.

Murder. Becky shook her head. She still couldn't believe it. Someone she knew personally had been murdered. And her boys knew him, too. She closed her eyes. How would she explain to Jamie and Tyler what happened to Mr. Neal? Was five too young to attend a funeral? She'd have to call Daddy tonight and ask his opinion.

"Mrs. Dennison," said the detective, "how are you holding up?"

Being called *Mrs.* Dennison irritated her, but whenever she insisted on *Ms.* she felt like a radical feminist. So most of the time she ignored it, like now. "Honestly? I wish I could go inside. I've got work to do." She glanced toward the back door of the farmhouse where yet another man carrying a canvas bag with the state police emblem on it entered. The door slammed behind him with a bang.

Detective Foster shook his head, and Jeff said, "It might be several days before you're allowed back inside. They've got to process everything."

"Several days?" Becky looked away so they wouldn't see the worry in her eyes. Several days without work meant several days without pay. She couldn't afford that right now, not with summer approaching. Her day care costs would double when school let out next month.

When she looked back at them, she found Foster watching her carefully. He didn't look as though he missed much. "Maybe tomorrow. The inside looks pretty clean so far. No sign of a struggle like in the barn."

Becky rubbed her hands on her arms. The sun had done its job warming the cool morning air, but she could not stop shivering. Every time she pictured Neal's body sprawled in the dirt, a chill shot down her spine.

Jeff scanned the paddocks where the horses grazed quietly. "Where's Lewis?"

"He went over to Shady Acres to check on a few things. He'll be right back."

Jeff slapped the bag against his thigh. "Look, Becky, I hate to do this but I'm going to need your shoes."

Startled, she searched his face. He returned her gaze apologetically. "My shoes? Why?"

Foster answered. "We need to match them to some prints we found in the barn."

Okay, that made sense. But she felt strange having her shoes confiscated, almost as though they thought she had something to do with the murder. Her face grew warm as she leaned against the car to lift her foot.

Jeff pulled on a blue rubber glove before taking the shoe. He immediately turned it over and showed the sole to Foster. There wasn't much tread on the bottom of her pumps, but dirt encrusted what little was there. The two men exchanged a glance.

"I've already told you I was in the barn this morning." She struggled to keep her voice even. Detective Foster would certainly notice if she acted defensively and might interpret that as guilt.

"Are you in the barn regularly?" Foster watched her closely.

Becky shook her head. "I've been in there a couple of times, like when I need to take something to Neal. Mostly I stay in the office." She shifted her weight from her bare foot to the other. Why were they staring at her like that? "That's my job. I'm an office assistant, not a farmhand."

"Were you in the barn yesterday?" asked Jeff.

Becky went over the day in her mind. They were working on the next issue of the newsletter, and she'd been focused on that most of the day. "No. The last time was on Friday."

"Do you wear other shoes to work, Mrs. Dennison?" Detective Foster's eyelids narrowed. "Ones with narrower heels, perhaps?"

Narrower heels? Becky glanced at the wide one-inch heel on the pump in Jeff's hand. "No, I don't."

The men exchanged another glance, and Foster nodded.

"Do you know of any women who might have been in the barn recently?" Jeff asked as he put her shoe into a big plastic bag.

Becky slipped her other pump off and handed it to him. They must have found prints in the barn from a narrow heel. She couldn't remember ever seeing anyone except Neal go in there. He gave tours several times a week, but the visitors came into the office to watch videos of the stallions' championship races, and then followed Neal around the paddocks, listening to each horse's life story.

Still, it wasn't impossible for one of them to step inside the barn. "I suppose someone on a tour might have." Doubt sounded in her voice.

Foster pursed his lips. "Was there a tour yesterday?"

"No. The last one was Monday."

Foster looked disappointed, and Jeff shook his head as he zipped the bag shut. The prints they found must be fresh.

Tours! The conversation sparked Becky's memory. "Speaking of tours, we have one scheduled at eleven." She glanced at her watch. "No time to call them to reschedule. They'll be here any minute."

"When they show up," said Jeff, "we'll let them know their tour's been canceled."

At that moment Scott's pickup pulled to a stop in front of the house. They watched him back carefully into the grass, avoiding the overcrowded driveway, and pull around to the rear of the house. He parked close to the edge of the driveway and opened the door. Sam followed him out, leaping from inside the cab to the ground.

Her new boss crossed the grass toward them, the dog at his side, and fixed a direct gaze on Detective Foster. "I need to get to the feed bin in the barn. The horses have to eat."

The detective frowned. "Can't you borrow some horse food from Mr. Courtney's place until we clear the scene?"

Scott looked incredulous for a moment, then his expression became patient as he explained. "Horses have extremely fragile digestive systems. A sudden change in feed can cause serious problems. Something like colic can actually put an animal down. These horses are fed a compound specially designed for older horses, and we don't keep anything like that over at Shady Acres." He cocked his head. "If I knew what brand to get, I suppose we could go buy some."

Foster and Jeff exchanged a glance. "That would probably be best."

"We have an account at Simpson's," Becky volunteered. "They'll have records on the brand and all that."

As though reminded of her presence, Scott gave her a startled look. His gaze dropped to her shoes in Jeff's plastic bag. "What's going on?"

Heat crept up her neck. She seemed to be doing a lot of blushing this morning. "They just need to compare my footprints to some they found in the barn."

Why did he have to be so handsome? Her pulse quickened as she stood under the weight of his stare. Working with the guy wouldn't be easy if she couldn't control her reactions any better than this. She drew in a deep breath and returned his gaze with a calm smile. "Do you need any help feeding the horses?"

He looked down at her nylon-clad feet, and his lips twisted into a lopsided grin. "You're going to help barefoot?"

Her cheeks blazed. "Of course not. I'll, uh, I'll go home and get some more shoes."

A knowing smile lurked behind Jeff's eyes. Amber's boyfriend had returned. Becky ignored him.

"Actually," said Foster, "you might as well stay at home. You won't be able to get into the office today, and the fewer people we have hanging around here the better. We've got your statement, and we know where to find you if we need anything else."

Escaping for home sounded like an excellent idea. She looked at Scott, her eyebrows arched in a silent request for permission. He returned her gaze for a moment, confusion creasing his brow, before his forehead cleared. Apparently, he had just realized that running the Pasture meant he was her boss.

"Oh, yeah, sure." He flashed a smile. "No sense hanging around here today. I can handle the horses. We'll start fresh tomorrow, right?"

He looked toward Jeff and Foster for verification, but Foster wasn't ready to commit. "If we're finished in there."

Becky didn't waste another minute. Time to get out of here, pay or no pay. "Okay, I'll see you in the morning." She whirled and slipped into her car. The engine turned over a couple of times before it started, but when it did the men stepped away. She backed up as far as she could, then pulled onto the grass and followed the trail through the yard and onto the road toward home.

Scott emptied a scoop of feed into Fortune's feed bucket. The horse stood a short distance away and eyed him warily.

"It's okay, fella. You'll get used to me in a day or two."

Fortune didn't appear convinced. Scott had seen the way this horse responded to Haldeman, running to the fence to be close to the man whenever he was outside. The same stallion was keeping a cautious distance from Scott, even though he was delivering food.

Or maybe it wasn't the change in servers that made Fortune distrustful; maybe it was the smaller portion. Since Scott had no idea how much Haldeman generally gave the retirees, they'd have to make do with pasture grass and a couple of scoops of the Triple Crown Senior he'd picked up at Simpson's until he could get to the records. Hopefully by tomorrow the cops would let them into the office.

He was sure Haldeman kept a file on each of the horses, their eating habits and preferences and any medications they might be on. He'd ask Becky to pull the files for him.

Becky. He poured a second scoop of feed into the bucket. He didn't know what to make of her. She looked a little flustered when she left, barefoot and covered in dirt. But throughout the morning she'd handled herself well, after the initial shock of finding Haldeman's body wore off. From her phone call, he'd have pegged her for the hysterical type, not the kind to keep her composure under police questioning. Megan would have…

He stabbed the scoop into the feed bag and climbed behind the wheel of the golf cart to head for the next paddock. Why did he keep comparing her to Megan? She didn't look a thing like his former girlfriend, except for the eyes. He steeled himself against the wave of regret that thoughts of Megan always brought. He had to stop thinking about the past and focus on the task at hand. And that meant working with Becky to hold things together. Hopefully, she was happily married and totally in love with her husband. Theirs would be a business relationship, period. And he was the boss.

A smile tugged at his mouth. He'd never officially been the boss of anyone before. This temporary job at the Pasture was going to give him some great experience. If he handled it well, he might be able to land a job as general manager with the next breeder he worked for. Having someone like Mr. Courtney put in a good word for him when he was ready to move on would be worth a lot.

He pulled on the hand brake as he approached the feed bucket for Samson's Secret. Zach's comment about having more experience with stallions than Scott wasn't really accurate. He and Mr. Courtney seemed to have forgotten that

Scott's last job had been at a stud farm. But out of respect for his boss, Scott had kept his mouth shut. Though he could be a bit crusty, Zach had been nothing but kind to Scott since his arrival. In some ways, he reminded Scott of his dad.

Unlike Fortune, Samson ran toward Scott eagerly when he realized food was being scooped into his feed bucket. He shoved his head in after the first scoop as though starving.

"Take it easy, fella." Scott laughed as he gently pushed the horse's head back so he could add another scoop. "You can't fool me into thinking you're that hungry. I've watched you graze all morning."

As he left Samson's paddock, Detective Foster and Trooper Whitley came through the back door of the farmhouse. Foster's gaze swept the paddocks and stopped when he caught sight of Scott. Both men started toward him. Scott hopped into the golf cart and met them at the edge of the black plank fencing.

"Lewis," said Foster, "any idea what this is?"

Trooper Whitley held a scrap of paper in his blue-gloved hand. When Scott reached for it, he jerked it away.

"Fingerprints," he explained.

Scott nodded and shoved his hand into his pocket. The square of paper looked like newsprint and had two ripped edges, as though torn from the corner of a larger piece. Scrawled in blue ink across the white space were two sentences.

I need to see you. I'll come by tonight.

The handwriting was pretty, the even, rounded letters flowing across the paper. The *i* in *tonight* was dotted with a little circle.

Scott shrugged. "I'm not an expert, but to me it looks like a note written by a woman."

Detective Foster's lips pursed. "We know that. I'm asking about the paper it's written on."

Scott looked again. The scrap was torn from the page of a racing form. Bold print beside the blue scrawl listed statistics that might look like gibberish to someone with no knowledge of the industry, but were a horse's lifetime stats.

"It's probably torn from a page of the *Daily Racing Form*." He grasped Whitley's rubber-encased wrist and turned it over. On the back the large bold heading was torn, the last part missing, but enough of the name remained that Scott recognized it. "Lemon Sugar. She's a filly from Harwood Farm over in Lexington. She ran at Keeneland this week."

Foster's face remained impassive. The man was a master at hiding his reactions. "What day?"

Scott shrugged. "I'm not sure. I don't go to the races much."

"But you're a horse guy." Whitley gave him a surprised look. "You work for a breeder."

"And you think everyone who has anything to do with Thoroughbreds is a racing enthusiast." Scott laughed. "Would you believe I've never even been to the Derby?"

"Yet you recognize the name of a horse and even know the week it's scheduled to race." Foster's statement held a question.

"Professional interest." Scott shrugged. "I might not bet on the races, but I can tell you something about the record of every horse we've bred since I came to Shady Acres, and their lineage." He nodded toward the paper. "In this case,

I know the manager over at Harwood. He was bragging about that filly last week."

Whitley flipped the note over again and studied the handwriting. "Did the victim ever go to the races?"

"Haldeman?" Scott threw back his head and laughed. "He never missed. The man loved the sport. He was as close to a fanatic as anyone I've ever known."

"So he would have been at Keeneland this week when this horse—" Foster gestured at the note "—raced?"

"I'm sure he was."

Foster nodded while Whitley took out a plastic bag and sealed the scrap of paper inside.

"What else can you tell us about the victim?" asked Foster.

Scott looked away, considering his answer. He should be honest with the police, of course, but he hated to say anything bad about a guy who could no longer defend himself. "I didn't know him well." Foster watched his face, waiting for him to continue. "We talked some. I met him last year when I came to work for Mr. Courtney, and we ran into each other around the farm fairly often. He loved the industry, everything about it. And he loved these horses." Scott nodded over Foster's shoulder, toward Samson. "He was passionate about saving them. You didn't want to get him started talking about Ferdinand or Alydar."

"Who is Alydar?" asked Whitley.

Scott waved a hand. "Another champion who died. Doesn't matter. The point is, Haldeman seemed determined to save every stallion he could. He had a list of horses he was watching, mostly in Japan, and he was relentless about raising the money to go get them the minute the Japanese were finished with them."

"Relentless?" One of Foster's eyebrows arched.

Scott shook his head. "I don't mean that negatively. Haldeman was smooth, a real talker. Remember that he was a salesman before he founded this place. He could get a donation from anyone, and if it meant he could save another stallion, he'd try."

Foster examined Scott from between narrowed eyelids. "What are you not saying, Mr. Lewis?"

Scott looked at the grass between their feet. "Well, I don't know this for a fact, but the talk around town says Haldeman had an eye for the ladies. Especially rich ones. I've heard it didn't matter how young or how old a woman was, if Haldeman thought he could get money out of her for the Pasture, she was fair game."

"I see."

Scott raised his chin and looked the detective in the eye. "That's really just farm talk. I don't have any personal knowledge to base it on. Haldeman and I didn't run in the same circles."

"And what circles would those be?" asked Whitley.

Scott shifted his gaze to the younger man. "I have no idea who Haldeman ran with. I'm active in my church, and that's where I spend most of my free time."

Both men nodded, and Detective Foster looked toward the farmhouse. "I think we're going to finish up in there this afternoon. You and Mrs. Dennison should be able to get back to work tomorrow."

A man came out of the barn and gestured to Foster. He tossed his head in answer. "If you think of anything else that might be helpful, you'll give us a call?" He didn't wait for a response, but headed toward the barn.

Whitley fished a card case out of his black bag and slipped a business card out of it. Scott took it, saw that it had contact information for Trooper Jeffrey Whitley, and shoved it in his jeans pocket. He glanced at the trooper. "So you go to church with Becky and her husband?"

Whitley shook his head. "Just Becky. Her husband took off when her twins were babies, I guess. She was already divorced when I met her a year ago."

Divorced. So she wasn't happily married after all. But she had kids. "Twins?"

Whitley laughed. "Five-year-old boys, and they keep her hopping. You never met a rowdier pair."

Well, that settled that. Divorced or not, Becky Dennison just dropped off his radar screen. He had no desire to get involved with the single mother of two lively mischief makers.

FIVE

"Hi, Daddy," Becky said into the phone later that night.

"Hey, sweetheart, how's my best girl?"

She smiled at his light tone. He always sounded happy to hear from her. "I'm all right."

"Just all right?" Now he sounded concerned. "Is something wrong with the boys?"

"No, they're fine. I just put them to bed." She propped her slippered feet on the coffee table, something she insisted Jamie and Tyler never do. But the recliner had a Hot Wheels car stuck in the mechanism, and she hadn't found the time to pry it out yet.

"Out with it, then. What's bothering you?"

"Something terrible happened at work. My boss was killed, probably murdered, and I found his body this morning."

"Becky!" Alarm exploded in his voice. "Are you okay? Do I need to come out there?"

A tender smile curved her lips. Always her stalwart, if long-distance, protector, especially in the four years since Mom died. "I'm fine, Daddy, and of course you don't need to come. I just need your advice about the boys. They knew Neal, so I have to tell them something, but I'm not sure how to go about it. Do you think they're too young to go to a funeral?"

"Yes, I do." Not a hint of doubt in his voice. "But they're not too young to talk about death."

"You don't think it will affect them?"

"Sure, it will affect them. But maybe not as much as you think. They probably already know more about death than you realize. They've seen dead bugs and animals on the side of the road. And on television, no doubt."

He was right about that. She tried to monitor their television viewing, but even the cartoons were full of violence these days.

"I wouldn't tell them the man was murdered," Daddy advised. "Just say he died, and he's living in heaven now with Jesus."

Sadness gripped Becky as she realized that probably wasn't true. "I don't think Neal was a Christian. Any time I tried to discuss God or church he changed the subject."

"Well, then just tell the boys he died and leave it at that."

"Okay." She reached for her mug of herbal tea and inhaled the soothing odor of chamomile before she took a sip. "How are you doing? Everything go all right in that meeting you were worried about?"

Daddy worked for a software firm in Silicon Valley managing a staff of developers. She had only a vague idea of what they did. Sometimes when he described the details of his job she felt as if he was speaking another language.

"Smooth as silk. I talked them out of a big chunk of next year's budget to fund a new database platform in conjunction with the operating system switchover."

Like that. But she knew better than to ask him to explain what a database platform was and why it would cost a chunk of money. She'd be on the phone all night. "Good for you."

"Listen, are you sure you're okay? If this guy was murdered, are you in any danger?"

That thought had plagued Becky throughout the day. "I don't think so. It looked like there was a fight. Scott thinks maybe he surprised a burglar in the barn."

"The barn? What would a thief want from a barn? And who is Scott?"

"Scott is my new boss." Unease trickled into Becky's thoughts, but she made sure it didn't seep into her voice. "And I don't know what a thief would want. Horse equipment maybe. Some of that stuff is expensive. Or maybe it was teenagers looking for drugs. Whoever it was, the police will catch them soon. Don't worry about me."

His voice softened. "Worrying about you and my rascally grandsons is what I do best. I still wish you'd move out here so I could give you a hand with them."

Becky sipped her tea before answering. The thought of living near Daddy was attractive. But the cost of living was so high out in California there was no way she could find a job that paid well enough to support her and the boys. And she refused to move in with her father. No, she was better off staying here where at least she could be somewhat self-sufficient.

"It would be wonderful to see you more often," she admitted, as she always did, "but I'm not moving to California."

"Well, then." His voice trailed off. The faint sound of a keyboard tapping interrupted the silence. As usual, he was working on something as they talked. "Do you need any money?"

She smiled. "No, Daddy. But thanks for asking."

"You get any more checks?"

"I got one last week, in fact."

After their divorce, Christopher paid a total of three child support payments before disappearing. But four months ago, out of the blue, she started getting checks from the division of child support. When she called, all she could find out was that he'd taken a new job and his employer filed his social security number with something called the national new hire reporting database. They'd begun garnisheeing his wages. Becky didn't expect it to last, but it had been a huge relief to have extra money to put toward some of her frighteningly large credit card balances.

"If you need money, you'll let me know, right?"

How lucky she was to have such a supportive father. Even though he was on the other side of the country, she knew her boys would never go without the basic needs. She could count on him. And she'd never abuse the privilege. "I love you, Daddy."

"I love you, too, sweetheart. Don't forget to say your prayers."

SIX

Scott snapped the lid back on the feed bin, straightened and listened to the sound of rain pelting the barn's roof. He breathed a deep breath of damp morning air. Both the front and rear doors stood open in an effort to clear out the lingering odor of death that was probably only his imagination.

He'd swept up the loose dirt beneath the place where Haldeman had lain and covered it with straw. But Sam kept leaving the rug that served as his daytime bed to circle the area, nose to the ground.

A car pulled into the driveway. Becky's Chevy. His watch showed a few minutes before eight o'clock. The engine cut off, the driver's door opened a crack and a blue umbrella popped open above the roof. Becky emerged, the slick canopy only partially shielding her from the driving rain as she made a dash toward the barn. When she stepped beneath the shelter, Sam leaped off his rug and ran to greet her.

She stopped just inside and bent down to rub the dog's head. "Hello, Sam." Her gaze went to the place where Haldeman's body had lain until the coroner took it to the morgue yesterday afternoon. She looked up at Scott. "I see the police are gone. I hoped they would be."

Scott nodded. "They finished up sometime after

midnight. They're coming back this afternoon, though. They want to get your fingerprints."

Eyes wide, her hand flew to her chest. "Mine? Why?"

"It's nothing to worry about," he assured her. "They found a bunch of prints in the office and out here. They just need to be able to eliminate yours."

A vertical crease appeared between her eyebrows. "What if I don't want them to have my fingerprints?"

Actually, Scott asked that same question when they came for his. Until yesterday he hadn't been at the Pasture in months, and he didn't see the need. But Foster said since he was present at the scene of a crime when law enforcement arrived, they needed his, too. It felt kind of creepy having your fingerprints on file with the state police. "They said they'd call the county attorney and get a warrant if necessary."

"Oh."

She looked nice today in dress slacks and a pink sweater. He glanced at her shoes. Women's shoes, not sneakers or boots. Obviously not farm attire.

"You don't help with the horses much, do you?"

Her eyes went wide. "Neal never asked me to. I handle pretty much everything in the office. He even turned over the bank account a few weeks ago, so I make the deposits and write checks and all that." She swallowed convulsively. "Do you need help out here?"

Scott studied her. She looked frightened. "Are you afraid of horses?"

"A little," she admitted. "I've never been around them much. They're so…so big."

Scott laughed. "They're big, all right. And some of them can be temperamental, especially stallions. But they're also smart and love to have fun. They each have their own personality and quirks, just like people." He nodded toward the paddocks behind the barn. "You should get to know them, maybe help me take care of them. A lot of people would jump at the chance. We've got some real celebrities here."

Doubt clouded her features, but she said, "I'm sure you're right." Suddenly her face cleared. "Before I forget to tell you, a volunteer group from the university will be here after lunch to help groom them. They come every Friday afternoon."

That made sense. The university boasted an equine research center as part of its veterinary medicine program. Scott had instructed student volunteers over at Shady Acres more times than he could count.

He glanced through the doorway at the dark, heavy sky. "I hope it clears up." The clouds looked as though they had settled in for a while. He looked back down at Becky. "Would you do me a favor?"

"Of course."

"I'm sure Haldeman kept files on each of these horses, with vet records and the like. I want to take a look at them. And if you can find anything else that might help me figure out how things work around here, I'd appreciate it. Oh, and Detective Foster said if you run across anything in the office that might help with their investigation, you're supposed to call Trooper Whitley. I put his card on the desk inside."

Becky glanced toward the house. "Are you going to live in there, like Neal did?"

Scott had considered the question several times yesterday. Though it wasn't a bad idea to have someone on-site at night, the thought of moving into Haldeman's bedroom was not an appealing one. Scott rented a cottage from Mr.

Courtney on the far side of Shady Acres, and he'd come to the conclusion that it was close enough. "I don't think so. Sam and I did okay last night. Oh, yeah." He snapped his fingers as he remembered a detail the dog certainly had not forgotten. "Could you feed Sam? I didn't have anything to give him over at my place."

Becky's smile made her eyes shine even in the gloom inside the barn. She was a pretty woman. Sweet and whole-some-looking. When she spoke, affection for the dog warmed her tone. "I always feed Sam when I get to work, while Neal's out feeding the horses." She bent again and roughed the yellow fur on the dog's neck. "Come on, boy. Let's go get you some breakfast."

She nodded in Scott's direction as she popped her umbrella open. With a quick glance at the menacing sky, she dashed out of the barn and splashed across the wet driveway toward the house, Sam running ahead of her.

Scott watched until the door closed behind them. What was he thinking, encouraging her to get involved with the horses? If she helped care for them, he'd be forced to spend more time with her.

Maybe she'd forget his suggestion. Better for everyone if she stayed in the office and let him handle the horses.

Seated in front of Neal's two-drawer file cabinet, Becky looked up when the back door opened. Scott stopped just inside the next room to wipe his feet on a tattered but still-serviceable floor mat. Sam leaped off a shabby recliner where he'd been napping and went to greet his new master.

At least, she assumed Scott had decided to adopt the dog. Becky had been half-ready to suggest that Sam could come home with her. The boys would love to welcome him to the family, and he could still come to work with her every day. But he seemed to like Scott, and she couldn't afford to feed an extra mouth anyway.

From the office, which had once been the living room of the old farmhouse, Becky called to him. "I found the files you asked me to pull."

Scott appeared in the doorway between the two rooms. He leaned a shoulder against the frame.

"Thanks. Do you know where Haldeman kept treats for the horses? There aren't any in the barns."

"Sure, they're in here."

He didn't move as she slid past him in the doorway. The scent of horses clung to him, an earthy, pleasant odor that reminded her of the outdoors. She looked up into his solemn face. He was a lot less jovial than Neal, who had always liked to make wisecracks. And a lot more handsome.

She led him into the kitchen. "Their favorites are carrots and apples. Neal did live here, of course, so there's some food that will need to be disposed of."

She opened the refrigerator and showed him the nearly empty interior. On the shelves were several take-out containers which had probably been there for weeks, a bag of apples and an unopened half-gallon of milk. "He wasn't much of a cook."

Scott peered inside. "If that milk's any good, you might as well take it home. Your boys will drink it, no doubt."

Becky turned a quick look on him. How did he know about Jamie and Tyler? Had she mentioned them yesterday? No, she didn't think so. Her pulse quickened as she looked into his dark eyes. Did he ask around about her?

She tore her gaze away and closed the refrigerator. "Thanks. I'll do that. We keep treats for the horses here."

She opened one of the cabinets. Inside were a dozen or so bags of peppermint-flavored horse treats. "They prefer carrots, but—"

From the other room came the sound of the back door slamming. "Hello? Is anyone here?"

A woman stepped into view. She was model-thin and tall, nearly as tall as Scott. Her artful makeup, tailored skirt, boots and elegant suede jacket with fur trim looked out of place in the dumpy little farmhouse-turned-office. When she caught sight of them, she came into the kitchen. The odor of her sweet, musky perfume filled the room.

She stopped just inside, her gaze sweeping over Becky, who fiddled with the cross that hung from her neck. Suddenly she felt short and dumpy in her slacks and sweater. Superiority flickered in the woman's eyes as her chin rose a fraction, and she turned her attention on Scott, dismissing Becky with a flip of shining blond hair.

Her carefully shaped eyebrows rose as she gave Scott the same once-over. "My, my, my. And who do we have here?"

Becky almost laughed out loud. Nobody pronounced it 'he-yah' like that on purpose. That deep Southern drawl had to be fake, as fake as her tan. Who had a tan like that in April, anyway?

Scott crossed the room in two steps, his hand extended. "Scott Lewis. I'm taking care of things here at Out to Pasture for a little while."

The woman's movement was smooth, silky, as she took Scott's hand. Her other arm rose to cover their clasped hands, and her long fingers brushed slowly over Scott's skin. "I am Kaci Buchanan." She tilted her head and peered at Scott from the corners of her eyes. "Have we met, Mr. Lewis? Perhaps at the Thoroughbred Club?"

Becky had to stop herself from rolling her eyes. Judging by the number of syllables the woman got out of each word, she must love hearing her own voice. Every sentence was its own little production. Nobody would fall for that assumed accent.

Scott shook his head. "I don't think so. I'm not a member of the Thoroughbred Club. And I'm sure I'd remember if we met somewhere else."

"You simply *must* become a member, darling. *Everyone* is, you know." Still clutching his hand, she leaned forward until her face was inches from his. "I'd be honored to sponsor you, given your new position."

A smile broke on Scott's face. "Thank you, Miss Buchanan. That's very nice of you."

"Please call me Kaci. Everyone does."

They appeared to have completely forgotten about Becky. She pasted on a pleasant smile and took a step forward. "What can we do for you, Kaci? I'm afraid we don't have any tours scheduled this morning."

Arrogance flooded her delicate features as Kaci tore her gaze away from Scott. Apparently, the invitation to use her first name was not extended to Becky. At least she released Scott's hand, and with a quick glance in Becky's direction, he shoved it in the back pocket of his jeans.

"Why, aren't you the sweetest thing." Her chilly tone contradicted her words. "But I've not come for a tour. Neal gave me one personally." Her gaze slid back to Scott and a smile flirted with her lips as her tone warmed. "After hours."

Amazing. She managed to flirt with one guy at the same time she hinted at an intimate relationship with another. Pink spots appeared on Scott's ruddy cheeks. Becky bit back a grunt of disgust. Surely he wasn't taken in by this, this fake Southern belle.

He cleared his throat. "I suppose you've heard about Haldeman?"

Kaci's face became mournful. "Simply dreadful. And such a shock." She lifted a graceful hand to rest at the base of her throat. "Neal and I had a *special* relationship, you know. When I read the news of his demise in the morning paper…" An elegant and perfectly manicured hand fluttered dramatically around her collarbone.

Becky didn't believe her for a minute. She knew Neal dated frequently, and sitting in the same office during the day she couldn't help but overhear the occasional phone conversation. She had heard him mention the name Kaci, had passed along an occasional message from her for Neal to return her call. But she'd taken messages from many women.

Kaci apparently recovered enough to continue. "I came by to pay my respects to dear Neal."

Becky folded her arms across her chest. "So you won't be coming to the funeral?"

Kaci's smile stiffened, her gaze shifting to Becky. "This is the place he loved. I shall always remember him here, as he was the last time I saw him."

Scott nodded, his face full of sympathy, which made Becky's fingers dig into her arms. Puh-lease! "You're welcome to walk around the farm, see the horses again if you like."

She gave a short laugh and gestured toward her fancy leather boots. "Not dressed like this, darling. No, I'm heading to the track right now, where I can shelter from the weather in Mother's box." She half turned toward the door, and then stopped. "While I'm thinking of it, I left an item here not long ago. A personal item. I'd like to have it back."

Aha. Becky studied her through narrowed eyelids. The real reason for this visit had emerged. "And what might that be?"

"An earring." She shot a coy glance toward Scott. "I know just where it is. If you don't mind?"

Without waiting for permission she turned and went through the doorway toward the television room.

Becky speared Scott with an open-eyed glance. "Stop her," she hissed.

He held out his hands, confused. "Why? If she left something here, she has every right to get it back."

Becky gave him an incredulous look as she brushed past him on the way down the hallway. "The police might like to know about whatever it is."

He followed her, and found Kaci bending gracefully over the sagging sofa, her hand shoved into the crack behind the cushion.

"There it is." She straightened and rose in a smooth motion, her hand held out for their inspection. Resting in her palm was a large diamond earring. The way the stone sparkled in the room's dull light told Becky it was not an imitation.

"I can see why you'd want to get that back." Scott spoke to Kaci, but leveled a triumphant look on Becky.

"They were a gift. When I got home from my last visit and realized I was only wearing one, I knew it must have fallen out." Kaci practically purred as she gazed at the diamond. Then she closed her fingers around it. "I'd best run along. You will consider the Club, now, won't you, darling?"

She flounced out of the room. Scott grinned at Becky and lifted a shoulder before following. His amused expression soothed her feathers a little. Maybe he hadn't been taken in by the flirty floozie after all. Becky stood inside, watching through the window as he gallantly opened the car door. With a new wave of disgust she noticed that Kaci drove a gorgeous BMW convertible.

Kaci fluttered her fingers at Scott as she backed out of the driveway. Becky didn't wait for him to come back inside, but went into the office. He arrived as she lifted the remaining file folders out of the cabinet and deposited them with the others on Neal's desk.

"You didn't like her very much."

His dry tone made her turn a sharp look his way. A denial rose to her lips, but she bit it back. No sense lying. "I'm not crazy about fakes in any form."

His brows drew together. "Fakes? Do you know who that was? Kaci Buchanan is the daughter of Francine Buchanan, one of the richest and most influential horse breeders in the industry. She's not a fake. Kaci's the real deal."

"Oh, I don't mean the money." Becky twisted her lips. "You can't fake that. I mean her—the accent, the attitude. And especially her excuse for coming here." Becky thrust her chin in the air and imitated the Southern drawl. "Oh, darling, I want to remember dear Neal in the place he loved." She blew a raspberry. "Not likely. She was here to get that earring before the police found it and started asking questions about its owner."

Scott threw back his head and laughed. "Are you sure you're not the tiniest bit jealous?"

Becky drew herself up, outraged. "Jealous of what? Her money?"

She turned her back on him and reached down to straighten the pile of folders. Jealous? Of a society brat? Not a chance.

But when she remembered Kaci's arrogance as her gaze swept over her, her face heated with remembered shame. Kaci had probably never bought a pair of pants at Wal-Mart in her life. She probably didn't even have to pay for her own clothes, or her car, or anything. She definitely had never searched the couch cushions for change to buy gasoline.

And the way she flirted so blatantly. Even worse, Scott seemed to actually enjoy the attention, in a detached, amused sort of way.

Jealous? Okay, maybe a little.

She faced Scott. "I'm prepared to concede that I might have felt a touch of jealousy. But you have to admit, her whole attitude was strange."

"How so?"

"If she and Neal had a 'special relationship,' she sure didn't seem very upset by his death, did she?"

He considered that, then shook his head. "She didn't seem grief-stricken."

"As I said, she came here today for one reason only. To get that earring."

Scott's forehead dipped forward. "Granted. But you can't blame her for wanting it back. That diamond had to be worth a small fortune. She must have been frantic to recover it."

Becky wasn't buying that. "First of all, she doesn't look like the kind who'd be worried over the cost of an earring, no matter what it's worth. No, either she has some reason for not wanting the police to know she's been here recently, or she left that earring here on purpose."

"You mean so she had an excuse to come back and see Haldeman again."

Becky relaxed. At least he wasn't too trusting to spot

manipulative behavior. "Exactly. She went straight to it, which can only mean she planted it there."

Scott chuckled, shaking his head. "She's a conniving female, I'll give you that. But she wouldn't be the first to pull that stunt. There's nothing of any possible interest to the police."

"Maybe." Becky shoved the top drawer on the file cabinet closed and crossed the room to her desk. "But did you see her shoes?"

"Boots," he corrected. "And what about them?"

She slid into her chair, picked up a piece of mail and caught his gaze across the room. "They had high, narrow heels."

SEVEN

Scott had already started grooming Dark Diego when the students from the university showed up. The dark clouds had emptied themselves out midmorning, and the sun shining overhead had dried the horses enough that they could be groomed. His helpers, three girls and a guy, already knew about Haldeman's death when they arrived.

"I just can't believe it."

Scott lifted his head to look toward the place where the four were perched on the fence, arms dangling over the top plank, while he ran the currycomb gently over Diego's back.

The pretty brunette, who introduced herself as Patti, shook her head. "I mean, last week he was totally fine."

The boy beside her, Mike, gave her a sideways glance. "He was killed. It's not like you'd be able to see it coming last Friday." He turned toward Scott. "And you saw the body?"

His expression begged for details, but Scott refused to feed the kid's morbid curiosity. He ran the comb over the stallion's flank. "Yeah."

"So, was there, like, blood and gore?"

"Mike, you're disgusting." Rachel looked at Scott. "I'm going to miss Mr. Haldeman. He really loved these horses."

"I know he did." Scott gave the chestnut's hair a final

swipe with the currycomb. "Could you hand me the dandy brush, please?" He pointed toward the pouch hanging on a fence post.

Patti dug out the brush and passed it over the fence. Scott stepped back up to Diego's head and started at the top of his neck. As he flicked the brush expertly, Diego's eyelids half closed, and his lower lip quivered with pleasure.

"He likes this," Scott said.

The third girl, Teri, agreed. "Yeah, Diego loves it. Not like Alidor over there."

Scott glanced at the next paddock where Alidor grazed near his run-in shack. "A bit feisty, is he?"

All four nodded. "Mr. Haldeman didn't let us mess with him much," said Mike. "Not unless Alidor was in a real good mood."

"But we can groom the others," said Patti. "Do you want us to get started?"

Scott looked at their eager faces. Actually, he preferred to groom all the stallions himself, at least this first time. That way they'd have an opportunity to get used to him, and he'd be able to do a quick checkup on each of them. On the other hand, if the horses were accustomed to having these four around they might appreciate seeing someone familiar in Haldeman's absence.

"Sure, go ahead. I'll come around and give you a hand so I can check each one out."

With a nod they hopped off the fence and headed toward the barn. Their voices faded as they rounded the corner and disappeared inside. Scott went over Diego with the dandy brush and then swapped it for a body brush. The stallion stood with his ears perked forward, obviously enjoying himself.

He'd read Diego's file this morning. The stallion was something of a legend in the Florida racing circuit, having fathered more than five hundred stakes winners. An impressive record, and by far the most successful in terms of his career as a stud, though his lifetime earnings as a racer didn't come close to that of some of the horses at the Pasture.

Scott laughed at the horse's delight as the soft-bristled brush caressed his forelock. "Yeah, this is the life, isn't it? You've got a big space to run, tender spring grass, an automatic waterer, someone to bring your food every morning and night, and you get groomed every week to boot." He ran the brush over the horse's face with a slow, careful motion. "That's what retirement is all about, huh, boy?"

As Diego's ears flicked forward, Scott caught sight of a spot on his left ear. He lowered the brush and reached up with his other hand to touch an irregular place along the edge. Diego tossed his head away when Scott's fingers touched it. There was a nick along the edge, healed up but not scarred over.

"What'd you do to yourself, Diego? Get in a fight?"

No telling how old the cut was, but it wasn't fresh. The stallion probably cut it rubbing his head against the ground or something. Judging by the amount of dirt caked under his hair, Diego enjoyed a good roll.

"Hey, Mr. Lewis."

Scott looked up to see Mike coming out of the barn, grooming tools in his hands. The girls followed, and two of them peeled off to head in the direction of Gadsby's paddock. Rachel followed Mike toward him.

"Any idea where the other hoof pick went?"

Scott nodded toward the bag hanging on the fence post.

"There's one in there. Just let me finish up with Diego here and you can have it."

A polishing rag in her hand, Rachel shook her head. "No, he means the other one. There should be three, but one seems to be missing."

Scott's hand stopped halfway through a brush swipe. The fine hair at the base of his scalp prickled. Foster said he should be sure to let him know if anything came up missing. Of course, Scott wouldn't have any idea what might be missing from the Pasture's barn, because he didn't spend any time there. But these kids did.

He pulled the bag off the fence post and dumped the contents onto the ground. One hoof pick. He grabbed it and held it up.

"Is this the one you're looking for?"

Mike shrugged. "It'll do as well as any of them. But Rachel's right. Mr. Haldeman kept three sets of grooming tools on that workbench in the barn, and—" The young man gasped as he realized the implication of the missing tool. "Do you think somebody used a hoof pick to kill Mr. Haldeman?"

Staring with horror at the pick in Scott's hand, Rachel looked a little green around the gills. Scott turned the tool over and examined the business end. The metal point was sharp, but not razor sharp. It wouldn't be easy to kill a man with this.

An image of Haldeman's body rose unbidden in Scott's mind. Those gashes on his chest had been ragged and wide. Ugly. Not clean punctures or slashes that a sharp knife would make. And his neck had been covered in blood. So much blood. Scott hadn't seen details, hadn't wanted to see details, but it was possible a hoof pick could gouge a man's throat.

The hand holding the hoof pick trembled. Rachel gave

a strangled cry and turned away, while Mike's eyes were round as doughnuts.

"I think I'd better call the police," Scott said.

Becky finished totaling up the bank deposit and double-checked her numbers. Two days' worth of correspondence opened and dealt with, finally. It had taken her most of the morning. The phone wouldn't stop ringing, people calling to offer their condolences after reading the article in the *Lexington Herald-Leader.* Finally, she'd recorded a generic message and let the machine pick up the calls.

The mail had yielded a few small donations from individuals, as usual, and one five-hundred-dollar check from a man who'd taken the tour three weeks ago. Neal would be pleased with—

Becky's hand froze in the act of setting down the pen. She closed her eyes and let the fact of Neal's death sweep over her again. Hard to believe he wouldn't be coming through the door any minute, whistling in that tuneless way of his as he crossed toward the kitchen to get his afternoon cup of coffee. Though Becky didn't drink coffee herself, she'd made a fresh pot at lunchtime. Habit. Maybe Scott would want a cup.

Through the back door she saw a police car pull into view and park beside Scott's pickup. They'd finally come to get her fingerprints. She pressed her lips tight. She intended to tell those people what she thought about them leaving fingerprint powder all over the office for her to clean up. And no matter what Scott thought, she'd tell them about Kaci Buchanan's visit this morning, too.

Jeff got out from behind the wheel, and Detective Foster stood on the opposite side of the car. But instead of coming into the office they walked toward the barn. She slipped the deposit into the desk drawer and then crossed the room to look out the window. Scott and all four university students came out of the barn and stood talking to them. The kids looked excited about something.

Curiosity drove her through the door. She approached the group in time to hear Rachel say, "There are *always* three hoof picks. We do three horses at a time."

Foster glanced at Jeff, who opened his leather notebook and slipped the pen from beneath the metal clip. "Can you describe the missing tool?"

"Yeah," said Mike. "It looks just like the other two. Hold on a sec." The kid dashed into the barn and returned in a moment with a tool in his hand. "Exactly like this one."

A tool missing? Becky looked at the instrument in Mike's hand. A red plastic looped handle held a curved shaft of metal that tapered to a point. Was something like this used to kill Neal? It didn't look all that sharp, but somehow that made it an even more wicked-looking weapon.

Foster took the hoof pick from Mike and turned it over in his hand. He spoke Becky's thoughts. "It isn't very sharp."

He and Jeff exchanged a glance. Watching them, Becky realized the two had expected a dull instrument like this one. Her throat constricted, trying not to think about the damage that point could inflict.

"When was the last time you saw all three hoof picks?" Jeff's glance swept the four kids.

"Friday," said Teri without hesitation, and the others nodded. "Our group comes every Friday afternoon."

"Six of us," put in Patti. "Because there are three sets of grooming tools. Last week Kelly and Josh came, but they couldn't come today."

Jeff looked at Scott. "Could it be misplaced?"

Scott shook his head. "We combed that barn after we called you. They're not sure if a polishing rag is missing or not, but they all insist the tools are kept on the workbench."

"It was there last week." Mike's expression became stubborn. "We used all three, and we always clean them and put them back. And they're always there the next Friday."

Becky remembered something Neal said earlier in the week, something about…

"Bull!"

They all looked at her. Foster's eyebrows arched. "I beg your pardon?"

She gave an embarrassed laugh. "Bulldozer Buckaroo. He's one of the stallions, and Neal sometimes grooms him during the week. I think he did this week, on Tuesday. He came into the office at lunchtime talking about…" She closed her eyes, trying to remember Neal's exact words. "He said Bull had been rolling in the mud again. He said he thought Bull did it on purpose, because he liked being groomed."

"So you think he used the hoof pick on Tuesday and didn't put it back?" Patti asked.

"I suppose it's possible."

"Not likely." Mike's eyebrows drew together. "Why would he put all the brushes back where they belong but put the hoof pick somewhere else? That doesn't make sense."

Becky agreed. Neal wasn't exactly the most organized man she'd ever known, but it didn't seem likely he'd put all but one of the tools back in place.

Scott rubbed his chin with a finger, his expression pensive. "Maybe it got broken, or maybe he dropped it on the way to or from Bull's paddock."

Mike seemed determined to prove the hoof pick as the

murder weapon. "Then he would have bought another one." He swung toward Becky. "Did he?"

"No." She spoke with confidence. "He would have asked me to do that, and he didn't."

The detective nodded slowly, then held Scott's gaze. "You'll look around for it? Let us know if you find anything?" Scott nodded. "In the meantime, may we have this one? I'd like to show it to the coroner."

Scott lifted a shoulder. "Of course." He switched his gaze to Mike. "Could you run over to Shady Acres and ask Mr. Garrett if we can borrow a couple of hoof picks for the afternoon?" Mike nodded. "And Becky, do you think you could pick up a couple of replacements?"

"Sure." She'd stop by the tack and feed store when she made the bank deposit.

Jeff slid his pen beneath the clip and snapped his notebook closed. He looked at her. "We need to get some prints from you."

His expression held a hint of apprehension, as though he was afraid she'd put up a fuss. Truthfully, Becky had considered it after the mess they'd left in the office. But if having her fingerprints helped them catch Neal's killer, she wasn't going to argue about it. "Okay, let's get it over with."

They headed toward the house and Scott fell in beside them. The girls returned to the barn, whispering together, and Mike headed toward the road and Shady Acres.

Scott spoke in a low voice as they walked. "You know, if that hoof pick was the weapon that killed Haldeman, it supports my theory that he surprised a burglar. The grooming tools are kept right out in the open on top of that workbench. Either of them could have grabbed it during a fight."

Jeff kept his eyes ahead as he opened the door for Becky

to enter. Foster smoothed down the edge of his mustache with a finger and answered noncommittally. "That's one theory we're considering."

In other words, the police weren't going to discuss their investigation. Well, that was to be expected. Becky eyed Jeff as she stepped through the doorway. Would he discuss the case with Amber? Probably not. It would be unprofessional. But just because they were being tight-lipped didn't mean she should. While Jeff took her fingerprints, she intended to tell him about Kaci's visit.

EIGHT

"I'll see to it, Darrell. Don't worry about a thing."

Becky replaced the telephone receiver. Darrell Haldeman, Neal's only living relative as far as she knew, had been notified of his uncle's death by the state police. He'd called from his home in Texas to tell her he was making arrangements to fly to Kentucky the week after next. Instead of a funeral he'd decided on a memorial service to be held while he was in town. Becky would help with the arrangements on this end.

She eyed Neal's desk. Making service arrangements was one thing. Going through Neal's personal belongings was a different story entirely. She'd shut the door to Neal's bedroom and bathroom, and as far as she was concerned it would stay shut until Darrell Haldeman arrived.

But the desk was another matter. Its drawers held information about the Pasture, and therefore she needed to go through it to see if there was anything that might help Scott in his role of temporary manager.

Might as well tackle the biggest mess first. She sat in Neal's desk chair and slid open the deep drawer on the right. She'd seen Neal toss papers unceremoniously in there, with no thought of maintaining any sort of order. "It's my To Be Filed drawer," he'd told her with a grin.

"I'll be happy to organize it for you," she had offered.

But he'd declined. "Nah, I've got personal papers mixed in with the business stuff. Nothing important, though. All the horses' records are in their file folders."

If only Neal had been as organized with his personal records as he had been with the retirees' folders she'd given to Scott this morning. She peered into the drawer. "What a mess."

She pulled out the contents and piled them on the surface of the desk.

Two hours later, Scott stepped into the office. "What's all this?"

Kneeling on the floor, Becky looked up. "A bunch of junk, mostly, from Neal's desk. I started out trying to make a folder for everything, but there's such a mishmash of stuff here I decided it would be easier to try to sort it into broader categories." She gestured to the eight piles of papers, receipts and clippings spread over the floor.

Scott dropped onto the only seat in the office besides the desk chairs, a dilapidated old wing chair donated by someone years ago. Becky avoided it, because it smelled like a musty attic.

"What did he have in there?"

"Everything." Becky picked up the nearest pile. "There are hundreds of newspaper clippings. It's like he saved every article he ever read that had anything to do with horses or racing." She lifted the top one and held it up. "Here's one about Japanese races earning graded status, whatever that means. There's one on stud farms in Turkey and a bunch about individual horses. There's even an article in here about horse cloning." She put the clipping back with the others and reached for the next pile. "And there are dozens of letters from people who've been on the tour and wrote to thank him." She shook her head. "Why would he keep those? Some of them are two years old."

"No idea." Scott bent over and picked up a handful of register receipts from the pile nearest him. "Shouldn't these be in a financial file somewhere?"

"No, he was very good about filing financial records for the Pasture. Those are personal receipts, as far as I can tell."

Scott read from the top one. "Two pair of jeans and a men's shirt from Wal-Mart." He shuffled through the next few. "Shoes, groceries." With a shrug, he put them back on the pile.

"Here's something interesting, though I have no idea what it is." She crawled forward on her knees to reach the pile nearest the desk. "There are more than fifty notes in Neal's handwriting that look like this."

She picked up the top one, a paper torn from a spiral notebook, a couple of ragged ribbons waving from the edge as she held it up for Scott's inspection. Written on it were rows of numbers that made no sense at all.

Scott took it from her. "2.5—#5w—BC3—8-1 Pd 20." He read the numbers and letters on the first line slowly, then his gaze rose to catch hers. "This is the record for a bet. See here, up at the top, the date is November 4. That's the day the Breeder's Cup ran last year, so I'm guessing BC3 means the third race. The five is the number five horse in that race, the W means he bet it to win, and it went off at eight to one." He studied it a moment longer. "Two point five must stand for two hundred fifty dollars, and this says the horse won, so it paid two thousand dollars."

Becky gasped. "Two thousand dollars? On one race?"

Oh, what she could do with an extra two thousand dollars. There were a bunch of rows on that sheet in Scott's hand. Neal must have bet on dozens of horses.

"He got lucky on that one." Scott's eyes moved as he scanned the sheet. "Looks like he didn't come out a winner at the end of the day, though. He was out close to eight thousand dollars."

"Eight thousand?" So much for winning two thousand in one race. Becky's head swam at the thought of losing eight thousand dollars in a single day. She knew Neal liked to bet, because she overheard him talking on the phone quite a bit. But that was a lot of money! "Are you sure that's what those numbers mean, Scott?"

Scott shook his head slowly. "Not entirely. Every bettor has his own way of keeping tabs on his bets. We could check the track statistics for that day to be sure, maybe pull the racing forms over at the Keeneland Library."

"Oh!" Becky turned and picked up a pile of newspapers. The title on all of them was *Daily Racing Form*. "There were a bunch of these in the drawer, too."

Scott took the pile and rifled through them. "Here it is." He fanned the edges and flipped the paper open. "Yeah, here's the fifth horse. There's a note jotted on there, '2.5—30-1.'" He looked up at her. "That's got to be his bet and the horse's odds at post time. And this—" he held up the page from the notebook "—is his tally sheet."

Becky looked at the huge stack of papers with similar figures on them. She shook her head sadly. "Poor Neal. He must have had a real problem with gambling. I had no idea."

Scott put the racing form down and studied the figures scrawled on the paper, lines creasing his forehead. "I'll tell you what worries me is this last number on here. Looks like he added up his winnings and losses for the day and ended up in the hole eight thousand three hundred fifty dollars. But look below that."

Becky took the paper from his hand. At the bottom of the page, below the eight thousand number, another number had been scrawled. She sucked in a breath. No. That couldn't mean what she thought it meant.

She raised her eyes to Scott's. "Minus thirty-seven thousand five hundred dollars?"

Scott nodded. "And do you see those initials beside it?"

Becky did. "EJ. Do you know what that means?"

Scott's lips tightened. "I sure do."

Scott paid for a general admission ticket to enter Keeneland. It was close to the end of the afternoon, probably only a couple of races left to run, but there was still a steady stream of race enthusiasts filing past the ticket window beneath the track's big stone entryway.

He stepped through the open breezeway, passed the gift shop, and joined a throng in the paddock. A line of horses were at that moment being ceremoniously paraded beneath the huge sycamores and maples that towered over the paddock as they made their way toward the saddle ring. Scott slipped into a gap in the crowd next to the metal railing to admire them. The next race was for fillies, and these magnificent beauties pranced in their eagerness to get on the track.

A line of jockeys arrived as the trainers started saddling the racers, eyeing their horses and each other, their expressions grim or stern as they assumed their game faces to meet the challenge ahead. A small cluster of well-dressed people stood a little distance from each horse to watch the saddle and review procedure. The owners and their guests.

Though he didn't spend much time at the track, Scott had to admit the atmosphere of excitement and anticipation stirred his blood. Gambling didn't appeal to him at all, but these horses were supreme athletes, every one of them. They loved to race, and always gave it their all. He'd seen horses suffer an injury and continue to run on three legs with every ounce of strength in them. Not many human athletes would be that dedicated.

Scott scanned the faces lining the black railing. He caught sight of several familiar ones, as he knew he would. Regulars during the months of April and October, when Keeneland's race meetings were held, racing forms clutched in their hands as they studied the horses, trying to decide which ones looked like winners. A beautiful little chestnut filly skittered sideways when her trainer tried to place the saddle on her back, and dozens of hands clutching pens made marks on their forms, noting her nervous energy.

Finally, Scott caught sight of the man on the other side of the paddock, standing with his back to the clubhouse. He stepped away from the railing and picked his way toward the tall, lanky man wearing a gray fedora and a pensive expression. He sidled up beside him and stood watching the number five horse for a moment.

"So who do you like in this one?" He didn't take his eyes off the horse as he spoke.

The man cast a quick glance his way. The corner of his mouth twitched. "Some fine-looking fillies there."

Scott nodded. "You're Eddie Jones, aren't you?"

He didn't seem concerned at being recognized by a stranger. Well, a man in his profession wouldn't.

"That's right. Have we met?"

"Not officially, but we've got mutual friends." Scott

turned to hold out his hand. "Scott Lewis, assistant manager out at Shady Acres."

Recognition flared in Eddie's face. "You work for Lee Courtney."

"And Zach Garrett." Scott watched the man's face as he dropped Zach's name. Mr. Courtney, though the more well-known of the two men, would certainly not have dealings with a man like Eddie Jones. But Zach had been known to place an occasional bet off-the-record.

Understanding showed in Eddie's eyes as he assumed he knew the reason for Scott's sudden introduction. That was, after all, the way bookies met their new customers, on the referral of others.

But Scott hadn't come to Keeneland to place an illegal bet. "Actually, I've taken over temporarily for Neal Haldeman at Out to Pasture."

The man's eyes flickered briefly at the mention of Haldeman, though his tone was carefully even. "I heard about that. Quite a shock."

"Yes, it was. I was hoping you might be able to answer a question or two."

"Why ask me? I don't know a thing about it, other than what I read in the paper."

Scott leaned forward and lowered his voice. "I've been going through some of Haldeman's records, and I found several—" he paused for effect, studying the man closely "—mentions of you in them."

Eddie's smile tightened as he returned Scott's gaze. "I'm not surprised."

Nor pleased, judging by the way the man's nostrils flared.

"I was just wondering how much Haldeman was into you for."

Eddie turned slightly away, his gaze going to the paddock where the number five horse was saddled and ready to be mounted. "I'd have to check."

Scott prodded. "Ballpark."

The man tapped pursed lips with a forefinger. "I'd say close to thirty." He looked back at Scott. "Why do you want to know?"

Scott held his gaze. "Just wondering whether this information is important enough to warrant turning it over to the police."

A bitter smile lifted the edges of his mouth. "Haldeman is no good to me dead, if that's what you're insinuating. A debt like this one isn't going to be paid out of his estate. Nor is it collectible from his relatives."

"No, but people like you have been known to apply pressure on occasion."

Anger flashed in the man's eyes. "Trust me, I wouldn't do someone in for thirty."

Scott held his hands out. "I'm not accusing you of anything. Just trying to get some answers."

He studied Scott for a moment. "I assume if you found mention of me, you found others, as well. Haldeman spread his business around pretty evenly. Word on the street is that he was down some fairly big numbers, all told."

Scott actually hadn't looked at Haldeman's files after his conversation with Becky. He'd wanted to get here before the last race. But he made a mental note to go through the rest of those tally sheets, see if he could find any other initials.

"My, my, my, look who's here."

Scott turned as the familiar female voice drawled in his ear. He shouldn't be surprised to see her here. She'd told them this morning she was on her way to the track.

"Miss Buchanan."

"Kaci, darling. Remember?" He took her outstretched hand, and she pressed it with her other one, her fingers rubbing in a caress over his skin as she had done this morning. Her gaze flickered over his shoulder. "Am I interrupting anything important?"

Scott flashed a quick look at Eddie, suddenly damp under the collar. He'd hate for anyone to think he was betting with a bookie. "No, nothing at all. We were just discussing a mutual friend."

Eddie eyed Kaci with a slick smile. "In fact, I was just leaving. Ma'am." He touched a finger to his hat before walking away. Scott thought he looked relieved to have an excuse to escape. He slipped into the crowd flowing toward the track and was quickly lost to sight.

Kaci lowered her voice, still clutching his hand. "I want to get up to the box for this race. But apparently I'm to have a visit from the police this evening." Her blue eyes caught his, her gaze hard.

"Really? Why?"

Her eyes moved as she searched his face. Then her mouth relaxed into a smile. "If it wasn't you, then it must have been Neal's secretary." Her voice dripped scorn at the mention of Becky. "The housekeeper called my cell phone about an hour ago to tell me the police stopped by with a few questions. Someone must have given them my name as a person of interest." Her smile stretched into a sly grin. "Of course, I am quite an interesting person, to those who get to know me."

Scott shifted his weight, suddenly uncomfortable. He wasn't used to females flirting so openly with him. "I'm sure you are," he managed.

The clear trumpet notes sounding the call to post cut through the murmur of the crowd, signalling the race was about to start. The speed of the people moving toward the track increased. Kaci glanced over Scott's shoulder.

"I must go. Mother's filly has a good chance of breaking her maiden in this one, and I don't want to miss it."

Scott gave her hand a final squeeze and released it. A racehorse's first win, or breaking its maiden, was a celebrated event among breeders and trainers alike. "Of course. Good luck to her."

Kaci fluttered her fingers in his direction and hurried toward the clubhouse elevator. Scott stood, indecisive, as the crowd surged around him. He could look for Eddie again, try to continue his conversation. But he didn't really need to. He'd gotten what he wanted from the guy, a verification of Haldeman's illegal betting activity, and a number.

The paddock area had emptied. Scott made his way toward the exit, remembering the flare of anger in Eddie's eyes and in his voice. True, thirty thousand dollars was probably not a big deal to a guy in Eddie's business. Not a big enough debt to kill a man over. But if Haldeman owed money to several people, and if each of them found out, it would certainly make someone worry that he wasn't going to get paid very quickly. He might want to apply a little pressure, to make sure his debt got settled first. And that kind of pressure could turn physical at the drop of a hat. Fistfights had been known to erupt for much less reason. And a fistfight could turn nasty quickly.

Especially if there was a handy weapon nearby.

NINE

"Now boys, *please* be on your best behavior. We want to show our manners to Mr. Lewis, don't we?"

Becky eyed her sons in the rearview mirror as she turned into the driveway of the Pasture. Jamie, intent on the colorful plastic man in his hands, nodded obediently in answer to her request, but Tyler's face bore its usual stubborn expression.

"Why?"

Becky let out an exasperated sigh. "Because he's my new boss, and I want to make a good impression on him. I told you that."

The boy fixed her with a look so like his father's that Becky's heart stuttered in her chest. "Will he really fire you if me and Jamie act up?"

How could a child who had not seen his father since he was six months old speak in the same voice and look at her with Christopher's eyes? Genetics, she supposed. She lived in Christopher's shadow every day of her life. It just wasn't fair. Yet she loved these tiny replicas of their father more than she loved her own life.

She shoved the shifter into park. "You never know." She locked eyes with Tyler in the mirror. "He certainly won't be impressed with an assistant whose sons act like savages. He might not let me bring you back again."

She watched the dark head nod as he acknowledged the truth in her words, and breathed a sigh of relief. Her goal for this beautiful Saturday morning was to finish labeling the files for all that junk in Neal's drawer while the kids watched Saturday-morning cartoons on the TV. After she made up a few of the hours she missed Thursday afternoon, she'd promised the boys a trip to the park to feed the ducks.

Neal's truck still sat in the driveway, unmoved since Wednesday night. Today, Scott's truck was parked along-side it, and both the front and back barn doors stood open. Neal usually left the front doors closed. A small difference, but one that served as a reminder that Neal was no longer in charge of Out to Pasture.

The moment she turned the key and cut the engine, the boys tumbled out the back doors and took off at a run toward the barn. Becky gathered her purse, watching through the windshield as Sam greeted them, his tail whipping back and forth while they petted and hugged him. She opened the car door, her pulse speeding up when Scott stepped to the wide barn doorway to meet her sons.

"Hello, there! You must not be strangers, or my guard dog wouldn't be licking your faces."

"Sam knows us." Jamie stared at him with serious eyes. "He's our friend."

Scott grinned at her, but he answered Jamie with utmost seriousness. "I can see that."

Jamie stood straight and stuck out a hand. "Pleased to meet you. I'm Jamie Dennison."

Becky hid a smile. At least Jamie had listened to her

lecture on manners this morning. Maybe Tyler would follow his brother's lead.

Scott returned Jamie's greeting formally. "Nice to meet you, Jamie. I'm Scott Lewis."

When Scott released his hand, Tyler shoved his forward. "I'm Tyler. Are you going to fire my mom if I act like a savage?"

With a groan, Becky leaned against the hood of her car and shook her head. Out of the corner of her eye she saw Scott considering his answer. "Probably not," he told Tyler, "but I might ask her to keep you in the office so you won't get in my way out here. Only big kids who behave themselves can help with the horses, you know."

Tyler's face lit with excitement at the suggestion of helping with the horses. "I'm a big kid. I'm in kindergarten."

Scott grinned at her over the tops of two dark heads. "Good. I can use some helpers today."

Becky opened her mouth to protest. She didn't come to work on a Saturday to play with horses. She had things to do in the office. And she couldn't dump the boys on Scott while she went inside.

Her protest died unspoken as a car pulled into the driveway. The sunlight gleamed on the polished hood of a gold Mercedes Roadster. It slowed to a stop midway down the driveway, the sun's rays reflecting off the windshield so that Becky couldn't see the driver clearly. She glanced at Scott, who shrugged.

Becky approached the driver's door and stopped beside the tinted windows. After a moment, the window opened a few inches, revealing a woman in large dark sunglasses with a tan print scarf covering her head.

Odd. Sometimes people came on Saturdays for a tour,

but she hadn't made note on the calendar of anyone scheduled for today. Maybe this woman was out for a drive and
stopped in when she saw the sign by the road.

"Hello." Becky dipped her head toward the window.
"Are you here for a tour?"

The dark glasses hid most of the woman's face, but her
lips, unadorned with lipstick, tightened into a crooked line
for a moment before she answered. "No. I...uh, no."

Was that a sob that broke her voice? Becky couldn't be
sure, but the skin on her arm prickled with sudden suspicion.
Could this woman be the mysterious "L"? Maybe the owner
of the footprint returning to check out the scene of her crime?

"What can we do for you, Ms...." She let her tone rise,
an unspoken request for the stranger's name.

"Keller." The woman's lips snapped shut. She faced
forward, staring through the windshield at the place where
Scott and the boys stood near the entrance to the barn,
watching them.

The boys! Fear clawed at Becky's throat. What had possessed her to bring the boys here today? Neal's killer was
still on the loose, and maybe even sitting here now, with
her fancy car pointed directly toward them.

The woman drew a shuddering breath and spoke
without facing Becky, the eyes invisible behind the glasses.
"I... I just wanted to look around, if that's okay?"

A sob stuttered her voice. That sounded like genuine
grief. Becky took a step toward the window, her suspicions beginning to fade. Did killers grieve over their
victims? The scarf was knotted beneath an untidy mass of
dark hair at the back of her head. The woman's rather large
nose was red, the nostrils rubbed nearly raw. Either she was
suffering from a bad cold, or she had recently indulged in

a violent crying spell. A shuddering breath gave evidence of the latter, and compassion warred with suspicion in Becky. Maybe she wasn't a killer after all. A friend of Neal's, perhaps?

"I don't know if Mr. Lewis has time to conduct a tour this morning." She cast a glance toward Scott.

The woman killed the engine and got out of the car. When she stood, she towered a full head over Becky. That wasn't unusual. Most people did.

Scott stepped forward, the boys and Sam tagging along. He held out his hand. "Hello, I'm Scott Lewis. I'm taking care of things around here for a little while."

The woman's hand froze in the process of stretching out to take Scott's, and a sob escaped her lips. Her shoulders hunched forward and her hands rose to cover her face, glasses and all, as she succumbed to a fit of weeping.

"Oh, you poor thing." All her suspicions melting at the sight of the woman's grief, Becky rushed forward and put an arm around the sobbing woman's shoulders.

The boys stood openmouthed. A grown woman blubbering like a child wasn't something they saw often. Becky squeezed the shuddering shoulders and made soothing noises while Scott watched, his extended hand clenching and unclenching.

After a moment, the woman pulled a much-used tissue from the pocket of her jacket and scrubbed at her red nose. "I'm suh-sorry to act like a fool. I just—" Another heave robbed her of words and she shook her head violently, knocking her glasses lopsided on her face. She shoved them up to perch on top of her scarf like the eyes of a giant insect.

Grief could ravage the looks of even a beautiful woman, and this woman was no beauty to begin with. Despair had wreaked havoc on her face. She folded the ragged tissue and attempted to blot at her eyes, the lids of which were so reddened and swollen that discerning their normal shape was impossible.

With a huge intake of breath, she shoved the damp scrap of tissue back in her pocket and thrust her hand toward Scott in a belated greeting. "Please forgive me for being rude, Mr. Lewis. My name is Isabelle Keller, and I'm a…" Becky thought she might sob again, but instead she swallowed hard and continued with obvious difficulty. "I was a friend of Neal Haldeman."

Isabelle Keller. Becky knew that name. Isabelle's father was a well-known real estate mogul who had bought and sold half the land in central Kentucky at one time or other. His name was in the newspaper almost every day. Becky had spoken with Isabelle on the phone several times, and had overheard Neal arranging to pick her up for dinner just last week. At the time Becky had noted that his attitude on the phone was deferential, unlike his tone when he spoke with women like Kaci Buchanan.

Neal had certainly moved in lofty circles.

Becky placed a hand on the woman's arm. "Miss Keller, I'm so sorry for your loss. Please accept my condolences." Isabelle's lips twisted in her effort to hold back another sob. "I'm Becky Dennison, Neal's assistant."

Recognition cleared the lines from her forehead and she took Becky's hand. Becky kept her expression kind as she returned the woman's troubled gaze.

"I remember. Neal said—" She stopped, struggling to maintain her composure, then continued. "Neal said you were a big help to him, that you were going to organize things in the office. He was so glad to have you." Fresh tears pooled in her eyes. Fumbling in her pocket, she withdrew the abused scrap of tissue again. "I'm so sorry. I didn't think anyone would be here today."

"Mommy?" Jamie edged toward her, his gaze fixed on Isabelle as he laid a hand on Becky's leg. His loud whisper rasped over the sound of the woman's sniffle. "What's wrong with that lady?"

"Jamie." Becky infused her tone with warning as her stern expression told her son to hold his tongue.

Scott cleared his throat. "Tell you what, boys. I could use some help feeding the horses. Think you guys could give me a hand?"

"Wow!" Tyler ran toward her, bouncing on his toes. "Can we, Mommy? Please?"

Becky lifted her gaze from their pleading faces to Scott's. The twins could be a handful, and she really hadn't intended to dump them on her boss. Scott nodded almost imperceptibly toward Isabelle and then the house. Obviously, he'd rather deal with them than a crying woman.

Becky laid a hand on each boy's shoulder. "Okay, but only if you promise to do exactly what Mr. Lewis says. And no fighting. And no standing up on the golf cart."

Jamie's eyes lit up. "We get to ride on the golf cart?"

"Woo-hoo!" Tyler pumped a fist into the air.

Scott nodded toward Isabelle and then with an unmistakable air of relief, headed toward the barn, flanked by excitedly leaping boys.

Becky smiled into Isabelle's tear-streaked face. "Perhaps you'd like to come inside. I can put on a pot of coffee, or maybe make some tea."

Isabelle hesitated. "Tea would be good, if it's herbal."

"It is."

Becky placed an assuring arm around her and guided her toward the back door. Inside, she steered Isabelle into the kitchen and gestured toward a seat at the small table in the center of the room. She ran hot water into the large glass measuring cup she used to make her own tea every morning. While that heated in the microwave, she placed a boxed assortment of herbal teas on the table and got two clean mugs from the cupboard. She set the unchipped one in front of Isabelle.

A comfortable silence, broken only by the occasional sniffle, descended between them as they each selected a pouch from the box. When the microwave dinged, Becky poured water over Isabelle's tea bag, and peach-scented steam rose from her mug. She retrieved a box of tissues from the office, which drew a brief smile of thanks from her distraught guest.

As Isabelle stirred a package of sweetener into her mug, Becky dunked her tea bag rhythmically in the steaming water. The sharp odor of mint from her mug mingled with the peach. She kept her gaze on the swiftly darkening tea. "Have you known Neal a long time?"

"We met at a Christmas party." Isabelle reached for a fresh tissue as she shook her head. "Four months ago. It seems much longer."

There could be only one possible reason for such grief for a man she'd known such a short time. Becky swirled her tea bag and spoke softly. "Were you in love with him?"

More tears rolled unchecked down her red cheeks as Isabelle nodded. "From the first moment. He was so handsome and funny. And passionate." She looked up quickly. "About the horses, I mean. He told me all about them, and he spoke as though they were his children."

"In a way, I think they were."

A brief smile took her lips. "That's what Father said. But that's only because—" She bit back whatever she'd been about to say with a hard swallow.

Becky pulled the tea bag from her mug and sipped, breathing in the sweet odor of wintergreen. She judged the woman to be in her early thirties, not much older than Becky. "His death must have come as such a shock."

She nodded miserably. "We were to have dinner Thursday night, a special dinner. When he didn't arrive to pick me up, I thought—" She broke off and stared into her mug. When she continued, her voice was soft. "Father said it wouldn't last, that Neal was only interested in me because of money. He forbade me to give him any." Her tear-filled eyes rose to lock with Becky's. "But he never asked. Not once since the night we met. So he couldn't have been after my money, could he?" Her voice held a note of desperation.

Though she'd only worked with Neal two months, Becky had seen him pursue donations for the Pasture with charming single-mindedness. Would he have dated a woman only to get money for his precious horses? Possibly. But only temporarily, perhaps a dinner date or two. Surely he wouldn't continue a relationship for months under false pretenses.

Becky blew the steam from her tea and sipped, aware that Isabelle waited fearfully for her answer. Neal was gone, and there was no reason for the poor woman to wonder for the rest of her life whether the man she loved had loved her in return. Tears of sympathy stung her eyes, and she replied with a confidence she didn't feel. "Of course not. Neal had too much integrity for that."

Isabelle seemed to draw comfort from her certainty. Her mug still untouched, she leaned against the back of the chair. "If only Father had known him better. And he would have had the opportunity soon."

Her mouth snapped shut. She clutched the mug with both hands and hesitated, clearly holding back something. Becky remained silent, confident that given the opportunity, whatever Isabelle had to say would spill forth.

The woman's gaze rose to meet with Becky's. "Neal would have made a wonderful father. I know he would."

Staring into the mournful dark eyes, Becky's jaw went slack. What was she saying?

"Isabelle, are you pregnant?"

Isabelle's chin trembled as she nodded. "I know it was soon, and we didn't plan for this to happen. I planned to tell Neal that night. Then he didn't show up for our date, and he didn't answer his phone. I didn't sleep at all, worrying that he'd found out about the baby and was angry with me. Which was silly, I know, because no one knows except me, but I couldn't imagine why he would stand me up. Then I read yesterday's paper."

She broke down again, deep sobs racking her body as she drooped over the table. Becky lifted the hot tea mug out of harm's way and laid a hand on her arm. What could she say? She knew no words of comfort equal to this woman's devastating circumstance.

After a moment the sobbing eased and Isabelle raised her head. This time she sipped the warm tea Becky pushed toward her, and as she did her tears quieted.

"What will you do?"

Isabelle drew a deep breath. "I'll raise our baby alone. Father will be furious when I tell him. He may even throw me out." She lifted her chin. "If he does, I'll get a job. I went to college. Surely someone will hire me."

Becky hoped she was right. She knew all too well the trials in store for a mother struggling to raise her children alone. It was certainly a different life from the one Isabelle enjoyed now, with her Mercedes and her rich father.

She reached across the table to cover Isabelle's hand with her own. "You'll be in my prayers."

The woman blinked, and then her features softened. "Thank you."

TEN

Scott steered the boys toward the barn. He glanced backward and felt like a couple of cement blocks had been lifted off his chest at the sight of Becky and Isabelle Keller disappearing through the office door. Thank goodness Becky had arrived before the weepy heiress.

"Was that lady sad?"

Both boys watched him with round, dark eyes and solemn expressions. They looked a lot alike, enough that they might be mistaken for one another at a quick glance. But when he looked closer, Scott saw that the one who introduced himself as Tyler was a little taller, and Jamie's face was more slender. And thank goodness Becky didn't dress them alike. Jamie wore a red nylon ski jacket, and his brother an electric-blue one.

Tyler shoved his brother's shoulder. "Duh, stupid. Why else would she be crying?"

Jamie rounded on him, anger blazing in his eyes. "Don't push me, Tyler. Mommy said not to fight."

Scott stepped forward and looked down on both of them, taking advantage of his intimidating height to forestall a scuffle. "If you're going to fight, you'll have to go in the house with the women. I can't have you upsetting the horses."

Eyes wide, they both nodded. Scott addressed Jamie. "Yes, I think that lady was sad. She must have known Mr. Haldeman." He snapped his mouth shut. What had Becky told her sons about Haldeman's death? Better to keep quiet than to say anything that might confuse them.

The edges of Jamie's mouth drooped. "I don't like it when ladies cry. It makes me upset."

Out of the mouths of babes. Scott glanced toward the back door of the house before nodding at Jamie. "Me, too."

He stepped into the barn, the boys and Sam following. He picked up the pouch into which he'd placed the various morning medications that needed to be administered.

"Shotgun!" Tyler sprinted across the dirt floor.

Jamie raced behind him. "No fair! I want to ride up front."

"Too bad." Tyler leaped onto the cart's front bench, and smirked at his brother. "I called shotgun first."

Did they argue like this all the time? Scott hadn't been blessed with brothers, and his only sister was six years older. When they were kids he liked to pester her, of course, but they never really fought. She would have squashed him like a bug.

"Nobody gets shotgun." He let his stern gaze slide from Jamie to Tyler. "Except Sam. That's his seat."

Tyler pouted for a second, but then shrugged and climbed over the seat back to the bench that faced the rear of the cart. Scott hefted the bag of feed he'd filled earlier and deposited it on the floorboard in the front. Jamie climbed up beside his brother.

"Up here, Sam." He slid behind the steering wheel and patted the bench. The dog leaped up to stand on the seat, then began licking the back of both boys' heads. Grinning at their laughter, Scott guided the cart through the barn and out the back door.

The warm sunlight dazzled his eyes, but a cool breeze still held a latent trace of winter as it blew the scent of sweet hay into his face. He buttoned the collar of his denim jacket and eyed the fencing as he steered between the paddocks. The top plank on his left would need to be replaced soon; Rusty had done a number on it. Since he had read through all the files concerning the stallions' diets, he knew the horse didn't have a mineral deficiency. He was probably just bored. Scott made a mental note to spray the fence with Chew Stop and to check Rusty's mouth for splinters.

He halted the cart beside Gadsby's feed bucket. The boys and Sam leaped to the ground as the gelding caught sight of them and trotted across the grass in their direction.

"Wow, look at him!" Jamie's eyes grew round as Gadsby neared. "He's a giant horse."

Tyler propped a foot on the bottom fence rail and, with a hand on his hip, spoke with authority to his brother. "He's not a giant. He's regular size. Isn't he, Mr. Lewis?"

Scott eyed the horse. "He's good-sized, but he's not a giant."

Tyler leveled a smirk on Jamie. "Told you."

Scott opened the top of the bag and grabbed the scoop. "He is a movie star, though."

"Wow." Jamie eyed Gadsby with awe. "What movie was he in?"

Scott emptied the scoop into the bucket, then added a second. "*Seabiscuit*. It's about a famous racehorse from a long time ago. You should ask your mom to rent it for you. It's a good story, and you'll see Gadsby."

"Gadsby. That's a great name." Admiration flooded Tyler's voice as he gazed on the happily munching horse.

His hand rose, but halted just outside the fence as he looked up at Scott. "Does he care if I touch him?"

Scott hesitated. Gadsby was one of the gentler horses in residence at the Pasture, but no sense taking chances. "In a minute, when he finishes eating."

The boys nodded, and they all watched as Gadsby chewed. The cool morning air seemed to magnify the sounds of the horse's teeth grinding the fiber. The sunlight gleamed on the smooth lines of his back and turned his coat a deep auburn.

"Gadsby is what's called blood bay," he told the boys, "because his coat is that rich, red color. And you see the way his mane, tail and the lower part of his legs are darker? Those are called dark points."

Jamie, far more cautious than his brother, eased up to the fence beside Tyler, his gaze fixed on Gadsby. "You're smart about horses, aren't you?"

Grinning, Scott ruffled his hair. "I've learned a few things. I've been around them since I was younger than you."

Two pastures away, Bull called toward them with an impatient whinny. Toward the front of the farm, Fortune answered. Everybody was hungry this morning.

"I wish we had a horse." Tyler leaped off the bottom plank and ran over to the golf cart. "Can I feed the next one?"

"Don't you want to pet Gadsby when he finishes eating?"

The boy shrugged. "He takes too long."

Scott shook his head. The kid had the attention span of a Chihuahua. "Okay, let's get moving. Yes, you can feed the next one." Jamie's mouth opened, and Scott spoke before he could complain. "They get two scoops, so you can each do one."

He climbed up in the golf cart and waited for Sam to settle beside him before releasing the brake.

As the cart rolled forward, Tyler shoved a hand into the air. "I'm first."

"No fair!"

Scott heaved a sigh.

When Becky followed a much calmer Isabelle through the back door, a flash of fluorescent green whizzed within a few inches of her head and bounced off the doorjamb. Startled, she threw her hands up to protect her face. A blur of yellow fur zoomed by her.

"Sorry, Mommy!"

From across the yard, Tyler turned a guilty grin her way as Sam retrieved the tennis ball and bounded toward him.

She leveled a frown on her son. "Young man, you've got to be more careful. That almost hit the glass. And me."

He ducked his head, then raced after the dog to try to wrestle the ball out of his mouth, Jamie running after them. At least they were both getting a lot of exercise today, running in the yard with Sam. Maybe tonight they'd go to sleep early.

Scott left his position near the barn and crossed the driveway as Becky followed Isabelle to her car.

Clutching her sunglasses, the heiress took a step toward him. "Mr. Lewis, I hope you'll forgive my earlier behavior."

Scott shoved his hands into his jeans pockets. "No apologies necessary, ma'am. I'm sorry for, uh, your loss." He shot a quick glance at Becky, a clear plea for rescue.

Hiding a smile, she stepped forward and took Isabelle's slim hand in hers. "Good luck. Don't forget, I'm here if you need someone to talk to."

The woman's smile wavered, but she held on to her composure. "Thank you. For everything."

She slid into the Mercedes, but before she shut the door she looked out over the paddocks. Then she directed a trembling smile toward them. "Goodbye."

Scott moved forward to stand beside Becky as the car backed onto the road and then pulled away. A bird in a branch overhead scolded when they walked beneath a thickly leafed sugar maple toward the boys.

"I guess she was upset about Haldeman." Scott's statement held a question.

Becky nodded. "She's in love with him."

"With Haldeman?" Disbelief twisted his features.

Sam raced by them as they reached the edge of the driveway, the boys hot on his trail, shrieking with laughter.

"Why do you say it like that?

He watched the boys romping in the grass. "I wouldn't think Haldeman was the type to appeal to a rich heiress like her."

"Well, he did. And apparently the feeling was mutual."

Scott's gaze slid sideways, skeptical. "I find that even harder to believe. If he was in love with Isabelle Keller, why was Kaci Buchannan dropping earrings in his sofa?"

Tyler caught up with the dog and threw both arms around his neck to restrain him while Jamie pried the ball out of his mouth. Becky watched her sons, struggling to come up with a plausible explanation in Isabelle's favor.

"Neal wouldn't want to be rude to Kaci," she said slowly. "She's too prominent."

Scott snorted a laugh. "You mean she's too rich."

"Isabelle is rich, too. At least, her father is."

Scott lifted a shoulder. "Yes, but Kaci is beautiful as well as rich."

Anger flared on behalf of her new friend. At least, she

hoped that was the reason. She still felt a bit of antagonism toward Kaci, the arrogant blonde.

"Beauty is more than looks. Apparently Neal recognized that." She snapped her jaw shut.

He twisted his head to stare at her, surprise coloring his features. "She really made an impression on you. What did she say to make you defend her like this?"

Becky watched the boys a moment before answering. Jamie held the ball high above his head, clutched in a white-fingered grip, while Sam sat patiently in front of him, his stare fixed on his toy. Finally Jamie threw it, and then wiped his hand on his jeans as the dog raced across the yard in hot pursuit.

"I guess I just feel sorry for her." She glanced at Scott, then away again. "She's pregnant with Neal's child."

Scott gave a low whistle. "That must have been a shock."

"Neal didn't know. Isabelle was going to tell him the night he was killed."

"I didn't mean Neal." He pivoted on his boots to peer at her. "How much do you know about her father, Mr. Keller?"

"I know he's rich. He's in the paper all the time."

"Yeah, and did you catch that article about him a few weeks ago?"

Becky knew the one he meant. "One of his employees accused him of assault."

"That's the one." He shoved a hand in his jeans pocket. "Apparently that wasn't the first time he's been accused of slugging an employee, but nothing ever comes of it. I thought at the time that the guy making the accusation would probably drop the whole thing and get a big check in return."

They stood in silence. Sam's excited barking sounded

loud against the backdrop of a distant whinny from the pasture across the street. Becky battled guilt as she watched Tyler toss the ball high into the air. Why hadn't she kept her mouth shut? What a lousy friend she turned out to be.

And what if Isabelle's father was angry with her? If he hit his employees, was he the kind of man who would hit his daughter? Or her lover?

"Whoa!" Scott took off at a run.

Startled, Becky looked after him. Her heart skipped a beat when she saw the tennis ball bounce inside Alidor's paddock. Sam, well trained by Neal, didn't go after the ball but stood obediently on this side of the fence. Tyler raced across the grass, his little legs pumping as hard as he could push them. From the far side of the paddock, the fiery stallion noticed the new object in his territory and started to run toward it.

"Don't go in there!"

Thankfully, Tyler stopped when Scott shouted. He turned a question-filled face toward him, but then stepped backward as Alidor arrived at the tennis ball and blew a loud snort. The stallion tossed his head and pawed at the ball.

Scott came to a stop beside Tyler and put a hand on his shoulder. His voice carried back to her. "Alidor doesn't like it when strangers go in his paddock. I found that out the other day. Let's see if we can find another tennis ball for Sam. I'll get that one later, when there aren't so many people around to upset him."

Jamie fell into step beside them as they headed toward the barn, but peeled off to come toward her. "I'm hungry."

Becky glanced at her watch. Eleven-ten. "You should have eaten more breakfast. It's not lunchtime yet."

"Actually," said Scott, giving her a sheepish smile, "I'm

kind of hungry myself. You interested in grabbing a hamburger somewhere?"

"Yeah!" Tyler ran to her side. "Please, Mommy?"

Becky's throat closed around any words she might have
tried to force out. Was Scott offering to take them out? No,
better not assume that. He was probably just suggesting a
friendly lunch, Dutch treat. Unfortunately, she couldn't
afford a restaurant, not even fast food.

"I have peanut butter sandwiches in the car." She didn't
look at Scott's face, too embarrassed to claim poverty.
"Remember our picnic at the park, boys?"

"We're gonna feed the ducks," Jamie informed him.

From the corner of her eye she saw Scott shrug. "Peanut
butter keeps. And I think Sam would love to go to the park
after lunch and chase a few ducks."

She looked up, and her pulse danced when he smiled
into her eyes. This good-looking man actually wanted to
spend his Saturday afternoon with her *and* her boys? Either
they'd behaved themselves better than she could have
hoped while she was inside, or he found her…

No. She wouldn't go there. He probably just didn't want
to sit around the Pasture alone all afternoon.

She found herself nodding, and the twins let out a yelp
of delight. How much could a burger cost, anyway?

ELEVEN

Scott pulled the truck into the Pasture's driveway. He parked, then threw back his head and gave in to a jaw-stretching yawn. He'd always been an early bird, but five o'clock on Sunday morning was stretching the point, even for him.

Somebody had to feed the horses, though, and they needed their morning medication. Life on the farm didn't stop just because it was the Lord's day.

"And somebody has to feed the dog, too, huh, fella?"

Sam lifted his head off the bench seat, and his tail thumped sluggishly. Even the dog thought five o'clock was too early. He'd follow Scott around on his morning chores, and then probably take a snooze in the barn while Scott attended church.

He got out of the truck and clutched his jacket together as a cold predawn wind whipped it open. He ducked his head to shield his neck with his collar and trotted toward the house with Sam on his heels.

He twisted the handle on the storm door, fumbling with his keys. Gripping the correct one, he extended it toward the inside door—

And stopped.

The inside door stood open. He stared at it, thoughts

spinning. Did Becky close it yesterday? Yes, he remembered standing by the truck, waiting for Jamie to run inside
and grab his backpack. When the boy ran out, Becky pulled
it closed and locked it with her key. He didn't open the
house at all last night when he came back to the Pasture,
just the barn.

He stepped forward through the door to get a look at
the handle. Yeah, it was scarred and bent. Somebody
jimmied the lock.

What could they hope to steal from the office of a non-
profit organization like the Pasture?

Whatever they were after, they'd ransacked the place.
The front room was a wreck. The couch cushions had been
slashed open, as was the pathetic old armchair in the corner.
The brochure rack had been thrown to the floor and the
contents scattered everywhere. Odd, though. The television
and DVD player were still in place. Not a random burglary,
then. From where he stood he could just see a corner of the
office, the floor littered with papers. All Becky's work or-
ganizing the contents of Haldeman's desk, wasted.

Sam pushed past him and headed for the kitchen.

"Sam, come."

The dog reluctantly returned. They stepped outside, and
Scott unclipped his cell phone to call the police.

The hallways of Grace Community Church were filled
with Sunday morning worshippers. Becky kept her voice
pitched low as she glanced over Amber's shoulder to be
sure no one overheard. "And after lunch, he spent a couple
of hours at the park with us." A steady stream of people
filed past them through the busy church hallway on their
way to the sanctuary.

She felt like a teenager giggling over a guy with her friend, but a girl needed someone to bounce things off. After Scott insisted on buying their lunch at McDonald's, she'd been going crazy trying to decide if it was just a friendly gesture on his part, or if she'd actually been on a date.

"How did the boys act around him?" With a hand on her arm, Amber moved her against the wall to let a group of green-robed choir members pass. "Did they seem jealous?"

"Not at all. Except of each other. They both kept trying to monopolize Scott's attention." A smile curved Becky's lips as she remembered Jamie parading each of his men out for a personal introduction to Scott. "They obviously liked him a lot."

Amber frowned. "That's not good."

"It's not?"

"You don't want them to appear desperate for male attention. That will drive him away as quickly as a clingy woman."

Becky hadn't thought of that. Amber's logic made sense, though. Neediness in any form was a guaranteed man repellent.

"I don't see what I can do about that." The crowd thinned to a few stragglers, and they headed slowly for the sanctuary doors as the first strains of the organ prelude reverberated through the church. "They are desperate for male attention, poor things."

Amber drummed her fingers on her Bible as they walked. "The next thing to do is get him alone. Let him see that you're a self-assured woman, totally at peace with yourself and your singleness." She peered sideways at Becky. "You can do that, can't you?"

At peace with her singleness? Until a few days ago Becky would have answered, "Absolutely!" But since Scott took over at the Pasture, her decision to remain single after her divorce five years ago was wavering.

Becky met her friend's gaze with a hesitant grimace. "Maybe."

Amber's eyebrows shot upward, but her whispered response was drowned out by the organ's chords. As they entered the sanctuary they passed the acolyte, a cherub-faced girl in white who stood like a statue, holding the candlelighter for an usher's match. Becky followed Amber down the center aisle to slip into a half-empty pew on the left.

Becky placed her purse beside her feet and settled onto the hard pew. She leaned over and whispered in Amber's ear. "Where's Jeff? I thought he'd be saving us a seat."

"He got called in to work this morning. A robbery or something."

Becky nodded, then faced the front of the sanctuary. Something else she'd spent a considerable amount of time considering last night was whether or not to tell Jeff this morning about Isabelle Keller. The decision to report Kaci Buchanan had been a no-brainer. No matter what Scott said, Kaci's visit to the Pasture for that earring looked suspicious.

The choir filed into the loft from a door to the right of the baptistry. A sudden swell of the organ's music indicated the end of the prelude. Beside her, Amber picked up two hymnals from the pew in front of them and handed one to Becky with a smile. Becky nodded her thanks and flipped the book open, her thoughts far from the morning's worship service.

Isabelle's visit, on the other hand, was a perfectly natural move for a grief-stricken woman. Nothing at all of interest for the police.

Even so, she felt a flood of relief at Jeff's absence this morning.

* * *

Scott shifted on the seat cushion as the screen behind Pastor Greg's head changed to display his third and, hopefully, final sermon point. The man next to him glanced his way, and Scott flashed an apologetic smile. He couldn't force himself to concentrate on the message this morning, but at least he could sit quietly so he didn't distract others.

He should probably have stayed at the Pasture while the police combed through the house. But he'd answered all their questions as best he could, then they shooed him away. After the horses had been fed and doctored, there wasn't much for him to do except stand around in the barn and watch the stream of police officers going in and out of the house. When Trooper Whitley told him he might as well go home, he'd jumped at the chance to leave. A good worship service was just what he needed today.

Unfortunately, the praise music had failed to direct his attention where it should be, to the Lord. And Pastor Greg might as well have been chanting in Latin for all Scott was getting out of his sermon.

What could a thief have been after? The only thing he'd noticed missing for sure was the petty cash box, but Becky kept less than fifty dollars in there. Of course, a thief wouldn't necessarily know that. Whitley and Detective Foster refused to talk about it, but another officer mentioned the possibility that a burglar had read of Haldeman's death in the newspaper and knew the house would be empty. That made sense, but a shadowy doubt niggled at Scott. Why hadn't the television and DVD player been taken? There was more to this than the cops were admitting.

The break-in wasn't the only thing on Scott's mind this

morning. Despite his determination not to fidget he shifted on the seat again, drawing another glance from his neighbor.

Why did he offer to take Becky and the boys out to lunch yesterday? He'd been set for a solitary afternoon in the office, going through Haldeman's records to see if he could discover the extent of the man's gambling debt. Instead, he ended up throwing stale crackers to a flock of fat ducks and teaching kids to hand-walk across the monkey bars.

He smiled, remembering Tyler's victory dance when he made it all the way to the other side unassisted. Jamie, the less athletic of the two, couldn't manage to get past five rungs before dropping to the ground. But he had an incredible mind for detail, and his face came alive as he told the stories behind about forty of those toys he carried around in his backpack.

Becky had done a great job raising those two, if Scott was any judge. Sure, they argued a lot, and occasionally even got physical with each other. But she was quick to step in, and he could see they respected her.

He crossed his right leg over his left, shifting away from the man beside him. He'd enjoyed the afternoon more than he expected. Especially Becky. She wasn't one of those women who watched from the sidelines. No, she got right in there and tried to cross the monkey bars, too. She didn't make it even as far as Jamie, but she faced her failure with a laugh and good grace.

It couldn't be easy raising two boys alone. She spoke of her father living out in California, and said she didn't have any other relatives close by. She never mentioned her ex-husband, but according to Trooper Whitley, he left when the boys were babies.

Thoughts of Becky's ex conjured up another memory,

one he'd prefer to forget. Megan, her face streaked with tears, begging him to understand why she was returning to her ex-husband, to her marriage. A wave of the familiar pain threatened to latch on to him again, but he fought against it, crossing his arms over his chest. She'd sworn the marriage was over, that it had ended long before the divorce made it final.

She'd lied.

Movement at the front of the room interrupted Scott's thoughts. The worship team stepped into position to play the final song as Pastor Greg invited the congregation to join him in a closing prayer. Scott uncrossed his legs and leaned forward. But though he bowed his head and closed his eyes, his thoughts refused to follow the pastor's words. His own turmoil tumbled out in a private prayer.

Lord, I know I swore I'd never again get involved with a divorced woman.

That oath was two years old, and he had remained true to his vow. In fact, the desire to date anyone seemed to have left along with Megan. The pain of his broken heart lingered. He wasn't about to risk another disaster. Every time he considered asking a woman out, that ache in his heart made it easy to walk away.

Until yesterday.

Lord, Becky is different. She's alone, like I am. So if You—

Music cut into his private prayer. The pastor must have said Amen, but he didn't hear it. Scott scrambled to his feet along with the rest of the congregation and returned the smile of an older woman across the aisle. Words to one of his favorite praise choruses projected onto the screen. He closed his eyes and added his voice to those of his fellow worshippers.

As he reached out with his heart and his hands toward his heavenly Father, peace washed over him. He wasn't alone in this. When the time was right, he'd know whether Becky was the one God had picked out for him or not.

TWELVE

Becky fought against a sudden attack of nerves as she pulled into the driveway for work Monday morning. Amber's words echoed in her mind. *Let him see that you're a self-assured woman, at peace with your singleness.* At the moment she felt neither self-assured nor at peace. In fact, the fluttering in her stomach made her want to throw up.

She caught sight of Scott inside the barn, standing at the workbench with his back toward her. When she cut the engine, music from his radio seeped through the shut windows of her car. The volume must be high enough that he didn't hear her arrive. Clutching the steering wheel with both hands, she closed her eyes and spent a moment bolstering her nerve.

There's nothing needy about me. I'm self-assured. At peace with my singleness.

And she really should be, too. This thing with Scott would probably lead to nothing, and that was best. It was absolutely nuts to become romantically involved with the boss. Everybody knew that. If it didn't work out, she'd be the one looking for a job, not him.

But he certainly was easy to be with. And he seemed to genuinely enjoy spending time with the boys Saturday.

Most single men ran screaming at the mention of one child, but two? And twins? She couldn't forget that the whole outing had been Scott's idea, not hers.

Regardless, she couldn't sit in the car all day. If he turned around and saw her staring at him, he wouldn't think she was needy. He'd think she was strange.

Gathering her purse and lunch bag from the passenger seat, she opened the car door and stood. Sam bounded out of the barn, tail flapping like a flag in a tornado.

"Good morning," she shouted toward the barn as she stooped to greet the dog.

Scott whirled, his face lighting with a smile that brought a warm flush to hers. "Hey, Becky. I didn't hear you." He leaned across the workbench to flip the radio off, then came toward her, wiping his hands on a dirty rag that probably did more harm than good. "How was your Sunday?"

"Good. Relaxing." She hefted her purse strap onto her shoulder. "Yours?"

His lips twisted sideways for a moment before he answered. "Interesting. We had a little excitement here yesterday."

"Oh?" She looked out across the paddocks and their peacefully grazing occupants. Everything appeared to be normal.

"Yeah. I almost called you at home, but the police didn't think it was necessary."

"The police?" Her eyes widened. "No one else has been hurt, have they?"

He shook his head. "Nothing like that. The office was broken into Saturday night."

"Oh, no! What did they take?"

"The petty cash box is about all I could see. The place is pretty much a shambles, though. They went through both desks, dumped everything out. I tried to clean up yesterday afternoon." He ducked his head. "It's still a mess, I'm afraid."

Becky's hand flew to her collarbone. A thief went through her desk? She mentally reviewed the contents. Thank goodness she didn't keep anything of any personal value in there. Still, to have someone going through her desk left her feeling violated.

"The checkbook!" She put a hand on his arm. "Oh, Scott, I keep the Pasture's checkbook and bank statements in my desk."

"They were still there." He covered her hand with his warm one, and she tried to ignore the thrill that shot up her arm. "I found all that stuff on the floor. But I still think we need to contact the bank this morning, tell them what's happened and maybe even close the account. Just in case they got the account number."

She shot him a quick smile and pulled her hand away. "I'll do that."

"Thanks. I started trying to put things back in folders, but I couldn't figure out what went where." He grimaced. "I just piled everything on your desk for you to sort out."

She couldn't help laughing at the chagrin on his face, and her nerves steadied a little. "Don't worry about it. I'll take care of things in there." She pulled a face. "I suppose there's fingerprint powder all over the place again?"

"I'm afraid so."

She heaved a sigh. "Great. I'm going to need a new bottle of cleaner soon."

"Oh, that reminds me." He pulled a crumpled piece of paper out of his back pocket. "Before all this happened I made a list of things we need to do this week. Some meds and other supplies are running low, and I'd like to get Doc Matthews out here to take a look at Kiri's Kousin. There are a couple of lesions on his flank region that I hope aren't ringworm."

He was suddenly all business. Her gaze dropped to the paper he thrust toward her. Was he going to completely ignore Saturday? A flicker of disappointment threatened to melt her smile. Okay, she could do that.

She started toward the house, nodding. "I'll give him a call as soon as his office opens. Anything else?"

"Remember those tally sheets of Haldeman's?"

She stopped and turned. Those were part of what she'd hoped to get organized and filed away on Saturday, before her day was preempted. "Of course."

"After you get everything figured out in there, could you look through them and give me a list of all the initials you see, along with anything that looks like a dollar amount?"

"You mean like the one we found for EJ?"

Scott's expression was grim. "Yeah. Like that one."

She studied him closely. "If you think those tally sheets had anything to do with Neal's death or with this break-in, we should turn them over to the police."

His grin disarmed her. "I doubt if they do. I'm just curious how much he might have been down, all told. If it's only a few dollars, the police won't care."

Becky certainly didn't think thirty-seven thousand, five hundred would be considered "a few dollars." In her world, twenty dollars at the end of the month seemed like a fortune.

"Sure, I'll do that first thing." She turned back toward the house, Sam at her side.

"Thanks. Oh, and Becky?"

She looked at him over her shoulder.

"Jamie and Tyler are great kids. I had a good time Saturday."

Her heart suddenly light, she returned his smile. "Thanks. We did, too."

Drawing on every ounce of poise she possessed, she headed into the house without looking back. Her step was light enough that the boys would have accused her of skipping. A few seconds later, she heard the heels of his boots striking the driveway as he returned to the barn.

Sam scooted inside when she opened the door, and ran ahead of her through the sitting room. Becky followed, steadfastly ignoring the mess. Scott said he cleaned up in here? The place must have been a disaster. The sofa had been gutted, the side chair was missing and the rack in the corner tilted awkwardly to one side. It was empty, too, which meant she'd have to print more pamphlets.

She thrust that thought away. All in good time. She'd need to clean up the office before worrying about the front room.

As she stepped into the kitchen, music from Scott's radio reached her ears. She smiled, picturing her handsome boss working in the barn.

"He had a good time, Sam." She roughed the yellow fur on the dog's neck, then practically danced over to the corner where his bowls were kept. "He said my boys are great kids."

Sam followed close on her heels, his gaze fixed on her hands as she picked up his water bowl, emptied it and filled it with fresh water for the day. When she set it down, he ignored it. He was more interested in food first thing in the morning.

"Of course, just because he had a good time once doesn't mean anything." She picked up the empty food bowl. Sam's ears perked forward. "A couple of hours at the park with the kids is one thing. An actual date with their mother is entirely different."

That sobering truth dampened her mood and slowed her step as she crossed the kitchen to the pantry, where the giant fifty-five-pound bag of dog food was stored. The door handle was covered in black fingerprint dust, as was every surface in the room. Her lips tightened as she used a paper towel to twist it open. She tugged at the open top of the bag, tilting it toward her so she could scoop out Sam's breakfast.

"We're going to have to add dog food to that list of things Scott said we need, aren't we, Sammy Boy?"

She reached way down into the bag and grabbed the handle of the cup she kept stored inside. When she scooped the cup into the chunks of food, it struck something hard near the bottom.

Odd. She tapped the cup on whatever it was a couple of times, then grasped the edge of the thing. The object was square and solid, but a crinkling sound told her it was wrapped in plastic. She slipped her fingers beneath it and lifted it out.

A plastic sack from the grocery store in town where Neal shopped. Strange. A peek inside told her the block-shaped object was wrapped in a second sack.

The hair on her arms prickled. Neal had buried something in the dog food. Was this what the burglar was after? Or maybe it held a clue as to the identity of his killer. She carried the package over to the kitchen table and set it on the scarred Formica surface. She wouldn't open it, but a quick look couldn't hurt, could it? Peeling away the layers of filmy white plastic, she glimpsed a rectangular object.

Another thick layer of plastic surrounded it, this one secured with wide strips of masking tape. But this plastic was clear.

Becky sank into the seat, her thoughts whirling at the sight of the item in the bag.

A gigantic stack of hundred dollar bills.

THIRTEEN

"The pantry door was closed, just like always." Becky leaned against the kitchen wall, staring at Detective Foster and Jeff. She tried to resist looking toward the bundle of cash on the table, but her gaze kept straying back to it.

Scott, too, kept glancing that way. It was a huge pile, at least a foot long. They hadn't handled it anymore before the police arrived, but after Jeff unwrapped it, she'd counted twenty-five bundles banded in white paper straps.

"How many bills do you think are in each bundle?" Scott looked at Detective Foster.

"A hundred." The detective answered without hesitation. "That's how they're delivered to the bank from the Federal Reserve."

Becky did a quick calculation. Her eyes went wide as she looked again at the money. If those were all hundred dollar bills, there was two hundred fifty thousand dollars on that table.

"Tell me exactly how you found it." Jeff's pen hovered above the paper, ready to write down her words.

"I was scooping dog food out of the bag, and I felt it in the bottom. I didn't know what it was, so I pulled it out."

She glanced toward Detective Foster, half expecting to

be scolded for tampering with evidence. In retrospect, she should have left it where it was and called the police as soon as she realized something was in there. If she'd known what the bundle contained, she would have.

Foster didn't reprimand her. "How was the package situated in the bag?"

"Exactly like it is now, but wrapped in those two grocery sacks." She nodded toward the discarded sacks beside the money. "It was lengthways, and all the way at the bottom. We're running low on dog food so I was scooping deep."

"How long have you had that bag?" Jeff asked.

Becky closed her eyes, trying to remember. Had Neal bought any dog food since she started working here in February? She didn't think so, but she'd only taken over the job of feeding Sam about a month ago.

She shook her head. "Sorry. It's been here at least a month, but beyond that I have no idea."

They looked at Scott, and he shrugged. "I'm newer than she is."

Jeff glanced at Foster. "Do we need to call the crime lab back?"

Foster pushed the edge of his mustache into his mouth and chewed thoughtfully. Then he shook his head. "They dusted in here yesterday. Whoever burgled the place Saturday night was obviously looking for the money, so if they left any prints we've got them."

Becky caught Scott's eye with a raised eyebrow. Was he going to mention the tally sheets?

He turned to Detective Foster. "Actually, Becky came across something that might be important when she was going through Haldeman's desk on Friday. Apparently the man was a frequent gambler, and we think he might have racked up some fairly significant debt."

Foster and Jeff exchanged a glance. "Like about two hundred fifty thousand dollars' worth?"

Scott shrugged. "We don't know yet. We just found some tally sheets that led me to believe that he's been doing a good deal of betting under the table."

The detective turned to Becky. "Show me."

"They're right in here."

Becky went through the sitting room into the office, the men trailing behind her. She clamped her jaws together at the sight of the mess the burglar had left. Both desks were piled high with a disarray of papers and folders. How could she find anything in this clutter?

She turned to Scott. "Do you remember which desk you put them on?"

He considered, then shook his head. "No, I don't. Sorry."

He went to Haldeman's, and Becky went to her own desk. Together they began sifting through the jumble. She resisted the urge to organize as she went, to put things into piles for filing. Time enough for that later, after the police left.

Foster and Jeff watched in silence as the minutes ticked by. The detective passed the time by chewing on the edge of his mustache.

Scott finished first. "They're not over here."

Becky flipped through the final handful of papers, then shook her head. She raised her head to catch Scott's eye. "Here, either. The thief must have taken them."

"It makes perfect sense." Scott stared into the expressionless face of Detective Foster. "Haldeman had a gambling problem. He hit it big on a bet somewhere and made a boatload of cash. Someone he owed knew about the money and figured he kept it hidden in the barn. The guy broke in, Haldeman heard him, they fought and Haldeman got killed."

The detective's face might as well have been carved from stone. Scott shifted his gaze to Trooper Whitley. "It even explains why Sam was confined in the house that night. Haldeman left him here to guard the real location of the cash while he investigated the barn."

Beside him, Becky nodded. "That does make a lot of sense."

Whitley looked skeptical, but at least he had showed some expression. "So where did he get the cash?"

"From one of his bookies, probably." Scott hooked his thumb through a belt loop. "There are always races to bet on, and a confirmed gambler likes the big odds. Occasionally, one is bound to pay off. Maybe after the bookie turned over the money, he decided to come back for it. If we can find the guy who paid Haldeman that money, we might just find the killer."

"It does make sense," said Whitley.

Scott nodded. Now they were getting somewhere. "Haldeman recorded the initials of the bookie he placed each bet with on those tally sheets. We were going to compile a list of them today." He waved at the mess. "Still, it shouldn't be too hard to find out who Haldeman did business with." He crossed the floor and stopped in front of Detective Foster. "So what's our next step? Interrogate the bookies?"

The detective's expression took on the texture of granite. He awarded Scott a chilly smile. "Thank you for your opinions, Mr. Lewis. We'll keep them in mind. But for obvious reasons we can't discuss our investigation with you in any detail. And I must advise you against doing any investigative work on your own. Leave that to the experts."

Scott shoved a hand in his pocket. He felt like he'd been slapped down. They weren't even going to talk to him about it, and after he'd turned over all the physical evidence he'd uncovered. He was just trying to cooperate, and he really could help. He had connections.

But they probably had more connections than he did. They didn't need his help. He should just focus on the horses, do his job and let the cops do theirs.

Still, they didn't have to be so condescending.

"I understand." He clipped the words short.

"So, is that it?" Detective Foster's gaze swept from Scott to Becky.

Becky shrugged. "That's all we know."

Whitley clicked his pen and closed his notebook with a snap. "You'll let us know if you discover anything else missing?"

Scott unclamped his mouth long enough to answer. "You bet."

Whitley's lips twitched. "Pun intended?"

Ha, ha. Scott rolled his eyes, and the officer turned away chuckling. Becky followed them to the back door, but Scott stayed where he was, staring at the piles of junk everywhere. Whoever broke in here wasn't concerned with hiding his or her tracks. If it had been him, he would have searched for the money carefully and tried not to leave a trace that he'd been here.

The storm door slammed, and moments later Becky returned to the room. "You didn't tell them about EJ." Her voice held a touch of accusation.

Scott lifted a shoulder. "They didn't ask."

"They didn't know to ask."

"Hey!" He held out his hands, fingers splayed. "We told them about the initials. You can bet they know every bookie in the state. They'll probably have a list of Haldeman's buddies by the end of the day, which is more than we'll have."

She folded her arms across her chest. "Why do I get the feeling you're planning to make your own list?"

"Well, I do have a few contacts. Won't hurt to ask a question or two." His glance slid away from her shrewd stare. He hadn't mentioned his conversation with Eddie Jones, and didn't see any reason to now. "If I discover anything important I'll turn it over to them."

"Mmm, hmm."

He fought the impulse to squirm under her stare. Which was ridiculous. He wasn't doing anything wrong, just following up on a hunch that Detective Foster obviously didn't think had merit. It wasn't like he was doing a real investigation or anything. He was just going to talk to a friend. He returned her stare.

She turned away quickly, but not before he saw a flash of emotion in her eyes. Concern, maybe?

"Do me a favor, would you, Scott?" She busied herself with shuffling papers into a neat stack as she spoke. "Be careful. I've lost one boss already."

Her head was lowered over her desk so he could only see the top of her head, but there was no mistaking her tone. She was worried about him. Warmth flooded his gut. It had been a long time since a woman felt protective enough about him to worry.

He made a snap decision. "Listen, I was wondering if you ever have any free time? You know, without the kids. Like maybe for dinner or something?"

She looked up, her wide eyes searching his face. A smile tugged at the corners of her mouth.

"It has been a long time," she admitted.

"How about tomorrow, then?"

"On a school night?"

He didn't even think about that. He fiddled with a paper clip on the surface of the desk. "Oh. Yeah. Sorry. I forgot."

"It's okay. I can probably manage to find a babysitter, as long as we don't stay out too late."

The thin metal rod of the clip jabbed into his finger as he straightened it. He dropped it on the desk and shoved his hand into his pocket. "So I'll pick you up at seven?"

The smile broke free, igniting her eyes. "That sounds good."

He couldn't believe he was doing this. He hadn't been on a date in years. He stood rooted to the floor, staring into her face until a pretty blush stained her cheeks and she looked away.

"Great." He turned toward Haldeman's desk, changed his mind, and swiveled to march toward the door. "I'll get directions to your house later."

Sam leaped off the cushionless couch to follow him as he escaped to the barn.

FOURTEEN

Scott paced down the center aisle of the horse barn, nodding at a pair of guys mucking a stall on his right. They were working late today. The stable boys usually tore out of here at four o'clock, and it was almost five now. At the far end of the barn, he tapped on the glass window of the door to the Shady Acres Farm office, then cracked it open.

"Zach, can I chew your ear for a minute?"

His former boss looked up from the desk, and a smile brightened his craggy face. "Sure thing. Come on in."

Scott sat in the seat across the old wooden desk's scratched surface. The room felt stuffy, thanks to the space heater Zach always ran when he was pushing papers. The gruff farm manager said he could take any amount of cold as long as he was doing something physical, but his fifty-five-year-old joints stiffened up if he sat still too long.

Zach rocked back in his desk chair, work-roughened hands folded across his stomach. "How's it going over there at the Pasture? You handling everything? You know you can call me if you need any help with those stallions."

"Thanks, but it's going great." Scott crossed his legs and rested his forearm on his knee. "Except we had some more excitement this morning."

He filled Zach in on the robbery, and Becky's big find of the day. As he spoke, the older man's jaw inched open until it gaped.

"You gotta be kidding me. Two hundred fifty *thousand* dollars? In a bag of dog food?" He gave a low whistle. "Do the cops think the guy who killed Haldeman was after the money?"

A grunt of disgust escaped Scott's lips. "Who knows what they think. But it fits, you know?"

Zach nodded, his thick gray eyebrows high. "It sure is a lot of money. Men have been killed for less."

"We found something else the other day. Apparently, Haldeman was into Eddie Jones for a fairly significant chunk of change. And Jones wasn't the only one Haldeman owed."

"I'm not surprised. He liked to play the ponies, no doubt about it." Zach speared him with a gaze. "You don't think Jones killed him, do you?"

"I don't know." Scott kept his face impassive. "But I did have a talk with him Friday afternoon out at Keeneland, and I mentioned finding his name in Haldeman's records. And guess what's missing after the break-in?"

Zach steepled his fingers and tapped them in front of his face as he studied Scott through narrowed eyes. He shook his head. "I don't peg Jones as a killer, but he'd eat a load of manure for that kind of cash. And if Haldeman caught him snooping around the place, and they got into a fight?"

Scott sat against the hard chair back. "That's what I thought, too. And if it wasn't Jones, it could have been someone else. Unfortunately, I don't know who Haldeman did business with." He caught Zach's eye. "Do you?"

A slow smile spread across the older man's face. "Now

why would you think I'd have any idea about something like that?"

Scott returned his grin. "Just a wild guess."

He chuckled. "Well, I have been known to place a wager every now and then." His hands dropped to the desk, and his expression sobered. "But I never talked to Haldeman about it. He might have used Edwards, or Kavanaugh, or maybe McMatthews. Jones would know."

"He would?"

Zach nodded. "They always know who else their customers are playing with, especially if the numbers start getting big. Makes sense, if you think about it."

It did. A smart businessman knew the total debt level of his customers. Especially a customer whose tab was growing.

Of course, Eddie had no reason to share that information with Scott. But it couldn't hurt to ask, could it? They didn't have a chance to finish their conversation at the race track the other day after Kaci interrupted them.

"I guess I'll have to pay Eddie another visit." Scott got to his feet. He might be able to catch him at the track. Oh. Today was Monday. No racing at Keeneland on Mondays.

"You don't happen to know where I can find him, do you?"

Zach glanced at his watch. "He'll be down at O'Grady's in another half hour."

O'Grady's was a sports bar in downtown Lexington. Scott had heard of it, but since he didn't make a practice of hanging out in bars of any kind, he'd never been there.

Zach put his hands on the edge of the desk and rolled his chair backward. "You want me to go with you? I got a thing tonight, but I can cancel it."

"Thanks, but that's not necessary."

Zach paused in the act of standing. "You sure about that?"

A rush of gratitude washed over Scott. "I'm sure."

The older man lowered himself back into the chair. He rolled up to the desk and caught Scott's gaze. "Be careful, son. Some of these guys don't take kindly to questions."

Scott nodded and slipped through the door quickly so the heat didn't escape. As he walked between rows of clean stalls, his step felt light. Zach could be crotchety, and the stable hands trod lightly around him, but when push came to shove, he was a loyal friend. The second person today to exhibit real concern for Scott's safety. It was enough to make a man stop and count his blessings.

"Please, Amber. The boys would be so excited."

Becky hated begging, but she was desperate. She propped the phone with a shoulder and pressed a sticky label on a file as she waited for her friend's response.

"I don't know." Amber's voice held so much reluctance Becky could almost see the scowl on her face. "I don't have any babysitting experience, you know."

"You don't need experience." Becky glanced at the wall clock. Four fifty-eight. Close enough. She crossed the room and locked the front door, phone still pressed to her ear. "You like kids, don't you?"

"Selectively." Becky chuckled at her dry tone. "Let me be honest with you," Amber went on. "Your boys scare me! They're rowdy and loud, and yesterday at church I saw one of them sucker punch the other for no reason at all."

Becky cringed. Tyler. She tried to keep the pleading out of her voice. "They would be on their best behavior with you. They love you."

"Why can't you just hire a teenager?"

"The truth?" She sat on the edge of the desk. "I can't afford a teenager. I figured you'd let me take you out to lunch after church one Sunday as payment."

"I don't know, Becky."

Amber still didn't sound convinced. Frustrated, Becky tapped her toe on the carpet. She did have a Plan B, though it came with far more strings than she liked. "I guess I could call Pastor Vaughn and Donna. They might watch the boys for me, if I beg them."

"You are desperate if you're willing to subject yourself and your love life to Donna's questions." A resigned sigh blew through the phone. "Okay, I'll do it."

Grinning, Becky hopped off the desk. "Thank you so much. I owe you big-time."

"Yes, you do. And lunch won't take care of this debt. I'm going to hold it over your head for a while until I figure out an appropriate payment."

"Anything. I promise. You are the best friend a girl can have."

"Yeah, yeah. I'll see you tomorrow a little before seven."

Becky dropped the phone into its cradle and almost skipped around the desk to get her purse from the bottom door. She had a date! Just wait until she told Daddy.

As she slammed the drawer shut, the phone rang again. She hesitated. The office officially closed at five.

She snatched it up. "Out to Pasture."

"My, my, my. If it isn't the little *secretary*."

No mistaking that voice. She'd recognize that fake drawl anywhere. "Hello, Miss Buchanan. What can I do for you?"

"You?" A haughty laugh sounded. "Not a thing. I'm calling for Scott."

The comment set Becky's teeth on edge, but she kept

her voice professionally polite. "He's not here. May I leave him a message?"

"I don't *think* so." She paused. "On second thought, yes. Tell him how much I enjoyed seeing him the other evening, and that I can't wait for the next time."

A hot flush dampened Becky's neck. Scott was with Kaci recently? Since she'd been here when Kaci made her appearance Friday morning, and Kaci said *evening,* she must be referring to a different time. A date, maybe? A sick knot formed in Becky's stomach.

"Did you get that down, or do I need to speak slower?"

The knot exploded into anger at the insult.

"I got it. You can't wait for the next time." Becky snapped the words. A catty comment shot from her mouth before she could stop it. "Should I ask him to check his couch for your other earring?"

"Oooh, the pony has a kick." Kaci's voice lowered, but lost none of its stinging conceit. "By the way, little pony, I don't appreciate having the police show up at my home unannounced, asking awkward questions. It makes for an uncomfortable evening."

A few uncomfortable evenings wouldn't hurt the haughty woman, in Becky's opinion. But her hackles were standing at full attention now, and she found herself wanting to punch back. "The police asked us to keep them informed. And even you must admit, having a prominent person stoop to such a blatant trick to get a man's attention is a little bit suspicious." She rushed on, anger causing blood to roar in her ears. "It must have hurt your pride to have Neal's attention directed some-where else."

Her laugh was genuine. "Trust me, darling, that filly

isn't in the same class as me, on the track or off. She's an upstart, that's what she is. Neal was only dallying with her."

Fierce loyalty rose up in Becky "You're right. She's not in the same class. Isabelle Keller's got more class in her little finger than—"

"Isabelle? Neal was involved with Isabelle?"

The surprise in Kaci's voice dumped icy water on Becky's anger. If she didn't know about Isabelle, then who was Kaci talking about?

"Uh, well, I…" Becky stammered her way into silence. She couldn't very well say anything else without betraying Isabelle's confidence.

Thank goodness Kaci didn't push for details. "He was a busy man, wasn't he? Not surprising, though. Neal knew how to treat a woman. If he chose to spread his charm widely, who cares?" Her voice hardened. "But my earring was a private concern, and of no interest to the police."

"If you've done nothing wrong, then you've got nothing to worry about."

"Oh, I am not worried. Merely annoyed." She paused. "Given your social standing, perhaps you aren't aware of the risks involved in annoying a Buchanan."

Becky's heart thump-thumped. "Are you threatening me?"

Kaci laughed. "A warning only, darling. Keep in mind that ponies can't run with Thoroughbreds in *any* race. They just don't stand a chance."

A click sounded in Becky's ear. She stood in place, the dead phone in her hand. There wasn't a single doubt in her mind what Kaci's warning was about. Scott.

She replaced the receiver and picked up her purse. Her

spirits, so high a few minutes before, now hovered somewhere in the vicinity of her shoes.

How could she compete with someone like Kaci Buchanan?

O'Grady's was a hopping place on Monday nights. Scott found a parking place on the street and walked three blocks to the busy little bar. The patrons spilled out onto the sidewalk in front of the building, many of them puffing on cigarettes they couldn't take inside.

Scott held his breath as he made his way through a cloud of smoke and into the bar. As the door closed behind him, he stepped to one side to let his eyes adjust to the dim light. The pungent odors of beer and bourbon prickled his nostrils.

A polished bar ran the length of the long room on the left, and when he could see he recognized a few of the people perched on stools there. A row of tables lined the opposite wall, each with four chairs and most of them full. Television sets hung suspended from the ceiling throughout the place. A loud shout went up from two of the tables to his right, and several men jumped to their feet, fists thrust into the air.

He spotted Eddie at the far end of the bar, his head bowed as he listened to the man next to him. A customer, probably. The man's hands moved constantly as he spoke, and occasionally Eddie nodded.

Scott made his way to the empty stool beside Eddie's customer and slid onto the seat. The man, whose back was turned toward Scott, kept talking, but Eddie looked up. Their eyes locked.

Scott had the sense Eddie was not surprised to see him tonight.

"What'll you have?" The muscled bartender swiped a damp towel across the bar in front of Scott.

Asking for iced tea in this place probably wasn't a good idea. He might get more than he bargained for. "A Coke's fine."

The guy's expression didn't change. He tossed a cocktail napkin onto the bar and turned away to get Scott's Coke. Scott watched as he scooped ice into a glass, then poured soda from a hose. Beside him, the man's voice droned on, low enough that Scott could only make out a word here and there.

"…seventh…carry me…handle another fifty…"

"I can do that." Because Eddie faced him, his voice carried to Scott's ears clearly. "Just make sure you're here on the seventh."

The man got off the stool, uttering profuse thanks, as the bartender returned with Scott's Coke. With a nod in his direction, Scott slid his glass, napkin and all, across the bar in front of the vacated stool.

"Mind if I sit here?" He moved onto the stool without waiting for an answer.

Eddie cocked his head. "It's a public place."

"I was hoping we could continue our conversation."

Eddie picked up a thin straw and folded it with a finger and a thumb. "I thought we finished the other day."

"Ah, but more has happened since then."

A smile flashed onto his narrow face, gone as quickly as it appeared. "I heard you had some excitement out at the Pasture. Something about a robbery?"

Scott studied him. Was the man mocking him? Hard to tell with that sardonic expression. "I figured you might know something about it."

Eddie picked up his glass, which had a sliver of lime perched on the side, and sipped. "I don't know anything more than I read in the paper this morning. Apparently the thief got away with about fifty bucks?" His shoulders jerked with a silent laugh.

He was mocking him. Scott was sure of it. He kept a tight rein on his temper. He was here to get information from the guy, not antagonize him. "And a couple of other things, as well. But he didn't find the real stash. I did."

Eddie's expression remained unchanged. He sipped from his glass again, then set it on the bar. "Here's where I'm supposed to ask what you found."

"Two hundred fifty thousand dollars in cash."

If Scott hadn't been watching him closely he would have missed the flicker of surprise, the quick movement of his eyes.

"That's a lot of money. Too bad Haldeman didn't use it to pay his debts before he cashed in his chips."

What a callous attitude. An intense dislike for the man in front of him came over Scott. Here was someone who made a living from other people's weaknesses. He didn't care for his clients one bit, that was obvious. "Yeah, it might have saved his life if he had."

The man straightened as he turned on his stool so that he faced Scott directly. Angry white lines creased the skin around his tightened lips. "I don't like what I think I hear you saying."

Scott stiffened his spine, too. He'd tried hard to keep the accusation out of his voice. Apparently he failed. "All I'm saying is on Friday I told you Haldeman had records mentioning your name, and Saturday night they were stolen. A day later a wad of cash turns up. Now those things might be coincidence, but when you add them to the fact that

Haldeman was killed in that same place just a few days before, it starts to stink."

Fury shone in Eddie's eyes as he slipped off the stool to glare down at Scott from his full towering height. "The only stink I smell around here is you and your insinuations."

"Is there a problem, gentlemen?"

Scott looked away from the fury in Eddie's face. The bartender, hamlike hands on the surface of the bar as he bent across it, slid a menacing stare from Scott to Eddie. Around them, all conversations had ceased as the nearby patrons watched openly.

Okay, not a good idea to continue this. Besides, he wouldn't get a list of Haldeman's other bookies from Eddie now. Nor did he need to. He'd come in here looking for information, but he might have gotten more than he bargained for. If Scott's hunch could be trusted, he was staring at the man responsible for Haldeman's death.

He stood. "No problem. I was just leaving."

He pulled a few dollars out of his pocket and threw them next to his untouched drink. With one more look into Eddie Jones's furious face, he turned and walked to the door, aware that dozens of eyes watched him go.

FIFTEEN

Becky stood inside the back door staring across the Pasture's paddocks. When she arrived for work an hour ago, Scott was already out on the cart doing his morning chores. Looked as though he'd just finished with Dark Diego in the farthest pasture.

She bit back a yawn and resisted the impulse to rub her tired eyes. Sleep had proven elusive most of the night. Instead, she replayed her conversation with Kaci over and over. By the time she finally dozed off, she'd come to the conclusion that the footprints in the barn probably didn't belong to the snooty Kaci. Nor did she believe they belonged to Isabelle. But Kaci evidently knew the identity of a third woman, probably the same one who signed the note they found "L."

Outside, Scott turned the cart around and headed toward the barn. Becky stepped back from the door. Hopefully he didn't see her watching. She returned to her desk and her task of refiling the last of the documents the thief had dumped on the floor.

Of course, she could simply call Kaci and ask her the woman's name. But subjecting herself to another conversation with that conceited snob wasn't an appealing thought. No, much better to let the police handle things.

Becky fought against an uncharitable smile at the thought of the police paying a second visit to Miss Kaci Buchanan. With her compliments.

"Good morning." Scott's voice preceded the banging of the back door. His footsteps went into the kitchen, followed by the sound of water running.

"Hello," she answered. "How was your evening?"

He stepped through the doorway, gulping from a glass. "Interesting." His gaze fell to her clean desk. "Hey, you've about got it whipped."

"I do. And I'm proud to say the files are in better shape now than they were before." She picked up the sticky note on the center of her desk and kept her expression impassive as she held her index finger toward him, the yellow square stuck on the end. "You've got a message."

He crossed the room with three long strides to pluck the note off her finger. Becky straightened the position of the pad and placed the pen beside it, trying not to watch as he read.

"Hmm." A puzzled frown drew lines on his forehead. Then it cleared as he folded the paper and shoved it in his pocket. "Oh, I forgot to tell you to add a bottle of Hoof Heal to the list of supplies from Simpson's. Have you already placed the order?"

Unspoken questions burned on Becky's tongue, but she managed to control herself. "Yes, but they haven't delivered yet." She reached for the phone. "There's probably time—"

"Is anyone here?"

Becky identified the voice calling from the back door at the same moment its owner stepped into the office. Detective Foster, followed by Jeff. Good. Their presence would save her a phone call to tell them about the third woman. She bit back a greeting when she saw their solemn expressions.

Scott must have noted the same, because his tone was guarded. "What can we do for you this morning?"

Foster's eyes flicked to her before settling on Scott's face. "For starters, you can tell me where you were around one o'clock this morning."

Scott's spine stiffened. "Why do you want to know?"

"Would you answer the question, please?"

Why was the detective acting so politely hostile? Becky caught Jeff's gaze and raised an eyebrow. He gave a very slight shake of his head, then stared pointedly at Scott.

Scott's shoulders rose as he pocketed both hands. "I was in bed."

"Alone?"

"Of course alone." A smile flashed onto his lips. "Sam slept on the couch."

Foster's expression did not change. "What time did you get home, Mr. Lewis?"

"Around nine, I'd say. I spent some extra time with Thunder last night because his hooves needed attention."

"And before that? Did you go anywhere at all last evening?"

Scott's eyelids narrowed. "Actually, yes, I did. But I get the impression you already know that."

The detective dipped his forehead, conceding the point. "We have statements from several witnesses who said you were at O'Grady's Tavern in Lexington last night around six o'clock."

Becky looked quickly at Scott. She didn't think he was the kind of guy who frequented bars. Church, yes. But a bar? She shifted in her chair, suddenly uncomfortable.

He nodded, his lips tight.

Foster continued. "And that you had a conversation with an Edward Jones?"

Becky's eyes widened as the name registered. That had to be the EJ from Neal's betting records. Relief washed over her. Scott just went to the bar to talk to Neal's bookie. Thank goodness. She'd had enough of men who thought a bar was a great place to hang out.

"You want to tell me what all this is about, Detective?" The stubborn set of Scott's jaw must have told the detective he wasn't going to answer any more questions blindly.

Foster nodded toward Jeff, his gaze never leaving Scott's face.

The trooper stepped forward. "Mr. Edward Jones was murdered in his home around one this morning. The killer broke through a rear window and surprised him in bed."

A loud gasp escaped Becky's open mouth. Another murder?

Surely no one could mistake the shock on Scott's face. His chin dropped as he stumbled backward to sit heavily on the surface of the other desk. He opened his mouth, closed it, swallowed hard, and then managed to choke out, "How?"

"We thought you might tell us."

Becky cringed at the accusation in Detective Foster's tone.

Scott's eyes went wide. "You can't think I killed Eddie Jones?"

Jeff answered. "The witnesses who place you at the bar also say you and Mr. Jones argued, and that you left in a hurry."

"That's right. I left because he got hostile, and the bartender was about to throw us both out."

"Why did he 'get hostile'?"

Scott's chest rose as he drew a deep breath. "Because I accused him of breaking into the Pasture's office, and insinuated that he had something to do with Haldeman's death."

Detective Foster closed his eyes and shook his head. "Mr. Lewis, I warned you not to try to investigate this case on your own."

"If you suspected Edward Jones of anything, you should have told us instead of trying to talk to the guy yourself." Jeff's voice was hard.

"Okay, yeah. In retrospect, that would have been the smart thing to do."

He sounded so defeated that Becky tried to infuse as much confidence in her smile as she could when he glanced her way. His lips curved upward in response.

Then he folded his arms and asked, "Am I being arrested?"

Becky sat forward on the edge of her chair, waiting for the answer. Surely no one could seriously suspect Scott of such a monstrous act. When Detective Foster didn't immediately deny it, she threw a panicked look toward Jeff, but he refused to meet her eye.

The silence stretched uncomfortably before Foster finally answered. "Not at this time. But we need to get your statement. And until further notice, it would be unwise to leave town without letting one of us know." Scott stared at the floor, his lips tight. "We'd also like to take a look at your truck and your home."

His head jerked up. Detective Foster returned his glare with equanimity.

Finally, Scott gave a single nod. "Go ahead. I have nothing to hide."

Jeff stepped toward the door. "If you'll come with me, then."

Scott followed him out of the house. As Detective Foster turned to leave, Becky rose from her chair.

"Detective, I have something I need to tell you."

He turned a polite expression her way.

When she heard the back door close behind Scott and Jeff, she cleared her throat. "It concerns that note you and Trooper Whitley found. I have a feeling Kaci Buchanan knows who L is."

His eyebrows arched. "What makes you think so?"

Becky repeated their conversation, leaving out the parts about Isabelle and Scott. "So she obviously knows Neal was involved with another woman."

He pressed the corner of his mustache into his mouth as he studied her for a moment. Finally, he spoke. "Mrs. Dennison, we've already disturbed Miss Buchanan once. She was entirely forthcoming, and we specifically asked if she knew of anyone else who might have visited Mr. Haldeman's barn. She denied any such knowledge."

"Then she lied." Becky raised her chin. "Something I have no doubt she can do with a great deal of skill."

A real smile curved Foster's mouth. He spoke gently. "Perhaps it was not me she lied to."

Becky felt a flush creep up her neck. "Why would she lie to me?"

"Perhaps to upset you?"

He stared at her until she looked away. She had to admit the possibility that Kaci would lie just to mess with her.

"That's possible," she conceded. "But I don't think so. She sounded too surprised when I—" She snapped her mouth shut.

"Yes?"

Becky chewed on the inside of her lip. She hadn't

planned to say anything about Isabelle. But under his piercing stare, she couldn't hold back.

She stared at the floor between them. "We were discussing another of Neal's girlfriends, Isabelle Keller."

"The daughter of Hugh Keller." His voice was flat.

She nodded. "Kaci didn't know about her, and obviously thought I was talking about this third woman. When I mentioned Isabelle's name, she was surprised." She looked up. "So that's why I don't think she was lying. Not to me, anyway."

He studied her a moment longer, then gave a single nod. "If we have reason to question Miss Buchanan further, I will certainly ask her to verify her previous statement about not knowing any other women who had opportunity to visit the barn here."

What did *if we have reason* mean? "You mean you're not going to—"

"Thank you, Mrs. Dennison. And now, I will stress to you the same thing I told Mr. Lewis yesterday. Do not attempt any further investigation on your own. Leave it to the professionals."

Feeling as though her hands had been slapped, Becky managed a sulky nod.

SIXTEEN

"After they searched Scott's truck, they took him over to his house and searched there, too. But they didn't find anything, of course."

Becky kept her voice low, glancing down the hallway toward the boys' bedroom.

"Jeff never mentioned a thing." Amber scowled. "But he never talks about his cases until they're over. Police rules or something." She winced as a crash echoed down the hallway, and threw an anxious glance at Becky.

Becky flashed an apologetic grimace as she trotted toward the boys' bedroom.

"All right, misters, stop it this instant!"

Entangled like a pretzel on the floor, they froze. Identical looks of surprise turned her way. Both were playing a less-than-friendly game of tug-of-war with a yellow dump truck.

Becky spoke in her sternest voice. "If you don't want to spend the whole week in time-out, you had better behave yourselves tonight. Aunt Amber is doing Mommy a favor, and I don't want you to make her sorry she did."

Tyler scowled and released the truck to fold his arms across his chest. "I don't know why we can't come, too."

A quick reply came to mind, but Becky stopped herself. Was this the jealousy Daddy told her might occur? She'd dated only a couple of times since her divorce, and the last time had been over a year ago when they were four. They were older now, closer to the age when they might really resent a man claiming their mother's attention.

She dropped to her knees, careful to avoid the assortment of cars and connecting blocks scattered around the floor. "You can't go because Mr. Lewis and I want to spend some time alone so we can get to know each other better. You'll have fun here with Aunt Amber."

Jamie spun a wheel on the upturned dump truck. "He could get to know me and Tyler, too."

"I'm sure he'd like that another time. Besides, we're going to a fancy restaurant where there won't be any other kids and you can't make any noise. You'd get really bored."

Tyler scowled. "Then why do you want to go?"

She laughed and ruffled his hair. "Because they have cool things to eat, like snails."

"Eeewww, yucky!"

Both boys rolled on the floor, clutching their stomachs and making gagging noises. When she tickled their tummies, the gagging turned to giggles.

After as much roughhousing as Becky could comfortably handle in a skirt and panty hose, she got to her feet.

"Mommy?"

Tyler looked up at her, his expression serious, dark eyes full of concern. Was this it? Was this where they'd ask her if she still loved them even if she liked Mr. Lewis?

Her heart twisted as she looked down into the beloved little face. "Yes, sweetheart?"

"Sam's not going is he? 'Cause if Sam goes, I get to go, too."

Jamie leaped to his feet. "Me, too. I want to go with Sam."

She kept the laughter out of her expression. "No, Sam is not going."

"Okay." Their concerns resolved, they returned to their task of picking out the perfect toy to show Aunt Amber.

Becky went back to the living room, chuckling.

The doorbell rang. Two tornadoes sped past her, each shouting, "I'll get it!"

They opened the door before Becky could stop them. When she caught sight of Scott on the front stoop, her protest died on her lips. She'd never seen him in anything but jeans. Tonight he wore dark tailored pants, a gray dress shirt and a sport coat. His model-like good looks made her mouth dry. This gorgeous guy was here for *her* when he could have someone as beautiful as Kaci Buchanan? What did she do to deserve this?

"Hey, guys, how's it going?" Scott's smile widened when he looked up at her. "Hello. You look fantastic."

Be still my heart. "Thanks."

His gaze swept the room, and she allowed hers to follow, seeing her cramped home with fresh eyes. The furniture was nearly as shabby as the Pasture's before it got ripped to shreds. And what was that smell? Why had she cooked fish sticks for the boys' supper tonight, of all nights? Heat flooded her face, and she grabbed Amber's arm to pull her forward. "Scott, I'd like you to meet my friend, Amber Craig. Jeff Whitley is her boyfriend."

Scott's smile was nothing but polite as he shook her hand. In return, Amber examined him with a friendly but curious gaze.

"I've heard a lot about you, Scott." Her eyes widened and she glanced quickly at Becky. "Uh, I mean from Becky. Not from Jeff. He would never talk about a suspect. Uh, not that Becky said—I mean, she told me…" She winced and lowered her eyes. Becky cringed. So much for making a good impression.

Thank goodness for kids who forgot their manners. They interrupted what might have become an awkward moment by tugging on Scott's arms.

"Come see our toys, Mr. Lewis," Tyler urged.

"Sorry, boys, we need to get going." Becky glanced pointedly at her watch, then at Amber. "Do you have any questions before we leave?"

Amber's face had gone from red to white at Becky's announcement. "About a million. What do they eat? When is bedtime? Do they go to the bathroom alone?" She wore a please-don't-leave-me-alone-with-them expression that made Becky chuckle.

"They've already eaten, eight-thirty, and yes." She gathered the panicky woman in a quick hug. "Don't worry. You'll be fine."

Becky pressed a quick kiss onto each of the boys' cheeks and slipped outside after Scott. When the door closed behind her, she leaned against it and wiped an imaginary bead of sweat off her forehead.

Scott laughed. "I take it this is her first babysitting job."

"Yes, and she had to be coerced into it." She cast an anxious glance over her shoulder. "I hope she'll be okay."

"Don't worry, Mother Goose." He placed a hand at her back and propelled her toward his truck. "She looks like she can handle your little goslings."

"Hey!" Becky pulled away from his touch and whirled

to walk backward so she could look at him. "I don't want to be Mother Goose tonight. I want to be Cinderella, going to the ball." She reached the truck and leaned against it, tilting her head to cast a flirtatious grin up at him.

Admiration lit his eyes. "I'll be Prince Charming to your Cinderella any day."

He leaned toward her, and butterflies took flight in Becky's stomach. But instead of kissing her, he grabbed the door handle and opened it for her.

When she had stepped up into the truck and slid onto the bench seat, he placed an arm on the back and bent forward to capture her eyes in an intense gaze. "I have only one request for the evening."

She would have promised him anything if only he would go on looking at her like that. "What is it?"

He grinned. "Let's not talk about the Pasture, or Haldeman, or murder suspects, or anything related to any of the above."

On that, they were in wholehearted agreement.

At ten-twenty, Becky closed the living room door behind her and sank against it with a rapturous sigh.

"Welcome home," whispered Amber from the couch. "Did you have fun?"

"Oh, Amber!" She closed her eyes and let a dreamy smile take her lips. "It was the most wonderful evening I've ever had. He is handsome and kind and smart and considerate. And a strong Christian! I think he knows the Bible as well as Pastor Vaughn." She grinned triumphantly. "We'll see tomorrow, because he's coming here for dinner and then to church with us!"

"I'm glad you had a nice time." Amber sounded tired.

As her friend struggled to her feet, Becky looked around the room. "What happened in here?"

The place was a disaster. Toys were strewn everywhere, the curtains dangled off the rod at one end and a brown handprint had been smeared across the television screen. Jamie was curled up in a slumbering ball on the floor, while Tyler had collapsed across the coffee table, his feet still on the floor. Drool puddled beneath his open mouth on the table's surface.

"I made a critical mistake." Amber's lips twisted at her blunder. "I tried to bribe them into being good with chocolate."

Becky's hand flew to her mouth. "Oh, no."

Scowling, Amber nodded. "They were wound tighter than a couple of springs."

A hint of concern crept into Becky's voice as she stepped farther into the room to examine her friend. She looked as if she'd been mugged. "What is that gunk in your hair?"

"Peanut butter." She tried to wipe off a blob of goo with her fingers and managed to rub it in even more. "One of them, I have no idea which, came up with the great idea of slathering the chocolate bars with peanut butter."

"Oh, Amber, I'm so sorry. They're usually—" She stopped. She was about to say the boys were well-behaved if you were firm with them, but the look on her friend's face warned her now was not the time to share child-raising tips.

"Yeah, whatever."

Becky winced at Amber's caustic tone. She bent to pick up a candy wrapper, then started to lay a hand on Tyler's back to rouse him and send him to bed.

"Don't!"

Amber's loud hiss made her jerk her hand back. "Don't what?"

"Don't wake them until I'm gone." She dashed into the kitchen and returned in a second, purse clutched in her hand and a frantic expression on her face. "Just give me a thirty-second head start. Good night. See you at church."

She ran from the house without a backward glance. The slam of the door shook the dangling curtain rod off the wall.

SEVENTEEN

"Samson's Secret is one of the friendliest horses we have here at the Pasture." Scott slapped the old bay's neck affectionately as six tourists gathered around him. "He was found abandoned in a field in New Jersey, nothing but a bag of bones living on rainwater and whatever wild grass he could find. The authorities checked his tattoo and realized who he was, a champion who had made more than a million dollars during his career. He still holds the six-furlong track record at Arlington." Scott shook his head. "It was like finding Babe Ruth living under a bridge."

"He's a beautiful horse." The woman reached a tentative hand toward Samson, smiling when he allowed her to rub his nose.

"Here, give him this." Scott pulled an apple out of the bucket he carried and halved it with his pocket knife.

She did, turning a wide grin on her husband when Samson took it eagerly from her fingers.

Scott laughed. "Besides being the friendliest, he's the best eater. Probably remembers what it was like to scavenge for food."

"What's wrong with his ear?" One of the men pointed.

Scott stepped closer to the fence to grasp Samson's halter.

The edge of his ear had a cut, fairly fresh. It looked clean, but he should probably put some antibiotic ointment on it to keep it from getting infected. Have to remember to do that.

He looked at the man and shrugged. "They get little nicks and cuts every so often, especially the ones who like to roll on the ground or rub against the fence."

His cell phone buzzed on his belt. He unclipped it and glanced at the number. Lee Courtney.

"Excuse me a minute." He nodded toward his audience before stepping a few feet away. They drew together in a tight cluster around Samson, who appeared to be enjoying all the attention.

"Scott Lewis."

"Scott, this is Marion. Lee would like to see you this afternoon, if you have time."

Scott wanted to get his evening chores done early so he could relax and enjoy Becky's church. But of course he'd make time for his boss. "You bet. What time?"

He heard a paper shuffle, then Lee's assistant said, "He's free around four. Just come on up to the house."

"I'll be there." Hopefully the meeting wouldn't take too long. He was supposed to be at Becky's at five-thirty.

Scott closed the cover on his phone and returned to the tour.

At three fifty-five Scott rang the doorbell at the Courtney residence, a magnificent antebellum mansion at the northernmost edge of the five-hundred-acre farm. Graceful white columns formed a two-story portico that always reminded Scott of *Gone With the Wind*. He could easily picture Scarlett O'Hara seated on a settee, batting her eyelashes behind her fan at a host of adoring beaux.

As he pressed the doorbell, he realized his cell phone was missing from his belt clip. He'd laid it down on the workbench this afternoon and forgot about it. Hopefully he'd have time to run back by the Pasture and pick it up before he went to Becky's.

The door opened, and Scott smiled a greeting at Marion, Lee's indispensable assistant.

"Right on time, as usual." Marion allowed him to press his lips to her cheek as he stepped inside. "He's out on the veranda. Do you remember the way?"

"I think so."

Scott had only been here a couple of times, but he'd been given the grand tour. Soft strains of classical music drifted down the wide, curving stairway, punctuated by the sound of his boots echoing on the tiled floor until he stepped into a carpeted den. There, eight-foot French doors that opened onto the veranda had been thrown wide to let a soft, rose-scented breeze flood the room. When he stepped outside, he found Lee seated in a white wicker chair, well shaded from the bright afternoon sunlight that bathed an enormous rose garden. Water trickled down multilayered porcelain bowls in a fountain in the center of the garden.

"Scott, there you are." The old gentleman laid his book on a glass-covered table beside him and stood to shake Scott's hand. "Have a seat."

As Scott sat in the chair he indicated, Marion stepped through the French doors bearing a tray.

"Ah, Marion, you always know what I want before I ask." Lee beamed up at her, his blue eyes twinkling beneath thick gray brows.

"Of course I do." She set the tray on the low table and winked at Scott. "That's why you keep me around."

She poured two tall glasses of lemonade from a frosty pitcher and set one before each of them. When she disappeared back into the house, Lee picked up his glass and held it to his lips.

He looked at Scott over the rim. "How are things going down at Out to Pasture?"

"Fine. I'm getting to know the horses and have spoken with most of the regular donors. You know, introduced myself, assured them that their help is still appreciated and necessary."

"Good, good."

Scott crossed his legs. "Several of them wanted to know when the board would meet to discuss the Pasture's future." Scott didn't mention that two donors had questioned him closely to determine if he was interested in taking the job as the Pasture's director on a permanent basis. He'd been flattered, but if he passed that along it would sound like bragging.

Lee sipped his lemonade, then held the glass in both hands and stared into it. "That's why I wanted to talk to you. I've had a few calls this morning from some of the board members."

So maybe he didn't have to blow his own horn after all. Maybe some of those donors had contacted the board on his behalf. He picked up his own glass and waited for Lee to continue.

"Frankly, Scott, they're concerned. They question my decision to put you in charge."

Scott sat immobile, searching the old man's face while his words sank in. Someone didn't think he could handle the job? Blood surged uncomfortably in his ears as the silence between them deepened.

He leaned forward to set his glass back on the table.

"I'm stunned. You might not remember this, but I have a lot of experience working with stallions."

Lee waved a hand. "Your experience isn't in question. Your maturity is."

"My maturity?" He shook his head. "I don't understand. Do they think I'm too young to handle the job?"

Lips pursed, Lee studied him. Scott resisted the urge to squirm beneath the older man's searching glance.

"I'll be honest with you. Neal excelled in many ways, but his personal habits were, shall we say, less than professional in some areas. Out to Pasture was his creation, his dream-child. But on more than one occasion his reputation had a negative impact on the organization."

Scott leaned back in his seat. "I can see how that would cause the board some concern. But what does it have to do with me? I don't have a bad reputation."

Lee moved his book to pick up the folded section of a newspaper beneath it. He held it toward Scott. "Have you seen this?"

Scott took it. A glance at the top showed him it was today's *Davidson County Post*. He started to tell Lee that he didn't take the small-town paper when his gaze caught on a headline.

Man Strangled In His Own Home

He skimmed the account of Eddie Jones's death, exercising a huge amount of self-control to keep his face impassive when he found his own name mentioned. The reporter had spoken with someone at O'Grady's, probably the same person Detective Foster questioned.

…A witness, who wished to remain anonymous, told police that a few hours before his death Jones was seen at O'Grady's Tavern arguing with the manager of Out to Pasture, a farm for retired Thoroughbred stallions. Scott Lewis, who took over management of the retirement farm after the previous manger was murdered last week, was unavailable for comment.

"Nobody ever asked me for a comment." He looked into Lee's eyes, willing the man to believe him. "Honestly. I was there all day yesterday and today, and nobody from the paper has been by."

"I've already called Jeffries, the owner of the *Post*. He said no one answered the phone last night in the office."

"Has he ever heard of leaving a message?" Anger seeped into Scott's voice. Surely there were laws against this kind of treatment by the press. Even a small-town newspaper was subject to the law, wasn't it?

"Is it true?" Lee leaned forward to tap a finger on the article. "Do you associate with characters like this Jones?"

Scott flinched at the disapproval in the old gentleman's tone. He leaned forward, forearms resting on his thighs. "No, sir. I do not associate with Jones. The bare facts here are true, but I don't gamble at all, and I don't drink." He met Lee's gaze without flinching. "I went to the bar to ask him about the break-in because I thought he was responsible for it. He didn't like my questions, and got a little uptight. I wasn't even there ten minutes."

Lee's eyes narrowed as he subjected Scott to a soul-searching stare. Finally, he nodded once and sat back with a relieved smile. "I knew you'd have an explanation. I'm never wrong about a man's character."

Scott sagged with relief. He picked up his glass and gulped, more for an excuse to look away than because of thirst.

Lee took the paper from his unresisting hand and buried it beneath his book. "I'll give the board members a call, explain things. Don't worry about it."

"I appreciate that." Sensing that he was being dismissed, Scott stood.

Lee stood, as well, and extended his hand. "Thanks for coming by. The board is meeting on Friday, so I'll give you a call and let you know how it goes."

Scott found his way to the front door alone and exited the house. Frustration tensed his jaw as he stomped down the porch stairs. Thank goodness Lee believed him, and he'd explain Scott's involvement with Eddie Jones to the board. But what about the others who read that article?

He slid behind the wheel of his truck and slammed the door. Instead of turning the key in the ignition, he stared across the gentle swells of green farmland. He could just glimpse the roof of the Pasture beyond the Shady Acres horse barn.

He'd never had a boss express anything close to displeasure in him, and the experience rankled. He needed to keep his reputation spotless if he had any chance of landing a job at another Thoroughbred farm. Or, as he'd begun to consider, of keeping the job at Out to Pasture permanently. Who would hire him to manage a multimillion dollar enterprise if they thought he was reckless with his personal finances?

He shook himself as he turned the key. The engine roared to life. He was going to a prayer meeting tonight, and a good, long prayer was exactly what he needed.

But first, dinner with Becky and Jamie and Tyler. A

glance at his watch told him he had just enough time to get home, shower and get over to her house. She'd left work an hour early, probably to get dinner ready for him. He didn't care if she served tuna fish sandwiches and potato chips, he was just looking forward to an evening with her. Something about Becky relaxed him. She was so easy to talk to, so insightful and smart. He loved that ready smile that ignited her eyes.

He punched the gas pedal. If he hurried, he'd have time to stop and pick up some flowers, as he should have done last night.

EIGHTEEN

Becky checked the address on her note and compared it to the number etched in gold on the plaque in the front yard of what she could only describe as a modern mansion. Three elegant stories, tall graceful windows, glittering crystal in the wide double doors. She battled a fit of nerves as she turned onto the circular driveway. Maybe she should have called Isabelle first. The police might already have been here, and it would be so embarrassing to be thrown out on her ear. But if they hadn't questioned her yet, Becky wanted to warn her that they might be coming.

Feeling like a poor relation, she pulled her bedraggled car beneath the arched portico and cut the engine. She clutched the steering wheel, gathering her nerve, then got out of the car. She paused in the act of locking the doors. Nobody would bother breaking into her old Chevy in a ritzy neighborhood like this one.

The exquisite front door opened the moment her foot reached the topmost brick step. When it did, cigar-scented air rushed outward. A dark-haired man who seemed to be all legs looked down on her from a lofty height, his expression one of polite inquiry. When she noticed a slight flaring of his hawklike nostrils, Becky bit back a nervous giggle.

"I'm here to see Isabelle Keller. My name is Becky Dennison."

"I'm sorry," he said, in a voice that denied it, "but Miss Keller isn't home this afternoon."

She *knew* she should have called. She gave the man a bright smile. "Will you tell her I dropped by, and ask her to call me?"

"Lawrence, who're you talking to?" A man's deep voice sounded from somewhere inside the house.

Lawrence turned his head and spoke without moving. "Someone to see Miss Keller."

"Well, don't leave her standing outside. Bring her in."

Lawrence paused only a second, long enough for Becky to wish she'd taken the time to refresh her lipstick, then stepped backward and opened the door wider. Becky stepped into an entry hall that belonged in Buckingham Palace. Marble everywhere, on the floors, the staircase, the tops of antique tables scattered all around. When the door closed behind her, the late-afternoon sunlight pouring through the glass cast dancing rainbows across the floor.

Movement to her right drew her attention. A man stood from a wing chair and stooped over an ashtray to put out his cigar before coming toward her. This man wasn't much taller than Becky, with a thick neck and muscular arms that bulged like one of Jamie's toy action figures. She recognized him from the newspapers.

"Mr. Keller, my name is Becky Dennison. I'm a friend of Isabelle's."

His hand engulfed hers, and he studied her face with small, piercing eyes. "I don't think I've heard Izzy mention your name."

Becky fought the impulse to look away. "Actually, we just met last week when she stopped by the place I work."

"And where is that?"

"Out to Pasture. I work in the office."

Something flared in his eyes that made Becky want to take a step backward. But it was gone before she could identify it. "I see. Please come in and sit down." He gestured toward an empty wing chair on the other side of a marble-topped table from his. "Can I have Lawrence bring you a drink?"

As she sat, she noticed a half-full glass beside the ashtray. From the smell of it, it was something alcoholic. At four-fifteen in the afternoon?

She perched on the edge of the seat cushion, ankles crossed, and held her purse in her lap. "No, thank you. I can't stay long."

With a glance of dismissal at Lawrence, Mr. Keller reseated himself and turned to look at her full-on. "You're the one who found the money. In a bag of dog food, I heard."

Becky straightened. She didn't know the discovery was public information.

He must have seen her surprise, because he explained. "I have friends at State Police Headquarters in Frankfort."

She remembered what Scott said about charges against Mr. Keller always being dropped. "I see."

Ice clinked against the sides of his glass when he picked it up. "Did my Izzy talk to you, tell you she'd been seeing Haldeman?"

Becky watched his hand as he swirled the liquid. Those hands were huge, and strong. Strong enough to kill a man with a hoof pick? Or maybe strangle him in his sleep?

A tickle of fear made her palms begin to sweat. She wiped them on her slacks. "Yes, she did."

A blast of humorless laughter shook his shoulders. "He was toying with her. He did that, toyed with women just to get money out of them for those precious horses of his. I warned her, but she wouldn't listen." His jowls drooped as he stared at the carpet in front of his chair. When he spoke again, it was almost a whisper. "She wouldn't listen. And now what will happen to her?"

He knew. Becky was suddenly sure that Isabelle's father knew of her pregnancy.

"Mr. Keller," she said gently, "maybe he did toy with women in the past, but a man can change. Maybe Neal really loved Isabelle."

"Ha!" He jerked upright and some of the liquor splashed out of his glass onto his pants. He didn't appear to notice. "He didn't. Know how I know?"

The last came out slurred. The man was drunk.

Lord, please get me out of here in one piece!

Becky kept her voice calm, though fear was creeping up her spine to brush prickly fingers at the back of her neck. "How do you know?"

He went still, staring into her eyes for a long moment. "Because I paid him to leave her and the baby alone. Gave him two hundred fifty thousand dollars. And he took it." He held the glass to his lips, staring into it. "He took it."

"How long have you known about the baby?"

"Since Izzy found out. She took one of those test things, and left it in the trash can. Lawrence found it, brought it to me." He jerked his head upright and glared at her. "Don't tell her I know. I want her to come to me on her own."

Becky sat back in the chair. The money had come from Isabelle's father. A bribe. Not a horse race. Had Neal told his bookies he had the money to pay them off? Who knew about it besides Mr. Keller?

She leaned forward. "Did you break into Out to Pasture to get your money back?"

He put his head back and laughed. "You're smart, you are. You should work for the police. They wouldn't have been able to figure it out if I hadn't told 'em."

"You confessed?"

He shrugged. "It's okay. I turned over everything I took. Fifty bucks in cash, which made it look like a real robbery, and the files. I figured they'd be happy to get those records, once I saw what they were. They probably can't use it as evidence, but at least they have it." He shook his head. "Never thought to look in the dog food, though."

If he broke into the office, did he also break into the barn? She couldn't help staring at those strong hands.

He followed her glance and laughed. "No, I didn't kill him." He flexed his fingers into a fist. "I could have, I was that mad. But I figured paying him off was a better way. And I was right. Izzy will see that sooner or later. She didn't know about the others, she believed him when he told her he loved her. But I knew better. I had him watched. He was having an affair with a married woman at the same time he was seeing my Izzy."

"An affair?" Becky's clutch on her purse tightened. "Mr. Keller, do you know who he was seeing?"

"Of course." He set the drink down. "Leslie Stevens. His next-door neighbor's wife. The scumbag."

Becky's mouth fell open. No way! She had met Leslie several times, because she came to the Pasture often. She and her husband, Nick, were regular donors.

"Did you tell the police?"

He scowled. "Why should I? The woman has bad taste in men, but I see no sense in dragging her into a mess. Let the dead stay dead, and leave the living alone, that's my motto."

Becky watched him pick up his cigar, glance at her and put it down again. She stood.

"I really must be going, Mr. Keller. Please tell Isabelle I stopped by."

He didn't get out of the chair as Becky practically ran to the front door. She felt the weight of his stare on her back as she slipped outside, not breathing freely until she was in her car with the doors locked.

She glanced at her watch. She couldn't be late picking up the boys. The day care center charged a dollar a minute after closing time. And she had to get home to put dinner on before Scott arrived. Now's when she wished she had a cell phone, so she could call the police before the boys got in the car. She had to tell them she'd discovered the identity of the L in the note.

"What are we having?"

Jamie's tone, as usual, told Becky he expected the worst. She'd managed to regain her composure before she arrived at the day care center by reminding herself that there was nothing time sensitive in the revelation of the mysterious L. She could pull Jeff Whitley aside at church tonight. That would be soon enough.

"Cheeseburgers, Tater Tots and a salad."

"Woo-hoo!" Tyler danced in his seat, arms pumping the air. Thank goodness for seat belts.

A glance in the rearview mirror showed her Jamie's scowl. "I don't like salad."

"I know you don't. But you can at least eat a tomato and a cucumber."

She grinned at his dramatic sigh of woe.

As she turned the corner onto her street, Becky looked automatically toward her house. Odd. There was an unfamiliar car in the driveway. And was that a man sitting on her front stoop?

Her pulse picked up speed as she slowed the car. Had Mr. Keller realized he'd talked too much? Did he send someone to her house to warn her to keep her mouth shut?

"Who's at our house?" asked Jamie.

"I don't know."

She'd drive right past, go around the block and leave. But where could she go? She faced forward while trying to get a look at the guy as she drove by. Maybe she'd go to Amber's house. Maybe—

Her foot slammed the brake pedal. The car came to a screeching halt just beyond her driveway. She knew that man.

She pulled forward to the curb in front of her next-door neighbor's house and parked.

When she turned off the engine, the rear door opened and Tyler tumbled out to the sidewalk, Jamie right behind. Becky jerked her door open and grabbed their shirts before they got three steps away from the car.

"You two stay here." She directed her sternest stare at both boys. "Do not move. Do you understand me?"

Her tone promised dire consequences, and they got the message. Wide-eyed, they nodded and backed up to lean against the car. She took a bracing breath and faced her house. This could *not* be happening. Not tonight. Not in front of the boys.

Becky reached the car as Christopher bent down to eye-level in front of Jamie. "How 'bout you, big guy? Do you play ball, too?"

Jamie nodded slowly, his dark eyes suspicious.

Christopher straightened. "Good, because I brought you guys a present."

Tyler's expression lightened. "What kind of present?"

"Everything you need to set up your own practice field in the backyard. A real batting tee, and helmets, and a practice screen, a glove for each of you, and a couple of real Louisville Slugger bats."

Becky bit back a sarcastic comment about the cost of all that equipment. Apparently having his paycheck garnished hadn't reduced him to poverty level.

Tyler was duly impressed. "Wow!" He did a victory dance on the sidewalk.

Jamie wasn't as easy to win over. "I already have a glove."

"Not like this one, buddy." Christopher's face lit with enthusiasm. "This is made out of top-grade premium steer hide, with extra padding in the palm to protect your hand from stinging line drives."

"Where is it?" Tyler raced toward their driveway. "Is it your car?"

Christopher straightened and called after Tyler. "Yep. Drove it all the way from Florida. That's where I live, right down the street from Disney World."

Jamie's gaze flicked from Becky to his father. "You live by Disney World?"

Christopher was pushing, true, but at least he seemed to be pushing the right buttons.

He grinned at Jamie. "That's right. But I haven't ever gone. I've been waiting until you guys could go with me."

As she walked down the sidewalk, the man stood. "I thought that was you."

"Christopher, what are you doing here?"

"I came to see my wife and sons." He flashed the lopsided grin she remembered so well. Her stomach clenched in response.

"Ex-wife."

"Whatever."

He hopped down the concrete stairs and came toward her, arms extended. She took a step backward, warning him with a glare to keep his distance.

"Whoa, a little touchy, aren't you?"

"And why wouldn't I be?" She didn't even try to filter her tone. "Did you expect me to welcome you with open arms like nothing's happened? After *four years* without a word?"

His hands dropped to his sides. "Trust me, I wasn't any good for anybody these past few years. You wouldn't have wanted me around." His voice softened. "But a day hasn't gone by that I didn't think of you and the twins, Becky."

Was that actual contrition she heard in his voice? She eyed him suspiciously. Chris could charm a T-bone from a hungry bear. It was one of his talents.

"And now?"

He looked her straight in the eye. "I'm getting things back on track. I've got a steady job down in Florida doing landscaping for a big corporation." His shoulders jerked with a silent laugh. "They actually pay me to dig in the dirt. Turns out I'm good at something after all. Wouldn't my old man have been surprised if he'd lived?"

Becky fought against a wave of sympathy, which made her angry. She didn't want to feel sorry for the man who deserted her with two little babies. "You were good at lots of things," she said, grudgingly. "Just not good at sticking with them."

"Yeah, well, that's all changing." He craned his neck toward her car. "Are those the boys? I'll bet I won't even recognize them."

Oh, he'd recognize them all right. He saw them every day in the mirror. Becky realized anew how much her sons looked like their father.

"I wish you had called first, Christopher. They were babies when you left. They don't remember you. I need to prepare them."

"Prepare them for what? I'm their father." His smile tightened. "I figure since I'm paying child support, I might as well exercise my visitation rights."

She spoke through clenched teeth. "You don't pay for the privilege of seeing your children. You pay for the responsibility of raising them. And you haven't done your fair share of that."

"I know, I know." He held his hands out, fingers splayed, and took another step toward her. "Are we going to argue about this right now? I've come a long way, and I'd like to see my sons." His arms dropped to his sides and he tried another smile on her. "I've looked forward to seeing you, too, Becky. I've really missed you."

For one instant, time stopped. A bird in a distant tree fell silent. The light breeze that tickled her hair stilled. Even her heart seemed to pause in her chest.

How many times had she dreamed of hearing those words from Christopher? She fell in love with him on the first day of their freshman year in high school, and had never loved another. After he left she'd lost count of the number of nights her aching heart kept her awake in bed,

knowing he would never share it again. Why sh⸺ when so many other women welcomed him to the⸺

The wind stirred the grass at her feet. The bird ⸺ its song. Her heart thudded to life. The Lord had ⸺ her hurts, healed the wounds Christopher had i⸺ But the scars remained, and they were a little more⸺ than she'd realized.

"I'm a Christian now, Chris. I live a different l⸺ the one we shared."

A scowl drew his eyebrows together. "Your fat⸺ to you, did he?"

She smiled. He always disliked Daddy. And the⸺ was definitely mutual. "Yes, my Father got to me.⸺ the one you think."

"Mommy?" They both turned to look at her car.⸺ had taken a few steps toward them. "Can we ⸺ house now? Jamie's gotta go to the bathroom."⸺

"Would you look at him!" Christopher's face⸺ a wide grin of genuine delight.

Before she could react, he ran down the ⸺ stopped in front of them, his arms thrown w⸺ guys. It's me, your long lost daddy."

The look Tyler threw her way was pu⸺ only she'd had time to talk to them first,⸺ expect. She infused her smile with as m⸺ she could, and nodded at him.

Christopher picked Tyler up and ⸺ "You play ball, don't you?"

The boy looked uncertainly ⸺ started T-ball."

"I thought so. Look at that." He⸺ Tyler's arm. "That's the arm of a b⸺

She cast a look of warning his way. He was good at making promises he couldn't keep. She wouldn't stand by and watch him disappoint her sons.

"Come on. Let's go put up the practice screen." He held out a hand toward Jamie.

The boy hesitated, looking toward his mother as though for permission. What could she do? He had been a louse of a husband, and a completely absent parent. But he was their father.

She unclenched her jaw enough to give Jamie a reassuring smile. "Let's do that."

Christopher grinned with triumph when Jamie clasped his hand. Together they jogged down the sidewalk, Becky following slowly behind.

Twenty minutes later, the doorbell rang.

"I'll get it," shouted both boys.

"No, let me."

Becky rushed to grab a paper towel to wipe the raw hamburger off her hands. She'd tried to call Scott, to explain why she had to cancel their plans this evening. But she wasn't able to get him on his cell.

She stepped into the living room, still wiping her hands, to find that Jamie had beaten her to the door. Scott stood on the front stoop, holding a bouquet of spring flowers. His eyes locked on to hers, and the smile that spread across his face warmed a cold spot deep inside that had appeared the moment she saw Chris on her doorstep.

Then Scott looked down. The living room was covered with packages and baseball paraphernalia. Christopher and Tyler knelt before a metal frame, the netting on the floor ready to be stretched on.

At the sight of Christopher, Scott's expression froze.

Becky stood speechless as Christopher got to his feet, stepped around the packages and approached the door.

"Hi, I'm Christopher Dennison." He extended his hand toward Scott. "Becky's husband."

Scott's gaze sought hers. The hand holding the flowers dropped to his side. She had never seen a face so full of pain.

She took a step forward, reaching toward him. "Scott, let me—"

He didn't wait to hear her explanation. Helplessly, she watched him turn on his heel and walk away.

Becky swallowed against a lump of tears that had lodged in her throat as she placed the receiver back in its cradle. Scott wasn't answering his phone. Not that she blamed him for dodging her calls, but if only he would let her explain.

She shook her head. Explain what? What could she say that would erase the pain, the look of betrayal he had given her? She covered her face with her hands and pressed against her eyeballs. She would never be able to forget the look on his face, the flowers thrown into the front yard, the screech of his tires as he zoomed out of her driveway.

"Hey, you okay in here?"

She dropped her hands at the sound of Chris's voice, and turned away so he wouldn't see the tears in her eyes. "I'm fine. Are the boys in bed?"

"Yeah. Thanks for letting me tuck them in." He scooted a chair out from the table. "I even listened to them say their prayers."

Becky picked up the damp dishcloth hanging over the faucet and swiped it over the already spotless countertop. "That's good."

"So, did you get your boyfriend on the phone?"

The sarcasm in his voice made her whirl toward him. "He's not my boyfriend," she snapped. She didn't bother to hide her anger as she continued. "And you are not my husband, Chris. Why did you say that?"

"Hey, calm down." He threw up a hand as though to ward her off. "I was just trying to—"

"To what? Scare him off?" Her pulse pounded with barely suppressed rage as she glared at him. "You have no right to even talk to my friends. You show up here after all these years and expect to step right in where you left off. Well, trust me, that is not going to happen."

The last came out in a hiss as Becky tried to keep her voice down so the boys wouldn't hear her from their bedroom.

Chris rose from the table and crossed the floor in two steps. She backed up until she was pressed against the sink, a thrill of fear coursing through her. Would he hurt her? Chris had never gotten physical with her during even the stormiest part of their marriage. He wouldn't start now, would he?

No, that look on his face wasn't anger. It was something else, something equally alarming.

He spoke softly. "Becky, I'm sorry. I don't know what came over me when that guy walked through the door. I think I was jealous."

He inched forward, and she leaned backward as far as she could. Even so, she felt his breath on her cheek when he whispered, "I want you back, Becky. I love you."

NINETEEN

When Becky's car pulled into the driveway Thursday morning, Scott's jaw clenched. He kept his gaze fixed on the halter he was cleaning while Sam leaped off his bed and ran to greet her. If she had any sense of decency at all, she'd head for the office without trying to talk to him.

"Scott."

So much for decency.

He kept cleaning.

"Please let me explain."

He forced his tone to remain cool, to deny the heat that tried to creep into his throat. "No explanation needed. Your husband came back. End of story."

"He's my ex-husband."

Apparently the guy didn't appreciate the distinction. But Scott didn't want to argue with her. He kept his teeth clamped shut.

She took a step into the barn. Out of the corner of his eye, he saw her hands twist around each other. "I haven't seen him in over four years. I had no idea he even knew where we lived anymore."

He risked a glance at her face. Her eyes pleaded with him to understand. Just like Megan's had done. Oh, man, he'd been here before, and it wasn't any easier the second time around.

"And he showed up out of the blue begging you to take him back."

She blanched. "Something like that."

Scott set the halter down on the workbench and rubbed his eyes. They itched from a long, sleepless night where he replayed the scene in Becky's living room over and over in his mind. It was like the rerun of a pathetically sad movie. He was the lovelorn sucker fated to have his heart broken by the heroine. He couldn't figure out why God kept letting him fall for women destined to return to their husbands.

Part of him wanted to believe in Becky, in her inherent goodness and kindness. The guy he'd seen last night didn't look like someone she'd be attracted to. His sarcastic grin looked as though it could hide a cruel streak. But some women seemed to fall for men who hurt them. He just didn't think she'd turn out to be one of them.

He had to know one thing, though.

"Do you love him?"

A cricket chirped from the corner of the barn, its rhythmic song amplified by the silence between them. Becky couldn't look at Scott's face. She'd agonized over that question all night after Chris left to go back to his hotel.

"Yesterday I would have said no, without hesitation."

Scott dipped his head, forcing her to look up at him. "But today?"

"I don't think I know what love is anymore." Unshed tears clogged her throat. "My marriage was a mistake from the beginning. He didn't want a family, didn't want kids. All he wanted to do was party and have fun. He didn't change. I did. When I got pregnant, I wanted to settle down." Her fingers dug into the flesh on her arms. "But he says he's grown-up, and he wants his family back."

"And you think he deserves a second chance?"

His gaze seemed to penetrate to her soul. She didn't look away, but let him see all the pain and uncertainty that had kept her tossing and turning throughout the night. "Everyone gets a second chance, whether they deserve it or not. That's what Jesus is all about."

Now it was his turn to look away. He went back to the bench, picked up the strip of leather he'd been toying with when she arrived. "Well, I hope it works out for you. I'm sure the boys will enjoy having their parents back together again."

Pain squeezed her chest as she watched his profile. Why did Christopher have to pick now to resurface? *Lord, it's just not fair!*

Or maybe it was God's timing. Maybe He sent Chris back to stop her from developing a relationship with Scott.

Sam nosed at her hand, a not-so-subtle reminder that he hadn't eaten breakfast. She started to turn toward the house, then realized she needed to tell Scott about yesterday.

"I almost forgot. I found out something important."

He turned a look of polite inquiry her way, and she bit back another wave of sorrow. She would probably never see his warm smile again.

She filled him in on Mr. Keller.

His eyebrows arched when she revealed the identity of the mysterious L. "So did you call the police?"

"No. I was going to, but then I realized they'd show up at her house. What if her husband doesn't know about the affair?" She nudged a clump of dirt with the toe of her shoe. "I'd just hate to be the cause of another wrecked marriage."

"So what are you going to do?"

Becky had thought about that in the middle of the night, too. "I'm going to go see Leslie this morning. I'll tell her what I heard, and urge her to go to the police on her own."

Scott studied her a moment, then gave a nod. "I'll go with you."

"Oh, you don't have to do that." The conversation would be awkward enough without a man there.

But he refused to budge. "There's a murderer running around loose, and for all we know, he's aware of their affair. It might be dangerous. I can't let you go alone."

As she walked toward the house, Sam racing in front of her, Becky admitted that she felt relieved not to have to face Leslie Stevens alone.

The Stevens farm was only half the size of Shady Acres, but what Nick Stevens lacked in space, he made up for in flamboyance. Becky drove by every morning on her way to work and loved gazing at the elegant horse barns, with their spired roofs and candy-cane paint job. A new one had been erected right after she came to work at the Pasture, and she'd been amazed at how quickly it came together. A beautiful clear pond fronted the property, hidden jets spraying water high into the sky to be caught by the wind and sprinkled on the crystal surface.

Becky rang the doorbell twice at the Stevens home, but no one answered.

Scott shielded his eyes from the bright April sunshine and looked over the grounds. "Let's see if she's down at the barn. There are several cars over that way."

"I hope Nick isn't there." Becky hopped up into the pickup. "What will we say if he is?"

Scott lifted a shoulder as he started the engine. "He probably won't be. I think he spends a lot of time at his office in Lexington. But if he is, I'll keep him busy while you get Leslie off in a corner somewhere."

Beyond a large pasture where a half-dozen yearlings grazed, they drove by a couple of small paddocks, each with its own resident horse. One ran along the fence on Becky's side, keeping pace with the truck, and she admired the way the muscles rippled along its hindquarters.

"Hey, that's a stallion." She turned to look at Scott. "I didn't realize the Stevenses kept stallions."

"Oh, yeah. They board three studs and manage a syndicate. Lee Courtney owns shares in a couple of them."

Neal had spoken of syndicates that owned and bred stallions, but Becky had only a vague knowledge of the process. All she knew was that Neal had identified a couple of horses owned by syndicates that were close to retiring, and he hoped the owners would send them to the Pasture when they stopped producing.

They turned the corner at the end of the paddock, and Scott inched past three horse trailers parked along the fencerow.

"Looks like they're busy today," he commented. "You might have a hard time getting Leslie's attention. She's pretty involved at the breeding shed."

Breeding? A flush crept up Becky's neck. She hadn't anticipated walking in on horses breeding with Scott there. In the months since coming to work at the Pasture she'd learned enough about the Thoroughbred industry to know those involved in the breeding process viewed it with a clinical, businesslike detachment. But she hadn't managed to develop that attitude yet.

She turned away when her cheeks started to warm. "Maybe we should come back later."

Thank goodness Scott didn't seem to notice her discomfort. "We're here. Might as well see if she's in." He got out of the truck.

Fighting to control the flush that she was sure had turned her face scarlet, Becky hopped to the ground and followed him into the small barn that was, apparently, a breeding shed.

It was bigger inside than she had expected, probably twice as big as the barn over at the Pasture, but instead of sweet hay, the place smelled of horse sweat. There were people everywhere. Three men surrounded a chestnut-colored mare, one with a firm grip on her halter while the other two rubbed her neck and spoke in low, soothing voices. Someone stooped behind her doing who-knew-what, while someone else stood to one side holding a small camcorder. Beyond the open back door came the sound of impatient neighing.

To the right of the door, two men bent over a desk, flipping through papers. One straightened at their approach. "May I help you with something?"

Scott thrust a hand toward him. "Scott Lewis. I'm the manager of Out to Pasture. This is Becky Dennison, who works with me."

"Jason Rawlins." He shook Scott's hand and nodded a smile in Becky's direction. "Nice to meet you."

"I heard Stevens had a new manager," Scott said. "Sorry I haven't made it over to say hello."

He dismissed Scott's apology with a shrug. "I haven't managed to get out much myself. I figured things would be busy here, but nothing like it has been."

Jason looked toward the mare, who whinnied and

pranced in a circle. The man holding her halter skipped along with her, speaking in a low voice.

Why did Scott look so suspicious all of a sudden? He gestured in the horse's direction, but he kept a close watch on Jason. "She's a beauty. And unique. You don't see nite-eyes like that very often."

Becky looked at the horse. She was pretty, as far as Becky's uneducated opinion went. But nite-eyes? How could he tell, when it was daytime?

Jason looked as confused as Becky felt. But he didn't admit it, either. His gaze flicked to the mare, then back at Scott. "Yeah. Real unique."

Scott's lips pursed, and he studied Jason through narrowed eyes. "So, have you been in the business long?"

"Long enough." Jason cast a quick glance behind him. "Are you here as witnesses?"

Becky spoke quickly, in case Scott should decide they could stay and be witnesses as the mare was bred. "We're looking for Leslie."

"Oh." Jason glanced around the barn. "She was here a minute ago. She must have stepped out back to check on the stallion."

He seemed embarrassed, eager to get rid of them. His head jerked toward the desk, where the man he'd been talking to when they came in waited patiently for him to return. "You can go on out there and see if she's around."

Becky grabbed Scott's arm and pulled him toward the rear exit. "Thanks. We'll do that."

They stepped into the sunshine, and walked a few steps away from the barn.

Scott glanced behind him and spoke in a low voice. "Something's not right about that guy."

"He seemed okay to me."

"It's breeding season. Why would he be surprised at being busy? And I don't think he knows what nite-eyes are."

"So?" Becky tilted her head and admitted, "Neither do I."

"You're not managing a breeding shed." He shook his head. "Nite-eyes are growths on the inside of the knees. No two horses have identical nite-eyes. That guy obviously didn't know that."

"Shh." Becky dipped her head in the direction of a woman coming toward them.

Leslie Stevens walked with a confident stride that swung her dark ponytail, pulled through the back loop of a white cap. Becky had liked Leslie since the time she welcomed Becky to her new job as Neal's secretary with the gift of a vanilla-scented candle. She said it would, "give the place a woman's touch." Becky had been pleased by the gesture, especially coming from a wealthy horse breeder and one of the Pasture's major donors. Looking back on that incident now, she wondered if the gift had been a bribe to keep Becky's mouth shut in case someone questioned Leslie's close friendship with Neal.

Recognition showed on Leslie's face as she approached, and Becky thought her smile faded a fraction when they locked eyes, although that could have been her imagination.

Leslie smiled at Scott when she came close enough to shake his hand. "I've been meaning to stop by and congratulate you on your new position. Well deserved, I'm sure." She sobered. "Even though it came about under sad circumstances."

"Temporary position," Scott corrected.

"Not for long, I'll bet. The board would be insane to let you get away. You're exactly what the Pasture needs."

Becky agreed, but they had more pressing matters to discuss this morning. "Leslie, we need to talk to you about something important."

Fear darkened the eyes that turned Becky's way. She knew what was coming, Becky was sure of it.

"I expected the police. Not you." Her voice was heavy with dread. "I guess it was only a matter of time before the gossip chain started buzzing."

"We didn't hear about your relationship with Neal through gossip." Becky watched her face, saw confirmation there instead of denial. "Hugh Keller told me."

"Isabelle's father." Leslie shook her head sadly. "That poor girl. I told Neal not to hurt her. She was too vulnerable to get involved with someone like him."

Scott glanced at Becky before speaking. "The police found a handwritten note in Neal's truck, arranging a meeting for the night he was killed."

Leslie's shoulders sagged, and tears sprang to her eyes. "I figured they would. Given the circumstances, slipping Neal a note wasn't my smartest move."

Two men came out of the shed and headed toward the paddock where a stallion pranced and tossed his head. She turned slightly so they wouldn't see her tears. An unexpected wave of compassion washed over Becky at the grief apparent in the woman's face, and she stepped sideways to block her from view.

"You really cared for Neal, didn't you?"

Leslie didn't answer immediately. Her lips trembled as she lifted her chin to look out over the pasture behind Becky. Finally, she nodded. "He was easy to fall for. So outgoing, so passionate about his work. But we were wrong to have an affair." Her struggle to hold back her tears contorted her face. "I cared for Neal, but I do love my husband."

"You have a strange way of showing it." Disgust twisted Scott's features.

Leslie blanched, then nodded. "I made a terrible mistake. Nicky deserves better. The night Neal was killed, I was going to break it off. I did break it off. I went to his house around eleven-thirty, after Nicky was in bed." Her lips twisted in a humorless smile. "That was our regular routine."

"Was he alive then?" Becky asked, her voice low.

She nodded. "I told him I couldn't see him anymore. He said he understood. He knew it was the right thing to do. But while we were talking, one of the horses got really agitated. Neal turned off the lights so we could see outside, and we saw a figure run toward the barn."

"Could he tell who it was?" Scott asked.

She shook her head. "It was too dark. I was afraid Nicky had followed me, that he had caught us just when I was trying to make things right. But instead of coming to the house, whoever it was went into the barn. We saw a dim light, like a flashlight. Neal thought it must have been someone breaking in."

Becky was beginning to get the picture. "So Neal went out to surprise them, leaving Sam in the house to protect you."

Fresh tears welled in her eyes as she nodded. "I waited a long time, but he never came back. Finally, I couldn't stand the suspense anymore. I tiptoed out to the barn, and that's when I saw his body." She bent forward and buried her face in her hands. "He was dead. There was so much blood."

Scott still eyed her with suspicion. "Why didn't you call the police?"

Becky knew the answer before she gave it.

"I know I should have, but I panicked! Nicky would have to know, and what's the point in that? The affair was over." She looked from Becky to Scott, begging them understand. "You're not going to tell him, are you? He'll be devastated."

Becky placed a hand on her arm. "Of course we're not."

"But you need to go to the police." Scott's voice was hard.

Leslie's gaze flew to his face. "I can't do that!"

"You really have to, Leslie." Becky tried to infuse as much persuasion into her voice as possible. "They found the note and your footprints in the barn. It's only a matter of time before they find out about your relationship with Neal, just as I did. Then they'll come to question you, maybe in front of your husband."

Leslie closed her eyes, her face a mask of pain. She drew a shuddering breath, and gave a single nod. "You're right. I'll call them this morning."

TWENTY

"We should tell the police ourselves."

Becky had never seen Scott so stubborn.

They sat at their desks in the office at the Pasture, Scott scowling across the room at her, his legs spread out before him. Becky struggled to control her rising temper. The man didn't have a compassionate bone in his body.

"She said she'd call them. I believe her."

His eyes rose to the ceiling. "You're too trusting."

"And you're too suspicious."

"She's an adulterer and a liar. Her husband deserves to know. I don't understand why you want to protect her."

Becky winced. Maybe she was being a little too soft on Leslie. But Leslie had realized her mistake. She'd taken steps to end her affair. What was wrong with wanting to protect her marriage from a devastating blow? Becky understood. She'd suffered the devastation of a failed marriage herself. She certainly didn't want to do anything to sabotage someone else's.

"I'll talk to Jeff at church on Sunday," she promised. "If she hasn't called them by then, I'll tell him."

Arms folded across his chest, Scott inhaled a long, slow breath. "I'll tell you who I'm suspicious of. Jason Rawlins."

Honestly, he seemed to have taken a real dislike to the poor guy. "Just because he doesn't have a lot of experience is no reason to suspect him of murder."

"How could someone with almost no experience land a job managing a breeding shed with someone as important as Nick Stevens?" He shook his head. "It just doesn't make sense. I wonder if Nick even knows what an idiot the guy is. He seems to leave the day-to-day running of the farm to Leslie."

"Well, Leslie is no dummy. If Jason didn't know what he was doing, she would see it."

Scott gave her a sad smile. "Some women are way too soft when it comes to men with a string of excuses."

Becky looked down so he couldn't see her cringe. So that's what the foul mood was all about. "Scott, I've said I'm sorry. What more do you want from me? Do you want me to find another job?"

"Of course not." He stood and strode across the room to the doorway, avoiding her gaze. "I'm probably not going to be around here much longer anyway."

What did he mean by that? Would he actually quit because of her? She couldn't let that happen.

"Scott, wait."

He stopped, but didn't turn to face her.

"You need to know something. Christopher lives in Florida." She bit her lip. She hated what she was about to say. "If we get back together, the boys and I will have to move there. So please don't leave the Pasture because of me."

She couldn't see his face, but the muscles in his shoulders tensed. A red flush stained the skin on the back of his neck.

"Don't worry. It won't be because of you."

What in the world did he mean by that? She didn't get

the chance to ask him to explain, because he hurried out of the room. At the sound of the back door slamming, Becky lowered her face into her hands and fought a wave of tears.

"He says he's changed, Daddy." Becky sliced into a piece of mail, the phone propped on her shoulder. "I think maybe he's grown up."

She'd sent him an e-mail first thing this morning, giving him the news of Christopher's return. She wasn't surprised when her phone rang at exactly eight-thirty California time.

"I don't believe it."

A check fluttered out of the envelope when she extracted a letter. She added it to a short pile of others. "You wouldn't. You never liked Chris."

"For very good reasons. He's a troublemaker who got my little girl suspended from school."

In the center of the room, Sam slept sprawled on the floor in a shaft of sunlight. He whimpered, his legs jerking in response to some dreamworld canine crisis.

She chuckled into the phone. "That was ten years ago, and I was just as guilty of skipping school as he was." But Daddy would prefer to blame someone else than acknowledge that his only daughter used to have a wild streak.

"A leopard doesn't change his spots, sweetheart. Especially a no-good, two-timing leopard."

"I changed my spots," she reminded him. "They've been washed clean."

"Has he become a Christian?"

She thought of the way Chris's face hardened last night when she told him she'd accepted the Lord. "No."

"Well, then, he's still a loser. Tell him to hit the road."

She tsked in his ear. "That isn't a very Christian attitude."

"I'll pray for him." From his tone, Becky didn't want to know what Daddy would ask the Lord to do with Christopher. "But that doesn't mean I want him hanging around my little girl. Or my grandsons."

She sobered. Laying down the letter opener, she rested a hand on the desk as she spoke into the phone. "He's their father. All the books stress how important it is for kids to have a relationship with their fathers. Even men who are not especially good parents. Jamie and Tyler will have to learn to deal with him sooner or later." Her voice became soft, remembering how the boys clung to Chris when he left last night. "But I think he could be a good father, given the opportunity. You should have seen them, Daddy. He got down on the floor and played with them, and they loved it." Amber's words came back to her. "They need a man around. They're starved for male attention."

"Then move them out here," he bellowed.

Wincing, she jerked the phone away from her ear. "Even if they were all the way on the other side of the country, Christopher would still be their father." She closed her eyes. "And my ex-husband."

Cell phone static crackled during a long pause.

"You're not thinking of going back to that jerk, are you?" His voice became stern. "Rebecca Ann, don't you even consider it. I'll come out there and turn you over my knee."

She laughed. "I'd like to see you try. Listen, Daddy, I've got to go. We've got a tour scheduled at noon, and a car just pulled into the driveway."

"I'll call you tonight. We're going to finish this conversation."

"After nine, okay? Love you, Daddy."

"Love you, sweetheart."

Becky replaced the receiver. For a moment she didn't move, just stared at the telephone. If she reconciled with Chris, Daddy would be furious.

But Tyler and Jamie deserved to have a relationship with both of their parents. And they were her first priority. As their mother, she had to put their welfare above her own. Didn't she owe them the opportunity to grow up with a father who loved them? Who loved her, even if she wasn't sure she returned his affection any longer?

After Chris left last night she had taken her Bible to bed and poured through the pages. The concordance in the back pointed her to the part that said an unbelieving husband could be won over by his wife, and her heart sank when she read it.

But she wasn't his wife anymore! If they hadn't divorced, her choice would be clear. She would stay with Chris and pray that God would reach him through her. But they *had* divorced. Did God want her to reconcile with a spouse who wasn't a Christian?

Her nails bit into the soft part of her hand as she banged a fist on the desk. It wasn't fair! She had needs, too. Didn't she deserve to be with someone she could love whole-heartedly? Would her mistakes of the past continue to reach into her future, to make her miserable?

Angry tears prickled in her eyes. In the old days, God sent an angel or a prophet so there was no question about what He wanted them to do. If only He would send a messenger to her now, to point her in the right direction.

She snatched a tissue from the box on her desk and scrubbed at her eyes.

It was the guessing that would drive her crazy.

* * *

"I don't like those green things," Jamie informed the server at the pizza restaurant.

He sat in the booth on Christopher's right, Tyler on the left. Alone on the opposite bench, Becky glanced up at the woman, who stood with her pen poised over an order pad, then back down at Chris. "We usually get half with double cheese and half with pepperoni and sausage."

With a grin, he slapped the menu closed. "Those are my two favorites. Bring us an extra large. And a pitcher of beer."

Becky couldn't believe her ears. What was he doing? She leveled a hard stare across the table, nodding toward Jamie.

"What?" Chris affected an injured expression. "Okay, fine. You can drive. Here."

He tossed his car keys across the table. They slid off the edge and dropped into her lap.

"Chris, I don't think it's a good—"

He stopped her with a look. "Not a big deal, unless you turn it into one."

She glanced at Tyler, who was watching her with a puzzled expression. All the parenting books said it was vital that parents not argue in front of the children, that it damaged their sense of security. So far she'd never had to heed that advice— there'd been no one to argue with. But she planned to discuss this with Christopher later, when the boys were in bed.

She smiled up at the woman. "I'll have a Diet Coke, and they'll each have a Sprite."

Their order duly recorded, the server left. Chris leaned back, put a hand on each twin's head and rumpled their hair. "So, what do you say we go to the ball field tomorrow and practice running the bases?"

"Yeah!" Tyler turned an eager face toward her. "Can we, Mommy?"

"I have to work until five, but after that we could."

Chris shook his head. "It'll have to be during the day. I've got plans tomorrow night." He winked at her. "Can't come to town and not get together with my old buds, can I? But I could pick up the boys after school and drop them off when you get home. You know, my first official visitation, like the court says I get."

Becky shifted on the padded bench, not meeting Chris's eyes. He was right. The court said he could have the boys one night a week and every other weekend. But he'd never exercised that right, not wanting the responsibility of caring for two babies. Still, if she agreed, she'd have to sign a form giving him permission to pick up the boys from school. She wasn't ready to do that just yet.

The server arrived with their drinks and placed them on the table. Chris immediately poured beer into a frosty glass mug and chugged half of it. The pungent smell brought back a dozen memories of the old days. None of them good.

Becky toyed with the car keys and tried not to look disapproving. What did he have going on tomorrow night? Was he meeting up with one of his old girlfriends? Suspicion burned in her mind, and she hated it. When she was pregnant, she'd caught him with other women so often she'd been reduced to a raving maniac whenever he said he was going anywhere without her. That life had been long ago, but the old feelings resurfaced with surprising speed.

Would it be different this time around? It would have to be. Chris knew his sons now. Surely he'd want to be a positive influence in their lives. He probably was just going to see some of his old friends, as he said. She shouldn't jump to conclusions.

"Hey, look, there's one of those claw games." Chris leaned against the back of the booth to straighten his legs so he could dig in his pocket. He dropped a handful of change on the table. "I've got some quarters. Let's go play. I'll show you how to win, guaranteed every time."

Tyler took off across the restaurant at a gallop, Chris right behind him, the beer mug in his hand. Jamie slid out of the booth more slowly. Instead of following his brother and father, he stood at the edge of the table, his face solemn, staring at the pitcher.

He spoke in a quiet voice. "Mommy, is that drugs?"

Startled, Becky's gaze flew to his face. Where had her five-year-old heard about drugs? Were they already teaching drug prevention in kindergarten?

And how should she answer? He'd just seen his father take a big drink. She jingled the keys in her lap, uncomfortable, and forced a smile to her face. "No, sweetie, that's not drugs. It's beer. Grown-ups sometimes drink beer."

"Do you?"

She shook her head. "No, I don't."

Thank goodness Jamie didn't press the matter. He nodded slowly, then turned toward the claw machine.

His face lit up. "Hey, there's Mr. Lewis!"

Becky's heart thudded in her chest as Jamie took off at a run. Scott, here?

"Mr. Lewis!"

A dark-haired missile darted toward him and tackled his thighs. Startled, Scott looked down at Jamie Dennison, then up at the man standing next to a toy machine. Becky's ex-husband. Just his luck to run into Dennison at the town's only pizza restaurant. Next time, he'd let them deliver.

"Hey, Jamie, what are you doing here?"

The little boy tilted his head back to look up at Scott. "We're getting pizza. Cheese for me, and pepperoni for Tyler."

Focused on the game, Tyler said, "Hi, Mr. Lewis," but didn't take his hands off the controls.

"Well, if it isn't my wife's boss." Becky's ex straightened and put an arm on the top of the machine. He leaned against it, a smirk on his face. Instead of washing his hair, he'd pulled it back in a ponytail tonight, not a nice look, in Scott's opinion. His other hand held a mug of beer. Startled, Scott eyed him carefully. Surely the idiot wasn't planning to drive his sons home after drinking beer. Maybe he should make a phone call to Trooper Whitley to tip him off.

A movement in the center of the restaurant drew his attention. Becky rose from a booth and turned slowly. Tension tightened her features, but as she locked eyes with him, he thought he saw a flicker of relief. His throat constricted as she gave him a hesitant smile.

Lord, she's so pretty, so sweet. What's she doing with a jerk like this?

"Is Sam here?"

Scott tore his gaze away from Becky and looked down at her son. Jamie searched behind him, as though expecting to find the dog following along.

"He's waiting in the truck."

"Can I go see him?"

Dennison put a hand on the boy's shoulder, his gaze fixed on Scott. "Not right now, *son.*"

Scott ignored him and smiled into Jamie's disappointed face. "Another time."

He went to the counter and gave the cashier his name. Thank goodness, his pizza was ready and waiting. He tossed a twenty toward the woman. Just get him out of there fast.

Becky stepped up beside him. He didn't look at her, but out of the corner of his eye he saw her hands clutching at each other.

"Scott, I'm so sorry."

The woman counting out his change was taking way too long. He watched as she peeled open a new roll of pennies with agonizing precision.

"Sorry for what? For wanting a pizza?"

"No, for…" She glanced over her shoulder.

Scott followed her gaze in time to see Dennison drain his beer mug. He turned a hard look on Becky. "I hope you're not drinking, too."

She stiffened. "Of course I'm not."

Finally, the cashier held his change toward him. He shoved it into his pocket without looking at it, picked up the pizza box and turned toward the door.

Dennison stepped into his path. "What's your hurry, Lewis? Why don't you join us for a beer?"

Excitement lit Jamie's and Tyler's faces. Beside him, Becky uttered a sound of protest.

Scott clamped his jaw shut against a sharp retort, but managed a stiff, "Thanks anyway."

Dennison lifted his empty mug in farewell. "Another time, then."

Yeah. Next time a mule wins the Derby.

Vowing to give up pizza for as long as he lived in this small town, Scott made his escape.

TWENTY-ONE

The minute Becky's car came to a stop, the back doors flew open and the boys tumbled out. She took her time gathering her purse and her nerve, glancing through the windshield to watch them run toward Scott in the barn.

She stood in time to hear Tyler explain, "Dad's going to pick us up in a few minutes, so we can't help you feed the horses today. But we can throw the ball to Sam till he gets here."

"Here it is!" Jamie raced over to the dog's blanket, stooped and held the ball aloft.

Sam danced in a circle, which set both boys laughing. They ran off toward the grass to begin their game.

Becky stepped up to the barn's entrance but didn't go inside. "I stopped to get them on the way back from the vet's office." She held the bag of ointment toward him, proof that she'd been on an official errand. "I just didn't think it was a good idea to let their father pick them up at school."

Scott came toward her slowly, his eyes searching her face with an intensity that made her stomach flip-flop. "Why isn't that a good idea?"

She gulped, and her gaze dropped to her shoes. "I'm not sure why."

"Well, I think—"

Whatever he thought remained unsaid. Tyler's voice interrupted. "Jamie, I'm telling! You're not supposed to go in there!"

Becky turned to see what misdeed Jamie was performing.

Her heart skipped a beat.

There was her older son, crawling between the two bottom fence planks into Alidor's paddock.

In the far corner, the stallion raised his head as he noticed movement inside his territory. The powerful horse stamped the ground and then headed for Jamie, trotting at first but quickly picking up speed. Pieces of grass spit up behind him where his hooves butchered the turf.

By the time Becky's feet became unstuck Scott had already sprinted halfway across the yard. Alidor was barreling toward Jamie when Scott reached the fence and vaulted over like an Olympian. Heart pounding, Becky froze as Scott ran toward the stallion, arms waving above his head, shouting, "Whoa, there!"

Nostrils flaring, Alidor diverted his attention from the boy to the man. He stopped in front of Scott, neck extended. Scott leaped backward in time to escape the snap of the Thoroughbred's teeth.

Jamie picked up something in the grass and ran for the fence.

When Scott danced sideways to avoid a second attempt to bite him, the horse changed his approach. He whirled around to present his backside and raised a hind leg. Scott didn't wait around for the kick but made a dash for the fence and leaped over.

Not as gracefully the second time. His boot caught on the top plank and he went sprawling face-first in the grass.

Becky ran forward and dropped to her knees beside him. "Are you okay? Is anything broken?"

He didn't answer. Should she call 9-1-1? She drew breath to shout at Tyler to run inside to the phone when Scott moaned and rolled over onto his back.

"That was kind of a klutzy move, wasn't it?"

Relief flooded through her. She threw herself forward to give him a fierce hug. "That was the best move I've ever seen anyone make."

Embarrassed, she straightened. Scott lay in the grass, looking up at her with an expression of pure astonishment. What must he think of her? Last night he sees her out with her ex-husband, and today she's practically rolling in the grass with him.

She turned to find Jamie and Tyler watching. When she spoke to the older twin, her voice came out sharp. "You are in so much trouble, young man. What in the world were you doing? Don't you know you could have been killed?"

His dark eyes went round and his lower lip quivered. "I saw this." He held it toward her. "I thought it was a man."

She looked at the object in Jamie's hand. A clear glass tube with a red lid. What in the world would make the boy think that was a toy? True, the lid was bright red, and might look the color of the trim on some of his action figures. Maybe if the sun glinted off it just so.

Scott rolled over on his side and sat up with a grunt. He took the object and held it up to the sunlight.

"It's an empty test tube. How'd that get in Alidor's paddock?"

A test tube. She hadn't seen one of those since high school science class. Way back then she'd done experiments, mixing chemicals, looking at specimens under a microscope.

Where had she read about microscopes lately? Seems like she'd seen something in the paper, something about…

Becky's eyes widened. She grabbed Scott's arm. "Do you remember that article we found in Neal's file? The one on cloning?"

His brow creased. "Yeah, so?"

Becky jumped to her feet and ran toward the house. Inside, she flipped through the files, scanning the neatly labeled tabs until she found the one she wanted. She shuffled the papers inside. Where was…there.

When she got back outside, the article clutched in her hand, no one had moved.

"It's right here." She waved the clipping in Scott's face. "It's talking about the first successful horse cloning in the U.S., in Texas."

He looked, but made no move to take it. "Okay. But surely you can't think this has anything to do with Alidor."

A car pulled into the driveway. Becky closed her eyes and dropped her head forward. Christopher's timing was perfect.

The boys raced across the grass toward him. Becky followed more slowly as Scott got to his feet.

Chris got out of the car and leaned against the hood, his arms folded. His eyes bored into hers as she approached. "Having a little romp in the grass, are we?"

Becky looked at the boys, then gave him a stern look. "Christopher, please."

"I just don't like catching my wife with another man."

Anger flared in Becky. "Ex-wife. I know exactly how you feel," she snapped.

At least he had the decency to flush. She set her teeth together until her jaws ached as she helped the boys into the backseat and made sure their seat belts were fastened.

Jamie avoided her eye, probably hoping also to avoid punishment for his stunt. She patted him on the leg and whispered, "We'll talk later."

Straightening, she turned to Christopher. "You will be careful, right?"

"Sure, I will."

She dipped her head, forcing him to lock eyes with her. "No drinking. Not even one beer."

The cocky Christopher-grin twisted his lips. He held up two fingers. "Scout's honor."

"You were never a Boy Scout." She stepped away from the car, her heart wrenching in her chest as he got in and slammed the door. Her babies were about to go on their first visitation with their father without her. *Lord, please, please, please keep them safe!*

"Have them home by six," she called as the car backed out of the driveway.

Christopher waved out the window, and then they were gone.

Her lower lip quivering much as Jamie's had earlier, she turned toward the office. Scott stood by the back door, watching. "You could have gone with them if you wanted. There's nothing pressing going on this afternoon."

He was trying not to look at her, and that suited her fine. If he said anything nice, she might just burst into tears.

She raised her chin. "No, that's okay. It's good for them to be without me every now and then."

"Well." He cleared his throat, then gestured toward the newspaper clipping still clutched in her hand. "About that article."

"Oh." She held it toward him. "I read it when I filed it away. That test tube reminded me of the procedure they describe in there. It says here they take a skin cell sample from the horse, and the DNA is placed into an unfertilized egg that's had the nucleus removed. Then they implant the egg into a fertile mare during breeding session."

Scott's head jerked upright, his gaze fixing on Alidor. "Skin cells? Does it say where on the animal they get them?"

"I don't think so." She looked up at him. "But it *is* breeding season."

He took the article and scanned it. As he neared the end, he shook his head. "It doesn't." He caught her eye. "I've found odd nicks on the ears of a couple of the horses."

The prickling sensation on the back of her neck had nothing to do with the light spring breeze that stirred the leaves above her. "Do you think Neal was cloning the stallions?"

Scott shook his head. "It doesn't make sense. Why would anyone want to clone a Thoroughbred? The Jockey Club won't register cloned foals. They specifically address that in the regulations. Clones can't race, and they can't be bred, so what's the point?"

Becky had no answer for that. "You're right. It doesn't make sense. But I have a feeling it's true."

But Scott kept staring at the article. "Lee Courtney needs to know about this."

"I don't believe it of Neal." Sitting in an armchair, Mr. Courtney removed his reading glasses but continued to stare at the article in his hand.

Becky shifted forward on the elegant sofa cushion and crossed her ankles. They'd closed up the Pasture office an hour early after Scott called Mr. Courtney's secretary and arranged a meeting at his house.

Beside her, Scott tapped the test tube in his palm. "I know it's far-fetched. Nobody would be stupid enough to think they could clone a Thoroughbred."

Mr. Courtney's thick eyebrows rose. "Not as far-fetched as you think. Over in Europe they've made remarkable progress in equine cloning procedures. The Jockey Club is monitoring the situation. Used to be the clones weren't as hardy or as healthy as the originals. I've heard that's changing. Of course, up until now they've experimented on workhorses and pets. But it's only a matter of time before someone tries it on a Thoroughbred." He leaned back in his chair, shaking his head. "I just didn't think about it happening here. Still the Pasture is the perfect place, isn't it?"

Becky thought of the horses they had at the Pasture. Champions, all of them. Millionaires, Neal used to say, because most of them had amassed millions during their racing and breeding careers. "If someone's going to clone a horse," she said slowly, "naturally they'd try for a champion."

Mr. Courtney nodded. "Exactly."

"So you *do* think Haldeman might have been trying to clone the horses," Scott said.

"Not for a minute." Mr. Courtney's chin jutted forward as he fixed a gaze on Scott. "Neal Haldeman had his vices, no doubt, but he loved the industry. He would never do anything to interfere with the natural process of breeding a champion. Never."

Becky leaned forward. "If someone else was trying to collect skin cell specimens from the horses at the Pasture, and if Neal caught them…"

She left the thought unfinished, but judging by their serious expressions, both men followed her logic.

Scott shook his head. "But who would do something so risky? And why? You can't register a clone."

"I don't know why. Maybe just to say they succeeded." Mr. Courtney's lips twisted with disgust. "I can think of only one person who would try something stupid like cloning a Thoroughbred. And he has access to the Pasture, since his property adjoins mine on the back side."

"Nick Stevens?" Becky cast a quick glance toward Scott. Would he mention Nick's wife, Leslie, and her affair with Neal?

Mr. Courtney nodded. "Exactly. He's an upstart, an amateur. He has no respect for the industry, for the breed."

Becky shifted and avoided the older man's glance. That he didn't like Nick, a competitor in the breeding industry, was common knowledge, but to accuse him of this crazy scheme, and maybe even of murder? She didn't believe it.

Scott shook his head. "I still don't understand why. What would he get out of it?"

"Who knows?" The older man stood, a signal that their meeting was over. "I think you should turn this over to the police. Let them sort it out."

Becky got to her feet and took the newspaper clipping Mr. Courtney held out to her. "Thank you for meeting with us on such short notice."

He waved a hand. "Any time. That's what I'm here for. And I was going to call you this afternoon anyway." He shifted his gaze to Scott, a smile tweaking the edges of his mouth. "The board met today. They've authorized me to offer you the position of director of the Pasture on a permanent basis. If you want the job, it's yours."

Becky whirled toward Scott. "That's wonderful news! Congratulations, Scott."

Instead of the wide smile she expected, Scott looked as though he'd just been handed a prison sentence. He stared at the floor in front of him, lips pursed. Didn't he want the job?

"They've decided I'm not disreputable after all?"

Mr. Courtney laughed and clapped him on the back. "They all know that was a misunderstanding. I explained it to them. And several of our donors have been vocal in their support of you. You're the right man for the job."

"I'll have to think about it, Lee." Scott cleared his throat. "I have another offer I'm considering as well."

Ah. So that's what he meant the other day when he said he might not be around much longer. Becky glanced at Mr. Courtney.

The old gentleman didn't seem surprised. "I heard a rumor Francine Buchanan's looking for a new manager over at her place."

Buchanan? Her face went cold as the blood drained away. Scott was going to work for Kaci Buchanan's mother?

"Assistant manager, actually." Scott lifted a shoulder. "But the general manager there is a few years from retirement."

Mr. Courtney watched him a moment, then nodded slowly. "Might be a good opportunity. But don't forget, Zach isn't too many years from retirement himself. I'll be looking for someone to take over Shady Acres before long."

Becky plucked at the hem of her sweater, feeling like an intruder in this conversation. Was it wrong to want Scott to stay at the Pasture when she, herself, was considering leaving? What did it matter that he spent time with Kaci? Becky had no claim on him.

But the thought of Scott with the tall blonde made her green with envy.

Scott flashed a quick smile at Mr. Courtney. "I'll pray about it and let you know next week."

He was silent as they left the house and climbed into the truck. Becky stared out the window as he pulled down the driveway, grasping for something to say. She had no right at all to offer advice about which job he took, but everything in her wanted to scream that he should turn down the Buchanan job and stay at the Pasture.

He broke the silence in the truck as he pulled out onto the road. "I'm going to wait until tomorrow to call the police about Stevens."

She twisted in her seat to face him. "I think Mr. Courtney is right. We should call them now."

One arm extended, the hand draped across the top of the steering wheel, he stared through the windshield as he answered. "I don't think we have enough to make a convincing case. Yet."

Becky narrowed her eyes. "What do you mean, yet?"

"I've been thinking about that guy, Rawlins. Why would Stevens hire him to run the breeding shed when he doesn't know squat? Well, maybe he doesn't know about horses, but maybe he does know about cloning procedures."

"You think Jason is a scientist?" Becky shook her head. The guy didn't look like her idea of a cloning specialist.

Scott shrugged one shoulder. "I don't know what he is, but there's something not right about him. And he's just one more strange circumstance hovering around Nick Stevens."

Becky knew what he meant. "You mean his wife having an affair with the manager of a farm full of retired champion Thoroughbreds?"

Scott nodded. "What if he discovered the affair? If Stevens wanted to get a skin sample from one of the stallions, what better time to do it than when he knew Haldeman was busy with Leslie?

"Okay, so why aren't we calling the police now?"

The truck slowed and Scott's knuckles whitened on the wheel as they neared the driveway of the Pasture. "Because unless we have something other than a suspicion, they won't listen. Nick Stevens is a pretty important guy in this town, no matter what Lee says. They won't do anything on a vague suspicion, and we'll look like alarmists."

The same way they didn't do anything about Mr. Keller. Becky hadn't heard a single word about him being charged for the break-in. "Money talks in this town," she said drily.

"Exactly. But if I get proof, then they'll move."

The truck turned into the driveway, and Becky clutched the seat belt to keep from sliding sideways. "What kind of proof?"

He shoved the shifter into park and turned toward her. "I've been thinking. All that DNA work would need a pretty fancy laboratory. Now, maybe Stevens has connections over at the university or something, but that would be risky. Plus, he's got tons of money. If it were me, I'd build my own laboratory."

Becky's eyes rounded as she followed his train of thought. "His new barn."

Scott smiled. "I want to get a look inside that barn."

TWENTY-TWO

Becky arrived home to find Chris and the boys pitching a baseball back and forth. Jamie and Tyler ran to hug her when she got out of the car.

"Mommy, you should have seen how far I hit the ball." Tyler's little chest swelled. "Dad said it was a triple for sure."

"And I have a good arm," Jamie informed her. "I might be a pitcher, or maybe a shortstop."

Chris ruffled his hair, laughing. "You'll have to work on catching those line drives, though."

She smiled as she unlocked the house. "With all the practice you're getting, I'll bet you boys will be the stars of your team."

"Yeah!"

When she pushed the door open, the boys tumbled inside. Jamie ran to put his ball glove in the bedroom, but Tyler stopped and turned an inquisitive glance toward his father.

"You coming, Dad?"

Chris shook his head. "I've got to get going, but I'll see you tomorrow, okay?"

"Okay." The boy followed his brother down the hallway at a trot.

"Tomorrow?" She raised an eyebrow at Chris.

"Yeah, I told them we'd all four go to breakfast and then spend the day together. I hope that's okay."

"How did it go?" Becky searched Chris's face. "You didn't have any problems?"

"Nah." Chris's face scrunched. "Well, not at first. After a while they wanted to come home. Kept asking when you'd be here."

Poor Chris. It must be hard to realize your sons aren't comfortable being alone with you. She laid a hand on his arm. "They'll get used to you. Give them time."

He leaned against the doorjamb and looked at her in the old way, the way that made her feel as though he could see all the way inside her.

"Listen, Beck." She ignored a flutter in her stomach. Nobody had called her Beck in more than four years. "I'm leaving early Sunday to get back to Florida. I've got to go to work on Monday. Are you coming with me?"

Was he kidding? She shook her head. "I can't just pick up and go. I have a job, responsibilities here."

Hope flared in his eyes. "Then you are coming eventually?"

Her gaze dropped. "I don't know."

"What's stopping you? We were good together once. We could be again." The twins' arguing voices drifted down the hallway, and he grinned. "We could be even better now. A real family."

"Why, Chris?" She searched his face. "Why do you want me back? I'm not the same person I was. I won't party with you like I used to, and I won't want you to, either. The boys need a positive influence in their lives."

"There's nothing wrong with a little partying every now and then." When she opened her mouth to protest, he laid a finger gently on her lips. "I said a little. Not like before. I've grown up, Beck. I'm ready to be a father, and a husband."

Her mouth went completely dry. Never in her wildest dreams did she expect to hear Christopher talking like this. "I'm a Christian now," she blurted. "I'm going to raise the boys in church."

He returned her gaze without flinching. "I can deal with that." A corner of his mouth lifted. "You never know. Maybe I'll even come with you every now and then. On special occasions."

Did he mean it? Was Christopher really ready to settle down? And would he really consider coming to church with her? He looked sincere. Once upon a time, years ago, she would have given anything to hear him say he wanted to be a father to the boys and a husband to her.

But now…

"I'll think about it."

"Well, you might want to hurry." He leaned forward, until his face was inches from hers. "We have a lot of catching up to do."

She stepped back quickly, out of kissing range. She wasn't ready for that yet.

His eyes danced with humor as he straightened. "I'll see you at nine in the morning."

"I don't know, Daddy." She rinsed milk residue out of a plastic cup and set it in the top rack of the dishwasher. "He seems sincere."

"I can't believe I'm hearing you. This is the guy who cheated on you when you were pregnant with his sons. Maybe you've forgotten all the tears you cried on my shoulder, but I sure haven't."

A lively song from a children's DVD sounded from the other room, punctuated by childish giggles. She switched the phone to the other shoulder.

"I haven't forgotten, but things are different now. I'm more mature, for one thing."

"One mature person can't support a marriage on her own."

"I know that."

The last supper dish loaded in the dishwasher, she wet a dishrag to wipe the table.

Daddy's voice lost its angry edge. He became serious. "Becky, what's going on? There's something you're not telling me, something more than just wanting a father for Tyler and Jamie. What's pushing you back to this guy?"

She tossed the dishrag into the sink and dropped into a kitchen chair. "Daddy, I've made so many mistakes. I wonder sometimes if this is God's way of giving me a chance to make things right."

"Hold on. You think *God* sent that lowlife back to you?"

"Have you ever considered that maybe I'm the only way He will ever get through to Chris?" Elbow on the table, she leaned her forehead on her fingers and massaged a dull ache behind her eyes. "I keep remembering that verse that says a believing wife can win her husband."

A long pause. "So that's what this is all about. You think you sinned when you divorced, and now you've got to make it up to God by going back to the guy."

Becky cringed at the heavy sarcasm in his voice. Or maybe it wasn't his tone, but the fact that he had just hit at the heart of her feelings. She hadn't thought it through, but that's exactly what she felt. She had to make it up, not only to God but also to her boys.

"Listen, Becky. I could pull out the Bible to try to

convince you that you're making a fool-headed mistake. The one about not being unequally yoked comes to mind. I'm no Bible scholar, but I'll bet I could find more.

"The point is this. You don't fix past mistakes with new ones. And going back to Christopher Dennison would be a colossal mistake for you and the twins."

"You don't know that." She straightened and placed her hand on the table. "You haven't talked to him in almost five years."

"Maybe I don't know the reasons, but I feel it in my bones." He stopped, then went on more gently. "That's it, sweetheart. I feel it, and I think you do, too. You know I'm not real smart when it comes to the Bible, but one thing I do know. God tells us what to do. The trick is learning how to ignore ourselves and listen to him. I just don't think you're listening hard enough."

A hush stole over the kitchen. Becky went still. From the other room, the sound blared from the television as though from a great distance. Daddy's words had the ring of truth. She'd been so busy feeling guilty, she hadn't prayed about this situation with Chris. Or, she realized with a sudden rush of emotion, about her relationship with Scott. She'd assumed she knew the answers, but she'd never asked the questions. How could she possibly make the right decision if she hadn't even taken the time to pray?

Her grip on the phone relaxed until it was almost a caress. "Thanks, Daddy. I know what I need to do now."

Dressed in black, Scott hugged as close to the fencerow as he could. He'd left his truck over at the Pasture and snuck onto the Stevenses' property through the back part of Shady Acres. Nick and Leslie's house, tucked in a back corner at the end of a long, smooth driveway, glowed like a light-house in a storm, a landmark on the otherwise dark farm.

Feeling like a criminal, he nearly jumped out of his skin when a dark horse in the paddock beside him whinnied softly.

"Shh, there now." He pitched his voice low, soothing. "Nothing to worry about. I'll be in and out in no time."

Wispy clouds moved across a fingernail moon, throwing strange shadows on the whitewashed side of the new barn. Thoroughbred breeders liked to erect fancy barns, and this was one of the better-built ones Scott had seen. Sturdy construction, thick siding, neatly trimmed windows with elaborately designed shutters. Nicer by far than the plain little cottage he rented from Lee Courtney. And about ten times the size. Situated as it was on the northernmost edge of the farm's cleared land, and backing up to a thick copse of trees, this out-of-the-way location was the perfect place to hide a laboratory.

He came to the place where he had to leave the sparse cover of the fenced pasture and cross a packed dirt road to approach the barn. A big cloud raced across the night sky, blown by a spring breeze, and Scott waited until it covered the moon. In the resulting darkness, he dashed across the road and into the deep shadows on the far side of the building.

He peeked around the corner. Not a movement anywhere. Light shone through windows up at the Stevenses' home about a hundred yards distant, far enough away that he couldn't see anything through them. If anyone happened to be looking out, hopefully they couldn't see this far, either.

He figured there'd be another door in the rear, like the barn at the Pasture. Sure enough, there was an entrance on this side. Probably one on the opposite side, as well, the one that faced the house. Hopefully it wouldn't be locked.

When he pushed, it moved beneath his hand. It was not latched. Ready to dart into the trees at the first sound or sight of movement, he slid the door open inch by painstaking inch. Just enough to slip through.

Inside, the building was like a cave. His sneaker squeaked on the floor, the sound echoing with a hollow ring in the otherwise silent interior. The place smelled fresh, like new paint and raw timber. He shut his eyes tight, trying to adjust them to the pitch black, then opened them again. Still too dark to see anything. Well, at least the windows were all shuttered. Nobody would see his flashlight.

He pulled a slim penlight out of his back pocket. Heart thundering, he twisted the cap.

Amazing what a dim light could do in a dark place. He aimed the narrow beam toward the front of the barn, noted a half-dozen empty stalls. Nothing in that direction. Looked like any other horse barn.

He pointed toward the rear, and his pulse quickened. The entire back fourth of the barn was walled off. A small window punctuated the left of the partition, shuttered from the other side. On the right, a door. Shut.

Scott moved as silently as he could, each step placed with careful precision. The door was sure to be locked. If it was, he couldn't bring himself to break in. Maybe the shutter on the window wasn't latched and he could push it in enough to see.

He grabbed the doorknob and twisted.

It turned. Not locked.

He eased it open a crack and pointed the flashlight inside, expecting to see shiny metal surfaces and microscopes. Instead, the beam illuminated an ordinary bedroom. A single bed stood in one corner, and beside it, a four-drawer dresser with a small television set on the top. Lining the back wall were a small table with two chairs, a half-sized refrigerator and a cabinet with a microwave oven. Beside the dresser a door stood open and he glimpsed the corner of a toilet.

In the next instant, his dark-accustomed eyes were blinded by a flood of bright light. His penlight clattered to the floor.

A voice echoed in the empty barn behind him. "I have a gun pointed at your back. If you move an inch, I'll shoot you."

TWENTY-THREE

Scott went statue-still, hand over his eyes. The police? But then the voice registered, and he knew who stood behind him. If only it *was* the police!

"Turn around slowly. Keep those hands where I can see them."

He did as he was told. "Listen, I know this looks bad. I can explain."

Nicholas Stevens didn't look receptive to his explanations. His glower deepened when he recognized Scott, and he gripped the shotgun tighter to his side.

"Lewis. I should have known. I can smell Lee Courtney's stink all the way over here."

"You've got it wrong, Stevens. Lee doesn't have any idea I'm here."

Scott tried to keep his gaze locked on Nick's face, but it kept sliding downward like metal to a magnet. He'd never had the barrel of a gun pointed in his direction. Not a good feeling.

Nick's eyelids narrowed. "I don't believe you. Courtney and all those other blue bloods have had it in for me since Leslie and I bred our first foal. I don't know what he sent you over here to do, but I think I'd better call the police and let them figure it out."

"Honest, Nick." Scott kept his hands in front of him, in full sight. "I came on my own. I wasn't planning to do anything bad. I wanted to get a look inside your barn, that's all."

The barrel dropped a fraction. "You have about thirty seconds to explain why, and it'd better be good."

Scott wished he had good explanation. At the moment, a horse cloning scheme sounded about as far-fetched as little green men from Mars.

"Well, it's kind of strange, really." He gave a laugh, at which Nick's scowl only deepened. "See, we've found a couple of things over at the Pasture that led us to believe Haldeman might have been involved in an experiment." Yeah, an experiment. That sounded good. "But it would have required a scientific laboratory." He cleared his throat. "I, uh, got to thinking about this brand-new barn, and, well, here I am."

"You thought I had a laboratory in my barn?" The barrel slipped farther as lines creased Nick's brow. "What kind of laboratory?"

"It gets a little crazy here." Scott tried to keep his gaze straight. "A horse cloning laboratory."

Nick's stare became incredulous. "You think I'm cloning horses?"

"It wouldn't have occurred to me at all, except I met your new shed manager the other day. Frankly, he didn't seem to have much experience. Made me a little suspicious."

His lips twisted. "Well, you got that right, anyway. He doesn't know the first thing about horses. But he's Leslie's kid brother, and she insisted on hiring him."

Scott rocked back on his heels. Leslie's brother? "So he's not a scientist?"

Nick's laughter echoed off the vaulted ceiling. "Scientist? He's a high school dropout. Hasn't held a job longer than six months in his life." He nodded toward the room behind Scott. "Leslie had that apartment put in for him, and moved him here from Phoenix. Against my better judgment, but she's softhearted. Said she'd keep an eye on him. She's more involved in the day-to-day operations of the place than I am, so I agreed."

Never in his life had Scott felt more like an idiot than he did at this moment. "Listen, Nick, I'm sorry. I let my imagination get the better of me. I shouldn't have."

Nick studied him for a long moment, then finally shouldered the shotgun with a shrug. "It's all right. I can't say I like you sneaking around my farm in the middle of the night, but I guess since Haldeman's death we're all a little jumpy."

Tension melted out of Scott's shoulders as the menace of the shotgun was removed. "Thanks. You're more understanding than I deserve."

Nick cocked his head. "Do you really think Haldeman was cloning horses?" His eyes widened. "Man, some of those old stallions over there were top-notch in their day."

Scott nodded. "I know. But if he was, I don't know how he did it. He had to be working with someone."

Nick's right hand went up, palm facing Scott. "Not me. You can search every barn on my farm if you want. You won't find a laboratory anywhere." He grinned, which went a long way toward taking the edge off Scott's guilt.

Scott shook his head. "Thanks, but I'll take your word on that. I think I'll let the police handle it from here."

"Sounds like a good idea to me."

Nick turned, indicating that Scott should precede him out of the barn. Scott did, but kept his eye on the shotgun, just in case.

Nick noticed him staring at it. He hefted it in his hand and laughed. "It's not loaded. I was standing outside having a smoke when I saw you cross the road. I grabbed it out of my pickup, but forgot to get the shells out of the glove compartment."

Scott grinned. "Now you tell me."

"I'm hungry, Mommy. When will he get here?" Tyler didn't normally whine, so his nasally tone told Becky he was more anxious than hungry.

When Chris didn't show up by ten, she'd fed the boys cereal. She glanced at the clock. Almost twelve-thirty. And still no answer in his motel room. For the fiftieth time she wished she'd asked who he was meeting last night.

"I don't know, sweetheart. Do you want a peanut butter sandwich?"

His head drooped. "No."

Jamie sat on the couch, watching television without a word. Occasionally he looked over his shoulder, out the window toward the driveway. His sad little frown nearly broke her heart. She'd gone through this countless times during the last months of her marriage. She'd grown accustomed to hours of gut-wrenching worry, wondering whether she should call the hospital emergency room to see if Chris had been in an accident.

But she wasn't five years old. Becky's teeth clenched. Chris had better have a good explanation for disappointing the boys.

She picked up the remote control and pressed the Off button. Neither twin protested, an indication of how anxious they were.

"Boys, listen to me." She waited until both sets of eyes

were fixed on her. "I know you're worried about your daddy. Do you remember what we do when we're upset about something?"

Jamie raised a tentative hand as though he was in school, and Becky hid a smile.

"We pray?" he asked.

She nodded. "That's right. Do you want me to pray with you now?"

"Okay."

Tyler slipped off the couch to his knees, Jamie right behind him. They placed their arms on the cushion, and clasped their hands together like they did every night before she tucked them in bed. Eyes closed, their dark heads dropped forward.

Her heart twisting in her chest, Becky joined her boys on the floor and bowed her head.

"Dear Lord, Jamie and Tyler are worried because they don't know where their daddy is." She cracked an eyelid open and saw Jamie nod in agreement. "But You know where he is, because You know everything. So we ask You to watch over him and keep him safe."

"And don't let him be in a wreck," said Jamie.

"And let him get here soon," Tyler added.

"And most of all," Becky continued, "let him know how much You love him. In Jesus' Name, Amen."

"Amen," they chorused.

Smiles lit their eyes as they both threw arms around her. Hugging them for all she was worth, Becky added a silent prayer of her own. *And please guard their hearts, Lord. I can't stand to see them disappointed.*

"There he is!" Tyler leaped up and ran to the front door, his brother a half second behind him.

Becky stood at the window, watching as the twins dashed across the yard to the car. Chris got out slowly and closed the door with exaggerated care. Dark glasses obscured his eyes, but even across the distance she saw his grimace as Tyler grabbed his arm.

How many times had she seen him move like that? About a million. He was hungover.

Opening the door, Becky stepped out onto the front porch. "Boys, you go on inside. I want to talk to your father for a minute."

Strangely subdued, Tyler obeyed without arguing. Jamie looked up at Chris once, then followed his brother past her and into the house.

Chris sank onto the concrete steps and lowered his head to his hands. "I gotta siddown a minute."

The back of his hair had an unbrushed tangle, ends hanging limply down past the collar of his T-shirt. Though fury at his disregard for his sons' feelings brought angry words to the tip of her tongue, she was surprised to feel the stirrings of compassion. He looked like a miserable wretch.

She sat down beside him, careful to keep space between them. The smell of sour beer wrinkled her nose. Whether it emanated from his clothes or oozed from his pores, she couldn't tell.

"You look terrible."

"I feel worse." He spoke barely above a whisper.

"Did you have a good time?" Her voice dripped sarcasm which she doubted he heard.

A pain-filled smile lifted the edges of his lips. "As far as I can remember."

Becky shook her head. Thank the Lord she had out-grown that behavior. Maybe one day Chris would, too.

"I ought to lecture you about disappointing your sons." He didn't react at all, and she continued. "But I'll save that for when you're completely sober. In the meantime, I want to tell you that I've made a decision."

He lifted the corner of one hand and tilted his head to peer at her through a bloodshot eye from the side of his sunglasses. "I can tell from your expression. You're staying here, aren't you?"

She nodded. "I'm sorry, Chris. I'll do whatever I can to make sure you have a good relationship with Tyler and Jamie." She softened her voice. "But the fact is, I don't love you. Marrying you again would be just one more big mistake. I'm sorry."

He bent double, his head hanging between his knees. For a moment he didn't say anything. Then he raised his head. "Yeah, well, I figured that from the way you were looking at your boss the other night."

A blush heated her cheeks, but she kept her mouth shut. She didn't owe him anything, including an explanation.

Chris heaved himself to his feet, groaning. "I gotta go. I need a little hair of the dog. Tell the boys I'll call 'em later."

Becky watched him lurch toward his car. Though Jamie and Tyler would be heartbroken, that was much better than letting them spend time around their father in this shape.

As he slid behind the wheel, she stood. Two little faces, so much like Chris's but fresh and clean and unpolluted by the harsh life he'd lived, watched her anxiously from the window. She forced a smile, fighting against a sadness that threatened to make her cry. He was their father. As their mother, she always would make sure they were safe, but she couldn't shield them from him completely. He probably loved them as much as he was able, but they'd just have to get used to being disappointed by him.

Starting now.

Scott looked at the sore on Kiri's flank. Doc Matthews had said it wasn't ringworm, and he put some ointment on it, but the place hadn't cleared up. In fact, it looked worse, as if it had become infected.

Doc, like most everyone who had anything to do with horses, was at Keeneland this last Saturday of the spring races. No chance of getting him out here until Monday.

But they kept some antibiotic ointment over in the Shady Acres farm office. He could use that for a day or two. Sure wouldn't hurt, and he had to do something.

"Come on, Sam." He whistled for the yellow Lab. "Let's go across the road."

A lone stable boy occupied the Shady Acres barn, seated at a bench in the tack room. Scott heard the tinny notes and rhythmic thump of bass from his headphones, smelled the leather cleaner on the rag he rubbed over a saddle. He jumped like a nervous cat when Scott tapped him on the shoulder.

He jerked the earphones off his head. "Mr. Lewis, you scared the daylights out of me."

Scott grinned and nodded toward his iPod. "You'll go deaf if you're not careful, Ben."

Ben rolled his eyes. "You sound like my mother."

Laughing, Scott left him to finish listening to his song and headed toward the office.

His keys jangled as he unlocked the windowed office door. Inside, the surface of the desk was littered with files and untidy stacks of paperwork. He crossed to the metal cabinet along the back row and slid the door open. Inside, he scanned across the various bottles and tubes, looking for the one he wanted.

Not here. Maybe Shady Acres was out of the antibiotic ointment, too.

One more place to look. The junk drawer. The bottom desk drawer served as repository for everything that either didn't have a permanent storage place, or that someone didn't want to take the time to put away. Scott sat in the rolling chair and yanked on the handle.

Locked. That was odd. They never bothered to lock the desk drawers, because the office stayed locked whenever nobody was in it. Scott sorted through the keys on his ring, grasping the smallest one between his fingers. He slipped it into the lock and opened the drawer.

What a mess. It was even more full than when he last looked. He pawed through a variety of stuff, pushing aside a stapler, a ball of metal wire, a roll of duct tape. Where was that tube of ointment?

He'd just about decided he was out of luck when he grabbed a grooming cloth and shoved it to the front of the pile. It unrolled as it moved, uncovering an item that had been wrapped inside.

Scott's hand halted. He stared. Blood roared in his ears in rhythm with his pulse.

A hoof pick.

Barely breathing, Scott gawked at the tool as his mind raced. Maybe there was a plausible explanation for a hoof pick to be in the junk drawer. Even though it should be in the tack room with the rest of the grooming equipment. Maybe it was broken or something.

Careful not to touch it, Scott dropped the cloth over the red plastic handle and picked it up. It wasn't broken. He examined the metal hook closely, almost afraid to find the telltale signs of blood. It was clean, thank goodness. A little too clean, maybe? Shouldn't there be dirt or something on it?

Stop it. The boys keep the equipment clean.

Pulse pounding, he set the tool on the desk. Was this the instrument of Neal Haldeman's demise?

Only one other person had keys to this desk. Zach Garrett.

Scott leaned back in the chair, unable to tear his gaze from the hoof pick. No. He refused to believe it. Zach had been nothing but kind to him since he came to Shady Acres. They didn't have a lot in common outside of the horses, but he was a nice guy. Not a killer.

Cold fingers slid up his spine, and the hair on his arms rose. Zach had wanted the temporary job over at the Pasture. He'd been irritated when Lee gave it to Scott. Why would he be eager to walk away from the Shady Acres manager position with the responsibility and staff and all the prestige that went with it?

Was Zach in cahoots with Haldeman to clone the stallions?

No. This had to be another misunderstanding, just like the one with Nick Sanders. There had to be an explanation.

And Scott wanted—no needed—to hear it.

TWENTY-FOUR

The ringing of the telephone interrupted their movie.

"I'll get it!" Tyler jumped up from the living room floor and ran for the phone in the kitchen.

"Want me to pause it, Mommy?" Jamie, in control of the remote tonight, held an eager finger above the button.

"Sure."

Becky glanced at the wall clock. A few minutes past six-thirty. About time Chris called. The boys had waited all afternoon. In a blatant effort to soothe their aching feelings, Becky had splurged on a supper of junk food and a movie rental.

She heard Tyler's high-pitched, "Hello?" from the kitchen, followed by a pause. "Hi, Mr. Lewis. I'll get Mommy."

Scott calling her? A sudden attack of nerves made her want to giggle, but she bit it back. She'd itched all day long to call him, to tell him about her decision. But what would he think? That she was chasing him? That she was man-hungry? Images of the tall, gorgeous Kaci Buchanan taunted her and kept her from picking up the phone.

But now he was calling her.

"Go ahead and press Play," she told Jamie. "I'll catch up with the movie in a minute."

She intercepted Tyler in the doorway and took the phone from him. He scooted past her, grabbed a handful of chips from the bag on the coffee table and returned to his place on the floor in front of the television.

"Hello?"

"Becky, it's Scott." His voice sounded odd, tight.

"What's wrong?"

"Nothing. I don't know. I found something."

She sank into a chair, listening with growing disbelief as he described his discovery in the office at Shady Acres.

"So you called the police, right?" Her voice came out in a squeak, and she lowered it. "Please tell me you called the police."

"Not yet. I have to talk to him, Becky. I've been falsely accused before, and I won't do that to anyone else. I've worked with Zach for almost a year now, and I owe him that."

"You don't owe him a thing if he *killed Neal.*" She hissed the last words, glancing toward the doorway to make sure the twins were still in the living room. "And don't forget that bookie. Two people are dead, Scott. If he's responsible, he might come after you, too."

"That's why I called you. I don't want to go over there without someone knowing where I am. I'm sorry to pull you into this, but I didn't think I should call Lee. Zach might have a perfectly logical explanation for that hoof pick, and then he won't thank me for calling his boss."

Her insides clenched into a knot. She wanted to scream at him, would have, if the boys hadn't been in the other room. "Scott, this is a mistake." She let a note of unabashed pleading saturate her tone. "Please call the police."

He ignored her. "It's six-thirty now. I'm at my house,

and I can see his place from here. It's dark. I know he went to Keeneland today, but he should be home soon. I want you to do me a favor." He paused. "If you don't hear from me by eight o'clock, call the police."

His tone chilled her to the bone. "Scott, I'm afraid. Please don't do this."

"I'll be fine. Promise me you won't call the cops before eight, okay?"

She hesitated. "I don't think—"

"Please, Becky. I'm counting on you."

She couldn't think straight. Her gut screamed *No,* but he was counting on her. She couldn't deny him. She heaved a loud sigh into the phone, another indication to him that she was going against her better judgment. "Okay, I promise not to call the police until eight o'clock. But the moment that second hand hits—"

"You won't have to. I'll be in touch before then." Relief made his voice sound almost normal. "One other thing. Say a prayer for me, okay?"

Her hand trembled so violently the phone slipped away from her ear. "I will. Please be careful."

The line went dead. Becky sat at the kitchen table, her heart pounding. He should not do this alone. If Zach Garrett killed Neal and that bookie, he was a dangerous man. Scott was too trusting. He needed someone else with him, someone to make him see reason. If only she had a babysitter she could leave the boys with on short notice.

After Tuesday night, she wouldn't dare ask Amber. What about...

No. She would *not* call Chris. He'd said something about "hair of the dog," which meant he was probably drunk again tonight.

Her hands balled into fists, and she pounded on the table. Oh, how she hated this helpless feeling!

Lord, please keep Scott safe.

The doorbell rang. Becky's teeth clamped together, her jaw tightening with frustration. She did not have the patience to deal with Christopher tonight. And if he thought he was going to come around the boys if he'd been drinking, he had another think coming. She'd just have to send him away, that's all. Tyler and Jamie wouldn't understand, but—

Jamie's excited voice pierced the air. "Grandpa!"

Becky's head jerked upward. Daddy, here?

She leaped up from the chair and ran into the living room. Each twin had hold of one of Daddy's hands, and both hopped like overinflated basketballs, squealing their excitement. Becky threw her arms around her father's neck and hugged for all she was worth.

"I'm so glad to see you." Her voice came out choked. She pulled back and looked at him through pools of tears. "What are you doing here?"

He gave her a stern look. "I caught a 6:00 a.m. flight out of LAX, and it cost me a fortune. I'm here to make sure you don't repeat the biggest mistake of your life."

She hugged him again, laughing. "Thank you. Oh, thank you, Daddy." She straightened. "And you're just in time. I desperately need a babysitter!"

Becky pulled her car into the dirt driveway behind Scott's pickup. She cut the engine and sat with her hands clutching the steering wheel. A chorus of crickets sang a peaceful counterpoint to her twanging nerves. When Scott saw her on his front stoop, he'd think she was no better than

Kaci, blatantly chasing after him. Either that, or he'd be ir-ritated with her.

Too bad. There was no way she intended to let him face a possible killer alone. Steeling herself, she dropped her keys in her purse and stepped out into the cool night air.

The door jerked open when she raised her hand to knock. Judging by the annoyance on his face, he'd chosen the second reaction.

"What are you doing here?" His gaze searched the car behind her. "You didn't bring the boys, did you?"

"Of course not." She drew herself up. "I came to help you. You can't confront Zach by yourself."

The cleft in his chin deepened as his lips tightened. "I certainly can, and I will."

"Scott, be reasonable." Becky adjusted the purse strap on her shoulder. "If there are two of us, he's less likely to try anything."

The next instant, Becky found herself jerked roughly through the door. Scott's fingers bit into her arm as he pulled her to one side and slammed the door shut. He released her, crossed to a window and pulled back a curtain to peek through it.

"He's home. I don't want him to see you."

She couldn't help looking around the tiny room curi-ously even as she asked, "Why not?" A plain three-cushion sofa, a coffee table and a small television on a cheap metal stand were the only furnishings. Very sparse. Very male.

Scott wasn't watching her. He had his eye up to the crack in the curtains and spoke without turning. "Because if it turns out he's responsible for Haldeman's death, I'd just as soon he not know you're involved." He whirled to face her. "I want you to go home."

She folded her arms and said, "Not a chance."

"But who will call the police if something happens to me?" His stare became suspicious. "You didn't call them before you came, did you?"

Becky returned his stare. "Of course not. I promised, didn't I?"

He peeked out the window. "He's leaving again." The irritated look he turned her way would have made her flinch if she hadn't been trying so hard to look stubborn. "I'm going to miss my chance to talk to him."

An idea sparked. "Let's follow him. Maybe he's going to grab a bite to eat or something. It'll be much safer if you confront him in a public place."

Scott's forehead wrinkled as he considered her suggestion. "Well…"

"Come on!" She grabbed his arm and pulled him toward the door. "He'll get away from us if we don't hurry. I'll drive."

Scott jerked his arm away. "Why should you drive?"

She smiled sweetly. "Because I'm parked behind you."

Scott's fingers cramped from his tight grip on the armrest of Becky's car. "He turned right. Past that white truck."

She took her gaze off the road to glance his way. "I saw him."

He had to admit, she'd done a good job of following Zach's car on the fifteen-minute drive to Lexington, never losing sight of his taillights, but staying far enough back that he wouldn't notice. Once they hit the city limits they got a little closer. But instead of going to a restaurant, as Scott hoped, Zach seemed to be going to someone's house. The car was winding through the quiet streets of a sprawling neighborhood. Not a lot of traffic here to hide them.

"There." His finger left a smudge on the windshield. "He pulled into a driveway. Don't get close to the house."

"I won't."

Becky pulled the car over to the side of the road and cut the lights. Enough cars were parked up and down this residential street that theirs should go unnoticed. They watched as Zach got out of his car and went inside the house without knocking.

"I can't follow him in there. What if he's on a date or something?" Scott's hands knotted into fists. "If you hadn't showed up, I could have confronted him at home, before he took off again."

Becky caught him in a sideways look. "If you hadn't been so mule-headed about talking to him, the police would be doing this instead of us."

He turned away from her piercing gaze. Unexpectedly, his lips twitched. They were snapping at each other like old friends. He swallowed convulsively. Or sweethearts. His smile faded. Which they definitely were not.

He unclipped the cell phone from his belt. "As long as we're here, I'm going to sneak up there and have a look through the back windows."

Her head jerked upward, and her eyes searched his face. "Why in the world would you do that?"

Scott lifted a shoulder. "Call it a hunch. If Zach was involved with Haldeman in a cloning scheme, there's still the matter of the laboratory. Where better to hide it than in the middle of suburbia?"

Her eyes widened as his logic sank in. Then her chin lifted in that stubborn pose he was getting accustomed to seeing. "Then I think we should call—"

"The police. I know." He handed her the cell phone.

"If I'm not back in ten minutes, that's exactly what I want you to do."

He didn't wait to hear her arguments, but unsnapped his seat belt with one hand as he opened the door with the other. He slipped out, crouching, and closed the door as quickly and quietly as he could. The light inside had only been on for a few seconds. Hopefully, not long enough for anyone to notice.

Not that there was anyone to see. The streets were void of movement, though light illuminated the windows of most of the single-story homes that lined both sides of the street. Scott walked down the sidewalk with his arms swinging at his sides. If anybody happened to glance outside, he'd look as if he was just out for a casual stroll.

When he neared the house into which Zach had disappeared, he bent low and darted through the grass and into the side yard. Thankfully, there was no fence. Nor were there any windows on this side of the home, except for a single small one high up, probably in a bathroom. He leaned against the brick and willed his breath to remain even. If he'd known he was going to be sneaking around in the dark, he would have worn his black jeans and shirt.

There was a front window, but no shrubberies or anything else to give him cover. His best bet was to sneak around to the back and hope he could see something from there.

Placing each foot with exaggerated care, he crept along the side of the house. A peek around the corner showed no sign of movement. A privacy fence encased the yard behind this one, so he couldn't be seen from that direction. There was no fence on either side, but there was no sign of anyone there, either.

Four windows on the back of the house. The far two

were dark. Bent double, he slunk toward the first one, through which a bright light shone. With extra caution, he inched upward and looked inside.

A kitchen. Not a very clean one, either. The sink held a load of dirty dishes, and a couple more stacks littered the counter beside it. The stove, too, had pots and pans on it. In the corner, a garbage can overflowed.

Nothing moved inside. Scott strained his ears for any sound from within the house. A dog barked a few houses away, but from inside, nothing. Where was Zach, and why wasn't he talking to whoever lived here?

He moved on to the back door. The handle didn't budge. Probably a good thing. He might have been tempted to sneak inside if it had. The window in the door was covered on the inside with a curtain through which he could see nothing.

The other two windows looked in on empty rooms. Though they were dark, his eyes had adjusted enough that he could see there wasn't a stick of furniture in either one. And the doors were closed, so he couldn't see anything beyond them, either.

He sagged against the wall, disappointed. He'd hoped to find something to justify this harebrained jaunt, so he didn't look like a complete fool in Becky's eyes. Which was stupid, of course. What did it matter what Becky thought? She was going back to her husband.

She was probably right, and they should just call the police. But what if he accused his boss and friend of killing someone, and it turned out the hoof pick he found wasn't the murder weapon after all?

He headed back the way he had come. Maybe he could call Trooper Whitley or Detective Foster and tip them off that he'd found it, and they wouldn't have to tell Zach where they heard it from.

A sound halted him. Someone was coming around the corner. His glance circled the yard frantically, looking for cover.

A moment later, all thoughts of hiding fled. Two familiar figures stepped into the backyard, one with an expression of pure terror on her face. Becky.

In the next instant he realized why. The other figure, walking behind her, was none other than his boss, Zach Garrett. And he held a gun to Becky's head.

TWENTY-FIVE

Becky looked at Scott's face and saw her fear mirrored there. Zach's grip on her arm didn't hurt, but she imagined her skin burned where his fingers touched. He was a murderer, a cold-blooded killer. The barrel of the gun bumped the back of her head when he jerked her to a stop.

What if she screamed? Surely someone in one of these houses would come to investigate. But he might shoot her or Scott in the meantime.

"I think we'd better go inside." She felt Zach's breath on the crown of her head.

Scott's gaze was fixed on a point behind Becky. On Zach. "It's locked."

At that moment, the back door opened. Afraid to move her head, she stared straight ahead at Scott, but from the corner of her eye saw a thin man shove the door outward and step back inside.

She heard the smile in Zach's voice. "Not anymore. You first."

Scott locked eyes with her for an instant. Becky saw no hope in them at all, and an answering dread welled up in her. If she died, what would happen to Tyler and Jamie?

Would Christopher get custody of them? *No, Lord! Don't let that happen.*

Scott walked up the three concrete steps and into the house. Zach pushed her forward into a filthy kitchen. The smell of rotting food, probably coming from an overflowing trash can in the corner, assaulted her nostrils.

"You really should clean the place every now and then, Tenney." The gun barrel appeared in her peripheral vision as Zach used it to gesture toward a doorway to the right. "Down there, Scott."

The thin man's head jerked nervously toward Zach. "Perhaps you shouldn't take them below." He spoke in a high-pitched, nasally British accent.

"Can't leave them up here. You never know who's sneaking around, peeking through the windows." His laughter sent a shiver up Becky's spine.

Scott went through the doorway and down a set of narrow stairs. She followed, Zach on her heels.

"Go on in that room on the right," Zach instructed. "Might as well see what you came to see."

She followed Scott through a doorway. The room on the other side was not large, but had been refinished with a white-tiled floor and white walls. A long counter, spotlessly clean, took up most of the floor space in the center. Its surface was covered with equipment. The only thing Becky could identify was a microscope, but it had extra stuff attached to it that she'd never seen. Along the far wall was another counter, and atop this one was a machine that looked like a convection oven, with a digital panel on the front.

Zach released her, and she stepped up beside Scott, close enough to draw a scant amount of comfort from contact with his arm. His tight lips cracked in a brief smile that was really more of a grimace. She bit back her rising panic.

"You two stand over there." Zach pointed with his gun toward a corner, and with the other hand flipped open a cell phone. He punched a couple of buttons, then lifted it to his ear. "You on your way?" He nodded. "Good. We have company. Looks like you were right."

As he pocketed the cell phone, Scott stepped in front of her. "Let Becky go, Zach. She'll keep quiet. You have my word."

Zach's smile chilled her to the bone. "I'll wait for my partner. Then we'll decide what to do with both of you."

"Partner?" Becky's voice wavered, and she swallowed. "You mean Neal wasn't your partner?"

"Haldeman?" A humorless blast of laughter lifted his chest. "We tried. He wouldn't have a thing to do with us. Kept going on about the purity of the breeding process. It would have been easier with his help, but we've done okay in spite of him."

"They why did you kill him?"

Becky glanced up at Scott. How could he sound so calm with a gun pointed at his chest?

Zach shrugged. "I didn't mean to. It was an accident."

"You *accidentally* ripped his throat out with a hoof pick?"

Zach's features tightened. Becky put a hand on Scott's arm and squeezed a warning. *Don't antagonize the man with the gun!*

"He was on to us but he couldn't prove anything. Until he caught me in Alidor's paddock. Or," he corrected, "running out of Alidor's paddock. That horse is the meanest, orneriest stallion I ever met."

Ah. Now Jamie's discovery made sense. "You dropped a test tube in there while trying to get a skin cell sample from him."

Zach's gaze slid to her. "Found that, did you? Tenney dropped it, the fool. Didn't tell me until yesterday, though."

Becky glanced toward the stairs that led to the first floor. "Tenney's a scientist?"

Zach smiled. "You catch on quick, don't you? Yeah, he's a scientist. A cloning specialist."

"Why, Zach?" Scott's question sounded sincere as he looked at the older man. "You can't clone a Thoroughbred."

"Oh, but we can. Have, in fact. Twice. One mare's already pregnant with our first success, Dark Diego. And see that over there?" He pointed toward the ovenlike apparatus. "In there is the clone of Samson's Secret, all ready to be implanted."

Becky glanced around the room. There were no windows, no doors except the one they came in. No way out. And no way for anyone to see in, either. With Tenney keeping watch upstairs, no chance of a rescue.

"And then what?" Scott asked. "What are you going to do with a clone? You can't register it."

Zach sneered. "Sure you can. All you have to do is submit a Live Foal Report to the Jockey Club."

Scott's arm twitched. "You can't fake the DNA report."

Zach laughed. "I thought you were smarter than that, Scott. Think about it. In December, two foals will be born. One will be the clone of Dark Diego. The other was bred the regular way, from a mare and stallion the same color as Diego, and with similar markings. Their mating has been duly recorded. The hair we send to the lab for DNA testing will be from the second foal. But the pictures the Jockey Club gets with the Live Foal Report will be from the clone."

The muscles in Scott's jaw bunched before he spoke. "It won't work. Clones aren't as healthy as the original, so it will never win a race."

"Maybe not, but they might surprise you." The sound of a door slamming, followed by the low hum of Tenney's British accent drifted to them from upstairs. Zach continued. "Besides, racing isn't where the real money is made. You know yourself all the winners Alidor has sired. Over thirty-eight million earned by his offspring. Runners bred by his clone could do that, maybe even more."

"You can't breed a clone." Frustration seeped into Scott's voice, and his fist tightened. "The DNA of those foals won't match the Jockey Club's records, unless you forge them, too. You'll have to breed another true foal for every clone, and keep faking the reports. You'll get caught!"

Becky dug her fingers into his arm. Why was he trying to convince the guy? If he was going to talk, he should try to talk them out of here.

"That is not my problem." Zach leaned against the counter, his eyes flicking toward the door. "By the time that happens, I'll be sitting on a beach in South America, enjoying a retirement generously funded by my partner. Who you're about to meet, by the way."

Fear gripped Becky's throat. When the partner showed up, their lives could be measured in terms of minutes. *Lord, I don't want to die!* She moved a half step behind Scott, tilting her head so she could see the doorway around his shoulder.

When Zach's partner stepped through, her jaw went slack.

Leslie Stevens.

The woman's dark eyes moved as she looked from Scott to Becky, a thin smile on her face. "Now, Zach, are you giving away all my secrets?"

"I should have known." Scott sounded angry. Color stained his cheeks. "Nick was too forgiving the other night. I should have suspected he was guilty when he let me go without calling the police."

Leslie crossed the room to stand beside Zach, her eyes on Scott. "You're wrong. Nicky enjoys playing the role of big-time breeder, but he doesn't want to be bothered with the details. He's blissfully unaware of my plan, as is my baby brother, who's too dumb to know what he's helping with. Though Nicky should have had you thrown in jail for trespassing."

Becky searched Leslie's face. Where was the love she'd seen the other day? This woman's eyes glittered with a hardness that left Becky cold. "So you seduced Neal to try to convince him to go along with your scheme."

Leslie's gaze slid to her face. "No, I didn't seduce Neal." A smirk contorted her face. "I tried, but he didn't want to play. But at least my efforts kept him involved while Zach and our British friend collected the specimens they needed." She glanced sideways at her partner. "If only Zach had listened to me and tranquilized Alidor, Neal would still be alive. And that lowlife bookie would, too."

The look Scott turned on Zach was sad. "You killed Eddie Jones, too?"

"That was your fault." Scott jerked upright, and Zach nodded. "You told me about those tally sheets, and how you mentioned them to Eddie. I figured Eddie broke in and stole them to keep his name from coming up to the police. I couldn't afford to let them fall into the wrong hands. My name was probably on there right along with his."

"You're a bookmaker, too?"

His free hand waved in the air. "Hey, I'm building a

very nice retirement package." His grip tightened on the pistol. Becky's breath caught in her throat. "But Jones didn't have them."

Hugh Keller did. Becky thought of Mr. Keller's thick, muscular build. Zach was lean and fit, but he wouldn't have been a match for Mr. Keller. Poor Eddie Jones. Killed for something he had nothing to do with.

"What, the payment for cloning a champion wasn't enough?" Scott no longer sounded sad. He turned a glare on Leslie. "Two people are dead, and for what? For a crazy scheme that doesn't have a chance of succeeding."

"Oh, I *will* succeed." Leslie drew herself up and tossed her head so her dark hair flipped to her back. "I promise you, one day I'll stand in the Winner's Circle at the Derby. That blanket of roses will be on *my* horse. I'll show those high-class snobs what a true champion looks like." Dark fire glittered in her eyes. "Do you know what they called me in the owner's dining room at Keeneland? They called me an upstart. They said it loud enough for me to hear, too, those snooty women. I'll show them, one way or another."

Becky knew exactly which snooty women Leslie was talking about, at least one of them. Kaci's conversation echoed in Becky's memory. She'd called Neal's girlfriend an upstart.

A muffled thud sounded upstairs. Both Zach and Leslie looked toward the doorway, and the stairway beyond. Becky's mind raced.

"What are you going to do with us?" Her voice came out louder than she intended. They exchanged a glance.

"We can't let them go." Zach raised the pistol and pointed it at Becky's chest.

Scott stepped in front of her, shielding her from the

gun's path. "Where will it stop, Zach? Do you want to leave a trail of dead bodies all the way from Kentucky to South America?"

Leslie was staring toward the stairway. "Tenney?" she shouted. "What are you doing up there?"

Becky's nerves felt stretched to the breaking point. She grabbed Scott's belt and buried her face in his back. Her heart threatened to pound through her chest. *Lord, help us, please!*

Zach's voice grew soft, so soft she almost didn't hear it past the hammer of her pulse in her ears. "I didn't want to kill anyone. But now that it's done, I have to see it through to the end. I'm sorry, Scott. You're a good man."

Becky clutched the belt and pushed her face harder into Scott's back. This was it. Her death. Maybe Daddy would fight Chris for custody. Maybe—

"Police! Don't move. We've got the place surrounded."

Becky opened her eyes and risked a peek around Scott's back. An officer in a gray state police uniform ran into the room, another one directly on his heels. In the next instant, her protective barrier was ripped from Becky's grasp as Zach, moving so quickly he was a blur, shoved Scott's body out of the way. Scott fell to the floor. Pain shot through her scalp as Zach buried a fist in her hair. Her head jerked backward. Cold steel sent a shiver of terror through her skull as he shoved the gun into the base of her neck.

"Nobody move." His shout, inches from her ear, reverberated in her eardrum. "I swear I'll kill her."

Two figures slipped into the room, moving slowly. Detective Foster and Jeff Whitley. Her heart threatening to pound out of her chest, Becky's gaze locked on to the detective's. How could anyone look so calm in a situation like this?

Well, he didn't have a gun pressed to his skull, did he?

"Don't be stupid, Garrett," Foster said. "There are at least twenty cops around this house. You'll never get away."

Becky felt Zach's body tense. "They won't shoot me if I have a hostage."

Her gaze slid to Leslie. The brunette stood, paralyzed, her lips tight with fear as she stared at her partner.

"Let her go, Zach." Scott's voice sounded as calm as Foster's.

Becky wanted so badly to turn her head and look at him. She heard shuffling noises as he stood, but she didn't dare move.

"You know I can't do that." Zach's fingers tightened his grip on her hair.

"Come on, Zach. I know you. You don't want to hurt Becky. She's a woman. A mom."

"I don't want to," Zach whispered. "But I will if I have to. If you make me."

"I don't believe it." Scott's voice sounded closer. He was moving toward them, toward her. "You're a decent guy, Zach. You wouldn't make an orphan out of two little kids. I know you wouldn't."

The grip on Becky's hair relaxed a fraction. "Two kids?" Did his voice sound hesitant?

Becky stared straight ahead, at Jeff and Detective Foster. Foster didn't have a weapon, but Jeff's was pointed toward Zach. Toward her. She stared into his eyes, but his gaze was fixed on the man behind her.

Scott's voice was almost a whisper. "Yeah. Two boys. Little guys, around five or so. You have a brother, don't you, Zach?"

She heard a loud swallow inches behind her right ear. "You know I do. You met him a few months ago." The grip loosened more, and the gun actually moved away from her skin.

Detective Foster spoke. "You don't want to do this, Garrett. Give us the gun."

Becky felt his muscles go tense again. "Cops don't tell me what to do. I'm in control here, not you. Get out, all of you!"

A movement of his arm behind her. A flash of gray beside her head. The gun moved away from her head to point over her shoulder toward Detective Foster.

A blur to her left.

In the next instant, Becky was thrown to the floor, pain shooting simultaneously through the palm of her right hand where she landed and through her scalp as a handful of hair was ripped out. Scott landed on top of her and Zach. The gun clanged to the tiles and skittered away.

As one of the police officers dashed for the gun, Jeff and Foster ran toward her. They grabbed Zach and flipped him over on his stomach, Jeff reaching for his handcuffs.

Scott rolled away, and pulled her with him.

She was free. Relief melted her muscles as sobs clogged her throat. She was free.

Becky felt hands on her shoulders, pulling her upward. Scott, kneeling before her, lifted her up and into his arms.

She buried her face in his neck and surrendered to shuddering sobs. His arms tightened around her, hugging her close.

"You're okay now," he whispered, his breath warm on her ear. "It's over. You're safe."

After a blissful moment, Becky gave an embarrassed laugh and pulled away. "I'm sorry. I'm all right."

They got to their feet and she turned in time to see Leslie, hands cuffed behind her back, being led through the door. Zach cast one unreadable look in their direction before he, too, disappeared from sight.

Jeff and Detective Foster approached them.

The detective shook his head. "You two almost blew everything. We had Garrett under surveillance, waiting for him to lead us to his partner."

"You knew he killed Haldeman?" Scott directed his question to the detective, but kept a firm arm around Becky's waist.

Jeff answered. "We suspected, but we didn't have proof. Not until tonight, when we recovered the hoof pick from the desk drawer." He nodded at Becky. "At least one of you was smart enough to let us know what was going on."

"You took your time getting here," Becky scolded. She put a cool hand to her hot forehead. "I thought my boys were going to grow up motherless for sure."

Scott whirled on her. "You called the police. And after you promised not to!"

"I did not. I called my friend, Amber."

Her side felt warm where his hand lingered. Maybe she was giddy from her close brush with death, but she wanted to tell him right now, at this moment, how she felt. Heedless of Jeff and Detective Foster, she placed her fingers gently over Scott's heart and forced him to lock eyes with her. "I wasn't about to let the man I love walk into danger without backup."

Gulp! Did she just say the *L*-word? That wasn't what she'd planned to say. Blushing to the roots of her hair, she turned her head and started to stammer an explanation.

"The man you…" Scott turned her face toward him with a gentle finger beneath her chin. His gaze pierced her soul, and in the next moment Becky felt herself swept up into his strong arms once again. This time she hoped he'd never let go.

EPILOGUE

Cars lined both sides of the two-lane country road in front of Out to Pasture. All kinds of cars, Becky noted as she walked arm in arm with Scott past a brand-new Mercedes parked behind a beat-up old farm truck. Seems everyone in that part of the state had turned out for Neal Haldeman's memorial service.

The weather could be iffy in early May, but today the sun shone in a deep-blue sky, and the coats of the Pasture's stallions gleamed in the radiance of a truly beautiful Kentucky spring day. Most of them had taken up positions as far as possible from the unusual activity going on in the grass behind the office, but Becky bit back a grin when she noticed Alidor keeping a watchful eye turned their way. She pitied the poor unsuspecting soul who dared to get too close to the testy stallion. Thank goodness the boys were home with Daddy today.

A cluster of mourners had gathered around Neal's nephew up at the front of the rows of folding chairs, most of which were already filled. Just beyond them, she glimpsed the big poster of Neal's smiling face on its easel beside the urn containing his ashes. Mr. Courtney stood off to one side, his hands gesturing widely as he spoke with a man Becky didn't know.

When they neared the chairs, a tall figure approached. Becky's hand tightened on Scott's arm. Kaci Buchanan had certainly dressed for the occasion. Her wide-brimmed hat with a thick red ribbon looked more appropriate for boxed seats at the Derby than a memorial service.

The smile she turned on Becky could have frozen hot coals. But when her gaze slid over to Scott, her cherry-colored lips widened.

"My, my, my, you would certainly dress up a Winner's Circle in that suit." Becky's teeth ground together as the heiress's gaze traveled from Scott's head to his polished black shoes. Then a shiny lip protruded. "But I hear you declined Mother's offer."

"I did." Scott's smile might have ignited a flare of jealousy in Becky, but at the same time he covered her hand on his arm and squeezed. "Lee Courtney needs me to do double duty for a while here, until he can find someone to take over at Shady Acres."

Scott's gesture did not go unnoticed. Kaci's eyes narrowed. "Then you won't be taking the head position for Lee?"

"No, I won't. I've had enough of the breeding business for a while." Scott inclined his head toward Alidor's paddock. "I'm going to stay at the Pasture and make sure these old guys enjoy their retirement."

"Well." She leaned forward and tapped his chest with a polished fingernail. "Our loss is their gain."

Her chin lifted as she caught sight of someone behind them and moved on. Becky refrained from voicing any of the less-than-polite comments that itched the tip of her tongue.

"Becky, there you are."

Fingers plucked at her sleeve, and she turned to see Isabelle Keller. Becky searched the woman's face. Grief had etched lines around her eyes, but at least she no longer exhibited signs of uncontrollable weeping.

Becky released Scott's arm to take both of Isabelle's hands in hers. "How are you holding up?"

"Okay." She squeezed Becky's fingers. "I miss him terribly, but I know I have to be strong for the baby."

Becky glanced at the people in their immediate vicinity. "Is your father here?"

She shook her head. "He had another commitment." She tilted her head toward Becky and went on in a lowered voice. "He's in a bit of trouble with the police and is doing community service. I think it's to keep him out of jail."

Becky's gaze slid to Scott's. That confirmed an elusive comment by Detective Foster when they'd asked him directly why Mr. Keller hadn't been arrested for burglary, even though he had apparently turned over the tally sheets that led them to suspect Zach Garrett of killing Neal.

At that moment, a trumpeter near the front stepped up beside the urn. It was time to begin the service. The man raised a shiny instrument to his lips and sounded the tune familiar to everyone who had anything at all to do with horse racing—the Call to Post.

As the clear notes echoed over the softly rolling hills of Kentucky bluegrass, the sound of hoofbeats thundered and the ground seemed to pulse with the pounding of powerful hooves on the turf. Every stallion at the Pasture, ears erect, began to run around their paddocks.

"Look at that." Scott turned a wide grin on Becky. "They remember."

"They're paying tribute to the man who brought them

here." She smiled up at him. "And the one who will keep them here."

He slipped an arm around her waist and pulled her close. "Both of us will keep them here. We're going to do it together, for years and years."

Her heart swelling with deep contentment, Becky allowed Scott to guide her toward a chair. There wasn't another person in the entire world with whom she'd rather spend her Out to Pasture years.

* * * * *

Dear Reader,

As I researched *Bluegrass Peril*, I enjoyed several visits to the only farm in the United States that provides a home for retired Thoroughbred stallions—Old Friends, in Georgetown, Kentucky. Though I've taken a few liberties with my fictitious farm, Out to Pasture, the terrible fate of many retired champions is distressingly real. The horses in these pages are fictitious, but many are modeled after real horses in residence at Old Friends. Like the farm in this book, Old Friends was founded in response to the brutal slaughter of the famed champion Ferdinand.

The stallions at Old Friends have their own tales to tell, and they will enchant you and steal your heart when you visit. The farm's founder, Michael Blowen, is one of the most dynamic men you'll ever meet. His love for these phenomenal equine athletes, and his passion for ensuring they enjoy their retirement years, are contagious. I hope it goes without saying that the victim in this book is totally fictitious, and bears no resemblance to the vivacious, charismatic and very much alive Michael Blowen.

If your sympathies for these horses have been aroused, I encourage you to read more about Old Friends at: *www.oldfriendsequine.com.*

Virginia Smith

QUESTIONS FOR DISCUSSION

1 When the book opens, Becky is a young mom raising her children alone. What challenges do single parents face today? Where can they turn for help?

2 Scott falsely accuses his neighbor of wrongdoing. Have you ever accused a friend of something of which they are not guilty?

3 Becky questions whether her Christian duty requires her to reconcile with her ex-husband. How does her decision relate to the book's Scriptural foundation, Jeremiah 31:33b?

4 When he sees his daddy drinking beer, Jamie asks Becky, "Mommy, is that drugs?" How would you have answered?

5 Did Becky make the right decision in refusing to reconcile with Christopher? Why, or why not?

6 Becky is hesitant to report the identity of the mysterious "L" to the police. Why? How have your personal struggles had an impact upon your judgment?

7 When Scott discovers the missing hoof pick, he doesn't want to call the police. Why?

8 Have you ever known someone so driven by jealousy or envy that they perform unacceptable acts?

9 The killers were motivated by two different emotions. Which is the strongest motivator of human behavior—greed or jealousy?

10 What do you think should be done with retired Thoroughbred stallions?

*Powerful, engaging stories of romance, adventure and
faith set in the past—when life was simpler and faith
played a major role in everyday lives.
Turn the page for a sneak preview of*

HOMESPUN BRIDE
by
Jillian Hart

*Love Inspired Historical—love and faith
throughout the ages
A brand-new line from Steeple Hill Books
Launching this February!*

There was something about the young woman—something he couldn't put his finger on. He'd hardly glanced at her when he'd hauled her from the family sleigh, but now he took a longer look through the veil of falling snow.

For a moment her silhouette, her size, and her movements all reminded him of Noelle. How about that. Noelle, his frozen heart reminded him with a painful squeeze, had been his first—and only—love.

It couldn't be her, he reasoned, since she was married and probably a mother by now. She'd be safe in town, living snug in one of the finest houses in the county instead of riding along the country roads in a storm. Still, curiosity nibbled at him, and he plowed through the knee-deep snow. Snow was falling faster now, and yet somehow through the thick downfall his gaze seemed to find her.

She was fragile, a delicate bundle of wool—and snow clung to her hood and scarf and cloak like a shroud, making her tough to see. She'd been just a little bit of a thing when he'd lifted her from the sleigh, and his only thought at the time had been to get both women out of danger. Now something chewed at his memory. He couldn't quite figure out what, but he could feel it in his gut.

The woman was talking on as she unwound her niece's veil. "We were tossed about dreadfully. You're likely bruised and broken from root to stem. I've never been so terrified. All I could do was pray over and over and think of you, my dear." Her words warmed with tenderness. "What a great nightmare for you."

"We're fine. All's well that ends well," the niece insisted.

Although her voice was muffled by the thick snowfall, his step faltered. There *was* something about her voice, something familiar in the gentle resonance of her alto. Now he could see the top part of her face, due to her loosened scarf. Her eyes—they were a startling, flawless emerald green.

Whoa, there. He'd seen that perfect shade of green before—and long ago. Recognition speared through his midsection, but he already knew she was his Noelle even before the last layer of the scarf fell away from her face.

His Noelle, just as lovely and dear, was now blind and veiled with snow. His first love. The woman he'd spent years and thousands of miles trying to forget. Hard to believe that there she was suddenly right in front of him. He'd heard about the engagement announcement a few years back, and he'd known in returning to live in Angel Falls that he'd have to run into her eventually.

He just didn't figure it would be so soon and like this.

Seeing her again shouldn't make him feel as if he'd been hit in the chest with a cannonball. The shock was wearing off, he realized, the same as when you received a hard blow. First off, you were too stunned to feel it. Then the pain began to settle in, just a hint, and then rushing in until it was unbearable. Yep, that was the word to describe what was happening inside his rib cage. A pain worse than a broken bone beat through him.

Best get the sleigh righted, the horse hitched back up and the woman home. But it was all he could do to turn his back as he took his mustang by the bridle. The palomino pinto gave him a snort and shook his head, sending the snow on his golden mane flying.

Yep, I know how you feel, Sunny, Thad thought. Judging by the look of things, it would be a long time until they had a chance to get in out of the cold.

He'd do best to ignore the women, especially Noelle, and to get to the work needin' to be done. He gave the sleigh a shove, but the vehicle was wedged against the snow-covered brush banking the river. Not that he'd put a lot of weight on the Lord overmuch these days, but Thad had to admit it was a close call. Almost eerie how he'd caught them just in time. It did seem providential. Had they gone only a few feet more, gravity would have done the trick and pulled the sleigh straight into the frigid, fast waters of Angel River and plummeted them directly over the tallest falls in the territory.

Thad squeezed his eyes shut. He couldn't stand to think of Noelle tossed into that river, fighting the powerful current along with the ice chunks. There would have been no way to have pulled her from the river in time. Had he been a few minutes slower in coming after them or if Sunny hadn't been so swift, there would have been no way to save her. To fate, to the Lord or to simple chance, he was grateful.

Some tiny measure of tenderness in his chest, like a fire long banked, sputtered to life. His tenderness for her, still there, after so much time and distance. How about that.

Since the black gelding was a tad calmer now that the sound of the train had faded off into the distance, Thad re-hitched him to the sleigh but secured the driving reins to his saddle horn. He used the two horses working together to free the sleigh and get it realigned toward the road.

The older woman looked uncertain about getting back into the vehicle. With the way that black gelding of theirs was twitchy and wild-eyed, he didn't blame her. "Don't worry, ma'am, I'll see you two ladies home."

"Th-that would be very good of you, sir. I'm rather shaken up. I've half a mind to walk the entire mile home, except for my dear niece."

Noelle. He wouldn't let his heart react to her. All that mattered was doing right by her—and that was one thing that hadn't changed. He came around to help the aunt into the sleigh and after she was safely seated, turned toward Noelle. Her scarf had slid down to reveal the curve of her face, the slope of her nose and the rosebud smile of her mouth.

What had happened to her? How had she lost her sight? Sadness filled him for her blindness and for what could have been between them, once. He thought about saying something to her, so she would know who he was, but what good would that do? The past was done and over. Only the emptiness of it remained.

"Thank you so much, sir." She turned toward the sound of his step and smiled in his direction. If she, too, wondered who he was, she gave no real hint of it.

He didn't expect her to. Chances were she hardly remembered him, and if she did, she wouldn't think too well of him. She would never know what good wishes he wanted for her as he took her gloved hand. The layers of wool and leather and sheepskin lining between his hand and hers didn't stop that tiny flame of tenderness for her in his chest from growing a notch.

He looked into her eyes, into Noelle's eyes, the woman

he'd loved truly so long ago, knowing she did not recognize him. Could not see him or sense him, even at heart. She smiled at him as if he were the Good Samaritan she thought he was as he helped her settle onto the seat.

Love was an odd thing, he realized as he backed away. Once, their love had been an emotion felt so strong and pure and true that he would have vowed on his very soul that nothing could tarnish nor diminish their bond. But time had done that simply, easily, and they stood now as strangers.

* * * * *

Don't miss this deeply moving
Love Inspired Historical story about
a young woman in 1883 Montana who reunites
with an old beau and soon discovers that love
is the greatest blessing of all.

HOMESPUN BRIDE
by Jillian Hart
available February 2008

And also look for
THE BRITON
by Catherine Palmer
about a medieval lady who battles for
her family legacy—and finds true love.

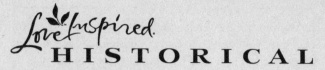

REQUEST YOUR FREE BOOKS!
2 FREE RIVETING INSPIRATIONAL NOVELS
PLUS 2 FREE MYSTERY GIFTS

YES! Please send me 2 FREE Love Inspired® Suspense novels and my 2 FREE mystery gifts. After receiving them, if I don't wish to receive any more books, I can return the shipping statement marked "cancel." If I don't cancel, I will receive 4 brand-new novels every month and be billed just $3.99 per book in the U.S. or $4.74 per book in Canada, plus 25¢ shipping and handling per book and applicable taxes, if any*. That's a savings of 20% off the cover price! I understand that accepting the 2 free books and gifts places me under no obligation to buy anything. I can always return a shipment and cancel at any time. Even if I never buy another book from Steeple Hill, the two free books and gifts are mine to keep forever.

123 IDN EL5H   323 IDN ELQH

Name	(PLEASE PRINT)

Address		Apt. #

City	State/Prov.	Zip/Postal Code

Signature (if under 18, a parent or guardian must sign)

Order online at www.LoveInspiredSuspense.com

Or mail to Steeple Hill Reader Service™:

IN U.S.A.: P.O. Box 1867, Buffalo, NY 14240-1867
IN CANADA: P.O. Box 609, Fort Erie, Ontario L2A 5X3

Not valid to current Love Inspired Suspense subscribers.

Want to try two free books from another series?
Call 1-800-873-8635 or visit www.morefreebooks.com

* Terms and prices subject to change without notice. NY residents add applicable sales tax. Canadian residents will be charged applicable provincial taxes and GST. This offer is limited to one order per household. All orders subject to approval. Credit or debit balances in a customer's account(s) may be offset by any other outstanding balance owed by or to the customer. Please allow 4 to 6 weeks for delivery.

Your Privacy: Steeple Hill is committed to protecting your privacy. Our Privacy Policy is available online at www.eHarlequin.com or upon request from the Reader Service. From time to time we make our lists of customers available to reputable firms who may have a product or service of interest to you. If you would prefer we not share your name and address, please check here. ☐

LISUS07

Love Inspired®

When Mule Hollow rancher Nate Talbert asked for a miracle to change his reclusive life, he wasn't sure he meant Pollyanna McDonald. The widowed city woman, her eight-year-old daredevil and menagerie of unruly pets had moved next door, driving him crazy. Yet Pollyanna's son was sorely in need of a father figure. Could he be the one to help?

Look for

Next Door Daddy

by

Debra Clopton

Available January

wherever books are sold.

www.SteepleHill.com

Steeple Hill®

LI87464

Love Inspired

TITLES AVAILABLE NEXT MONTH

Don't miss these four stories in January

FAMILY IN HIS HEART by Gail Gaymer Martin

Nick Thornton could tell Rona Meyers was a special person, so he'd offered her a much-needed job. And as he got to know her, he couldn't stop wondering if God was offering him a new beginning and a second chance at love.

NEXT DOOR DADDY by Debra Clopton

A Mule Hollow novel

When rancher Nate Talbert prayed for a change to his reclusive life, he got new next-door neighbor Pollyanna McDonald. But the menagerie of pets that she and her son cared for was driving him _crazy_. Could he handle the chaos that surrounded her?

THE DOCTOR'S BRIDE by Patt Marr

Everyone in town was trying to find Dr. Zack Hemingway a wife. Yet the one girl who caught his eye wasn't interested. Why was Chloe Kilgannon hiding from him? This doctor knew it would take some good medicine to get to the heart of the matter.

A SOLDIER'S PROMISE by Cheryl Wyatt

Wings of Refuge

Pararescue jumper Joel Montgomery had the power to make a sick little boy's dream come true. He was determined to follow through even if it meant returning to a place he'd rather forget. And meeting the boy's pretty teacher made his leap of faith doubly worth the price.

"[A] passionate love story rich in history and character-ization. She takes the reader back in time and place to an era where men are strong and caring and extremely possessive and defensive of their women. . . . This is an award-winning saga from a sensational author."

—*Rendezvous*

"*Cranberry Point* warms the heart, challenges the mind, and fills the soul with characters to treasure. Miranda Jarrett brings humor, empathy, and romance to her story by showing growth and compassion. The universal appeal of Cinderella finding her prince goes straight to the heart of every romance reader. In this book, Serena finds not only her prince in Gerald, but that he is charming. Tears, passion, and joy make this a golden chest of memories."

—Romancing the Web

"Five stars. Charming, witty, and oh-so-tender—a great book!"

—Amazon.com

"Miranda, you've outdone yourself. *Cranberry Point* is undeniably your best to date."

—Merry Cutler, Annie's Book Stop

THE CAPTAIN'S BRIDE

"As always, Ms. Jarrett takes the high seas by storm, creating one of her liveliest heroines and a hero to be her match. Readers are sure to delight in Anabelle's sometimes outrageous schemes and fall in love with Joshua. . . . Hurrah for a new series!" —*Romantic Times*

"A well-written book that is a joy to read. I'm all set to settle in with the founding of another dynasty of unfor-gettable, sparkling characters created by the marvelous Miranda Jarrett. As usual, Ms. Jarrett's heroes raise your blood pressure and make you want to claim them for your very own!" —*The Belles and Beaux of Romance*

Books by Miranda Jarrett

The Captain's Bride
Cranberry Point
Wishing
Moonlight

Published by POCKET BOOKS

MIRANDA JARRETT

Moonlight

SONNET BOOKS

New York   London   Toronto   Sydney   Tokyo   Singapore

This book is a work of fiction. Names, characters, places and inci-
dents are products of the author's imagination or are used ficti-
tiously. Any resemblance to actual events or locales or persons
living or dead is entirely coincidental.

An *Original* Publication of POCKET BOOKS

A Sonnet Book published by
POCKET BOOKS, a division of Simon & Schuster Inc.
1230 Avenue of the Americas, New York, NY 10020

ISBN: 0-671-03261-5

First Sonnet Books printing June 1999

10 9 8 7 6 5 4 3 2 1

SONNET BOOKS and colophon are registered trademarks of
Simon & Schuster Inc.

Front cover illustration by Fredericka Ribes
Tip-in illustration by Harry Burman

Printed in the U.S.A.

For Stan and Luna, the muses in fur
(and for L.H.S. and C.H.S.,
who thought it was about time
the cats got credit)

Moonlight

🎔 1 🎔

Boston
June 1725

*B*oston had never seen a more beautiful bride.

She stood with her groom in the middle of her father's grand new ballroom, her hand resting lightly on his arm as they waited for their first dance as husband and wife to begin. Her gown seemed to gather all the light of the two hundred candles into the luminous silver satin and gauze, her hoop-shaped skirts covered with swirling silk embroidery and crystals that sparkled like stars. Deep flounces of Bruxelles lace draped her elbows, and rows of tiny silk flowers outlined the front of her stomacher, emphasizing her tiny waist. The first notes of the dance began, and as she took her first graceful step a murmur of spontaneous admiration rippled through the guests.

Standing unnoticed in the shadows of the backstairs hallway, Amelie Lacroix smiled with satisfaction. Her work here was done for the night, and done well. If there'd been time for another fitting, she might have shortened the petticoat a hairbreadth, or used a darker shade of silk for the rosebuds, but these were details that only she noticed. The gown, and therefore the shy little bride wearing it, were an undeniable success, and so was the milliner's shop of the Mademoiselles Lacroix. After a triumph like this, Amelie and Juliette would have more customers than they'd ever dreamed possible, and as her reward Amelie let herself linger to watch a few stolen minutes more, forgetting her weariness in the tremulous joy of the young girl before her.

In a class where most marriages were made for profit or influence, this one was based on love alone, and Amelie had been privy to every delirious detail of the courtship as she'd stitched the bride's wedding clothes. Even now, as the newlywed couple danced, Amelie could see how their eyes glowed with devotion, how oblivious they were to everyone but each other. What must it be like, she wondered wistfully, to be so completely, utterly in love?

"If Richardson smiles any harder, he's going to burst," said an unfamiliar male voice behind her. "Look at him! Have you ever seen a prouder papa?"

"Mr. Richardson has every right to be proud," said Amelie without turning, her voice purposefully cool. She'd no intention of being caught criticizing a gentleman as wealthy and powerful as John Richardson, especially not to someone she didn't know. Besides, what could be gained by encouraging some stranger? He was obviously a guest at this ball, just as she obviously wasn't, and there was no point in blurring the boundaries between them any further.

"His daughter has never looked more lovely," she continued severely, "and she means everything to him."

"Everything that gold can buy," said the stranger

with wry cynicism. "And what better way to spend it, eh?"

But Amelie had heard, and said, enough.

"You will excuse me, sir," she murmured, lowering her eyes to avoid meeting the man's gaze as she turned to ease past him. But the feet that she did see were very large in their brass-buckled shoes, and standing, it seemed, a good deal closer to her than was proper. She felt trapped between him and the wall and the ballroom full of guests, and she did not like it.

"You *will* excuse me, sir," she said again. "I was just taking my leave."

"Before supper, before you've danced yourself? How can you wish this sweet little bride well if you don't stay to drink her health?" She felt his arm nudging against hers in an impulsive invitation she hadn't sought, an arm that was a match for those oversized feet. "Come, I'll take you in myself."

"No!" She eased herself against the paneled wall behind her, trying to escape by edging around him. The last thing she wanted was to cause a disturbance that would undo all this night's good, yet this giant seemed determined to do exactly that. Couldn't he see that she didn't belong here? True, she'd taken care with her dress—she always did—but her untrimmed silk dorea petticoat and jacket, narrow-striped blue on blue, her scalloped Holland cuffs, her neat ruffled cap with the periwinkle ribbon, were hardly worthy of the grandest wedding feast in the colony's history. And even if he'd mistaken her dress, as even observant men could do, at her waist hung the badge of her trade, the engraved silver chatelaine with a tiny folding scissors, needle-case, pin-box, watch, and spool-holder, each dangling from a jingling silver chain. "That is, you are kind, sir, but I truly must be on my way."

"Kindness has nothing to do with it," he said, that same easy bemusement she'd heard returning to his voice. "I'm being entirely selfish. There are damned few pretty women in this room, and I do not wish to see the prettiest one leave so soon. Unless, of course, she leaves with me."

That made her gasp. Gentlemen were seldom this audacious with her, this bold, this—this *flirtatious*, and indignantly she lifted her gaze from his feet to his face to tell him so.

Yet as soon as she did, the words vanished. She'd expected him to be another of Mr. Richardson's older merchant friends, portly and bewigged. But the man who stood too close to her was young and tall and lean and appallingly handsome, with glossy black hair falling carelessly to his shoulders.

The handsome face alone would not have been enough to leave Amelie speechless—she'd long ago mastered that part of Maman's careful lessons—but with this man, it was only the beginning. There was a boundless self-assurance to him, a physical presence that seemed barely contained by his well-cut evening coat, and that she found at once intriguing and disturbing. He belonged in the dark, wild forests to the west, or racing with the wind on the sea, and he might as well have dropped from the moon for all that he would have in common with Amelie's elegant little world of damask silks and taffetas, curled plumes and brisé fans. Clearly, too, from the warmth of his smile he was accustomed to felling females by his sheer presence alone, and in that first speechless instant, Amelie felt herself begin to sway and topple like every other woman in his path.

But as Amelie was quick to remind herself, she was not like every other woman. She'd spent her whole life making certain she wasn't, and she wasn't about to let this man make her forget that now. Instead she folded her arms over her chest and composed her face with the well-practiced severity that she used for collecting delinquent accounts, another excellent lesson she'd had from Maman.

"You shall let me pass, sir," she said evenly, "else I shall call for help."

"No," he said with exactly the same evenness. "You won't."

She looked up at him shrewdly. In the shifting candlelight his eyes were an astounding color blue and framed with lashes as thick and dark as his hair, a tragic waste on a man. "No?"

"No," he answered firmly as he rested one palm on the wall beside her shoulder, almost as if by accident. "If you're so blasted concerned about being seen with me that you'd rather scuttle away like a guilty crab, then you won't compound the sin by calling for the world as a witness."

He spoke lightly of her "sin," doubtless imagining the usual virtuous maiden's fluttering. Yet there was so much more at stake for Amelie, more than any man could ever comprehend, and defiantly she lifted her chin a fraction higher. "How can you be so certain of what I'll do?"

"I'm not," he said, "but I'm a man who likes to take chances."

"And you see me as a chance to be taken?"

"Oh, nothing so common as that." He turned his

head to one side, appraising her, and the candlelight shifted across the angled planes of his face. "But I do see a woman who cares too much about little Miss Richardson, or whatever her name is now, to spoil her wedding day by squawking about me."

He was right: she wasn't going to squawk. "Then you presume, sir, more than you see."

He shrugged. "It's much the same thing, isn't it? No matter what I see or presume, you're still a good friend to Miss Richardson."

"She needs friends," said Amelie, glancing back at the dancing girl. She looked happy now, radiant, but it had not always been so. "No matter what you think, not everything in life can be bought."

"True enough. No one's ever been able to put a price on love, have they?" The man followed her gaze. "Which is why that little lass is so important to you. You want to believe in love as much as she does."

Startled, Amelie flushed. What right did this man have to speak of love to her like this, or to guess the deepest secrets of her heart? She pursed her lips and shook her head, waving away his words as if they were not true.

But *mon Dieu*, they were. Though she'd dressed a score of other wealthy brides, Deborah Richardson Vandervert's wedding had been the first to make her weep with emotion and an unfamiliar, inexplicable longing. She was blessed with so much—an eye for beauty and the talent to make it visible to others, too; prosperity and independence; a loving sister and a cozy home to share with her—that she'd be selfish indeed to yearn for more. But with every tiny, measured stitch she'd taken in the silver satin, she'd caught herself wishing for the one thing she was never meant to have.

And struggling to accept the hardest of Maman's careful lessons.

But the stranger misinterpreted her confused silence. "These are good things, sweetheart," he said, softly, so softly for so large a man, "and I meant no insult by noting them. Women are expected to be beautiful, but it's rare to find one who's loyal and thoughtful in the bargain. Nearly as rare as finding true love like that pair there."

True love, true love: how had he guessed the name of the wicked, forbidden apple she craved so much? True love was the single thing that Maman had warned her most to distrust, true love the one sure, ruinous temptation for any woman to choose. Hadn't Amelie only to look at poor Maman herself for all the proof she needed of the folly of believing in true love?

"There is no such thing as true love," she said, her voice unnaturally sharp and harsh, "and any woman who lets herself believe otherwise is sure to come to grief."

But to her horror the music had stopped in the same second she began to speak, and her words—hateful words at a wedding, however true they might be— seemed to ring across the ballroom. Curious faces turned toward the hallway, and in the middle of them, on the far side of the room, stood John Richardson. Beneath his tall, curled wig his eyes were cold, critical, and as he scowled toward the doorway where she stood Amelie could already feel the iciness of his displeasure.

"Oh, no," she whispered, backing away farther into the shadows. She was horrified, humiliated, and if anyone saw her, the shop, which was also her home and Juliette's, could be ruined as well. She had come at Deborah's invitation, not her father's, and he would not be pleased to find a mere seamstress peeping at his grand amusements. All she could hope was that no one had recognized her voice, and all she cared about now was to get away as fast as she could. She clutched her skirt in a bunch to one side to keep from tripping and ducked beneath the stranger's arm, determined to run further into the shadows and away from disgrace.

Yet she'd barely turned the first corner of the hall when she felt the stranger's hand on her arm, gently pulling her to a halt. "There now, lass. No need to rush off so sudden."

She twisted around, glaring at him as she struggled to break free.

"Let me go, let me go *now!*" she whispered desperately. "I have to leave at once!"

"No one knew it was you, and even if they did—"

"But if I'd left long ago, when I was supposed to, after I'd dressed Miss Richardson, before I shamed myself, and—oh, I cannot let them find me still here in this house!"

He nodded, understanding, but still he didn't release her hand. "Then you don't want to go that way. That only leads to the servants' rooms upstairs."

"How would you know—"

"I've been here before." He pulled her in the opposite direction. "Come, this way."

She resisted only long enough to hear the footsteps behind them, coming from the ballroom. "Then hurry," she said, now the one tugging. *"Hurry!"*

But instead of turning back down the hallway, he threw open the first door and pushed her inside. The room was more of a closet, dark and close, with a single small, shuttered window outlined by moonlight, and she blinked to make her eyes adjust.

"Where are we?" she demanded, more panic in her question than she wished as he latched the door behind them. "You said you knew the way out!"

"I do," he said, his voice oddly reassuring in the darkness as she heard him prising open the window shutter. "Trust me, sweetheart."

But to her regret she realized she was already trusting him to have come this far. The more fool she, she thought dismally. Probably John Richardson hadn't even heard her, and what vanity to think a gentleman like him would recognize the voice of his daughter's dressmaker! Weariness had made her overreact, that was all, weariness and agitation over the wedding and then this persistent gallant had reduced her to an empty-headed, vaporish female. Now all she'd done was trade one disaster for another.

The shutter swung open with a squeak of protest, and the window followed. Though the stranger was only a large black shadow beside her, Amelie didn't have to see his face to know he was grinning from sheer anticipation.

"This is all a great adventure for you, isn't it?" she whispered fiercely. "You'd probably like it all the more if there was a moat full of hungry crocodiles, too."

He laughed, a low rumble in his chest. "It's better than that infernal ball of Richardson's, aye. Handsomely, now. Swing your legs over the sill and drop over the side. And I promise there's not a crocodile in sight."

Dubiously she peered through the open casement. They were overlooking the kitchen garden, and beyond the whitewashed fence lay Hanover Street. From there the walk home wasn't far—not above half a mile to the little brick shop on Marlborough Street, across from Old

South Meeting House—but first she had to reach the ground below, a disturbing distance away.

"There's nothing handsome about this," she said, inching back from the sill.

"I meant handsomely as in briskly, swiftly. Fast." He held the window open a little further for her, his arm brushing next to hers in the dark, the contact enough to make her skin tingle beneath her sleeve. "If someone in this house is searching for you, they'll come hunting in here before long. Look, it can't be more than six feet to the ground."

She did not like to think of herself as a coward—and if she were, she wouldn't be in this situation now—but to her six feet seemed as impossible as a hundred. "I do not believe I can do this."

"Oh, aye, sure you can," he coaxed, his voice as velvety as the summer night air around them. "But if you want, I'll go first and catch you."

That image—of her skirts and petticoats fluttering up while he waited below with a splendid view of her bare knees and garters—decided her. Before her resolution wavered, she gathered her skirts up as modestly as she could, slung her legs over the sill as he'd suggested, closed her eyes, and jumped.

Or fell. She landed hard on her feet with an undignified *ooof*, then lost her balance and toppled backward into the cushioned mound of her own petticoats, the tools on her chatelaine clinking in protest, her legs in their neat white stockings splayed out before her like a doll's.

"There, didn't I say it would be easy?" said the man as he appeared again beside her. His large, rough hand swallowed up hers as he raised her to her feet, as lightly if she weighed nothing at all. "But we should move away from the house before we're seen from the windows. Come, this way."

He led her down a narrow path of crushed shells, into a small copse of apple trees. Clusters of white blossoms weighed the branches downward, the same fragrant flowers that Amelie had pinned into the bride's hair earlier. The scent had intensified with the night, sweet and thick in the late spring air as moonlight washed the kitchen garden with silver, turning the mundane beds of new beans and lettuce into a magical, mysterious place. For an instant she forgot everything but the unearthly beauty of the moonlight's spell, exactly the fleeting, ethereal effect she'd been striving to create with silk gauze and crystals for Deborah Richardson's gown.

A magical place indeed, she thought, here among the cabbages, magical and romantic and not quite real, just like everything else about this evening since the stranger had first spoken to her. But because of that, and because of him, the garden was a dangerous place now, too, one she must flee immediately if she had any sense at all.

"I must go, sir," she said as she scanned the length of the fence for the gate to the street. "I've tarried too long as it is."

"In a moment," he murmured, drawing her into the center of the apple trees. She could see now that he must be close to her own age of twenty-five—young for a man, old for a woman—and that his expression had turned serious, shedding the easy charm for something darker, more unsettlingly seductive. "I'm not ready to send you on your way just yet."

She felt his hand settle on the back of her waist, the touch of his widespread fingers light and familiar, as if he'd every right to guide her this way. Guiding her, that was it: leading her, gentling her, reassuring her as they stood together in this fairy-tale circle.

Skittishly she twisted away from his hand, her skirts swirling around her legs as she turned back to face him. What was it about him that made her feel so off-balance and unsettled?

"What is it you want?" she demanded, surprised by the ineffectual huskiness of her own voice. "Why are you doing this?"

"Because it pleases me to help you," he said, his voice low, as if confiding a great secret. "Because *you* please me."

She shook her head, denying it while her heart thumped wildly in her chest. She'd never pleased any man before, at least not knowingly, and especially not by accepting help of any sort. Whatever would Maman have said?

"I didn't seek any assistance from you," she said swiftly. "I didn't need it. I owe you nothing in return."

He sighed ruefully. "I didn't expect anything, sweetheart. Leastways not as a reward."

She felt herself blush, realizing she'd somehow blundered. "That's not what I meant."

"No?" But he was gazing up into the night sky now, over her head. Moonlight silvered his black hair, and danced on the row of pewter buttons on his coat. "Did you know the stars all have names? Every last one. It's a shame you don't, too."

"That star, there," she said quickly, avoiding the question of her own name. In this unreal world she'd no more wish for him to know her identity than she in turn wanted to know his. Why should she, when she'd never see him again after tonight? "Do you know what that bright one is called?"

He came to stand beside her to follow the line of her pointing finger. "Ah, now that's the dog star. Not a very grand name for so fine a star, but I'd wager it's called something prettier in French, say, or Spanish."

"*L'étoile du chien*," she answered automatically.

Thoughtfully he glanced back down at her. "So you are not from Boston, either."

"Of course I am," she said, regretting the slip into Maman's language, the old-fashioned Bordeaux French that she and Juliette still spoke together at home. "Many Boston ladies speak French. I was born here, and I've never left, not even for a day, and I—"

"Hush," he ordered softly. "You've chosen your star, mademoiselle. Now make your wish."

She frowned, not understanding, or not wanting to. "My wish?"

"Your wish," he explained. "Even in a grim, righteous place like Boston, you're permitted to wish upon the first star you spy each night."

She didn't dare speak the wish that was in her heart, not in a hundred years, and she blinked back the inexplicable tears that stung her eyes. Steadfastly she tried to focus on her star again, and forget the man standing at her side and how much she wished he'd link his hand with hers again.

"I wish, I wish—oh, I wish for a good harvest for the farmers and a fair wind for the sailors!" she said at last, the words tumbling together in an agitated heap.

" 'Good harvests and fair winds'?" He chuckled, and reached out to lightly brush a stray curl from her forehead, the grazing touch of his fingertips over her skin enough to make her hold her breath. "I fear I'd wish for something a good deal more specific."

Amelie swallowed. "Would you?"

"Yes," he said as he bent to kiss her. "For your sake, mademoiselle, I'll wish for true love."

She was already trembling as his lips brushed across hers, and instinctively she closed her eyes, shutting out the stars and the moon and everything else except the touch of his mouth, his tongue, teasing and tempting in ways she couldn't have imagined. The only other time she'd been kissed had been long ago, an unpleasant and awkward experiment with the apprentice next door, who had been easy to refuse subsequently, even without Maman's threat of punishment when she'd learned of it.

But there was nothing unpleasant about this man's kisses, nor awkward about the way he gathered her into his arms as if he'd every right. With a shuddering sigh her mouth opened to his, and she tasted his heat as he deepened the kiss. Even with her eyes closed he was making her feel the magic of the moonlight, and she gave herself over to the fresh new wonder of it, drifting further into the pleasure of his kiss.

"Ah, sweetheart," he whispered against her cheek as their lips parted, his breathing as ragged as her own. "Seems you did need me after all, didn't you? Almost as much, I'd wager, as I need you."

You need me. Her eyes opened wide with shock as his words cut through the dizzy haze of pleasure. Too late she realized the truth of what he'd said. She'd behaved like a coy, cunning wanton, practically falling into the arms of a man whose name she didn't know. She'd behaved impulsively and foolishly, as if she'd nothing to lose. She'd forgotten all of Maman's lessons, betraying not only her mother's memory but her responsibility to Juliette as well. She'd forgotten who she *was*. And all she had to blame it on was the moonlight, and the man who'd dared whisper nonsense of the stars and true love.

"No," she said as she shoved hard at his chest to break their embrace. "*No.*"

As she turned away, she saw the confusion in his eyes, confusion and bewilderment and anger, too, all the same things she was feeling herself. That would be the last of what they'd share, and once again she fought the tears she'd no right to shed. Before he could see them, she ran, her skirts flying and her shoes crunching deep into the crushed shell path as she prayed he would not follow.

But when she finally found and unlatched the gate to the street, she was still alone, and as she hurried toward home, she told herself over and over again, how fortunate she was to have escaped as she had. She didn't need him—she didn't need any man—and the sooner she could forget this entire shameful evening, the better.

But for one moonlit moment, she'd almost believed.

The small brick shop was shuttered and dark for the night, but the windows to the back chamber where they worked still glowed with candlelight. Juliette should have been in bed by now, not sewing, especially not by the candlelight that gave her such headaches, and Amelie quickened her steps through the little alley to the back door. She caught her breath when she saw the broken window, smashed inward by something hard enough to have cracked the wooden mullion, too.

The muslin curtain lifted in the breeze, but there was no sound from inside the room.

"Juliette?" she called frantically, fear making her fingers clumsy as she jiggled her key in the heavy box lock to the back door. *"Juliette!"*

But as soon as she shoved open the door, she saw her sister, crouched down in her night-rail on the floor as she gingerly gathered up the shards of broken window glass with her fingers wrapped in a handkerchief.

"Juliette, praise God you are unharmed!" Amelie rushed forward to raise her sister to her feet. "I should never have left you alone for so long!"

"I was fine, Amelie, truly, at least until this." Half-heartedly she waved her hand with the handkerchief in the direction of the broken window. But though Juliette was trying hard to be brave, Amelie loved and knew her sister too well to be convinced. Juliette's face was nearly as white as the linen of her night-rail, her pale blue eyes too bright with fear and excitement, and even her fingers, the same fingers that could work so skillfully with a needle or scissors, were now knotting the handkerchief with uncharacteristic aimlessness. Six years younger than Amelie, Juliette had always been fragile, more fashionably delicate, just as Amelie had always been her vibrant, vigorous protector. With concern Amelie now slipped her arm around Juliette's shoulders and guided her to a chair.

"I'll tend to this, Julie," she said as she reached for the little broom used for sweeping up threads and scraps from beneath the worktables. "We'll have things back to rights in no time."

"But you're still wearing your good blue dorea!"

"And you're dressed for your bed, traipsing through broken glass barefoot as if it were clover in May."

Briskly Amelie swept the glass into the flat blade of the fire shovel. It didn't take long, for the single pane hadn't scattered far, but still Amelie berated herself with every short sweep of the broom. She shouldn't have dawdled so long at the Richardsons' house, and she certainly should never have gone into the garden with the blue-eyed stranger. How would she have felt if Juliette had been hurt while she'd been wantonly letting that man kiss her?

With a silent prayer of repentance, she dumped the glass into the bucket by the door. "Likely it was only apprentices or some other wicked boys bent on mischief," she said, striving to calm Juliette's fears as well as her own. "No doubt in the morning we'll hear of a half-dozen other broken windows among our neighbors."

But Juliette shook her head, hugging her arms across her chest. "It wasn't apprentices, Amelie. I know that much."

"Hah, then whoever else could it have been? A lady who didn't like the cut we gave her flounces?"

"Not a lady, no." Juliette turned in the chair to reach into the workbasket on the table behind her, rifling through the scraps of ribbon until she found a worn leather pouch that she held out to her sister. "And it wasn't a rock that broke the window, either. When I came downstairs, this was lying on the floor in middle of the glass."

With a frown, Amelie took the pouch. It was heavy in her hand, weighted as if filled with small stones, but as she untied the thong around the top, the contents made a muffled metallic clink.

"Oh, Julie," she said with awe as the glinting coins

spilled into her palm. "There must be twenty guineas in here!"

Juliette nodded, and handed her a folded scrap of grimy paper. "This was inside as well."

Amelie scooped the coins back inside the pouch and unfolded the paper. The words written inside were smudged, but their message was clear enough:

> Remain in Boston at your risk & peril. Flee
> while you can. Do not doubt me.
>
> A Friend

But Amelie did doubt, doubted very much. Breaking a window was one thing, but to do so with more gold than many men earned in a year was quite another. And what sort of self-styled friend would simultaneously threaten and reward them so grandly?

But if not a friend, then what enemy? Unbidden, the tall stranger returned to her thoughts: he would have wanted to save her now, too, to protect her from this new threat just as he'd done at the Richardsons.

"Oh, Amelie," whispered Juliette fearfully, as if she feared their secret friend were even now listening at the broken window. "What are we to do?"

Amelie tucked the note back into the pouch of coins and sighed. "Well, we shall not leave Boston, that is certain. I'll not be driven from my home and livelihood by some foolish note, and neither will you. And we won't keep the gold, either. What decent woman would?"

She wondered if this were some sort of calculated temptation for her and Juliette, a trap set by a rival to shame or disgrace them. Any unmarried woman who was successful in her own right could expect to have that success challenged by suggestive attacks on her reputation. It was the easiest way in the world to ruin a female competitor, and, in Amelie's opinion, the most cowardly, too.

She slid the pouch back into the workbasket. "I'll put that in the poor box at church tomorrow, where it can undo the mischief it's already caused."

But the fear remained in Juliette's eyes. "Shouldn't we speak to the constable?"

"The constable?" repeated Amelie, her brows raised in dismay at such a suggestion. "Oh, Julie, Maman would never wish us to do such a thing! The minute we asked a constable to call, all our custom would disappear—vanish! We're supposed to offer ladies a safe harbor of taste and refinement, a haven of respectability free of any sort of scandal. What kind of haven could we offer with a meddlesome *constable* in our shop?"

"And what ladies would wish to risk being showered by breaking glass?" asked Juliette, her voice full of misgivings. "What if this—this friend—returns when we do not do as he says? Can you imagine what the Richardson daughters would say if they knew that—"

"But this way they *won't* know, Julie. How could they, unless one of us told?"

Juliette sighed, letting her head droop forlornly. "Forgive me, Amelie. I didn't mean to be such a sorry coward. I only thought—"

"You don't have to think," said Amelie gently, coming to kneel on the bare, swept floorboards before her sister. She took Juliette's hands in her own, clasping her fingers tightly. "This isn't something we have to think about. We know what Maman would have done, and now we must do the same. We will be brave, because we must. We will keep this to ourselves, just between the two of us, and mend it the best we can."

She leaned forward to rest her forehead against her sister's, so close that she could feel Juliette's feathery breath upon her cheek. This was what mattered most in her life, this bond she'd always shared with Juliette, and not the careless, forgetful flirtation offered by men in moonlit gardens.

Even by tall gallant men with surprising blue eyes and pleasure in their kisses, and the empty temptation of love that could never be hers.

"Just us, Julie," she whispered fiercely. "Just us, and no one else."

❦ 2 ❧

$\mathcal{S}$he had needed his help, and he'd failed to give it.

It was as simple, and as complicated, as that, and once again Zachariah Fairbourne muttered an oath at his own incompetence. Not that swearing would help the young woman now, any more than it had helped the countless times he'd done it since she'd run away from him in Richardson's kitchen-garden.

She would have been hard to forget under any circumstances. Her sleek black hair, dark eyes, and golden skin made her exotic by Boston's blue-eyed standards, and the way her full upper lip pouted over the one below, sulky and tempting, was hardly the demure rosebud then in fashion.

Oh, aye, it had been a face worth remembering . . .

Standing there just outside the brilliance of the ballroom, her head resting wearily against the paneling as she'd watched the dancers, she'd intrigued him even more by the way she'd taken such care not to be noticed. In Zach's experience, women as beautiful as this one usually did exactly the opposite. Yet the stylish elegance of her clothing, the self-assurance of her manners, her obvious familiarity with the powerful Richardson family, even the ease with which she'd slipped into speaking fashionable, if unpatriotic, French, all told him that she was as much a lady as any in the ballroom.

So who, or what, had she been so desperate to avoid? She hadn't confided in Zach—damnation, she hadn't even told him her name—but she'd trusted him enough to follow him through the house and out the window into the garden. She'd been brave, and he'd liked that about her. She'd let him kiss her, too, a kiss that had raised a dozen more mysteries about her. But in the end, when she'd vanished into the moonlight, all he'd been left with was the nagging sense that he had failed her when she'd needed him.

"Mind yourself, you great fool!" bawled the red-faced driver of a passing wagon, barely in time for Zach to duck beneath a swaying load of fresh-milled timber. "I nigh knocked your damned head clear off, an' 'twouldn't be my fault if I had!"

But instead of swearing back at the driver for his insolence, Zach merely stepped close against a shop window and resettled his hat. The driver was right: he deserved to have his damned head knocked off and his pocket picked, too, wandering about Boston's narrow, crowded streets like a sleepwalker while he daydreamed of a nameless woman in shimmering blue silk. It had been like this for three days now, and it had to stop.

Muttering another oath, he fished the crumpled scrap of paper with his destination from his pocket. Better to help a woman who wanted his assistance than one who didn't, and he frowned down at the twisting feminine handwriting on the paper. Anabelle was his eldest cousin's wife, a lovely, charming lady whom the whole Fairbourne family either indulged or obeyed, depending on their relationship to her husband, Joshua.

For Zach, it was a bit of both: he was genuinely fond of Anabelle, but Joshua was the largest investor in the sloop the building of which Zach was overseeing here in Boston, a sloop that when finished would be his first command. Captain Zachariah Fairbourne had an excellent ring to it, and for the sake of his title he'd go on any number of Anabelle's little errands.

And this one was little, at least in weight. "One swan's-down muff," he read to himself, mentally hearing the words in Anabelle's bubbling voice. "Not woolen flannel, mind, but true feathers. Purest white, with no yellow, of a good size, lined with velvet capuchin such as I had before the cat chewed it to pieces. To be found at the Frenchwomen Lacroix's shop, in Marlborough Street, opposite the old Meeting House. Do not let them cozen you into paying too dear, Zach, they are very pretty merchants."

That made him smile again, as he had the first time he'd read it. It was bad enough that Anabelle would patronize French shopkeepers, considering how most of her husband's wealth had come from plundering French ships during the last war. But if Anabelle teased him about their beauty as well, then more likely the Lacroix sisters were wizened old crones, long past cozening any man into overpaying. He certainly wasn't about to fall into the trap of anticipation that Anabelle had so gleefully, and obviously, set for him. And to make him ask for something as blatantly suggestive as a muff—Lord, did Anabelle think he'd be in such sore need of amusement here in Boston?

He was still smiling when he found the Lacroix shop, exactly where Anabelle had said it would be, so near to Old South Meeting House that the shadow of the church's long spire fell across the doorway like an arrow pointing his way. Whether the sisters were pretty or not, they had clearly prospered at their trade. The wide windows of the little brick shop were framed by gleaming black shutters, picked out with gold, and the lavish signboard of a lady's plumed hat that hung over the doorway must have been the work of a master painter. Three well-scrubbed steps led to a heavy paneled door with more gold-work and a crescent-shaped window at the top that would have done justice to the finest house in town. But the finest house in town wouldn't have a bouquet of fresh flowers, daisies, and Queen Anne's lace, artfully tied with curled pink ribbons and pinned to the door, as a cheerful, beckoning welcome to all ladies.

In one window was a narrow worktable with baskets of thread where a seamstress could catch the best light of the day, while in the other was an assortment of the shop's wares: ribbons and laces, hats and fans, purses and pockets and a frivolously sheer embroidered apron meant for parlors, not kitchens.

But what captured Zach's eye at once was a length of striped silk, draped and bunched to shimmer in the sun. The cloth was an unusual shade of blue, to his eye the color of a running sea beneath a quarter-moon, and he'd only seen it in silk once before, glistening and rustling around the elegantly curved figure of the young woman in the moonlit garden. Unconsciously he leaned closer to the window, remembering how the silk and the warm, feminine body beneath it had felt in his arms, rustling softly against him as—

"Good day, sir," said the young woman as she opened the door to let a large gray cat dart outside and down the steps. "What do you buy this day? Have you discovered something that pleases?"

"Ah, aye, that is, good day to you, too, mistress." He cleared his throat and straightened, chagrined to have been caught with his thoughts wandering yet again. "You have, ah, many interesting items."

She laughed, less from amusement than to be pleasant. She *was* pleasant, he decided, a slight, cheerful young creature with pale blond hair and round cheeks that reminded him of peaches, and pleasant enough, too, to be the cozening shopkeeper that Anabelle had warned him about—correctly, as it turned out. But though pleasantry was certainly agreeable, even charming, it couldn't begin to compete with the memory of his mystery woman, and wistfully he glanced back at the blue silk in the window.

"You may deem them only interesting items, sir," she said, misinterpreting his glance, "but I'd wager your sweetheart or lady-wife would find them vastly more than that. If you please, I can show you fancies guaranteed to please the most discerning lady's eye."

Zach smiled wryly, Anabelle's request still in his hand. "The only lady I must please has already chosen her own fancy. A swan's-down muff, lined with—"

"Lined with purple capuchin velvet, for Captain Fairbourne's lady in Appledore, on Cape Cod. Her letter was most specific." The young woman stepped back to hold the door more widely open for him, all dimples and eager attention. "You must be her husband's cousin, Mr. Zachariah Fairbourne."

"More properly another Captain Fairbourne," answered Zach as he entered the shop, "though there are so many of those in the family already that I'll admit it confuses. And you are Mademoiselle Lacroix?"

"Mam'selle Juliette Lacroix, sir." She bobbed a quick courtesy, her pink-striped skirts rustling as they spread over the clean-swept floor. "Come, please make yourself at ease while I fetch the muff."

He watched as she disappeared through a curtained doorway to a back room. He was surprised to note the uneven halt to her step, nearly a limp, though her petticoats and shoes were carefully styled to disguise it. Not that most men would care; a girl this appealing likely had more than her share of flirtation, and besides, he'd always had a weaknesses for lighthearted little seamstresses. But this time, because of the lady in blue, he found he'd no serious interest at all, and with a shrug he turned back toward the window that held the silk.

He reached into the display to gently finger the cloth. Perhaps Juliette Lacroix could tell him the name of the woman who'd ordered it, and more importantly, how he could find her again.

"Here you are, Captain." Juliette's hands were tucked inside the fluffy white muff as she presented it for his approval, arching her wrists to show it to best advantage. "Exactly as Madame Fairbourne requested, is it not?"

Absently Zach nodded, searching for a way to ask about the blue silk. "Oh, aye, I'm certain it's exactly as Anabelle wishes."

"If she is pleased, Captain, than so am I." Impishly she raised the muff to her chin to blow across the swan's-down toward him. "And Madame Fairbourne *will* be pleased. Now is there something else I might show you? A pair of violet gloves to match the capuchin? Or something perhaps for another lady?"

He nodded, motioning toward the window. "That blue silk, there on the stand."

"The dorea?" She lay the muff on the counter and went to lift the fabric from the window, draping it over her arm. "An elegant choice! This is new arrived from the East-India House itself in the *Adventure*, and I know for certain we are the only house to offer it in Boston. It would work up most beautifully in a jacket, or perhaps a gown for afternoon."

"But you have sold some of this particular silk already, haven't you?"

"I told you, it is new arrived to this town, less than a fortnight." She pretended to study the fabric, clearly hedging. "Have you ever seen such a color?"

"Aye, I have," he said, "and in this last fortnight, too."

"Well, it is possible," she admitted with reluctance. "Anything in this world is. But Captain, if you wish to make certain that no other lady has this silk, why, then, you must buy the entire stock of it. There is no other way that I can guarantee—"

"*Juliette*." The single word was sharp, a warning, yet enough for Zach to recognize the voice instantly, before he turned.

Standing in the doorway from the back rooms, she was as beautiful as he remembered, the streaming sunlight taking away none of the magic that had gilded her in moonlight. Though she was dressed more simply today, in peach-dyed sprigged muslin that accentuated the color in her cheeks, she still held herself with the same inborn elegance, the same confidence, that had first attracted him at the Richardsons' party. But the anxiety he'd seen in her dark eyes then was here now, too, and the warmth of the laughter—and the kiss—they'd shared was again hidden away behind that same fear's defensive chill.

He'd have to tread lightly with her to bring back the warmth, very lightly indeed. And this time, he was determined not to let her vanish before he could.

He bowed from the waist, and smiled as if they'd only parted on the best of terms. "Good day, mademoiselle. Mademoiselle Lacroix, isn't it?"

Best of terms for him, that is. She, for her part, ignored him.

"Juliette!" she said again instead, more curtly this time, and still without directly acknowledging Zach's presence, or his question. "I shall assist this gentleman now."

Bewildered, Juliette let her glance slide from her sister to Zach and back again, the blue silk draped across her arm forgotten. "I do not see the necessity, Amelie. Captain Fairbourne was just—"

"Captain *Fairbourne?*" At last she looked his way, staring with as great distaste as if he'd been covered with a toad's green bumps, then launched into a rapid torrent of French that was far beyond Zach's limited Caribbean-learned vocabulary. Even so, he could understand the important things: that her name was Amelie, that Juliette was her sister, and that together they owned this shop; that she was as unhappy to see him as he'd been pleased to see her, and that somehow his being a Fairbourne only made that unhappiness infinitely worse.

Now Zach could see the resemblance between the sisters, more in their movements and in the way they stood than in their features or coloring. He watched as Juliette set the blue silk back into the window and dipped another curtsey to him, this time for farewell, before she hurried away to the back rooms. He was sorry that she'd been banished so abruptly, but he wasn't sorry at all that he'd been left alone with Amelie.

Amelie—an unusual name for New England, an elegant name that danced and spilled off the tongue. He couldn't wait to try it himself.

"You will be taking this with you, sir?" she asked, busying herself with wrapping the muff in a length of plain muslin to avoid meeting his gaze. Clearly, with her there'd be none of the charming foolishness like blowing across the swan's-down that Juliette had shown. With Amelie, everything was going to to be brisk and businesslike. Already she was trying so hard to pretend that he was nothing more than another customer, that they'd never met, never spoken, never kissed. With any other woman Zach would have been bemused by such determination. But for reasons he didn't entirely understand himself, Amelie Lacroix's show of indifference *stung*.

"I can have it sent to your lodgings if that would be more convenient, sir," she was saying as she bent over the muff. "We often do that for gentlemen who—"

"Not 'sir,' " he interrupted, keeping his voice purposefully low, confidential. "My name is Zachariah. Zachariah Fairbourne. But friends will shorten that to Zach."

"How convenient that must be," she answered, "for your *friends*."

He took two steps forward, closer to her, so that

only the wooden counter stood between them. "You could include yourself among their number, you know."

"No," she said lightly. "I don't believe I could."

"Aye, you could," he persisted. "You've every right, and Zachariah is a wicked mouthful."

"I would not know," she said with a mannered primness that he didn't believe for a moment. "Now, sir, pray tell me your wish for Madame Fairbourne's purchase, and then you may be on your way."

She smiled then, continuing to smooth the muslin-wrapped package, and looked up at him through her lashes without raising her chin. If they'd been in the moonlit garden still, the angle of her glance might have been winsome, even seductive, but now all Zach saw in her wide dark eyes was a challenge, a challenge for him to keep his distance.

Fortunately for him, he enjoyed challenges. He was a deep-water sailor, and a Fairbourne in the bargain. He'd been bred and born on challenges.

He watched as she lowered her gaze again and began to wrap a narrow cord around the package, deftly binding the loose ends of the muslin inward and together. She had pale, elegant hands with graceful fingers, but there was no mistaking the strength and capability in them as well, a capability that he found oddly seductive. Hands like that made a man think of what other things they'd handle with the same easy skill. She looped one end of the cord over the other to make a bow, and as she drew it taut Zach thrust his own finger foreword and pressed down hard on the loop to hold it fast.

"I will not be dismissed, and I will not leave," he said softly. "Not until you can tell me you're safe."

She didn't balk or pull away, only pausing for a moment to glance up at him again before she looped the ends of the cord over his fingertip, sliding it slowly across his nail as she tightened the ends. In comparison to her pale, elegantly kept fingers, her pinkie crowned by a flower-shaped garnet ring, his own hand looked barbarously large and rough, browned by the sun and criss-crossed with the endless small scars of a working sailor.

"You make no sense, sir," she said as the loop of cord grew smaller, tighter around his finger. "Why should my safety be your concern?"

He smiled, intrigued by the tension growing between them with each slippery tug of the cord in her hand. "Because, lass, you have made it that way."

"Then you can allow me to unmake it as well." Abruptly she snapped the cord, pinching his fingertip as the knot jerked free. "For of course I am safe. This is my shop, my home. Whatever gave you the notion that I wouldn't be safe here?"

"You didn't feel that way two nights ago." His finger smarted, though he'd be damned before he let her know it.

"That—that was nothing." Yet the way her pleated lawn cuffs fluttered and trembled over her hands as she clipped the cord proved it had been indeed very much something. She'd flushed, too, the warm peach color of her cheek deepening, and he remembered how much like a ripe, velvety peach her skin had been to smell, to touch. "And Mr. Richardson's house was not my own home. I am sorry if you were misled to think more than—than was intended. I was weary, and the hour was late. I forgot myself, that was all."

"Then it's sure as hell a good thing I remembered,"

he said, leaning his elbows on the counter to close the distance between them. "I've been worried about you, Amelie. Not even Richardson himself could tell me who you were when I asked."

Her eyes grew large and startled, the way they had when she'd turned to him in the garden. "Oh, no," she murmured anxiously. "You asked Mr. Richardson?"

"Him, and a good many others who were at his daughter's wedding." Why, wondered Zach, would Richardson's name bring such a reaction from her? The man was dour and over-bearing, proud of his power and position in Boston, but hardly the sort who'd even acknowledge his daughter's seamstress existed, let alone bother to terrify her. "I told you before, lass. I care what becomes of you."

"Don't." Deliberately she drew away from him, her expression turning resolute as she wound the remaining cord back onto its ball and tucked her sharp-tipped scissors into the center. "I don't need your concern, and I don't need your help."

"Perhaps you do, more than you realize." He tried to remember how the shop had looked from the street, if there'd been signs of private quarters on the upper floor or to the rear. "Do you and your sister live here alone?"

"That is truly no affair of yours!"

So, he concluded, they did unwisely live here alone. "Yet for the two of you, alone together in a city such as Boston—"

Up went her chin.

"Captain Fairbourne," she said, thumping the ball of cording and scissors on the counter for emphasis. "Sir. I know what the world says of women who dare to be independent of men. And I know that because

Juliette and I have chosen to run this shop—and have made it prosper, as our mother did before us—that there will be those in this town who will say cruel things about us, things that would never be spoken of a male tradesman."

"Amelie, I—"

"No, sir, *you* will listen!" *Thump* went the ball of cord again, emphatically close to Zach's hand. "I know what is said, and I know, too, that milliners and mantua-makers are always considered easy sport for fine gentlemen like you, as if toiling honorably for our living is but one step away from earning it basely in our bedchambers. And I won't hear another slanderous word—not one! I do not need the assistance of any protector, Captain Fairbourne, no matter how gallantly you may make your offer."

He looked down at the tight fist she'd made around the ball of cord, and smiled wryly. True, he *was* worried about Amelie's safety, but earlier, with her sister, he'd been thinking exactly what she accused him of now, and for that he well deserved this scolding.

He deserved it, aye, but he wouldn't make excuses for himself, either. What honest man would? As a mariner, even as a ship's officer, he never stayed in a place long enough to form any lasting ties with one special sweetheart. He preferred to keep his involvements uncomplicated, with the emphasis on shared pleasure instead of love, and because he himself was good company and indulgent, too, he'd always found plenty of delightful, delicious women eager to oblige him. This part of his life was simple, and it was easy, and he'd no regrets to haunt him at night.

Except, perhaps, the way things were now disintegrating with Amelie Lacroix.

He sighed, wishing they were back in the moonlight together. "Forgive me, mademoiselle, if my, ah, concern for your welfare has led me to—"

"There is nothing to forgive, sir," she interrupted swiftly, "and still less for us to discuss. Now I will ask again for you to tell me your lodgings, so that I might have Madame Fairbourne's package sent to you."

But though her words were brusque and businesslike, he could see the signs that undermined them, little things, like the way her voice had grown higher and rushed and how she'd nervously threaded her fingers in and out of the ball of cord. And that wonderful, tempting peachlike blush had stayed on her cheeks, if anything growing deeper.

"I'll tell you my lodgings only if you'll agree to let me buy you tea there tomorrow," he said evenly. "By way of letting me prove my concern for your well-being is only of the honorable sort, of course."

Incredulous, she muttered something in French that he didn't understand. "Have you always been this— this *obstinate?*"

"Since babyhood." He grinned shamelessly. "Or so my mama's told me."

"Then she and the rest of your family will understand perfectly when I write to Madame Fairbourne and tell her you refused to oblige her wishes." She plucked the package from the counter, clasping it to her chest with both hands and an unmistakable look of triumph. "Good day, Captain."

Zach's grin widened. *This* was the woman he remembered, overcoming her misgivings to jump boldly from the windowsill, and he remembered, too, why he'd wanted so badly to find her again.

"You would risk Anabelle's unhappiness to teach me

a lesson, mademoiselle?" he asked with mock seriousness, reaching out to her across the counter. He hooked his finger into the cord around the package, twisting it around, and pulled it tight to reel her in toward him. "You'd rather lose a devoted customer who could single-handedly keep you prospering?"

She backed away the one step she could before she bumped into the tall shelves behind her, the cord stretching in a tight little tent between them. Awkwardly she rearranged her grip to try to keep her hold on the package without letting her fingers touch his.

"I would if it meant I'd free myself from a conceited scoundrel who believed he knew what was better for me than I myself," she declared warmly. "I would in an instant!"

"Why, Amelie?" asked Juliette absently as she returned to the shop. "The man—"

Then she saw Amelie with the package clutched to her chest and Zach with his fingers twisted in the package-cording tugging her forward, and both of them looking as guilty as the sin they weren't committing. At least that was what Zach decided from the shocked expression on the younger sister's face.

"Forgive me, Amelie," she said hastily, beginning to edge away from the shop and toward the back chambers. "I did not realize that you and Captain Fairbourne—"

"Captain Fairbourne was leaving," said Amelie, glaring at Zach, who still held tight to the cord. "He is leaving *now*."

Zach smiled winningly. "True enough. We are just resolving the question of the package's destination."

"*Très bien, monsieur.*" Juliette smiled uneasily in return before she looked back toward her sister. "Amelie,

I only wanted to tell you that the boy from Mr. Swinley's shop says that Mr. Swinley cannot replace our window until Friday at the earliest."

"Until *Friday?*" repeated Amelie indignantly. "Friday, when he has already put us off once! I'm sure 'tis only one tiny window to grand Mr. Swinley, but to us it is a most grievous inconvenience!"

"Where's the broken window?" asked Zach. "If you wish, I could look at it for you, if you'll only—"

"No!" Amelie shook her head, and made a small puffing sigh of exasperation. "That is, no, thank you, Captain Fairbourne. We are perfectly able to handle this matter ourselves."

"Your capability astonishes me," said Zach, his smile gone. There were suddenly too many questions swirling unanswered around the sunny shop, far too many for this kind of flirtation to continue. Gently he unhooked his finger from the package, releasing it and Amelie as well. "You make me believe you've no wish for anyone else on this earth at all, except perhaps this Mr. Swinley."

"We swept up the broken glass from the floor in the back chamber ourselves when it happened two nights ago," explained Juliette. "There's nothing else left to be done until the glazier can come."

"Yes, yes, nothing," echoed Amelie, clearly unhappy with how much her sister had volunteered. "That is quite right."

Right, ha, thought Zach grimly. There was little *right* about any of this. When he'd jested about Mr. Swinley, he thought their window had been broken by some common accident—an errant broomhandle, say. But glass on the floor meant the window must have been broken inward, from something thrown or jabbed from the alley and after dark, none of which sounded to him like a common accident for a pair of pretty young women living alone.

"Two nights ago?" he asked, his mind already suggesting a wealth of disturbing possibilities. "The night when you and I—"

"The night I helped Mrs. Vandervert dress for her father's ball," said Amelie, her words rattling into a rush jitterish enough to make her sister stare. "It happened then, yes, but as Juliette says there was nothing serious, nothing remarkable about it. A nuisance, that is all. A mere nuisance."

"A nuisance," repeated Zach, "and doubtless, mademoiselle, one more thing you can handle yourself."

"Yes." With obvious effort she straightened her back and composed her features into bland, unemotional discretion, patting the package on the counter once for good measure. Expectantly she held a pencil and a card, ready to mark down his address. "Your lodgings, Captain?"

"As you wish." He would find a way to help Amelie and her sister both, but lingering in their shop, in the middle of all this awkward dissembling, wasn't going to be of any use to any of them. Blast, they'd probably already marked him for a great blundering oaf, and he couldn't blame them if they had. "You can send Madame Fairbourne's package to the Crescent, in Ann Street. I'll be staying there another month at the least, until my ship is ready. Good day to you both."

A month, thought Amelie dismally as she hurried forward to close the door after him. Her heart was pounding, her whole body so taut and on edge that she didn't know if she was close to laughing or weeping, and all of it the fault of a man she'd thought she'd never meet again.

But she had, oh, dear Lord deliver her, she *had*. He'd come out of the moonlight of her dreams and boldly into her shop and into her life, twisting her heart and conscience with the same ease that he'd twisted the cord on the package.

She'd thought at first she'd imagined his voice, rich and deep as he'd bantered with Juliette, and once again she'd been drawn toward it, and toward him, as irresistibly as a bee to a dish of sugar-water. With the morning sun streaming over his broad shoulders, he'd seemed too large, too aggressively masculine for the little shop, yet his smile, as shining warm as the sunlight around him, had held nothing but unabashed surprise and pleasure at finding her—*her!*—again. He'd told her again how much he wished to help her, yet in turn he'd made her as helpless as a new lamb, and as worthless, too.

A month at the least, he'd said, another month of him here in Boston. How was she going to survive it?

As she pushed the door shut after him, a round mass of gray fur squeezed its way through, adding a small scolding yowl of displeasure at having to hurry. Ignoring the protest, Amelie scooped the cat up into her arms and rubbed her face across the thick, warm fur.

"Oh, Luna," she murmured unhappily. "What am I to do now, eh?"

But while Luna didn't answer beyond wriggling into a more comfortable position in Amelie's arms, Juliette was not so obligingly silent.

"You know him, don't you?"

Amelie sighed, absently running her fingertips beneath the cat's plump chin. There was no more use in denying it than in asking the name of the "him" in question.

"Captain Fairbourne was a guest at the Richardsons' ball," she began carefully. "He thought I was a guest, too, otherwise I doubt he would have spoken to me at all."

"He knew otherwise today," said Juliette, "yet he seemed quite willing to speak."

"And how else would he be? A fine gentleman that handsome, that charming . . . You know how it is with men like that." Unhappily Amelie sighed again, realizing she was trying to convince herself as much as Juliette. "We were Captain Fairbourne's morning's amusement, no more, a diverting way to lighten an errand he'd no wish to perform in the first place."

"He didn't seem that way to me," said Juliette with unexpected stubbornness. "He was handsome, yes, but he seemed more gallant than you paint him."

"Oh, Julie." Amelie turned, hugging the cat tight. Her sister was too young to remember Maman's warnings, too vulnerable and innocent to understand their truth. Perhaps Juliette couldn't even remember Maman's face by now, the way she herself had, to her shame, forgotten their father's. She'd been only six when Papa had died, seven months before Juliette was born, and eighteen when Maman's frail heart had finally stopped forever.

"Grand families are so much alike," she began, even as she thought of how different in turn the grand ones were from her own. "The Cheseboroughs, the Clarkes, the Bowdoins, the Richardsons, and the Fairbournes, too, they can all afford to be gallant when it pleases them, and we can be charming to them, too. We need them, for they are the only ones in Boston wealthy enough to buy our kidskin mitts and Hungary-water, but they need us and what we sell to make them look as fine and comely as the ladies and lords they wish to be mistaken for."

"But, Amelie—"

"Nay, you must listen!" Amelie shook her head fiercely, knowing how important it was to make her sister—and her own wicked heart—understand. She'd been so fearful of being caught spying on her betters by John Richardson, but what she'd done instead with Zach Fairbourne had been infinitely more dangerous.

"You must listen, Julie," she said urgently, setting the cat down to better make her point. "You *must!* Gentlemen like Captain Fairbourne will be gallant, and we will be charming in return, but the moment we forget how empty and false by rights such gallantry is, the moment we forget how far our place in the world is from theirs, why, then we are lost, Julie. Lost."

Julie bowed her neat blond head over the broom in her hands. "Ah," she said. "Ah."

That was all, one tiny breath of a syllable, and Amelie prayed it was enough to mark the end of the conversation, and of Zachariah Fairbourne as well. If they were truly fortunate, the man would find other, more interesting ways to pass his time in Boston and forget all about the shop of the Mademoiselles Lacroix.

And most importantly, he'd forget every foolish thing that had happened in that moonlit garden, the way she herself likely never would.

In silence Juliette began the morning sweeping, the soft *shush* of the corn-broom brushing over the floor proof that the comfortingly familiar patterns of their life still existed, still continued.

"Did you finish the ruching for Dorothy Connelly's cuffs?" Amelie asked, brushing stray bits of Luna's fur from her sleeve. "I expect her this morning for fitting."

"It was done three days ago," said Juliette, doggedly concentrating on her sweeping instead of her sister, "as I understood her to desire, along with the wider trimmings for the petticoats."

She gave the broom a vengeful shove for emphasis, jabbing hard beneath the counter. "But what I do *not* understand is why, when you told me of Deborah Richardson's ball, of what everyone wore and how the table was laid and how anxious poor Deborah was for every detail to be perfect and and everything else important, you didn't tell me about meeting so fine a gentleman as Captain Fairbourne."

Amelie's face grew warm. She had never lied to Juliette, and she'd no intention of starting now.

"It he did not seem of any consequence," she explained haltingly, "especially after finding you with the broken window and that wretched note."

"So it is now somehow my doing, my fault, that you did not confide in me?"

"In a way, yes, I suppose it is," said Amelie defensively. "Why should I have worried you further, when I believed the man had vanished forever from my life?"

"Oh, pray, why indeed?" snapped Juliette as she shoved the broom back into its niche beneath the counter. She was so upset that she'd stopped compensating for her scarred leg, her dragging limp an unconscious but painful stab to Amelie's conscience. "As if a gentleman like Captain Fairbourne were the culprit, without anything more worthy to do than go about heaving bags of gold through windows!"

"I know nothing of the sort," said Amelie sharply. "I don't know what to believe of someone, even a gentleman, that I've scarcely met."

"Then I suppose I must be ignorant as well," answered Juliette resentfully, her eyes red-rimmed with angry tears her pride would not let her shed. "For I must *believe* what you say you *believed*, because you are Amelie and I—I'm only Juliette."

Amelie's eyes filled with tears, too, the stiff set of Juliette's shoulders and the reproach in her eyes unfamiliar, uneasy barriers that, for the first time, she was not sure she could cross.

"I have never spoken of you that way, Juliette," she began, searching for the right, true words that would breach the anger, "because I have never considered you anything less than another part of myself, the other half that makes me whole. Even our shop-board says so. Not our names alone, but who we are together: the Mademoiselles Lacroix."

"It was limned that way because no one would come for my name alone," said Juliette forlornly. "Because all the world already knew you're the clever one, the one who could make a belle from a milkmaid, there was no reason to spell it out in paint and gilding."

"It's that way because we are *sisters*, Julie." Across the polished counter Amelie reached out for the hand that was so nearly a match for her own, searching again for the trust and the love that had always been there before. "Because that is what matters most."

"Oh, Amelie." Juliette's face crumpled and the hard set of her shoulders collapsed as she reached for the familiar comfort of Amelie's arms.

Yet even as they linked their fingers, even as they embraced, even as they kissed each other's cheeks in apology and tried to smile and wiped away their tears— even then Amelie could still feel the unspoken danger looming there between them, exactly as Maman had always warned.

And that danger's name was Zachariah Fairbourne.

🏵 3 🏵

"*It* is not precisely what I had hoped, Miss Lacroix," said the heavyset woman as she scowled critically into the tall mirror beside Amelie. "It is not at all. But since you say the style is one the dear Princess of Wales favors, then I shall not quibble. No. If you are certain that these fussy sorts of furbelows across the stomacher please her majesty at present, then they shall please me, too."

Amelie smiled wearily, relieved that, at last, *something* had been deemed pleasing, and this interminable day might finally end. First Zachariah Fairbourne in the morning, and now Esther Drummer all afternoon.

"Then I shall be pleased, too, ma'am," she said, doubting that even the princess herself could be any more demanding or difficult than the woman before her. "I have it on the very best report, ma'am, that her grace is wearing no other style of bodice, and since you and the princess do share the same, ah, regal carriage, what suits one of you will most certainly suit the other."

Preening as she turned before the mirror, Mrs. Drummer smoothed the row of bronze-colored satin bows running across her sizable bosom. Her fingers were as inelegantly thick and ruddy as the sausages her husband had once sold, when he'd still been a mere butcher in Hampshire and before he'd come to Boston and built his fortune in supplying dubious beef to His Majesty's navy. Being a former butcher's wife was no sin in Amelie's eyes—she didn't give a fig where a customer's money came from, so long as there was sufficient to pay her own accounts—but a former butcher's wife who demanded to be treated like a duchess presented a sizable trial indeed.

"I suppose the Princess Caroline favors these ruffled cuffs as well?" asked Mrs. Drummer critically as she shook the deep, gathered bands of lace so they fell over her forearms.

"*Engageantes*, ma'am," murmured Amelie as she reached out to give one of the lace cuffs a final tweak. "They're called *engageantes*, meant to engage a gentleman's eye, to tease, to delight, and yes, they're worn by all the most fashionable ladies."

"French?" Mrs. Drummer sniffed contemptuously, her fingers lifting from the fabric as if they'd been singed. "Do not forget, miss, that I am a good and loyal Englishwoman. Mr. Drummer would not wish me to wear anything that is considered *French*."

Amelie raised one delicate brow, the strongest protest she could allow herself before so valued a customer. She understood the criticism, for Englishmen— and Englishwomen—had hated France since the first Norman stepped on English sand, and the last war, not four years past, had done little to ease their hostility. She understood the prejudice, but understanding

wasn't liking. There was a good chance that the ugly
note with the coins had been hurled through their
back window simply because their name on the signboard in front was French. Though Amelie considered
herself first a Bostonian by birth, English second by
default of that same birth in the colony of Massachusetts, and French only through her long-dead parents'
blood, she still resented this kind of blunt and unques-
tioning hatred by all of her fellow New Englanders of
everyone and everything French.

Though, if she were honest, not *quite* all of her fellow New Englanders. Despite his other glaring flaws,
Zachariah Fairbourne hadn't been shocked or disturbed
to learn her name was French, nor had he recoiled
from her as if she'd had some traitor's plague. On the
contrary, he'd called her "mademoiselle" in a way that
was almost approving and, like everything else he'd
said or done, had been thoroughly, and appallingly,
charming.

She'd liked that about him, how he'd accepted her
for what she was. Because it was so rare, she'd liked it
very much.

And, like everything else about him, she had to
remind herself now that such acceptance must not
matter at all.

"They're only scraps of lace, ma'am," she said as she
forcibly pulled her thoughts back to the stout woman
before her. "And even lace as fine as this Mechlin does
not have the power to make the wearer disloyal to the
crown. How else could the wife of the next king of
England wear them in perfect conscience?"

"That is true," admitted Mrs. Drummer with a final
disdainful sniff. Yet from the loving way she was stroking the elaborate lace, Amelie could tell that the

woman was already so fond of the gown that not even her husband's politics were going to keep her from owning it. "I suppose I could simply call them cuffs, instead of *en-en*-oh, whatever foolish trumpery you said."

"*Engageantes*," said Amelie as evenly as she could. No wonder she spoke French only with Juliette, and never before others. "But they will still look well above your hands, no matter what you choose to call them. Come, let me help you dress."

"You will have that sent to me by next week's end?" asked Mrs. Drummer as, red-faced from the exertion of changing into her own clothes again, she prepared to leave. "Mr. Drummer and I have been asked to dine with the governor, and I must have it in hand by then or not at all."

"As you wish." Swiftly Amelie tallied the other bespoke garments in progress in the shop, adding Mrs. Drummer's newest gown to the list. She was glad they were busy, but she was going to have to bring in two more seamstresses, perhaps three, to help with the plain sewing, or she and Juliette could never hope to be finished with everything by the dates they'd promised. "It will be ready, ma'am."

"I am pleased." Mrs. Drummer tugged on her gloves, bending to check her reflection in the small oval mirror on the counter. "But then you are so very artful with your stitchery, Miss Lacroix. There is no one to rival you in Boston. What marvels you worked with that sad little Richardson girl for her wedding! A sow's ear into a silk purse, that one, and a most costly silk purse at that. Not that Mr. Richardson minded the final accounting, eh?"

Amelie kept her expression cheerfully, purposefully

impassive. Discretion was an immense portion of her success, and often one of the hardest parts to maintain. "Miss Richardson made a most beautiful bride."

"Rather your cleverness made her into one." Mrs. Drummer smirked and snorted at her own heavy-handed wit. "Truly, you have no equal in anticipating a fashionable lady's needs and wishes."

Amelie chose to take it as a compliment, and graciously bowed her thanks. In truth her "cleverness" had painfully little to do with the shop's success; like every other mantua-maker, whether in Boston or London or even Paris, the lion's share of their profits came from selling the luxurious imported fabrics, and not from the sixteen hours that she and Amelie could spend toiling on a single gown.

Mrs. Drummer nodded with condescending approval. "But I would willingly pay every last cent of whatever exorbitant price you asked for such wedding-clothes for my own daughter. If only Betsey would rise from her sullen rump and catch herself a suitable husband! Where has the girl gotten to, anyway? Betsey! Betsey, you silly baggage, I am leaving, with you or without!"

"I am sure she is in back with my sister, ma'am," began Amelie as the girl came rushing down the hall to join her mother. Betsey Drummer was small and round, with a ruddy complexion and pale hair and eyes that gave her the unfortunate look of a startled rabbit. Hers was not the face that would "catch" the sort of grand husband that Mrs. Drummer had in mind, though the fortune she'd bring as a dowry would definitely help.

"Betsey," said her mother sternly. "I was just telling Miss Lacroix how much I should like to be ordering you wedding-clothes like your lucky friend Deborah Richardson's."

"Yes, Mother." Betsey blinked, silent acknowledgment that she'd suffered through this discussion many times before. "But Deborah isn't Deborah Richardson any more, Mother. She's Mrs. Philip Vandervert of Vandervert Manor."

"She's whatever I say she is to you, miss," said Mrs. Drummer curtly, "and if I hear any more of such impertinence, I'll take a willow-switch to you, see if I don't!"

"Yes, Mother. That is, no, Mother." Betsey bowed her head meekly, her tiny rebellion snuffed out as surely as a candle's flame.

"Betsey, wait, please!" Juliette hurried from the workroom, a small pocketbook worked in Irish-stitch in her hand. "Here, I didn't want you leaving this behind."

Mrs. Drummer frowned as her daughter flushed and squirreled away the little purse into her pocket. "Thank you, Miss Lacroix. Betsey would misplace her own head if had anything of value in it. Now hurry, you foolish minx, we are late already on account of your dawdling. Hurry!"

Mrs. Drummer's scolding continued down the steps and into the street, the sound of her voice stopping only when the noise from a passing cart drowned it out.

Amelie shook her head as she closed the door after them. "I'm glad you found the pocketbook before they left. Can you imagine what Mrs. Drummer would have done to poor Betsey if she'd discovered it missing at home?"

"More willow-switches, I'd wager," said Juliette without any irony, "and stale bread for supper while *she* dines with the governor."

Amelie shuddered. "I doubt that poor little creature has ever given her mother a minute's real trouble, yet have you ever seen a daughter kept on a shorter rein? To my mind, she has Betsey near to choking."

With a sigh, Juliette began sorting and refolding the pile of silk handkerchiefs rejected by Mrs. Drummer. "She'd wish nothing more herself then to be wed and away from her mother."

"Consider how perfect that poor man will have to be before Mrs. Drummer finds him acceptable!"

"But Betsey herself, I think, will be a good deal less demanding. She couldn't wait to tell me all about Deborah Richardson's wedding and her new Dutchman-husband and their house in New York, giggling and chattering until you'd swear she was another girl. And when Mr. Swinley's man came, she very nearly—"

"Swinley's man came?" asked Amelie with surprise. "I thought he couldn't possibly tend to our window until Friday."

Juliette shrugged as she piled the folded handkerchiefs back into their box. "He came, and he set in the new pane as well as the mullions around it. Swept up after himself and carried off his rubbish, too, and very agreeable the whole while."

"More agreeable than Esther Drummer, I'd venture." Amelie went to the back room long enough to retrieve her account book from her desk. She opened the heavy leather-bound book on the counter and began flipping through the pages to find this day's entries. Maman had always been scrupulous about entering every expense as well as every sale, an example that Amelie followed. "So how much did this agreeable rascal charge us?"

"That was the oddest part of it," said Juliette, "or perhaps the most agreeable. When I tried to pay him, he wouldn't accept it. Wouldn't even name a fee. He said Mr. Swinley had told him the reckoning was already settled."

"Settled?" Amelie frowned. With hard money perpetually in short supply in the colony, she would on occasion barter services or wares with another tradesperson, receiving a fresh coat of paint for the shop, say, in exchange for feather-trimmed hats for the painter's daughters. But George Swinley had neither wife nor daughters to make such an arrangement useful to him, nor was he the sort of generous man who'd want to make amends for having put a large job before a smaller one.

"That is not possible," she said slowly. "Who would have settled our reckoning for us, especially before the work was done?"

Juliette hesitated, clearly weighing her words before she spoke. Then she twitched her shoulders with another little shrug, this time of resignation. "You won't like the answer, Amelie. 'Twas your Captain Fairbourne."

Amelie gasped. "My Captain Fairbourne! He is no more *my* Captain Fairbourne than I am *his* Amelie Lacroix, to have my bills paid at his whim!" She slammed the leather cover of the ledger shut. "I cannot *believe* his audacity! Doubtless he expects me to fawn over him with gratitude, to praise him for his great and wondrous generosity in meddling in my business! In *my* business oh, *confound* the wretched man!"

She smacked the ledger with her palm, hard, so furious she could scarcely speak. The last thing, the very last thing, she needed was for George Swinley to begin telling the world that her expenses were being paid—paid in advance, and likely double the asking, too, for that window to have been mended so quickly—by some handsome young sea captain.

"I told you you wouldn't like the answer, Amelie," ventured Juliette. "But perhaps all Captain Fairbourne wished was to make amends for this morning."

"Don't you begin defending him, Juliette," warned Amelie as she searched through the bandboxes stacked on the shelves, impatiently shoving them this way and that. "*He* doesn't deserve your mercy, and it demeans you to give it. Where have you put that wretched white muff for his cousin's wife?"

"I already had Nathaniel take it to his lodgings," said Juliette, naming the neighborhood boy they used for deliveries. "But I recall the address, if that's what you want. The Crescent, in Ann Street."

"The Crescent." Amelie felt deep in her pocket, counting the coins with her fingers: more than enough to cover the window's repair. It was late afternoon, nearly five, but with the longer summer daylight she'd have no problem walking to Ann Street and back before dark.

And that, she determined, would be the last time she saw, heard, or received the tiniest assistance from Zachariah Fairbourne.

"I won't be long, Julie." The words clicked out in a familiar litany as she tied a wide-brimmed straw hat over her bonnet, adroitly looping the ribbons beneath her chin without bothering to look in the mirror. "Lock the front shutters and door while I'm gone, and don't answer to anyone. Lord knows we've no need for any more custom today, and if—"

"You don't know why he did it, Amelie."

Surprised, Amelie paused, the notched ends of the ribbons still pinched in her fingertips. The reason seemed so obvious to her that she couldn't understand why her sister couldn't see it, too. "Because he could, Julie. Because he wanted us to *know* he could."

"But you don't know *why*," said Juliette. "Maybe he did break the window himself. You said yourself you'd only scarcely met. He's a sailor, and sailors love their rum and mischief. Every night the watch gathers them up from the docks and takes them to gaol for disturbing the peace. He could have done it."

"No, he could not," said Amelie, more irritably than she wished. He'd been too occupied kissing her in the Richardsons' garden to have broken any windows, not that she was willing to grant him that particular alibi. "He's a Fairbourne, which means he's gentry, and not even seafaring gentry go about breaking windows and making empty threats to spinsters. Now come, lock the door after me, and promise you'll open it to no one until I return."

Juliette ducked her chin to sulk with more authority, and wrinkled her nose, too, for good measure. "You think as little of me as Mrs. Drummer does of Betsey. You're treating me like I've no more sense than a flea. A *naughty* flea."

"Oh, hush, Mistress Flea, I'll treat you exactly as you deserve." But Amelie's voice softened. "All I can remember is what happened the last time I left you in the shop alone."

Juliette's scowl faded. "And what about you, Amelie? Who's to see that you're safe with Captain Fairbourne?"

"With Captain Fairbourne?" In spite of all her wishes to the contrary, Amelie felt her cheeks warm as she opened the door. Confound that insufferable man and that one miserable kiss for doing this to her!

"Of course I shall be safe, Julie. I mean only to return his money and explain to him again that we do not welcome his attentions, and then home I'll come."

"Directly?" Juliette's eyes were anxious, begging silently for reassurance.

"Directly," said Amelie firmly. Despite Juliette's protests, there were still times when when she felt more like her mother than her older sister. "And don't fuss over dinner, not when we've so much seaming to do. I'll fetch us something from the cookshop on my way home."

"None of Mrs. O'Dunfree's old halibut pie, not in this heat." But Juliette's smile, the smile that was always as bright and predictable as the sunrise, this time faltered. "Be careful, Amelie."

"I will," promised Amelie, "as long as you will, too."

But as she hurried down the steps of the shop, carefulness was not first in her thoughts: resentment was.

Resentment, and unhappiness, and an open disgust with herself so irritating that she could barely contain it as she hurried along Marlborough Street, the shaped heels of her shoes clacking a staccato across the paving stones to match her temper. It was bad enough that, by succeeding with the glazier where she herself had failed, Zach Fairbourne had bested her in her own neighborhood, her own little community of tradespeople and shopkeepers. He'd treated her like some fluttery little female, not the successful woman of business that, like Maman, she'd worked so hard to become.

But what was far worse, and far harder to put back to rights, was the way his meddling presence had come between her and Juliette. She'd never kept secrets from her sister, and she trusted that Juliette had never kept any from her. But how could she explain to Juliette something as foolish as what had happened in Richardson's garden? After a lifetime of living by Maman's cautious wisdom, how could she possibly confess she'd so blithely ignored it, for no better reasons than moonlight and a handsome face? She'd already lost her self-respect. Losing Juliette's as well was beyond imagining. But instead she'd taken the coward's path and said nothing, an omission that still seemed to carry the same dreadful burden of an out-and-out lie.

And all of it, all, was the fault of Zach Fairbourne. *Captain* Zachariah Fairbourne, thought Amelie crossly. May Neptune himself come claim the man's arrogant soul! Why couldn't Zachariah Fairbourne have conveniently disappeared off to sea like every other faithless sailor-man? Lord knew there were already so many of them in Boston that the loss of one would be a blessing.

With an impatient twitch of her skirts she crossed Dock Square to Ann Street. She'd never walked this way; she'd no reason to. She supposed the crowded, crooked lane had been called in honor of the last queen, but like the unfortunate war that had born her name as well, there seemed to Amelie to be precious little grandeur here to merit such a regal title. Ann Street was too close to the water to have ever been fashionable, and the houses and shops crowded so tightly together proved it: squat, sturdy buildings, most with their rough-hewn clapboarding left unpainted to silver in the salt air from the sea, and most, too, with old-fashioned diamond-paned windows that swung outward to open, a sharp-edged hazard to unwary passersby.

Through these windows drifted the mingled scents of woodsmoke from a score of hearths, of well-browned cornbread, simmering onions and codfish, or a slice of salt pork sizzling in an iron skillet, for so late in the afternoon every goodwife was busying herself with the meal that would welcome her husband home. Fretful babies cried, a sleepy dog growled a warning, older children squabbled, and restless apprentices grumbled as they hauled one more heavy bucket of water for their masters from the common well in the square.

But as she walked further, the nature of the street began to change, and it was clear that the evenings here would not be as innocent. While most respectable tradesmen would use the long summer daylight to work until dark, sailors on leave from their ships were already beginning to straggle up from the wharves to the taverns and smaller rumshops. They were eager for amusement, ripe for excitement, and Amelie hurried her steps to avoid them as best she could, keeping her gaze resolutely ahead. But alas, no matter how much she strived to look stern and unapproachable, the mere fact that she walked alone was encouragement enough.

"Ah, lovey, give me a smile!" called one man with a greasy queue hanging clear to his waist. "Come share a pot o' ale with me, an' I swear I'll make you smile a-plenty!"

"Come with *me*, my pretty," leered his companion, another sailor in a short patched jacket, "and I'll make you a special gift o' what I've got hard an' hot in my breeches!"

Practically running now, she flushed as their coarse guffaws echoed behind her. Ordinarily she could ignore this sort of attention—an unmarried female in a town with so many sailors, apprentices, and soldiers had no choice if she wished to go out-of-doors—but because of the threatening note she seemed to have lost all her courage. She knew she was skittering like a frightened rabbit, but she couldn't make herself stop. The whale-bone in her stays dug into her ribs, while beneath that her shift clung damply to her body and her hat ribbon marked a sticky groove beneath her chin.

She darted across the street again, desperate to leave the men behind, and to her great relief saw the hanging silver moon of the Crescent Inn before her. On so warm an afternoon, the door stood open, and thankfully Amelie slipped inside.

After the bright bustle of the street, the inn's front room seemed mercifully cooler and calmer, and Amelie blinked as her eyes grew accustomed to the murky half-light. From what she could see, the inn seemed clean and neat enough, though considerably more modest than she'd expected for a Fairbourne.

"Them rogues from the wharves giving you trouble, miss?" asked a tall woman with a stiff-starched cap as she hurried forward, wiping her hands dry on a check-ered apron daubed with soapsuds. "I could hear them braying clear in the kitchen. Where's the watchman when a decent lady needs him, I ask you, miss? Still, still, no use in asking a question like that, seeing as we both know the answer."

Amelie smiled wanly, unwilling to admit how unsettled she'd been by the men in the street. Somehow she doubted the watch ever bothered overmuch with this neighborhood. From the taproom to the rear came enough noise to prove that there was already a good share of other rogues here at the Crescent, too.

"Sarah Isham, miss, your servant." The woman nodded, more with approval than in deference as she quickly surveyed Amelie. Anyone who claimed that dress did not matter had never been appraised by the keeper of a respectable tavern or inn; as humble as the

Crescent might appear, Amelie was willing to wager that the inn's mistress could tell the good-quality Indian muslin that she wore from the gaudy sort sold to strumpets more swiftly—and more accurately—than many of her own regular customers.

"Now you just sit here so long as you please, miss," continued Mrs. Isham soothingly as she tried to usher Amelie into a smaller room to the left of the hall, "until them braying jackasses pass by. Might I bring you a pot of tea to sip, or a taste of buttermilk?"

Amelie shook her head, and refused the chair in the tiny parlor as well. Such a sympathetic invitation was tempting, but she was determined to make this fool's errand as brief as possible.

"Thank you, but no. I've come here only to speak with a guest of yours, Captain Fairbourne. Captain Zachariah Fairbourne, that is."

"Oh, aye, and is there any other in this house?" The woman smiled with such undiluted warmth that she was almost doting: another eager victim of Zachariah Fairbourne's charm. "The finest young gentleman to follow the sea that I know, Miss, ah . . . ?"

"Miss Lacroix," said Amelie belatedly. "Of Marlborough Street."

"Miss Lacroix?" Mrs. Isham studied her again with undisguised suspicion, all of the goodwill gained by her genteel dress lost in an instant. "French, are you?"

Amelie stiffened. Of course she'd heard this before, but it never did grow any less offensive. "My parents were French, but I was born here in Boston."

Mrs. Isham sniffed as if she'd smelled milk that had soured. "Then you're like as not the same Miss Lacroix what sent the boy with a package to the captain this morning?"

Amelie nodded, wondering why his landlady felt the need to be so protective of her guests. "He is, I am sure, expecting me, if you will but tell him I am here."

At least this was most likely true. Why else would he have paid the glazier's bill unless he expected to be thanked for it?

But Mrs. Isham was of a different opinion.

"I am sorry, Miss Lacroix," she said sternly, pursing her lips in a way that showed she did not quite approve of women—*French* women at that—having packages delivered to gentlemen in her care, "but if you were expecting him to be expecting you, well then, you must expect to be disappointed, and so you shall. Captain Fairbourne is engaged in business at Heward's Yard, nor do I *expect* him before nightfall."

"It is on business that I wish to speak with him as well," said Amelie firmly. She was not about to let herself be scorned or outplayed by some Ann Street barmaid, especially not for the sake of Zachariah Fairbourne. "Now, if you please, I would like—"

"Mademoiselle Lacroix!"

He was always coming up behind her, always with the advantage of surprising her, and now, though her heart was pounding with unruly expectation, she silently counted to ten—in French—before she turned to face him.

And oh, how glad she was then that she'd taken those ten moments to compose herself!

He was standing in the open doorway, filling it, the slanting sun of late afternoon giving him a golden nimbus that he did not need. He was already too glowing, too vibrant on his own, with the kind of undeniable presence that made people behind in the street pause to watch, and Sarah Isham stand open-mouthed with admiration.

If a gentleman, like a lady, was to be judged by his dress, the way that Amelie believed, then from what he wore now Zach Fairbourne would have been nothing of consequence in the eyes of the world. He was outfitted like any other waterfront laborer in a red-and-white checked linen shirt with the neck open and the sleeves rolled carelessly to his elbows, a faded bandana knotted loosely at his throat; a worn, dark-red waistcoat, unbuttoned and flapping open, the pockets bulging fat with scraps of scribbled notes and bits of wood and twine; patched linsey-woolsey breeches with the knees unbuckled for ease. Sometime during the day he'd tied his black hair back haphazardly with a frayed length of purplish ribbon, doubtless fished from one of those same bulging pockets.

Yet instead of demeaning Zachariah Fairbourne, these workman's clothes somehow managed to magnify him. The shoved-back shirt sleeves revealed the strength of his sun-browned hands and forearms, and the unbuttoned waistcoat proved that the width of his shoulders and chest owed nothing to artful padding or hidden whalebone. These rough, homespun clothes emphasized his ruggedness in a way that no well-tailored silk suit ever could, and conversely would make that gentleman's silk suit seem like a self-conscious, studied bit of pure foppery. Clearly he was a man who cared more about directing his purpose in life than dressing for it, and a man who didn't care a fig for anyone else's opinion to the contrary.

Dangerous thoughts for a mantua-maker to have, Amelie told herself sternly, at least one who prized her livelihood. Yet still they filled her mind as surely as the man himself threatened to overwhelm her.

"Mademoiselle," he said again, his grin enough to make her—almost—smile automatically in return. His bow to her was swift, scarce more than a nod, a hasty acknowledgment to formality overrun by his natural impulsiveness as he came to stand looming over her. "Amelie. How happy I am to see you again!"

"I have come to you on business, Captain Fairbourne," she said, her voice sounding foolishly stilted and tinny even to her own ears. How she wished he wouldn't use her given name, his voice somehow turning it into a misplaced endearment. "Pray do not convince yourself that it's otherwise."

"Oh, aye, business." He folded his arms over his chest and drew his black brows together, all mock seriousness. "You have brought my little package from this morning yourself, then?"

"I have not," she said, more indignantly defensive than she'd intended. "That was brought here hours ago. I do not keep my customers waiting for their goods, Captain."

Mrs. Isham edged forward, laying her hand upon his sleeve. "I tried to tell her you were occupied, Zachariah, but she wouldn't hear it."

Amelie didn't miss that too familiar "Zachariah," even if it came from a woman old enough to be his mother. Older, even. Had the man no shame at all?

"I came to speak to you, Captain," she said, "on an important matter. A most urgent, important matter."

Mrs. Isham made a scolding murmur of distrust in her throat. "Desperate to see you, she was, Zachariah. But haven't I seen how them chits are with you before?"

"But Miss Lacroix isn't like the others, Mrs. I," he said softly, his gaze excluding everyone except Amelie. "Surely you can see that. Miss Lacroix is only like herself. If she says she must see me on an urgent matter, then she shall. Come, lass, we can go somewhere quieter where we can—"

"No, thank you," she said quickly, barely shifting away from his guiding fingertips as they reached for her arm. But she couldn't let him touch her again, for fear of what mischief he'd cause this time. She hadn't forgotten how he'd pulled her in like a fish flopping on a hook and line this morning, and she wasn't about to let him befuddle her like that again. "That is, Captain, I will not trouble you long."

She dug her hand into her pocket, drawing out a small handful of coins that she then held to him in her open palm. "I've come to settle my debt, you see. I can't allow you to pay my accounts. Here, now you must let me give you what you gave to Mr. Swinley."

He frowned, bending to stir the coins in her hand with one finger while she prayed he wouldn't notice how damp her palm had instantly become at his touch.

"You want me to take this?" he asked. "Because you cannot accept my help?"

"I can't accept your *money*," she corrected, raising her open hand a little higher in encouragement. "Consider what would be said of me if I did! Now here, take what I owe you, so we may be even."

He looked up at her over the coins, his eyes an even brighter blue than she remembered, and a good deal more predatory, too. "But you would have me take money from you?"

"Of course," she said uneasily. "Why not, when I owe it to you?"

"Why not?" He straightened, clasping his hands behind his back as if to remove them from temptation. "Because I cannot take it, that's why not. What decent man is going to accept money from a woman? Especially such a young and very pretty one?"

She felt her cheeks grow hot, not so much from his compliment but from the uncomfortable position he'd somehow led her into, standing in the very public doorway of an inn. "I suppose you were being—simply being kind to Juliette and me. Yes, kind. That must have been it. But now you must let me pay you back."

"For my kindness?" He smiled wryly, and gently folded her fingers over the coins in her hand. "You've said enough, Amelie. Now keep your coins, and this matter with them, to yourself, mind?"

"Your poor mam would never forgive you such a sin, Zachariah," said Mrs. Isham, scandalized. "Taking money from some French strumpet and her sister in exchange for your *kindness!*"

He shrugged. "There now, Amelie. You see how it is."

"But what am *I* to do with your money?"

"If you don't wish to keep it yourself?"

"I can't!" she cried with frustration. "For heaven's sake, that's the entire reason I've come to return it to you!"

"Well, then," he said slowly, considering. "Perhaps you could give it to Mrs. I here, and have her make up some sort of dinner basket for me. That's why I came back here in the first place, for something to bring back to the yard with me. But I don't think anyone would look amiss at me for taking dinner from you."

"Very well." Hurriedly she turned to the older

woman, handing her the loathsome coins. "Please prepare dinner for Captain Fairbourne, to that amount."

Mrs. Isham glanced suspiciously from her to Zach and back again, but still she took the money. "Aye, miss," she said, almost reluctantly, before she left for the kitchen. "As you please."

"Enough for both the lady and me, Mrs. I!" called Zach, but when Amelie gasped and began to protest, he rested two fingers lightly over her lips. "Hush, now, hush, and let her go."

She jerked away from his hand as if she'd been burned—which, in an inexplicable way, she almost felt as if she had.

"But you've tricked me!" she fumed. "You don't care about being called a—a male trollop! From the beginning, all you wanted was to have your own way!"

"What I wished was for Sarah Isham to leave us alone together to talk," he explained patiently, "which she wasn't about to do until she was given a reason to go that she couldn't ignore. And which you, quite conveniently, have provided."

"Why didn't you simply send her away?" said Amelie rebelliously. Her lips still tingled from the half-second when he'd touched them, her own mouth betraying her. "Why make me party to more of your foolishness?"

He smiled in a way that made her wonder if that sense of betrayal somehow showed on her face. "Sarah Isham is my mother's oldest, truest friend, and I could no more send her away than I could my own mam. If in turn she guards me as jealously as dog with a favorite bone, well then, I can find no fault her for that, for I know she acts on my mother's behalf."

"Oh," said Amelie. There wasn't much else to say except to apologize for having made such a horribly wrong assumption about him and Sarah Isham, and she wasn't about to do that. She remembered how much he valued loyalty, and apparently practiced it, too, in a way that surprised her. "I see."

"Then perhaps you can also see your way to telling me how exactly that back window of yours was broken."

"I told you before, it was an accident," she said automatically. "Not that it is any of your affair."

"What kind of accident broke your window seven feet above the alley? Did you accidentally hop up that high from the path and tap it with your thimble?"

"I don't have to explain anything to you." Her heart racing, she turned to leave, but he caught her arm and gently drew her back. He smelled of pine shavings and sea salt, the summer sun and hempen rope, and other, more complex things that seemed intuitively, mysteriously male. She refused to lift her gaze to meet his, but instead found herself staring at the dark hair that curled just below the hollow in his throat, a peculiarly interesting place she'd never noticed on any man before.

"You don't *have* to do anything," he said softly. "But I wish to God for your own sake you would tell me how it happened so I can help you. I know the window broke from the outside in; I could see that much for myself, and besides, there was no broken glass in the alley. And you *are* in some brew of trouble, Amelie, aren't you?"

"I am fine." She jerked her arm free, furiously rubbing the spot above her elbow where he'd held her. It wasn't that he'd hurt her arm—he'd taken care not to hold her that tightly—but that she needed to reassure herself that she was as wholly fine as she claimed.

"That is the other reason I've come, to tell you to stop meddling in my life. I am not in any sort of 'brew,' as you call it, leastways nothing that I cannot sort out for myself."

"Then what about that pretty little sister of yours?" he demanded. "Is she fine as well?"

"Of course she is," answered Amelie, though as soon as she'd spoken she caught herself wondering if it were true. She prayed it was, and the desperation of that silent prayer slipped out in her next question. "Why would anyone wish to frighten Juliette that way?"

"I never said they did, lass." He paused, watching her closely, his smile turning grim. "But you could tell me, couldn't you?"

"Here's your dinner, Zachariah," interrupted Mrs. Isham as she returned, using both hands to carry a large willow-basket covered with a blue cloth. "Mind you bring back my basket, too, else you'll get no breakfast."

Grudgingly she glanced at Amelie. "There's enough for you, too, miss, seeing as you paid for it. But if you do tarry, make sure Zach sees you home. I don't want you coming to any harm alone in the streets."

"Ah, Mrs. I," said Zach with a theatrical sigh as he struck his fist to his chest with an actor's broad emphasis. "How little you must think of my gallantry, that I'd let the lady wander about Boston unattended!"

Yet when he looked back to Amelie, he wasn't teasing. The shadows had lengthened just enough to make his face all contrasts, harsh darks and lights that could hide so much. She couldn't tell if he felt as agitated as she did, or if, standing there with his fist still pressed over his heart, he, too, had been left with more questions than answers.

Not that she'd learn it now. All he was willing to give away was a noncommittal sigh.

"Unless, that is," he said, his gaze intent on her, "unless the lady would prefer to be alone."

Amelie swallowed, her thoughts in turmoil. When he'd been dressed like a gentleman at the Richardsons' house, it had been easier to trust him. She wasn't nearly as sure now. But when she thought of facing the street outside as the sun faded, of walking past the men who would have grown even more boisterous and menacing as the evening began, and thought, too, of her sister waiting for her alone at home, she realized she'd already made up her mind.

"Thank you, captain, yes," she said as formally as she could, striving to regain the distance between them. "Thank you. I will accept your company, but I prefer to take my dinner at home with my sister."

She'd prepared herself for him to be angry, or at least to try to convince her otherwise. But instead all he did was nod, his expression and mood unreadable, and hold his arm out for her to take.

"Whatever you wish, lass," he said. "Whatever you wish."

4

"I never seen ochre-yellow on the sides o' any deep-water vessel," said Heward querulously. "Leastways not on any vessel a-comin' out o' my yard."

"Then who's to say this one won't be the first?" said Zach as patiently as he could. He thought all this business about paint had been settled last week, and though he didn't want to upset Mr. Heward, the shipyard's owner and masterbuilder, enough to delay his ship's launching, neither did Zach want to waste any of his own time disagreeing for the misguided sport of it.

Especially not now. He looked over Heward's white head, across the yard to where Amelie Lacroix stood. A shipyard was no place for a neatly dressed woman, as she herself had been quick to inform him. At least the workers had gathered their tools and left for the day, so she wouldn't be bothered by them. The yard sat on the edge of the bay, a trampled wallow of muddy sand, sawdust, and drips of black tar and paint, and he hadn't been surprised that she'd preferred to stay closer to the street, waiting on one of the warped planks that were laid across the ground as a makeshift bridge for walking. In the fading light, she looked like some pretty little bird balanced on her perch, her pale muslin gown over layers of petticoats swaying gently about her like well-feathered wings.

A pretty little bird, and a disgruntled one, too. Even from this distance, he could tell that from the irately exaggerated angle of her wide-brimmed hat and the stern way her hands were folded at her waist. She'd made it perfectly clear that they should have gone straight back to her shop instead of coming back here, where he'd this last stray bit of business to settle with Heward, and he suspected that she was keeping to the plank and away from him as much from pique as from fear of soiling her peach-colored shoes.

But while she wasn't happy, he was. When he'd wakened this morning, he would have sworn he'd never see her again, and yet since then he'd seen her not once, but twice. The first time he'd found her by accident, but the second she'd come looking for him. She'd had an excuse, of course, that folderol about returning his money. A woman as concerned with being proper as this one would need it.

But once she'd been there with him, crowded into the Crescent's tiny entry, the excuses didn't matter. She'd come to him, and as soon as he'd seen her he'd felt the same odd, overwhelming interest in her that he'd felt that first night in the garden. It was a desire that went well beyond mere carnal temptation, though that was definitely there, too, especially whenever she licked her little tongue across her pouty, top-heavy lips from vexation. It was more complicated than that, tied up with an odd need to know and understand everything about her. He wanted to help her, and he wanted to be worthy of the trust she'd placed in him.

He didn't know why he felt this way, or what she'd done to inspire it. He didn't know how long it would last, either. But discovering the answers with Amelie Lacroix was going to make an enjoyable entertainment indeed for his time here in Boston.

"Lamp black or deep red, now, those I can see," Heward droned on. "Those be decent, fitting colors on the sides of a vessel. But to go making a piebald mess o' her sides just for the sake o' being different, well now, that don't seem right."

But Zach wasn't listening, not really. Instead he was watching how the breeze from the water ruffled Amelie's petticoats around her neat, white-stockinged ankles, how the gathered pouf of ribbons at the back of her waist suggestively called attention to her bottom, hidden somewhere beneath all those petticoats. It hadn't taken Mrs. Isham to tell him that Amelie would need someone to take her home; women this pretty had no business wandering about this part of town after dark. How could he possibly let her run that sort of risk? And how could he pass by the chance to walk with her alone again with only the moonlight for company?

"An ochre strip along the wales, now, that might be agreeable," Heward was saying. "But nothing more, Captain Fairbourne, nothing beyond that."

She tapped her fingers restlessly together, staring out across the water, until she turned away from the bay and from Zach with an abruptness that made the board walkway shake and shudder beneath her feet. With her arms outstretched for balance, she lurched to one side, then overcompensated and jerked to the other as she clumsily began to make her way up the shimmying board toward the street.

"Where the hell is she going, anyway?" he muttered, watching her. "Didn't I tell her to stay where she was?"

But what he'd told her didn't seem to carry much weight, for she seemed determined, however awkwardly, to leave him.

Abandoning Heward in the middle of his lecture, Zach jumped from the overlook where they'd stood. In a handful of strides he was behind Amelie, who was still wobbling purposefully ahead. She'd bunched her petticoats in one hand to lift them clear of the mud, high enough that he could see she'd tiny pink diamond-shaped clocks on her white stockings, rising up across her ankle-bone to follow the curve of her calf. He'd never seen stockings like them before, or a female leg that began with such a pleasing shape to it.

She must have sensed all this admiration, or perhaps she'd only felt his footfall behind her on the plank they shared. But when she turned about to confront him, she stopped concentrating on her precarious balance and began to topple.

Instantly, without a thought, Zach reached out to steady her, his hands settling on either side of her waist. Fleetingly he considered how narrow that waist was, and how rigidly contained, too, thanks to the stitched rows of whalebone in her stays. But below, below the lacing and under the petticoats, she'd be soft, yielding, warm . . .

"Hoist 'em higher, my own honey-sweet!" called a man to the hooting appreciation of his friends, sprawled beside him on the bench before the tavern across the street. "Show us what you've got abast your garters!"

With a muffled gasp of outrage, Amelie dropped her bunched skirts as swiftly as a curtain falling.

"Steady, now, sweetheart, steady," said Zach, realizing how fortunate he was that she hadn't turned fast or far enough to catch him ogling those pink-clocked stockings of hers himself. "Don't pay them any heed."

"Hell, let the little chit go," called the man on the bench again. "Don't spoil the entertainment for the rest o' us."

"I am not a chit," sputtered Amelie as she tried to twist around to see his face. "You tell them! You're supposed to be a captain, a master. You make them listen!"

He barely swallowed his amusement, and the laughter that rose with it, in time.

"Shove off, now, lads," he called back, though that suppressed amusement took all the teeth from his order. "The lady is with me."

"Don't call me that, either," she said indignantly, wriggling with irritation in his grasp. "Can't they see for themselves that I'm not one of their usual waterfront trollops?"

As easily as if she were a doll, he lifted and turned her around on the plank so she faced him. He raised his hands from her waist, and at once she backed away—not far, only a step or two, so she wouldn't risk falling again, but far enough to make it clear she wasn't pleased.

"Look at me," she ordered, flicking her hands across her petticoats for emphasis. "Am I not dressed with perfect propriety? Is there anything in my attire to merit that—that kind of commentary?"

He looked as she'd ordered, frowning a bit from the effort of keeping the truth from his face. Taken piece by piece, the hat and the bodice and the petticoats and the heeled slippers and even those wondrous stockings, he supposed she *was* dressed with perfect propriety. Her bosom was well-covered, her hem stitched to a modest length. She would know what was proper, just as she likely knew the cost of every one of those pieces. Such conviction, and such knowledge, were her trade.

But no matter how many of those perfectly proper those articles might look on their own, the combined effect upon her person was entirely different. Perhaps it was because of her French blood. Zach had seen his share of Boston ladies: docile, bland creatures like John Richardson's daughters, silent women who glided through rooms with their eyes meekly downcast. Such proper women could never wear these clothes of Amelie's with anything like her natural ebullience and flair, or give each flick of the pale muslin the kind of unconsciously flirtatious swish that made it impossible for men to ignore her.

How could he fault those men on the bench outside the tavern? He felt the same way. She didn't look like a rich Boston gentleman's well-bred daughter; she looked like that rich man's mistress.

"What I see," he said finally, "is a comely young woman who hasn't the least notion of how to dress for a shipyard."

"As if I should know what *that* would be," she said, fortunately accepting his diplomatic answer for a literal one. "A bonnet made from wood-shavings, glossed with tar, and crowned with a curled gull's feather and a crest of quahog shells? A mantua sewn from bleached sailcloth, trimmed with tuffets of frayed hempen rope and sand dollars?"

Strange how when she described such a ludicrous image, he could almost picture it. "You could start a new fashion."

"More likely I'd lose what custom I have."

Behind her the man at the tavern called to her again, his suggestion this time more openly lewd.

"Vile man," she said, looking down with embarrassment. 'Tis not even dark, yet clearly he is already drunk."

"And darkness makes it more acceptable?"

She shook her head. "Decent men work with the sun. But sailors like those men seem to be at liberty to drink spirits and destroy the town's peace whenever they please."

"Sailors don't follow landsmen's time, lass," explained Zach. "Those men could have been working hard for a day and a night at sea, risking their lives without rest or small pleasures, before their captain granted them leave. A year may have passed since they last cleared their home port, if they have a place they call home at all."

"Loneliness is no excuse for drunkenness."

"Nor is strong drink a weakness that all sailors share."

Surprised, she raised her gaze beneath her hat's brim, her eyes shadowed beneath her lashes. "You would defend them, then?"

"No," he said, "especially not when they put you at risk. But I can understand the reasons why they act the way they do." He held his hand out to her. "Now come, there's something I wish to show you before we leave, or ask you, really."

"I shouldn't." Skittishly she glanced back over her shoulder, toward the town and away from him, rubbing one hand along her upper arm. He wondered what she'd felt when he'd held her waist, if his touch had been as tantalizing to her that it had to him. "I must go home. I'm already later than I should be, and I don't want my sister worrying."

"But you can't go alone."

"No." This time when she glanced back over her shoulder it was toward the tavern across the street. "But I did not think your offer would be withdrawn."

"It hasn't." He kept his hand outstretched in invitation. "All I'm doing is seeking your opinion before the light is entirely gone. It's a question of color, of fashion, and surely the most fashionable mantua-maker in the colony must have an opinion."

She hesitated, wavering, before finally slipping her hand into the crook of his arm.

"Only for a moment," she said warily, "and only for this opinion that you seek. Your sailors are not the only ones who must toil after nightfall, you know. And only as long as you do not expect me to jump from any more windows."

He laughed, patting her fingers, and began to lead her toward the hull of the unfinished ship at the water's edge. He hadn't expected her to agree, but now, with her hand tucked against his sleeve, he realized how glad he was that she had. When he stopped by the overlook to retrieve Mrs. Isham's dinner basket, he saw that Heward had disappeared, doubtless still disgruntled, leaving them with the shipyard to themselves. For that Zach was glad, too, because he could say whatever he pleased to her without risk of being overheard.

The sun had begun to slip down behind the church spires and the hills to the west, while the hazy summer dusk was already falling over the bay. The water had taken on that late-day glassiness, so smooth that the few small boats that crossed it left long, V-shaped wakes trailing behind them. The deep-water ships that lay farther out at their moorings were dark, angular shadows against the greying sky, with pinpricks of light to mark their lanterns. A handful of gulls wheeled and mewed overhead, while fiddles and off-key singing drifted out through the warm air from the taverns and rumshops.

"Is this your new boat?" asked Amelie, her voice full of misgivings as she stared up at the mastless hull, held upright by a forest of rough-hewn brackets and supports, looming before them on the sand.

Zach smiled wryly. He knew he shouldn't expect her to view it with the same loving affection that he did himself, but he still felt the protective inclinations of a mother toward an ungainly child.

"First of all, it's not a boat," he began. "It's a ship, more specifically a two-masted sloop. And, alas, she's not mine, but my cousin Joshua's."

She was leaning her head back so far to look that she'd placed her hand on the crown of her hat to keep it from sliding off. "But you're the captain. How can it not belong to you?"

"This is my first command, lass. Just because I'm qualified to be a shipmaster doesn't mean I'm prosperous enough to be her owner, too. Few captains are, these days."

She glanced at him suspiciously, her head still tipped back, and the first time this afternoon he'd seen her face without the hat's brim to shield it. "Don't tell me you're a pauper. You're a Fairbourne."

"I'm a Fairbourne, aye, but not one of the Appledore clan from the Cape." He sighed balefully. "My mother keeps the ordinary at the ferry in Westham, a tiny flyspeck to the north of Marblehead. I'm but a poor backcountry cousin that Joshua and Samson have taken under their more finely feathered wings."

"Well now, that's hardly anything to be ashamed of," she said stoutly. "To be a captain at your age is a very excellent thing. I should think you'd be more proud to have made your way on your own merits, than to have grown fat only on your father's gold."

"That wasn't much of a possibility." He squatted down to open the dinner basket, hoping she wouldn't be able to see how ridiculously happy her defense had made him. He owed a great deal to his older cousin Joshua for taking a chance on him—a great deal indeed—but he also knew how he'd had to work doubly hard to prove himself worthy of Joshua's trust, and to make him forget the bad blood that had simmered long ago between their fathers. Of course Amelie Lacroix would know none of this convoluted family history, but the fact that she did recognize his own accomplishment was a rare and welcome compliment anyway.

"So this is your, ah, your ship," she said, musing. "It would seem that it will be a good deal longer than a month before it is ready to sail."

"Oh, a month is more than sufficient." He rose, brandishing a roasted turkey leg. "She's almost ready for launching now. Then, once she floats, we'll step the masts and rig her out, fill her hold, and off she'll sail. Some turkey for you, or cornbread?"

"No, thank you. I promised my sister I'd dine with her." She sighed, as if the mention of her sister had been a reminder she'd rather not have had. "Now what is this opinion you seek of me?"

"A matter of paint." He swept the turkey leg grandly through the air to indicate the ship's length. "I am weary of the same sad colors that custom dictates for a vessel. Though I am considered a madman for suggesting it, I believe that an ochre stripe there, along the wales, would show most handsomely above a green and black hull. Now what say you to that, mademoiselle?"

"Not black, but blue," she said firmly, without the least hesitation. "The deepest, richest blue you can find, as close to a midnight sky without being ebony itself. And not ochre. Definitely not ochre, the color of Indian-squash and dirt, not for your pretty ship! She must fly, Captain, and to fly she must be colored like a dream: that midnight blue striped with the palest silver-white, like a new crescent moon, fresh and fair and full of promise. That is how your lady-ship must be painted, Captain, in those colors precisely."

He didn't answer at first, taking a contemplative bite from the turkey leg. What could he say? He'd sought her opinion, true, but more on a whim, a bit of well-intended flattery calculated to make her linger. He'd never expected to hear his ship, his precious new sloop, described with the same lush, lavish precision she'd use to conjure a new gown to one of her ladies.

But that wasn't the worst of it. *That* came when he realized her suggestion made sense. If he wanted his sloop to stand out from all others, the way he claimed, then he shouldn't fuss around with green paint or ochre, but commission Heward to mix the colors Amelie described. There wouldn't be another ship like her in any port.

He squinted up at the ship, striving to visualize the bare, waiting wood painted as Amelie described. The only time he'd kissed her, she'd glowed with moonlight herself. If he striped the sloop the way she wanted, every time he'd look at the sides he'd think of that kiss.

Which, despite her protests, could well be exactly what she wanted. Not that he needed any more reminding, not with her turning her face up to the sky one more time beside him.

His squint deepened to a scowl as he struggled to control his unruly thoughts. "Like a new moon, you say?"

"Yes." She nodded, a quick, precise little duck of her chin. "A mere silver sliver."

He glanced at her sideways, pretending to scold her by shaking the turkey leg. "Are you trying to set new fashions here on the wharfs as well as on Marlborough Street?"

"That's not my meaning at all," she said with an impatient flutter of her hand. "If I use all my art to dress a plain woman well, if I can make a gown that makes her feel beautiful, then she will *be* beautiful."

She raised her chin high and took one graceful spinning step backward, arching her back and circling her arms with her wrists and finger precisely cocked, as if demonstrating a delicious new dance from London. If any of those men on the tavern bench could see her now, Zach knew he'd have to fight them off with a pistol.

"You see," she continued, "if a woman can feel that beauty in her heart, then it will show in her face, her carriage, until the world believes it, too."

"But you *are* beautiful," he protested. "And I don't

see what the hell this has to do with painting my sloop."

"No, I'm not," she said with a triumphant smile. "I am altogether too dark for true beauty. My mouth is too full, and I've a great horrid bump on the bridge of my nose. But I've made you *believe* I am beautiful, which is most nearly the same thing. And so it will be with your ship. If you dress her to look fast and sleek, as if she could fly through the clouds as easily as water, then she will. She *will*."

He tried to smile in return. He couldn't tell which was making him more uncomfortable: her notion of "dressing" his sloop, or her claim that she wasn't beautiful. He'd never heard a woman say that about herself, especially one who so clearly *was*. It went against nature, somehow.

"Do not look so distressed, Captain," she said playfully. "You sailors have always believed the same. Why else would you give your ships such names as *Swiftsure*, and *Greyhound*, and *Speedwell?*"

"Not this one," said Zach quickly, relieved to be able to shift the conversation to more comprehensible matters. "Anabelle chose the name for this sloop, as a special favor from Joshua. At the launching she'll be christened *Diana*, after their daughter. Nothing about speed in that."

She glanced up at him skeptically, one brow raised in question. "Of course there is, Captain. And I venture Mrs. Fairbourne, being nobly born and schooled, knew perfectly well what she was suggesting. Diana may be her daughter's name, but it's also the name of the ancient goddess of the hunt, of chase and capture and evasion, too."

Zach cleared his throat, that earlier discomfort returning. It was common enough knowledge that the Fairbournes had made much of their fortune as privateers in the last war, capturing French ships for profit. But apparently it was also common knowledge—common enough for a French mantua-maker to know it, anyway—that Fairbourne ships had continued after the war to sail on the dubious side of the law, shifting from privateering to smuggling without pause. And Zach, as a new-minted Fairbourne captain, wouldn't be any different. Why else would the sloop be built with such sharp lines except for the speed that outrunning the customs officers required?

But to name the ship, *his* ship, so coyly after some pagan goddess of the hunt made him feel foolish and ignorant. He'd learned his letters from his mother, spelling out words from the Bible, the one book they'd owned, and along the way he'd picked up enough ciphering and calculation to be able to figure courses and keep his accounts. But he'd never had the kind of formal gentleman's schooling that could have taught him about heathen gods and goddesses, nor had he felt the lack. Not, at least, until now.

He threw what remained of the turkey leg into the water where it landed with a disconsolate *plop*. "Come, I'll take you home."

"Now? Without letting me go on top of your ship, Captain?" she asked, surprised and, to his own surprise, evidently disappointed, too. "I know that I'm already later than I should be, but—but I may never have another opportunity to visit a ship again, even one stuck in the sand without any sails."

For one long, moody moment he considered whether he wanted to do this or not. "I thought you didn't want to jump through any more windows."

"I don't see that I have to," she said, pointing to the ramp that the workmen used. "There seems to be a perfectly good walkway to the top floor."

"It's called a deck, not a floor. The main deck, or topsides." He sighed mightily. "Very well, then. Up you go, if you must."

"I must," she said sweetly, bunching her petticoats to one side so she could see where she was placing her feet as she began up the ramp. "Just as I must thank you for obliging me, however much it has so obviously pained you to agree."

He watched her scamper up the ramp, left behind, speechless and chagrined. He could do nothing now about the chagrin, but he certainly wasn't going to be left gawking by some impudent little seamstress. In a handful of long strides he was up the ramp and at her side, and ready with any number of clever retorts to her last remark. But as soon as he saw the expression on her face, he forgot his retorts and her remark and everything else in Boston that night.

"Look at the sky," she whispered in awe. "I never imagined the city could look like this!"

Zach had seen Boston from the deck of a ship—albeit on the water—so many times and in so many ways that he'd long ago lost count. But Amelie was right: this, this *was* different.

The sun had just disappeared behind the crest of Beacon Hill, leaving the signal tower a black arrow piercing the glow of the fading day, while on the lesser hilltops to the north the windmills sat idle, their fan-shaped blades like so many oversized flowers cut in sharp silhouette. Picked out, too, were the jumbled roofs and gables, spires and chimneys and cupolas of the city, a pattern of angles that twisted and turned to match the streets below. Far above the undersides of the scattered clouds were still streaked with orange, pink, crimson, vivid banners against the deeper violet of coming night. Behind them, over the water, the moon had already begun to rise, pale and luminous, and the first tiny pinpricks of stars glittered over their heads.

Impatiently Amelie tugged off her wide-brimmed hat to be able to better see the sky, letting the long ribbons trail in the breeze.

"Where Juliette and I live, at the shop, we can never see the setting sun, nor the rising one either, because of all the other buildings," she said as she turned in a slow circle, a little smile of blissful wonder on her upturned face. "How I wish I could capture the color of those clouds! I cannot even begin to give it a name. Not flame, nor peach, nor aurora, but all together, burnished into one, one I must remember always, just like this!"

He smiled at her side, her undisguised joy giving him more pleasure than she'd ever guess. He understood the rare beauty to be found in the sky and water, and understood, too, how rare it was that others could see it the same way.

"You have the soul of a poet, mademoiselle," he said softly. "Or perhaps the eye of a painter."

"A painter?" she scoffed, incredulous and amused. "A limner, daubed all over with colors and turpentine? What folly *that* would be for a woman!"

"But you do paint, in a way," he said, remembering the gown that the Richardson girl had worn. He'd never claimed an eye for fashionable dress, but the magic of that gown had been impossible even for him to ignore, or to forget. "No turpentine, true, but you do much the same with your ribbons and furbelows."

She nodded quickly, agreeing, her dark eyes bright with creative fervor. "Someday I will find a silk of this color, a watered moiré, and *la*, I shall make such a gown of this sunset!"

"Then you must come see it again when the sloop's afloat," he said impulsively. This was the way he remembered her from that first night in the garden, full of passion and unafraid to show it, and he would promise anything to keep her like this. "I'll take you out into the bay if you wish, away from the city to the open sea. Then you'll see what a sunset can truly be, and moonlight, too."

She turned toward him, tiny tendrils of dark hair dancing around her face, and he knew from the look in her eyes, soft as the summer evening itself, that she, too, was remembering the moonlit garden.

"Aye, I'll show you moonlight," he declared, flinging his arms out wide to encompass the entire night sky as he paced across the deck and back again. "I'll give you moonlight, Amelie, clear and bright and pure, without any landsmen's lanterns to steal its brilliance. That's the sort of moonlight you meant to see painted on this sloop, and the moonlight I mean to gather for you now!"

"You can't do that," she said, her voice breathy, low. "No one can gather moonlight, as if it were windfalls in an orchard."

"I could." He came to a stop directly before her, close enough to see that same moon doubly reflected in her eyes. "If you wish it, Amelie, I can."

He was certain, almost, that he could kiss her now, again, and she wouldn't stop him. But he wouldn't kiss her unless she wanted him as well, and he wasn't nearly as certain of that.

"You've only to ask," he murmured as he leaned closer to her. "You won't even have to say please."

Her smile wobbled. "Moonlight belongs to her, too, you know."

"Amelie," he whispered as he threaded his fingers through her hair, cupping her cheek in the palm of his hand to steady her. "What in blazes are you talking about?"

"Diana." She swallowed so hard she gulped; he could feel it against his hand. "She was the goddess of the hunt, true, but she was also the goddess of the moon."

He smiled, oddly reassured. Perhaps Anabelle had named his sloop more fortuitously than he'd first realized.

"Then you *will* come sail her with me," he said, slanting his face over hers. "Who would deny a goddess, eh?"

But before he could stop her, she'd twisted free, another graceful dance of a movement that left him aching with loss. He held out his hand, more in welcome than to pull her back, but she shook her head. She stood just beyond his reach, her hands clasped tightly together with the knotted ribbons of her hat looped over her wrist.

"She—Diana—is goddess of the hunt, and of moonlight, too," she said, her voice so sternly miserable that with any other woman there'd be tears on her cheeks as well. "But she's also a chaste goddess, one who never let herself be distracted by any man, mortal or divine, for fear she'd lose her powers. And so, Captain, I must be like her."

"But Amelie—"

"You mustn't call me that," she said with a little shake of her shoulders. "And you must not try to persuade me otherwise. It's my fault, of course. I should have insisted on leaving directly from the Crescent, and not—not made myself so agreeable to you. At least I am fairly certain that neither Mrs. Clarke nor Mrs. Cheseborough nor any other of my customers was here near the docks to watch."

She tried to smile again, and when she couldn't she pressed her hands over her mouth and closed her eyes until she could trust herself to speak again.

"Please, Amelie," he said gently. Although to take her in his arms would be the worst possible thing to do now, it might also be the best, and he kept his hands held out to her in case she made the choice he couldn't. "You—we—have done nothing wrong, not one blasted thing."

"For a man like you, no." She blinked her eyes open and this time she'd managed to compose herself enough that the sad smile held. "But for me, and my sister—oh, yes. No matter how I might wish it otherwise, I cannot change the world's ways. To sail with you on this sloop, to feel the wind on my face and waves rocking beneath my feet, to see that rare moonlight—all that would be unseemly and impossible for me. Most unseemly, but how wondrous, too."

Zach watched her walk away, her head bowed as she slowly made her way down the ramp to the beach, trailing her fingers along the rail. She wasn't running away again, not like the first time, but she didn't need to now, either.

He felt selfish and thick-witted, the worst kind of clodpate who can never do anything right around women. Hadn't he told her he'd protect her if she needed it, save her from whatever harm was threatening her?

And hadn't he just done exactly the opposite? His own mother toiled from dawn long past sunset as a tavernkeep and cook, and he'd seen for himself how hard it was for decent women to make an honorable living. If Amelie were to continue succeeding in her trade, she needed an impeccable reputation among the gentry that brought her the most custom.

But seeking him out at the Crescent to return his money, joining him to come to the shipyard, watching the sunset with him on a deserted ship after dark—any one of these would have been enough to irrevocably tarnish her good name. Yet still he'd insisted, thinking only of his own enjoyment and not giving a damn for all she'd had at stake. If this was helping her, then he'd sure as hell hate to see how he'd wish her ill.

Yet when he retrieved the dinner basket and joined her on the beach, he still had found no words of apology, and in silence they walked side by side through the darkening streets to her home. She was near enough that he could smell her scent, violets and lavender mingled, so close that her petticoats would brush against his leg. Yet in the ways that mattered most, they'd never been farther apart.

Most wondrous, he thought bitterly. Most bloody wondrous indeed.

❧ 5 ❧

"For once my sister did as I told her," said Amelie with relief as the shop came into sight. Though she and Zach had both taken extraordinary care not to touch one another as they'd walked from the dock, she had still skittishly shied closer to him whenever they'd passed a group of men, especially loud ones who'd been drinking. Though she hadn't been able to help it, it also hadn't really been necessary. The black mood that had settled over Zach as they'd left the yard showed not only on his face but in the very way he walked, and not even the most drunkenly ardent admirer would have dared cross him like this.

She tried to sound cheerful as she glanced over the shop. The front door was bolted tight and the shutters were latched over the darkened shop windows, while the only candlelight came from their private quarters upstairs.

"Locked up tight, as it should be," she said with approval. "At least tonight I'll know Juliette's safe."

"Tight as a drum," said Zach, the first words he'd

spoken since they'd left the shipyard. "But I wonder if your sister worries the same way about you."

"Perhaps not exactly the same way," admitted Amelie. She didn't know why she was telling this to him now, or, for that matter, why her steps had slowed as they drew closer to the shop across the street. "Juliette's younger, more headstrong, and though I would not call her careless, she doesn't always see risks the same way I do."

"Risks like me?"

She looked at him sharply, wondering if she'd misjudged him yet again. She'd trusted him this far, but it wasn't too late for him to prove her wrong. But even in the shadows of the street, his expression was both grim and carefully impassive, giving away nothing, and she sighed with frustration.

She knew she should simply thank him and say good night, and end this now, without making things any more complicated. Yet as little experience as she had with men, she still felt that she hadn't behaved honorably, if women were allowed to speak of honor in such matters. He was well entitled to this black humor. She had been too open in her enthusiasms, too free with her opinions. Small wonder he'd misunderstood her wishes. No, as she thought about it, he'd understood them perfectly well. She'd been the confused one, not him.

But why hadn't Maman ever warned her how hard it would be to be good?

"You are not so much a risk," she said carefully, "as a hazard."

He made a disgruntled snort. "I don't really understand the difference. Unless you're meaning to take out insurance against me as a threat to your livelihood, the way shipowners must to protect their cargos."

She relaxed a fraction. If he could make jests like this, then perhaps he wasn't as angry as she feared. "What wise and practical men those merchants must be. Though obviously men who have never met you."

"Not the way that you have, anyway." He touched three fingers to her shoulder. "Let's not keep your sister looking for her dinner."

"Wait." She stopped, swallowed, then spoke boldly, before she lost her nerve. "On the ship, on your sloop. You could have kissed me, but you didn't."

He let out his breath in a low whistle. "It wasn't from lack of desire, sweetheart, if that's what you're thinking."

"I don't know *what* I'm thinking, not about you!" she cried softly. "But why didn't you do it, when you had the chance? Why didn't you kiss me?"

"Why?" He dropped Mrs. Isham's dinner basket at his feet and reached out to cradle the side of her face in his hand again, the way he had on the ship, and she wondered wildly if he was going to kiss her now instead. She wanted him to; she knew that now. She was trembling, her heart hammering in her chest, and all he'd done was touch her face.

"Why?" he asked again, his voice raw with the same longing she suddenly recognized in herself. "Because, Miss Lacroix, to kiss you would be most unseemly. Very wondrous, aye, but most, most unseemly."

They both heard the scrape of the door's box-lock opening at the same time, and at the same time they separated with guilty haste to turn toward the sound. The front door to the Lacroix sisters' shop swung open, and a tall man stepped through it. The door opened wider, wide enough to show Juliette silhouetted, too, with a candlestick in her hand to light the man's way to the street. The man laughed at something she said, then leaned closer, into the circle of candlelight to kiss her cheek.

"That's Oliver Richardson," said Zach with a surprise that matched Amelie's own. "What in blazes is that milk-fed bastard doing here at this time of night? Buying garter ribbons?"

"I cannot say," murmured Amelie, her heart suddenly sick with uncertainty and worry for her sister. Everyone who dealt with fashionable Boston knew Oliver Richardson and his reputation as well. He was as much a roguish dandy as his father was piously severe, a spoiled young gentleman who spent gold nearly as fast as his father earned it. He had come to the shop a handful of times with his sister Deborah, an obviously disinterested bystander to her wedding. But now that Deborah was wed and gone from Boston, Amelie could think of no good reason for Oliver to be here in the shop, especially after the door should have been closed and Juliette alone. "I can't begin to guess why he's here."

"I can't, either," said Zach, his whole manner abruptly changed. He looked full of commanding self-assurance, the very picture of a captain despite his clothing, and eager to challenge the other man. But what startled Amelie was the way he also seemed primed to enjoy himself—and thoroughly—in the process. "He's one of the greatest asses in the colony."

"But what could a man like that want with Juliette?" asked Amelie, already suspecting the worst. Julie would be such easy prey for a man like Oliver Richardson! "Why must he bother with us?"

"Maybe we better go ask him," answered Zach promptly, "and ask him about that broken window of yours, too."

"No, wait, please," begged Amelie, seizing his sleeve to try to hold him back. As bad as it was to discover her sister alone with Oliver Richardson, the chance of a scandal would be infinitely worse if the watchman discovered a Richardson and a Fairbourne brawling in the street before the shop. "Oliver couldn't have broken the window! He was at his father's house that night, the same as we were!"

But Zach was already charging across the street, and all Amelie could do was grab the dinner basket that he'd left behind and hurry after him.

"Ah, Richardson!" he boomed with a heartiness that made Amelie wince. "What brings you here on this fine summer eve?"

Oliver turned slowly, unwilling to oblige anyone with haste, flicking the lace cuff back from his wrist. "Why, I believe it's a Fairbourne, isn't it?"

"It is," said Zach with an oddly cheerful menace, "though in return I won't bother to point out what sort of low jackadandy vermin you are."

"Oh, Zach, stop, please!" pleaded Amelie, already visualizing the end of her shop. Despite Oliver's lace cuffs and brocade waistcoat, he was a solidly built man, not half the mincing dandy he pretended to be, and she was horribly sure he'd welcome a scuffle as much as Zach. "Don't make trouble!"

Zach grinned wickedly at her, no reassurance at all. "I'm not making trouble, mademoiselle. I'm simply going to ask Mr. Richardson why he's here causing mischief in such a respectable house."

"He's not causing any mischief at all, Amelie," declared Juliette heatedly as she held the candlestick higher. "Mr. Richardson asked to enter to make a special purchase, and because his family is so partial to our house, I saw no harm."

Oliver raised his hand with affected grace. "Do not trouble yourself, Miss Lacroix. Since we've already said our farewells, I shall simply be on my way."

"A fine notion, Richardson," agreed Zach. "An excellent notion. Good evening to you both, mademoiselles. We'll leave you ladies to yourselves and both be on our way. *Now.*"

He bowed first to Amelie, then to Juliette, though he was careful to keep the other man always in sight. Left without a choice, Oliver did the same, backing away down one side of the street while Zach began down the other. To Amelie they looked for all the world like two distrustful mongrel male dogs, barely able to contain their growls. Except, of course, no dog would turn to wink and grin at her in bold-faced triumph the way that Zach now did, enough to make her gasp at his audacity.

But that was all she'd have to spare on him for now; now she was going to have to concentrate on her sister instead, a sister who had already flounced into the doorway with several of the choicest French words she was not supposed to know, let alone say.

"Juliette," she called firmly as she once again bolted the door. "I want to know exactly what Oliver Richardson was doing alone with you in our shop after dark."

"He is a friend, Amelie, no more nor less!"

"Oh, Julie, please do not lie to me!"

"As if you would ever believe any explanation I gave you!" retorted Juliette, the candle in her hand glimmering from the back room. "Besides, I wasn't walking about for all the world to see with some low-born sailor-man! Or have you conveniently forgotten that already as well?"

"Don't you talk like that, Juliette!" Angrily Amelie marched back down the hall after her, still lugging the abandoned dinner basket. "Oliver Richardson is a wealthy, worldly man who would think nothing of ruining you for the sport of it!"

"Oh, yes," fumed Juliette, "and *you* have done so much better with *your* Zachariah Fairbourne!"

"That is none—oh, Julie, what manner of foolishness is *this?*" She dropped the basket on the table to stare, appalled by the intimacy of the scene before her. The broad worktable had been cleared of fabric and thread and instead used for dining, with the remnants of a cold dinner still sitting on the plates: two plates, two forks and knives and glasses, two crumpled napkins, all in the coziest proximity.

"I wasn't going to starve waiting for you to come home." Juliette tossed her head and turned her back, instead climbing up the winding stairs to their bed-chamber, her heels clacking on the bare treads in angry haste.

"Julie, please—"

"And don't start telling me Maman wouldn't approve," shouted Juliette back over her shoulder, "because she wouldn't approve of *you*, either."

She was, of course, right, and furiously Amelie shoved the two chairs back to their places along the wall. As she cleared the table of the incriminating supper, she was so angry that the dishes shook in her hands, clattering against one another, so angry she could not begin to think of what to say next to Juliette, angry enough that she felt the rage eating at her from within, her stomach knotting and twisting in rebellion.

She threw open the back door for a breath of cooler air. She looked up at the patch of stars overhead, the sky squared off by their neighbor's roofs, and took a deep breath to calm herself, then another. She struggled to control her temper and think instead of better, happier ways to caution Juliette than by shouting. They'd never spoken to one another like that before, and she'd felt the peaceful foundation of her world shake with every ugly word. Yet not an hour past that same world had been filled with beauty and shared dreams and a tall man with blue eyes who'd made lovely, impulsive promises to her in the moonlight.

Strange how the same moon seemed so much less magical alone here on Marlborough Street . . .

It was then, shaking her head at her own misguided longings, that she lowered her gaze to the little patch of ground that was their kitchen garden.

Every nodding stalk of peppermint had been slashed to the ground, every onion yanked from the ground and crushed, every flat-topped cluster of yarrow torn up and broken. Even the spindly daisies that struggled to grow near the back fence had been snapped off, their little white petals torn and scattered. Everything had been destroyed, leveled, except for one lone garden stake thrust upright in the ground. On the jagged point of this stake was a note, a tattered scrap of paper with six words scrawled large enough for Amelie to read by the moonlight:

Leave Boston at once or suffer.
　　　　　　A Friend

But with a frightened little sob, Amelie realized it was already too late.

The sun had barely risen and the dew still clung like diamonds to the spider's web stretched beneath the eaves as Amelie dragged the wooden teeth of the rake through the limp green tangle of what had been her garden. Purposefully she gathered up the broken stems and withered leaves, the brown-stained petals and whatever else the robins and gulls hadn't already fought over, and dumped it all in a bucket for the scavenger-man to collect by their gate. Any other time, she would have thriftily saved the damaged plants to fertilize next year's herbs and plots, but now all she wished was to have them, and their memory, gone.

With each pass of the rake she strived to put her fear behind her. Dawn had made that easier, and work, hard work like this, made it easier still. Her hands sweated and itched inside the coarse leather garden gloves, but she couldn't risk her fingers becoming too scratched or roughened to work with fine silk and floss. Besides, there'd be plenty of time to change into her fashionable clothes before Juliette returned from the market, before they unshuttered their shop for the day. By then, too, she was determined to show the world—including whoever was threatening them—that nothing had changed at the Mademoiselles Lacroix.

"Wretched, stubborn root," she muttered as she pulled at a tenacious shoot. She'd bent her back into the task, determined to win, when she heard the rustle of the crushed shells on the path behind her. Instantly she spun to face the intruder, her heart racing as she clutched the rake in her hands like a soldier's pike.

But the intruder was remarkably unimpressed, even blasé. With a chirping good-morning mew, Luna trotted toward her, rubbing her plump gray sides against Amelie's oldest patched linen petticoats, now flecked with fur as well as leaves and twigs.

"Silly Luna girl," scolded Amelie softly as she crouched down and tugged off her gloves to stroke the cat, who in return butted her head into her mistress's hand to have her ears rubbed. "Didn't you find me the least tiny bit fierce?"

"I did," said Zach as he pushed the gate open with his fingertips, "even if the cat didn't. Good day to you, Amelie."

Amelie sighed, sitting further back on her heels with her arms around the purring cat. "Captain Fairbourne. Why am I not surprised to see you back here this morning?"

"Zach," he said as he came to join her. He was dressed with the same informality as yesterday, with the addition of a cocked straw hat that he now swept off in greeting. "I shall call you Amelie, Amelie, and you shall call me Zach. It's not difficult. You did it last night without much effort at all."

"I said a number of things last night that I shouldn't have."

"And a fair number of others that were well worth the saying." Tossing the hat lightly on his fingertips, he walked around her to peer down at the empty beds, their quahog-shell borders framing nothing now but churned dirt. "A bit early in the season for harvest, isn't it?"

"The work of some stray dog during the night," she

said quickly, telling the story that she and Juliette had agreed upon.

"In Boston?" he asked over his shoulder, openly and rather scornfully incredulous. "A town where dogs by law cannot exceed ten inches' height? All this digging and worrying was done by one of your tiny little Boston dogs, acting by his own tiny self?"

"I didn't see the dog and cannot vouch for his size," said Amelie defensively. Nor, unfortunately, had she or her sister considered this fault in their story. "I told you, it happened during the night. We were asleep."

"Now that is a pity." He prodded through the bucket of stems and leaves, selecting one to hold up to her. "For all that he was a mean-spirited and destructive little dog, he also must have been very accomplished. It would have been something to see, a dog using a knife to slash through a stalk like this. No wonder you challenged me with that fork."

She tried to look stern instead of smiling the way she wanted to at the ludicrous image of the tiny, knife-wielding dog. She wished both that she hadn't tried to dissemble to him, and that he in turn hadn't been quite so clever. "Why are you here, anyway?"

"Why?" he repeated, letting the question hang for a moment, unanswered and disturbing, before he dropped the incriminating stem back into the bucket. "Why, to collect my landlady's dinner basket, of course."

She hadn't realized she'd been holding her breath until then, when with relief she let it out. The imaginary knife-wielding dog was one thing; telling him the truth about the threatening note would be quite another.

"Mrs. Isham is a woman of her word," he was saying,

"and this morning she refused me breakfast because I'd forgotten her infernal basket—and my dinner—here last night. So by my reckoning that makes two meals you owe me now."

He was openly inviting himself to breakfast, with a beaming smile calculated to be refusal-proof. But this morning, Amelie found she didn't mind. She was still unnerved enough by what had happened last night that having Zach Fairbourne stay for breakfast seemed like one more way to help chase away her fears, and, though she was reluctant to confess this to Zach, his sizeable presence might make whoever was bothering her and Juliette think twice about doing it again. Even Maman might have been able to condone his visit for that reason.

Besides—and this she wouldn't even confess to herself—she also found she liked having him here for his own sake. He was making her smile, and after the ugly quarrel with her sister and finding the ruined garden, being able to smile was a welcome thing indeed.

"We don't keep much in our kitchen," she admitted apologetically. "In truth we don't even keep a proper kitchen at all, not with just the two of us, and especially not when it's so warm that things spoil in an instant. I cannot offer you a Mrs. Isham kind of breakfast. Coffee or tea and currant buns, too, if Julie hasn't eaten them all."

"Coffee will make it a feast," he said, his smile widening shamelessly as he bowed, then smoothed back his dark hair and resettled his hat on his head. "I'll want nothing more."

"As you wish." She wasn't the only one dissembling this morning. Likely in one morning he ate more than Juliette and she ate together in an entire week, but still she was touched by his willingness to pretend otherwise. "I'll fetch it out here directly."

Though she was smiling as she slipped through the door, she was also glad that he'd understood he was not to follow her inside. This was all new to her, exciting but unsettling. While of course she'd served gentlemen in the shop, husbands and fathers and uncles and brothers of female customers, she'd never entertained any gentleman in a private way like this, and the flustering nervousness she felt amazed her. It was also different from climbing aboard the *Diana* with Zach. Then, she'd been an outsider in his world, and now he was here visiting hers.

Swiftly she fanned the small fire in the work room back to life and hung the kettle from the crane over it, then took the four remaining current buns from their baker's basket and arranged them on a blue-flowered plate, in the center of the lacquered tray.

Anxiously she peeked out the open door, smoothing her pinner as she waited for the water to heat. He certainly was a comely man, and the thought alone was wickedly enticing enough to make her blood race through her veins. She wished she'd time to change her clothes now, to put on her stays so she'd have some sort of decent shape. In this worn old petticoat and bodice, with her hair functionally braided in a single plait down her back, she must look like some dowdy, lumpy farm woman from Woburn or Weston.

Zach sat on the lowest wooden step and leaned back against the others, wishing he could enjoy the warmth of the sun with a clear conscience. Retrieving Mrs. Isham's basket was in fact a reason for coming here, but he'd also wanted to see Amelie again. The memory of her face when she'd watched the sunset had stayed with him all night, awake and asleep, too, and though he'd a thousand other tasks to do this morning, he'd had to see her again before he tended to any of them.

Yet what he hadn't expected was to find another worrisome question waiting in her yard. It was obvious that she wasn't telling the truth about the destroyed garden. But if that unlikely dog hadn't done it, what—or who—had? Oliver Richardson? Some neighborhood scoundrel, the same who'd broken her window before? Could the quarrel he'd seen brewing between the two sisters have somehow ended out here? He shook his head, considering the puzzle. The only thing he knew for certain was that he wasn't going to leave her again until he had an answer.

He listened to her clattering around inside and smiled. He liked those cheerful, domestic noises; he always had, ever since he'd been a boy, though now that he was a sailor such moments were rare indeed. In fact if it weren't for the destruction of the garden in front of him, he couldn't have imagined a more peaceful place to be on this early June morning.

Well, not entirely peaceful. On the step beside him sat Amelie's enormous gray cat, her tail curled over her paws, her chin tucked up to display her chinly ruffs, and the most venomous look he'd ever seen from a cat coming his way from her round green eyes. If the statutes regarding the size of dogs in Boston had included cats as well, then this one would be the law-breaker of all time.

"Your cat is, ah, large," he called back to Amelie through the open door. "For a cat, that is."

Without blinking, the cat settled down lower on her haunches, rounding her plump, plush sides out even further, and licked her snub-nosed muzzle once. She must weigh twenty pounds, easy, guessed Zach. Maybe twenty-five.

"That is my pretty Luna," said Amelie. "She is a good-sized cat, true, but that is because Julie and I spoil her so dreadfully. It is not her fault. But she is my baby."

The devil's baby, maybe, decided Zach, unwilling to trust the cat enough to look away. He'd wager a guinea the hideous animal slept on Amelie's bed, too.

" 'Luna' means the moon, doesn't it?" he asked. It was hard to reconcile his pleasant association of Amelie in the moonlight with this ill-favored beast.

"Yes, it does." Amelie peeked her head through the door, and he'd swear that her own memories of their moonlit nights were making her blush. That was good: whenever she looked at the beast now, with luck she'd think of him. "We found her as a tiny lost kitten one night when there was a full moon, and because of her color, Luna seemed to fit for a name."

There was nothing tiny about the cat now. Jesus, she could take on a bull-terrier and win. From the glower in her green eyes, she certainly looked ready to take *him*.

"She doesn't like me," he said flatly. "She keeps watching me like I'm a mouse she'd like to devour to make herself even fatter."

Amelie laughed, a sound Zach wanted to hear more often, even if he had to become this wretched cat's breakfast in the process. "She is not that way, not my sweet Luna. If she's angry with you, it's because she heard you speak so much of that silly invented dog. Come here to me, pretty girl!"

She came out onto the step and set down a small dish of milk for the cat before she went back inside to return with the tray with his breakfast. Zach did not miss who came first. He would have to work on changing that.

Now he merely smiled his thanks as he accepted the coffee, strong and black, the way he liked it, even in the summer. The currant bun was fine, too, but then, given the company, he suspected most anything would taste good.

His mouth full of breakfast, he patted the wooden step for Amelie to sit beside him. With an unexpected shyness she accepted the step, though she chose to sit at the farthest end with her back to the railing, like a high-backed chair. She looked younger this morning, her hair coming down in little wisps from her braid and her face rosy from work. Compared to her usual correctness, she was nearly disheveled, enough for him to contemplate the tempting possibility of disheveling her further.

And, dear God preserve them both, she wasn't wearing stays, her breasts beneath the linen the soft, round, tempting shapes that that same God had made them.

Unaware of his thoughts, she carefully pulled her skirts over her knees and tucked them around her ankles, a providential gesture that reminded Zach of how, at sea, his crew would lash and batten down the hatches against a coming gale. It was also an action that was, he thought wryly, perhaps more apt than she'd realized.

"If Luna doesn't want me to talk about destructive little dogs," he began, "then how does she feel about Oliver Richardson?"

Amelie looked at him sharply, but said nothing, which he took as permission to continue as the cat settled beside her.

"He could have done this, you know," he said, lifting the coffee cup toward the ruined garden. "He was here. He had time. Now why the hell he *would* have done it escapes me, but he still could be your villain."

"He's not." She looked down at her lap, clearly troubled. "My sister said Oliver was with her when this must have happened, and I believe her."

"Ah." He hadn't expected that, not after he'd seen the way things were headed between the two sisters last night. "You've settled your, ah, differences, then?"

"I have made my feelings about Oliver Richardson clear to Juliette, as well as my expectations about her behavior. Beyond that, we have agreed that I—that I will trust her to do what is right." She glanced up through her lashes at him without lifting her chin, oddly seductive and defiant at the same time. "Not that it is any of your affair."

"I have a willful younger sister who seldom does what she should, either," he said, then realized from her expression that commiseration was not the wisest course for him to take, especially given the dubious husband his own sister had finally chosen. He didn't have much experience with this kind of delicate conversation, not with a woman, and he sensed he wasn't doing a particularly good job at it now. "Anyway, you're probably right about Richardson. If he was with your sister, then he wouldn't have been mucking around out here, would he?"

The frosty resentment in her eyes now rivaled that of her cat's. "He wasn't 'with' my sister. He took tea with her, that is all."

"Damnation, Amelie, I didn't mean it like that," he said hurriedly. "I'm sorry if it sounded that way, because I—I didn't. Mean it that way, that is. Oh, hell, that's worse, isn't it?"

"Yes," she said, so quickly that he could already feel himself twisting from the gibbet. "But since I don't believe you did intend to speak ill of Juliette, I shall overlook it."

"Thank you," he said, with more relief than a ship's full captain should ever reveal to anyone. "And besides, the watchman and the magistrate are likely to have a good idea who did this mischief if it wasn't Richardson. Even if they such rascals don't sign their work, there are ways to find them out."

She stiffened visibly. "I've no intention of telling the watch anything."

"Why the devil not? You can't let the rascal who did this run free about Boston." He set the cup down on the step. "You didn't report your window being broken either, did you?"

"I saw no need for the whole town to learn of my broken window." Though her voice had turned edgy and defensive, he could still hear the fear in it, too. She wasn't telling him everything, that was clear, not telling him the half. "I cannot afford the scandal such an inquiry would cause. What lady would bring me her custom if she must fear for her safety to do so?"

"But what about your own safety?" he demanded. "What's going to happen to you the next time this bastard comes back? You have to tell the watch, Amelie. You can't keep this to yourself."

"It is not what my parents would have wished me to do." She pulled the cat into her lap, cradling it fiercely like some sort of purring talisman. "Because they wouldn't worship the way King Louis ordered, everything they did or said was questioned and suspected. To go to the village watch or magistrate could mean risking their lives. Instead they learned to take care of themselves, and not to rely on others. It was— is—safer that way."

"But this is Boston, lass, not France!" protested Zach. Of course he'd heard of the plight of the Protestants in France, of how their persecution was encouraged by their intolerant papist king. He could understand why her parents had lived in fear of such dangerous authority, but not Amelie, not here in Massachusetts. "We follow English laws here, laws that are meant to protect every man and woman equally."

She shrugged, attempting indifference, but the woeful little way she tucked a loose strand of hair behind her ear betrayed her.

"For anyone named Fairbourne, of course it would seem so," she said softly. "And if I were called Amelie Richardson, or Amelie Mather, or a score of other grand English names instead of the lowly French one that is my own, then perhaps I, too, could believe in your English justice. But as it is, as I am, I cannot do it, Zach. I just can't."

She was saying the same things she'd said that first night they'd met, that she could trust no one beyond herself, and once again he hated the thought of her being so alone in such trouble. It was wrong; it was unnatural. Why couldn't she accept what he was trying to offer, the way any normal woman in a difficult situation would? Why couldn't she trust *him?*

"Damnation, Amelie, then let me come with you!" he said, rising to his feet with his urgency as he held his hand out to her. "I've told you before that I'd do whatever I could to help you, haven't I?"

But instead of looking up to him, she sighed mournfully and looked down at the cat in her lap, and when she spoke the words seemed muffled in the soft gray fur.

"Oh, Zach, you have said such lovely, wonderful things to me," she began with a patience that also, to his ear, seemed dangerously close to patronizing. "Things that I shall always remember, things I know you meant when you spoke them. But what if I did put my trust in you, Zach? What if I forgot who I am and who I must be, and accepted your help instead?"

"Would that be so bad?" he demanded. Why the devil did she only use his given name when she was going to refuse him something? "You've trusted me before. Why not again, now?"

That made her look up. But instead of the trust he'd expected, or at least hoped, to discover on her face, her dark eyes flashed with a challenge that matched Luna's, and two bright patches of angry pink glowed on her cheeks. "I've trusted you before, yes. But I've also answered that question from you before, too, Captain Fairbourne, and I see no reason to answer it again."

"Amelie—"

"No," she said. "No, and no, and no."

Before he could answer she'd lifted the cat from her lap to her shoulder like a baby and run up the steps and through the doorway, sweeping her free hand across the front of her apron as if sweeping him away, too. In two strides he'd jumped up the steps after her, but just as quickly she slammed the door shut, clicking the lock shut for good measure.

He stared at the locked door, his anger swirling with open disbelief. No woman had ever shut him out of her house like this before. He wasn't the kind of man who deserved such treatment. What had he done wrong, anyway? He'd offered her his help, help she most definitely could use, and she'd rejected it outright.

But far worse was realizing she'd also rejected *him*.

"Amelie!" he shouted, pounding on the door with his fist for good measure. "Blast it, Amelie, come out here and talk to me!"

Instantly the door flew open, and before he realized what was happening she'd thrust Mrs. Isham's now-empty basket into his startled hands. "You may be lord and master and king-captain-blowhard on board your precious ship, but *I* don't have to bow and scrape and obey your bullfrog bellowing!"

"A plague upon your bullfrog!" Irritably he tossed the basket away, only half aware of hearing it bounce and crash down the steps behind him. "I've never once made you do anything against your will!"

"Oh, no, not at all," she scoffed, folding her arms defiantly across her chest. "But what you *have* tried to do is to make my will the same as yours, and I won't have it."

As angry as he was, he found his gaze wandering downward from her face. Damnation, she must be doing this on purpose, distracting him by lifting up her breasts with her folded arms like this, practically offering them to him, the full, rounded flesh, unbound and unlaced, rising up from the gathered neckline of her shift.

He shook his head, forcefully trying to concentrate on what she was saying instead of what she was showing. He'd never realized before how important it was that women wore stays; not so much for the sake of their own whalebone-enforced respectability, but to keep men from lapsing into complete babbling idiocy. "What the devil does your will have to do with it?"

"Not *my* will," she said, flushed with the heat of her argument. "Your will, and I won't obey it."

He frowned down at her, struggling to make sense in what she said while he wondered how warm her skin would feel beneath his fingers, soft and warm, smelling and tasting faintly of peaches. "My will won't—"

"No, I'm the one who won't," she said impatiently. "Obey, that is. But it's your will that's trying to—"

"Oh, just to hell with it all," he said, and before she could confuse him more he hooked one arm around her waist and pulled her close and kissed her, kissed her hard. He felt her flailing beneath him, her hands pushing against his chest, just as he felt her last sputters of protest against his own tongue. Yet still he held her, pressing her back against the frame of the door, still he kissed her, and if in some distant corner of his conscience he considered how he was now guilty of forcing his will upon her exactly as she'd said, he ignored it.

He'd had enough of words; he wanted to make her understand in a way that she wouldn't forget. He wanted her to know how much he needed her, but more importantly, he wanted her to realize she needed him, too.

And so he kissed her, purposefully and directly, until he felt her hands turn quiet against his chest and then slip behind his neck, drawing him closer. He knew the instant she gentled, yielding, and he told himself he'd won.

But to his surprise, he hadn't, not the way he'd thought he would. When she opened her mouth to him she opened her soul as well, and as her breasts and belly and thighs pressed closer to his through the worn linen, the heat of the passion that simmered between them stunned him. She was kissing him back with a fervor that left him quaking and an unskilled eagerness that made him groan with frustration and rocked every conviction he had about women. When finally he broke away, he was shaking, his body hovering so near to boiling over that it took all his tattered willpower not to ruck up her skirts and take her here against the wall.

Her eyes were huge, her breathing wild, her mouth swollen and reddened from his kisses, her lips still parted even as she smiled.

"Dear God," she murmured, her voice low and velvety, "but you're a wicked man, Zach Fairbourne."

"Wickedness has nothing to do with it," he said thickly, amazed that he could string enough words together to make a sentence over the thumping din of his heart. "Though I wish to hell I knew what did."

"Maybe you've wished for too much," she whispered. "Maybe you should stop wishing on stars and moonlight."

"And maybe you haven't done it enough." He ran his hand along the curve of her jaw, feeling how her pulse was racing beneath the pale skin of her throat. God in Heaven, was there ever a man more sorely tempted? "I have to leave now, Amelie, but I swear I'll be back."

"No, Zach, I wish you wouldn't—"

"Hush." Lightly he pressed his forefinger across her lips to silence her. "That's not the kind of wish I had in mind for you. I'll be back because I want to know you're safe, you and your sister both. And I'll do it because I want to, mind?"

Before she could think of another reason against it, he kissed her quickly, a good-bye kind of kiss that wasn't supposed to make him think of anything more but did. Oh, did it. Hell, as roused as they both were now, simply being on the same side of the ocean with Amelie was too close. On legs that felt as weak as a new lamb's, he somehow managed to back down the steps, retrieve Mrs. Isham's basket, wave once more, and leave through the gate.

And wonder if leaving her like this was enough to qualify him for sainthood, or for Bedlam.

❦ 6 ❦

*A*melie stood before the looking-glass in the bed chamber she'd always shared with her sister and tried impassively to study her reflection while she pulled apart what remained of her unraveling braid. Her cheeks were flushed, but that could have been from her raking, and that, too, likely accounted for the sorry state of her hair. Her lips looked darker, almost bruised; perhaps she'd inadvertently bitten them as she'd worked, the way she sometimes did when she concentrated.

But there was no explaining away the change in her eyes, crying out things she'd never dreamed she'd experience. She didn't recognize the self that stared back at her, and even less could she recognize the woman who'd just behaved so shamefully on her own back steps.

She leaned her arm against the wall and pressed her forehead into it, feeling almost light-headed. Maman had warned her against men who'd seek her body for their sinful satisfaction, but she'd never said a word about the pleasure she'd find herself in a man's embrace. Her conscience twisted and turned, torn between her mother's memory and the kiss she'd just shared—again—with Zach Fairbourne.

She'd never behaved like this before with any other man; she'd never even considered it. But with Zach the easy familiarity of the early summer morning, of shared coffee and currant buns and teasing about a mythical little dog, had made this kiss seem almost inevitable, in the same way that the moonlight had graced their first embrace in Richardsons' garden. She couldn't deny that she'd enjoyed Zach's company as much as his kiss, or that her wicked inner self hadn't wanted him to leave. She'd wanted him, all of him, and she flushed miserably when she remembered how he'd been the one to break away, not her.

But why hadn't Maman warned her of this danger along with all the others? Did it mean that Maman had never felt this way when Papa had kissed her, that she hadn't warned against what she hadn't known? Or did it mean that Amelie herself was no better than a common slattern, a woman with passions as deep and coarse as a man's? And how could she possibly advise and warn Juliette when she herself had fallen—no, leaped, with eyes wide open—into the same glittering, delicious pool of temptation that she'd tried to warn her sister against?

She felt something brush against her petticoats and looked down. Luna gazed up at her with round green eyes and twitched her tail in acknowledgment, giving a plaintive little *chirrup* to encourage her mistress to pick her up.

"Oh, Luna-lass," said Amelie as she gathered the cat up in her arms and set her on the bed, dropping onto the coverlet beside her. The cat *was* spoiled, but then so was she, to have such a trustworthy and silent friend for her confessions. Gently she stroked the cat from the top of her silky head down the length of her well-padded spine. "I know you don't like him, Luna, but I do. I *do*, more than I ever should. He makes me smile, and laugh, and he makes me feel special, Luna, in ways not even you can understand."

In response the cat arched and rolled over on her back, front paws in the air as she indolently begged for her stomach to be scratched.

"Ah, then, perhaps you *do* understand, to be so shameless yourself," Amelie said softly as she obliged, running her fingers across the lighter fur of the cat's belly. "But it's not so easy for me, Luna, not by half. And if Julie learns how I feel about him—no, I should say when, because we cannot keep secrets, the way you can—when Julie learns of it, why, then I—oh, how could I have forgotten why I came upstairs?"

Swiftly she rolled off the bed and knelt beside it, sweeping her hand across the floorboards beneath the rope springs until she found the small battered trunk that held the shop's older account books. Like every conscientious tradesman and shopkeeper, she kept two sets of books, one a full-sized ledger, kept in her tall desk in the workroom, and a smaller duplicate, a pocket-sized book, to carry with her at all times in case the original in the shop were somehow destroyed. But once the pages were filled and the accounts settled, the books were stored here, and here she now hoped to find an answer, or at least a clue, before Juliette returned from the market, and the way she'd intended to have done before Zach had distracted her.

She pulled out the ledger that had ended in December and rapidly flipped through the pages to the last days, running her finger down the columns until she found the one name she sought. Then she sorted through the handful of loose papers that had been tucked into the back cover, searching for the corresponding receipt. Purring, Luna bumped an inquisitive nose against her hand, but gently Amelie pushed her aside. At last she found the paper she needed, signed in a gentleman's fulsome hand to mark the acceptance of a delivery of a bride's fine-hemmed linens to his house.

She spread the receipt on the bed, holding it flat with the edge of the ledger, and with a deep breath—though from anticipation or dread, she wasn't sure which—she pulled from her pocket the grubby, threatening note that had been left last night in the remains of the garden. Carefully she unfolded it, and set it directly beside the receipt to compare the writing.

The writer of the note had taken some care to disguise his hand, making some of the letters purposefully clumsy. The man who'd signed the receipt had done so with much less thought, automatically writing a name he'd written countless times before. Yet though she strived to find similarities between the two, looking for telltale loops or dashes or blots, she found nothing, and with a discouraged sigh she sat back on her heels. She thought she was being so clever, so perceptive, hunting like this for both their tormentor and a way to save her sister. She'd even let herself imagine explaining her cleverness to Zach. But all she'd accomplished was to prove that, while Oliver Richardson had signed for a delivery for his sister, he most likely hadn't written a single threatening word to the sisters Lacroix.

"Nothing, Luna, nothing at all," she said with frustration as she shoved the receipt back into the ledger. "Oliver is rich enough to toss away a bag of guineas, he's bold enough to have caused such mischief, and he might even have had a reason, if he'd decided he'd dallied too much with poor Julie. But instead I've only wasted—"

The cat started, her eyes round as saucers, at the sudden thump below them. Someone was at the door of the shop, an impatient someone, too, and Amelie rolled off the bed to peek from the window to the steps below.

"Oh, dear God in heaven," she murmured with dismay. The door pounding was the work of a heavyset footman in a powdered wig and overlaced livery. Behind him, leaning anxiously from the open door of one of Boston's few sedan chairs while two bearers waited, was his mistress, Mrs. Murray. Lucretia Murray was an elderly, spindly widow who nonetheless still liked to dress in the newest and most opulent of styles. She was one of the shop's very best customers, and one Amelie never kept waiting.

Never, that is, until now.

"Where can they be, Jacob?" asked Mrs. Murray with querulous agitation, her quavering voice still able to carry to where Amelie stood. "By my watch it is nearly a quarter past nine. It is not like them to be tardy. Knock again, do, to make certain they've heard you."

But Amelie had most certainly heard. She was already racing down the stairs, smoothing her hair as best she could before she stuffed it beneath the linen cap that she'd grabbed from a table. Hurrying down the hall and into the shop, she barely remembered to untie her pinner, tossing it behind one of the counters as she rushed to unbolt the lock.

"Good day, Jacob," she said breathlessly as she threw open the door. The man nodded stiffly in greeting, his bearing impeccable to his mistress behind him, but from the way he let his gaze drop disdainfully to Amelie's muddy, rumpled garden clothes, he made his contempt abundantly, silently clear.

"Are they open, Jacob?" called Mrs. Murray anxiously, craning to see from the chair. "Are they within?"

"Yes, ma'am, I am," said Amelie as cheerfully as she could, sidestepping the footman to curtsey toward the older woman. "And what do you buy this day, Mrs. Murray?"

"I hardly know yet." She beckoned impatiently for Jacob to come help her from the chair, leaning half her brittle weight on the footman's arm and the other on a silver-headed walking stick. Despite the warm summer morning, she was dressed in heavy green satin with a short beaver-trimmed cloak. Black netted gloves hid her hands and arms to the ruffles on her sleeves, with three heavy gold rings worn over her gnarled, net-covered fingers.

Step by labored step she came forward up the steps, squinting critically at Amelie as she unlatched and opened the shop windows for the day. "What have you been about this morning, missy? I'd turn out any serving girl who'd dare be so slovenly in my house."

Somehow Amelie found enough self-control not to flush, years of professional composure somehow seeing her through.

"I would never show you such disrespect, Mrs. Murray," she said with another graceful curtsey as Jacob led his mistress into the shop. "You cannot know how it does shame me to appear before you is such disorder."

"Then you must not do it," said Mrs. Murray with quavering anxiety. "Already you have vexed and worried me nearly beyond bearing."

"A thousand pardons, ma'am," soothed Amelie as she held a chair out for her, "and you have my word that it shall not happen again. I had a small, ah, event this morning in my garden that required my attention, and alas, it took more of my time than I'd anticipated."

"An event?" Fearfully the woman seized Amelie's hand in her own. "Here? What manner of event?"

"Nothing of any import," said Amelie quickly, giving her trembling hand a reassuring pat. She liked Mrs. Murray, enough so that she genuinely regretted distressing her like this. But she also now regretted mentioning the garden at all, for Mrs. Murray liked to gossip even more than she liked fashionable silks, and half of genteel Boston would know of her garden by week's end. "A, ah, a small dog somehow came through our fence and made mischief in our garden."

"A *dog!*" Mrs. Murray nodded fiercely, her jaws working as tenaciously as any mongrel terrier's. "*Dogs!* They are a bane to the streets and to all decent folk, the nasty, filthy, sneaking, vicious curs!"

Amelie nodded solemnly, wishing she'd been able to think of any other explanation than Zach's. Who would have guessed that stray dogs would be such a favorite topic for Mrs. Murray's outrage?

"Dogs," muttered Mrs. Murray again, jabbing her stick against the floorboards for emphasis. "A plague upon the vile creatures."

With a certain desperation Amelie lifted down a pasteboard box from the nearest shelf. "I have some fine new stockings that arrived this week, ma'am, cream-colored lisle with the most delicate openwork patterning in the leg."

She slipped her hand inside one of the stockings, carefully spreading her fingers to stretch the delicate knitting and display the pattern as she held it up to the window's light. "I know you've an elegant eye toward what's new from London, ma'am, and when you see the garters I've had sent to match, why, then you'll—"

"Was that the dogcatcher, then?"

Amelie paused and blinked, the stocking still on her hand. She did not wish to lose the sale or the customer, but even for Mrs. Murray this made no sense. "The dogcatcher, ma'am?"

"Yes, yes, yes," she said impatiently. "The dogcatcher. Was that he I saw before, skulking out through your gate? I came here earlier this morning, you know, hoping to find your shutters open, then went away when they weren't."

"Here?" repeated Amelie, too stunned to say anything more. "Earlier this morning?"

"Yes, yes, yes, as you know perfectly well." Mrs. Murray squinted at her, one painted brow shrewdly arching towards the front of her wig. "I saw him with my own eyes. A large, rough-looking man with black hair and a worn waistcoat. I saw him leaving your gate as if he'd every right, carrying a covered basket."

She leaned forward with excitement, lowering her voice like a conspirator. "Did he catch the foul beast in the destructive act, then? Did he kill the rascal outright? I'll vow he had the carcass in the basket, didn't he?"

What could Amelie possibly say? Of course Mrs.

Murray meant Zach, and if the moment weren't so hideous, she would have roared with laughter at the description of him as a rough-looking dogcatcher. Instead all she could imagine was how close she'd come to complete disaster: what if Mrs. Murray had decided to investigate, and had left her sedan chair to come creeping through the gate in time to see her so scandalously kissing Zach? If the tale of a dog destroying her garden would have traveled swiftly through the best parlors in Boston, then news of her kissing the Boston dogcatcher would have fair flown.

She'd already gotten mired in her first lie about the dog and the garden, and she'd no wish to make it worse by telling Mrs. Murray any more tales. But telling the truth would be equally damning and, tongue-tied and shamed, she bowed her head, unaware of how she'd curled her fingers into a tight knot inside the stocking.

"Oh, there, there, Miss Lacroix," said Mrs. Murray sympathetically, now the one patting Amelie's hand through the cotton stocking. "I know how you are suffering! What a trial it must have been for you to have called such a disreputable man to your home to perform such a disagreeable task—an outright affront to our gentle woman's sensibilities."

"That is most kind of you, Mrs. Murray," began Amelie, desperately determined not to make things any worse than they were. "But the man wasn't—"

"Hush, I'll hear no more," said Mrs. Murray archly. "Not about the man, nor the dog, nor even how disgracefully you are dressed this morning. It shall all be our secret, Miss Lacroix, between us alone. Now show me the garters to go with these sweet stockings, there's a good lass."

"But Mrs. Murray, I must tell you that—"

"My dear, you grow tedious," said Mrs. Murray, the tremor in her voice now a sign of irritation and warning as much as age. "I have told you this is our secret, and that is an end to it."

But as Amelie draped the ribbon garters—rose, violet, mint, satin stripes of royal and crimson—over her arm to show them off, her heart, and her conscience, were heavy with misgivings. Mrs. Murray could vow by everything that was most holy that this was an end to it, but Amelie knew it wasn't.

It wasn't by half.

Juliette shifted her market basket from one arm to the other, wincing as the twisted willow handle dug into the crook of her elbow. The basket was heavy, almost filled, her list nearly finished. She still hoped to find strawberries, ones that weren't hard and green or blotched with mold, for Amelie.

Though they were both pretending their quarrel was done, Juliette still sensed the unhappiness and disappointment hovering just behind her sister's smile, the same unhappiness that she, too, silently shared. And though they both pretended that the threats against them meant nothing, Juliette could feel the tension and the fear growing in their little shop. Juliette didn't expect a bowl of sweet June strawberries for supper to ease all of Amelie's troubles, but it certainly wouldn't hurt.

She slipped through the clusters of chattering housewives and farmer's daughters to the last makeshift display of vegetables, fruit, eggs, and a few corn brooms that the farmer had made over the winter. Though Boston still did not have a proper market with a roof and standing stalls—the city's selectmen and overseers could not agree on the location for such a building, nor, more importantly, on who should pay for its construction—the number of farmers and artisans who brought their wares to this square still made it the best and biggest market day in all New England. Juliette could see this farmer's strawberries, gleaming like rubies in a pine-needle basket, to the back of his goods, doubtless kept there to discourage sampling, and she leaned carefully across a crate of squawking hens to better consider the berries.

"I never expected to find you here, sweet Juliette," declared a man's voice beside her. "A true pearl cast before the swine, and before the chickens, too."

"Oliver, don't," she hissed, shifting her basket again so it hung between her and the only son of the richest man in Boston. She felt the heat rising to her cheeks, not so much from the overblown way Oliver was now sweeping his hat from his head to her, his forehead so low it nearly touched his well-shaped leg, but from the curious looks such a demonstration was already collecting. Swiftly she turned away, trying to disown his attention, but he caught her arm to join her.

"Aren't you glad to see me, sweet?" he asked mournfully. Not that Juliette, or anyone else, would believe mournful wounds from a gentleman dressed in an exuberant shade of plum superfine with silver lacing and matching embroidered buttons, his hair powdered and tied back with a silk bow nesting at his nape like a giant crimson butterfly.

Juliette sighed uncomfortably, tugging her arm free of his fingers. "Not like this, no. Oliver, I told you before I cannot afford a scandal. My sister—"

"Oh, lud, not the sainted word of your gorgon-sister again." He rolled his eyes dramatically toward the heavens. "Scandal will ruin you, scandal will destroy your little trade, scandal will see you die and rot in the very street."

"Stop it, Oliver." Juliette drew up short behind a horseless wagon, the load of firewood giving them a small measure of privacy against the rest of the marketgoers. "If you wish me to continue in this—this arrangement with you, then you must never mock my sister, and you must not call attention to us where others can see."

"You make more laws than a judge," he grumbled, though he did manage to screw his handsome features into something closer to contrition. "And here I thought you believed in love."

"I do," she said, her voice softening. "Do you think I'd be here now if I didn't?"

He smiled, a smile that would have meant infinitely more if it had reached his eyes. She could see that about him now, though at first she'd been too dazzled to recognize it. She still liked him, but now she had no delusions about Oliver's character, or the faults and flaws that not even his handsome face and plum-colored coat could compensate for. Idleness and self-indulgence had nearly ruined him for much of anything useful in life, but it was still Juliette's dearest hope that love could redeem him. Love, and the right woman to love him in return.

For why else, really, would she be here now?

"I didn't have the chance to thank you properly last night," he said, fumbling through his pockets, "not with that—er, your dear sister arriving home. Blast, I know I've something here for you somewhere."

"Keep it until Friday, as we agreed," said Juliette hastily, glancing over the top of the cart. Besides, she didn't want to be "thanked." Thanking made this all feel even more tawdry than it was. "Don't give me anything here. Someone might see."

"True, true. It's good for me that you're as clever as you are fair, the best sort of friend for a poor addled man like me." He gave his waistcoat pocket one final pat, then frowned. "So what the devil was your sister doing with that rascal Fairbourne, anyway?"

"I don't know." And she didn't, not in the least. Amelie had never before shown anything but benign contempt for men, and out-and-out scorn for the notion of falling in love. That had been part of the reason that Juliette had let herself become entangled with Oliver in the first place, to prove that Amelie was wrong about love. But with bewildering suddenness, Amelie appeared to have changed her mind, and with a gentleman who seemed considerably more agreeable than Oliver Richardson could ever hope to be.

And, as always, always happened, Amelie had once again done better.

"Well, she should watch herself." With the back of his hand, Oliver flicked a smudge of hair powder from his sleeve. "I know Father thinks the Fairbournes are acceptable, but by my lights they're simply low-bred, overreaching sailors, nothing better. They'll sully Miss Amelie's prim petticoats fast enough if she's not careful."

"Oh, Oliver, please." Her head was beginning to ache from the sun and her basket was heavy, and all she wished to do was go home. "I must go, or I'll be missed."

"Until Friday, then." Again he bowed, again too grandly for the market, but as he rose again, flushed with the effort of such gallantry, his smile for once was genuine. "For love, sweet Juliette. It's all for love, and there's nothing else in this world that comes close."

For love, repeated Juliette like a magical chant to herself as she trudged home alone with her head bent against the hot summer sun. *There's nothing else in his world that comes close. For love, for love, for love . . .*

And each time she whispered it, she prayed that Oliver was right.

"Your basket, Mrs. I," said Zach, setting it on the battered dining table in front of him as he dropped wearily into a chair. It was so late in the evening now that most of the tables here in the Crescent's back parlor were empty, the other guests long done with their suppers and shifted to the front barroom. "I hope it means at least I'll get my supper."

"With luck." She picked up the basket gingerly, as if half-expecting to find a coiled snake hiding inside. "Not that I thought I'd ever see *this* again."

"I told you I'd bring it back, and I did." He wasn't in the mood for her bantering this evening. He'd worked hard today, filling in for one of the caulking-crew who'd broken an arm, a laboring job that, as the new sloop's captain, he wasn't supposed to do. But given the choice between maintaining his captainly distance and dignity and making the sloop's hull properly tight and waterproof on schedule, the caulking had won, and he'd pulled off his shirt to toil side by side with the other men, swinging a heavy oak mallet against a hawsing iron in the hot sun until dusk. Now the caulking was done, but beneath his shirt his back felt as burned and tight as bacon left too long on the fire, and the muscles in his shoulders and arms that he'd forgotten he had ached in angry protest.

But the other advantage of such work was that it had given him time to think freely of Amelie: Amelie in homespun, kneeling in a patch of early-morning sunlight; Amelie smiling at him over the back of that infernal cat; Amelie breathless from kissing as she leaned against her door. He'd been able to think of little else, nor had he wanted to. She'd been enough.

When he didn't say more now, Mrs. Isham merely sniffed, a studiously noncommittal sniff this time, and took away the basket.

"That French chit laundered the covering-cloth and ironed it, too," she said as she returned with a pewter tankard of ale, a plate of chicken stew, and a hefty slab of cornbread. "Who would have thought she'd do that, seeing the kind of fancy airs she had about her?"

Zach took a long swallow of the ale, letting its comforting chill ease down his throat before he answered. He didn't want to quarrel with his mother's friend—while he was in Boston, she nearly *was* his mother—but he wasn't going to let Amelie go undefended, either.

"Miss Lacroix's not a chit, Mrs. Isham," he said finally, "as you could have seen for yourself if you hadn't been so busy looking for her 'airs.'"

"Hah." She bent forward to wipe away the ring of foam the tankard had left on the table. "You're the one she's keeping busy, Zachariah. You wouldn't be looking so peaked now if you'd been content to keep to your own bed last night instead of tumbling the likes of that one."

Zach sighed and set the tankard back down on the table, his pleasure in the ale rapidly fading. "I called on Miss Lacroix this morning to fetch back your basket, early this morning, after we'd each spent the night in our separate beds beneath separate roofs. Not that it's any particular affair of yours. Leastways it shouldn't be."

"I'm watching out for my friend Sally's son, and there's no sin to that." Crossly she wiped at the new ring Zach's tankard had left and pushed the plate with the stew closer to urge him to eat. "It's not that I'm blind, either. I know how it is with you and women, same as it is with most men. But I can't believe your poor father fought the French in the old war so you could lie with some French hussy twenty-five years later."

"I told you, I didn't lie with her." Zach dug his fork into the stew. His father had served on a privateer for one month, never once so much as sighting a French ship let alone fighting any Frenchman in mortal, patriotic combat, but that seemed beside the point now. "And she's no more a hussy than she's a chit, and since she was born here in this colony, I hardly think you can call her French, either."

"Oh, aye, she's French," said Mrs. Isham scornfully. "You can't shrug that off. Not that she wants to, not that one. Dressing above her station, calling on you so bold, keeping that foreign-sounding name of hers."

He glanced up at her, incredulous, his fork poised in midair. "It's her own father's name, and her mother's, too. Why should she cast it off just to please you?"

"If she wanted to belong here in Boston, she would," insisted Mrs. Isham stubbornly. "There's plenty that do. Mr. Bun-villy-ay, the tailor across the square that wed Mary Wilson, he became Mr. Bonney, and that chandler near Clark's Wharf trimmed that clumsy Dees-shar-dans to Mr. Gardiner. There's a journeyman goldsmith comes in here sometimes, too, as pleasant a young man as you could wish, who now calls himself Revere instead of Ree-wah-res, just to be obliging to his neighbors, he says. Now why couldn't that chit do the same, I ask you?"

She could ask all she wanted, decided Zach, but he wasn't going to answer, devoting himself instead to the plate of stew. Trading as he did in the Carribean, he'd met a great many Frenchmen in his voyages, and Frenchwomen, too, and to him they seemed much the same as the English: some were excellent folk, some were wicked as the Devil himself, and most fell in the happy places between.

Yet he wasn't naive enough to believe that there were more people in Boston who thought as he did instead of like Mrs. Isham. Hating the French was more than a pastime for Bostonians; it was a patriotic way of life, and he wondered uneasily if such unthinking bigotry could be someone's excuse for destroying Amelie's garden.

But Mrs. Isham wasn't about to leave him to his thoughts yet. With a quick glance back toward the front room to make sure she could be spared, she pulled a chair close to Zach's and sat close beside him, her brows knit with concern and her hand clutching the damp cloth on the table before her.

"I'm fearing for you, Zachariah," she said earnestly. "I've seen how you look at this woman. You're besotted, boy, befuddled and beamy so bad that your judgment's clear left you. So why her, eh?"

Zach looked at her wryly across the tankard. "Since when isn't it enough for a woman to be beautiful and charming?"

"When it's you, Zachariah," she said firmly. "For your mother's sake, I care what becomes of you. Boston's full of prettier women—prettier *English* women—and you'd only have to look their way to have them come running. Other times you've stayed here, I've had to shoo the lovesick creatures from my very kitchen. But now you're blind to them all except this one sallow little French hussy, and it's worrisome."

He began to correct her again, that Amelie wasn't sallow or little or even French, but the rest of what Mrs. Isham said made him pause. Since he'd met Amelie Lacroix at the Richardsons' house, he *had* been as good as blind to every other woman, and that wasn't like him, not at all. And it wasn't just because Amelie was beautiful and charming: that had made a good, quick, flippant answer, true, but if it were also the sum of her appeal, he wouldn't have become so uncharacteristically single-minded.

No, her appeal had to be more complicated than that, he thought as he carefully sopped up the rest of the stew's juices with the last bit of cornbread, so complicated and complex that he couldn't yet put his feelings into words.

Or maybe, instead, it was just as ridiculously simple.

He popped that last bite of cornbread into his mouth, and smiled at the older woman.

"I like her," he said softly, "because she needs me."

Skeptically Mrs. Isham cocked her head to one side, as if she couldn't trust what she'd just heard. "She told you that?"

"Nay, she'd never whisper a word of it," he said, still smiling as he pictured Amelie's proud little chin raised in defiance. "Likely she doesn't know it for herself, not yet. But she needs me, and I mean to be there for her."

Mrs. Isham shook her head, her expression clearly

perplexed as she rubbed the damp cloth around the table in a small circle.

"I don't know what that woman's done to bewitch you, Zachariah," she said uneasily. "I haven't heard nonsense like this out of your mouth since you was a little lad, when it was just you and your mam alone in that drafty house near the river in Westham."

But his mind was already impatiently racing onward, not listening to or interested in what she was saying about the past. "A good part of Boston comes through your door, Mrs. I. Have you overheard anything spoken against Miss Lacroix or her shop? Any threats or complaints?"

"I wouldn't. I've only to look at her to know she trades with the better sort, not them that comes to Ann Street for a pot of ale or rum." She shook her head, her uneasiness clearly growing. "What kind of trouble is the girl in?"

Briefly Zach told her what he knew, which, he had to admit, wasn't much.

"I don't like this, Zachariah," said Mrs. Isham. "Not with you meddling in her affairs like this."

"It's hardly meddling, not when someone's out to hurt her." He shoved the empty dish to one side, and leaned eagerly across the table, his earlier weariness forgotten. "She and her sister are all alone, Mrs. I, and they're too frightened by what's happening to go to the constable. But I can help them. I know it."

"Now you're acting daft," she declared unhappily. "Oh, I know you're tenderhearted, lad. You always have been, and I'm glad of it. But this woman's not another kitten you're saving from drowning. You've no real notion of what sort of trouble she's in, or who's behind it."

"Do you truly believe that's going to stop me?" he scoffed. "Being afraid that some low villain's going to come hunting for me next?"

"It's not the low ones that worry me, not in this town." She placed her hand on his arm, a caution more than a restraint. "Your life's full enough as it is, Zachariah. You're going to be a captain, a fine young gentleman with a grand new ship. Don't go tossing all that away for the sake of some chit you scarce know."

"I don't toss anything away. Mam taught me that, didn't she?" He grinned, and as he stood, he bent to kiss her on the cheek. "Don't worry over me, Mrs. I. I wouldn't have gotten as far as I have if I didn't know how to look after myself, would I?"

But Mrs. Isham didn't smile in return, her expression grim as she patted his arm one last time.

"Don't be pert with me, Zachariah, and don't be taking your dear mam in vain," she warned. "You just watch your back where that Frenchwoman's concerned, mind? Keep out of alleys, and keep clear of her bed. Take care, lad, and may God keep you safe."

He'd only intended to walk past the shop, to see for himself that all was safe and snug for the night. He'd promised that much to Amelie, hadn't he? Besides, by now it was far too late to make a decent call on anyone, let alone two young, unmarried women, and he could hardly pound on the door of a millinery shop and pretend he'd come on some urgent emergency, the way he might have done with an apothecary or surgeon. No, now he must content himself with lingering in the street, staring up past the shuttered shop to the darkened windows of the upper floor like any other moonstruck idiot who'd taken the time to wash, shave, and change to a fresh shirt to impress a woman who was already fast asleep.

At least, he thought wryly, he'd have no witnesses. Marlborough Street was empty, all its respectable inhabitants long since asleep and their fires and lights dowsed for the night so that every star shone brightly beside the moon overhead. With the town at rest, the gentle *shush* of the river and sea filled in the silence, and from the east, likely from one of the old elm trees that ringed the common, came the insistent hooting of an owl. Closer, perhaps as near as Bishop's Alley, was another sound of the night, the comforting, rumbling drone of the watch.

"Half past eleven," the man called, over and over, as he made his way through the streets with his lantern in hand, "and a clear, fine night it is."

Instinctively Zach shifted back into the shadows beside the shop. He had nothing to hide, but he'd still no wish to have to explain himself to the watchman. He bumped against the iron latch of the gate, eased it up, and slipped inside and down the narrow alley to the same small yard where he'd found Amelie this morning. There'd be no harm in waiting here until the watch was gone—already the man's drone was fading as he turned down another street—and besides, the place was so closely associated with her in his mind that simply to be here again made him smile.

The smile disappeared as he glanced at the neatly raked void that had been her garden. He knew from his mother how much women valued their gardens, their own tidy patches to make flowers grow for beauty and herbs and vegetables for nurturing. Amelie was no different, and he remembered how sorrowfully she'd trailed her fingers through the scattered yellow daisy petals before she'd swept them away. Whoever had ruined her garden had shown a keen sense of how to hurt her, a determined meanness that seemed somehow worse than the destruction itself, and that concerned Zach all the more.

If only she'd confide in him, then he was sure he could help her. If only she'd tell him all she knew . . .

He sensed the noise more than he actually heard it, a muffled thump from the far side of the steps. He wasn't alone in the yard, and hadn't been, and he cursed his own carelessness. No wonder Amelie didn't want to trust him, not if he could be as thick-witted as this. He could only hope the other intruder hadn't realized he was here and, with his heart pounding with excitement, he strove to find some shape or movement in the black shadows beside the steps.

As silently as he could he eased his way along the wall, carefully lifting the heavy rake Amelie had left propped against the railing. He tightened both his hands around the smooth wood, testing his grip. He'd been in enough brawls and scrapes to know that the first blow was often the one that won the fight; he had to be ready.

"Avast there, you bastard," he ordered sharply, the rake raised in his hands like a cudgel. "Quit your hiding, and show yourself."

But instead of showing himself, the man lunged forward from the shadows, hurling himself toward Zach. Instantly Zach swung the rake, hard, the other man crying out with pain as the heavy wooden handle struck him and he fell, his body scattering the crushed shells of the path.

"Who the hell are you, then?" demanded Zach as

he jabbed the rake at the groaning man at his feet. "And what the hell are you doing here at—"

And it was then, in the next sliver of a second, that Zach realized there'd been not one man lurking in the shadows, but two.

And realized also that it was too late to save himself.

7

"Luna?"

Amelie rolled over onto her back, listening. Beside her in the wide bed they shared Juliette sighed in her sleep and bunched her pillow more tightly beneath her chin. The up-and-down tick-tock of the little case clock in the front parlor echoed through the second floor, but beyond that and Juliette's sigh, there seemed no sound, nothing to ruffle the serenity of the night.

Yet there must have been something, something loud enough to awaken her as suddenly as she had been. The most likely answer was, of course, Luna. Though the cat spent most nights prowling through the neighborhood, Amelie kept one of the upstairs windows open so that Luna could crawl in (or out) from the top of the fence at will. Though the cat generally behaved herself, there were occasions when she'd investigated a basket of thread or a covered plate of food left from supper a bit too thoroughly, sending the basket or plate crashing to the floor in the middle of the night. Perhaps, then, somewhere in the house such a catastrophe lay waiting for Amelie to discover, and with a soft sigh of her own she swung her legs over the edge of the bed and rose to investigate.

Because the night was warm, she didn't bother with slippers or putting a shawl over her night-rail, and in bare feet she padded down the narrow, twisting stairwell, guided by the moonlight, to the workroom. There, because they'd begun shuttering all the lower windows at night after the one had been broken, she needed light to find her way. Cautiously she felt along the wall first for the flint and striker in the leather bag next to the hearth and then for the candlestick on the mantelpiece.

"Luna?" she called softly again, lifting the candle to cast its wavering light around the room. Everything looked as it should; nothing seemed to have been knocked over or pushed out of place. "Luna-lass, have you been making mischief?"

Swiftly she checked the hall and the shop, and there, too, nothing seemed amiss, nor did the cat present herself, which was, of course, most typically perverse of Luna. Perhaps, thought Amelie, she had in fact dreamed the noise that had wakened her. She'd become as skittish as old Mrs. Murray, and she shook her head at her own foolishness as she began to snuff out the candle and return to bed.

But before she did, she heard a scraping, scratching sound at the door: certainly not enough to be whatever had wakened her, but not usual, either.

"Luna?" she asked tentatively, leaning her head against the door to see if she could hear the noise again. "Luna-lass, is that you?"

The cat's disgruntled meow was unmistakable, and Amelie set the candlestick on the table to unbolt the door. "Luna, Luna, you naughty beast, waking me up like this, and clawing at the paint on the door, too!"

She cracked open the door and at once the cat squeezed in, flying past her into the room and down the hall without stopping. But to Amelie's surprise the door kept opening, too, pushing against her so hard that she gasped in panic as she tried to shove it back with both hands. Still the door kept pressing open, until, all at once, the entire lengthy weight of Zach Fairbourne staggered forward on top of her.

"Zach, please!" Amelie shrieked, fighting to keep her balance as she struggled against him. Yet as terrified as she was, she realized even before he didn't answer that something wasn't right. He wasn't pushing against her: he was falling, loose-limbed as an oversized rag doll. "*Grâce à dieu*, Zach, what is wrong with you?"

He muttered something she couldn't understand as he lifted his head heavily from her shoulder and tried to stand, his untied hair slipping back from his forehead. Then by the candlelight she saw the smear of blood across his temple, the glisten of it clotted in his hair, as he sagged against her again.

"Oh, Zach, oh, Zach," she cried softly, not really expecting an answer as she twisted clumsily around him to slide her shoulder beneath his arm and her hand around his waist, the better to support him.

But the unconscious weight of his body was nothing compared to the fear and guilt that pressed down on her soul. Had whoever was threatening her and her sister done this to Zach? If he hadn't come back here to look after her, the way he'd promised, then he would still be unhurt. It was her fault, all her fault, and she didn't try to stop the frightened sob that shook through her. How could anyone who'd been so wonderfully,

vitally alive and strong this morning be so deathly
still now?

"Amelie, are you—oh, Amelie!" Juliette stood on
the bottom step of the stairs, staring openmouthed
with sleepy bewilderment. "Whatever has happened to
Captain Fairbourne?"

"Help me, Julie, please!" gasped Amelie, and this
time her sister obeyed. Hurriedly Juliette shut and re-
bolted the door, then helped Amelie guide the unconscious man to the tall-backed armchair that had
belonged to their father.

With the candlestick trembling in her hand, Amelie
held the light close to Zach's face and gently brushed
back his hair. At least now to her relief she could see
that the blood was from a graze rather than an open
cut, not as serious as she'd first feared nor enough to
merit bandaging, but the purple bruise beneath the
scrape was already swelling into an angry lump. She
guessed he'd been struck on the head, which would
explain his groggy unconsciousness. But she'd no way
to guess the seriousness of the blow, or worse, how
long it would be before he woke. She was very skilled
at mending clothes, but people were a different matter altogether.

"What shall we do, Amelie?" whispered Juliette fearfully. "Perhaps this time we really should call the
watch."

"And how would you propose to do that, Julie?"
answered Amelie, tension making her tart. "Do you
wish to go blithely out that door without a thought
for who might be waiting there, to do to you what he
did to Zach?"

Juliette shook her head, quick, frightened shakes. "I

wasn't looking for more trouble. I only thought the watch might help, that was all."

Instantly Amelie regretted being sharp. "Oh, Julie, I'm sorry. But we shouldn't go to anyone else until Zach can tell us what happened himself."

She brought a bowl of water and a clean cloth to the table and began to dab at the blood in his hair and on his forehead as carefully as she could. She wanted to be competent, brave for Juliette's sake, sure of herself and of what to do next to help Zach.

That was what she wanted, and oh, God, she wasn't even coming close.

Juliette watched, anxiously twisting the drawstring from her shift in her fingers. "But what should we do until then? What should we do with—with *him?*"

"I'm not sure." Amelie swallowed, fighting the help-lessness that threatened to choke her. "We can't leave him here in Papa's chair, that's for certain."

"Does he have friends we might summon to fetch him?" asked Juliette. "I know the Fairbournes are from Appledore, but he must have friends here in Boston, too."

Briefly Amelie considered Mrs. Isham, before she re-membered how suspicious the woman had been of her. She'd be sure to blame Amelie for this happening to Zach, perhaps even have her taken to the gaol, and reluctantly Amelie shook her head.

"Until he wakes, he is our guest," she said, gently holding the water-cooled cloth on Zach's bruise. "He came to our door for help, and we cannot refuse it. Besides, it's the least we can do for him, considering how he was protecting us when—when he was hurt."

"He was?" Juliette frowned, her lips rounding with

confusion. "It would have been very nice of him if he had, of course, but whyever would he?"

"Because he just *was*." Amelie busied herself with rinsing the cloth in the bowl to avoid meeting the question that must, inevitably, be in her sister's eyes.

But for once, Juliette didn't hold back her misgivings. "Tell me, Amelie," she asked softly. "Captain Fairbourne—he's a special gentleman for you, isn't he?"

Reluctantly Amelie raised her gaze to meet her sister's, over the man himself. Juliette wasn't asking much—"special" could cover an endless range of possibilities—but to admit to even that much would have meant that she'd also be confessing it to herself. She told herself she wasn't sure, she wasn't ready to make such a step, and then she looked back down at Zach's face. He hadn't hesitated, had he?

"Yes," she said, her heart thrumming wildly to hear it spoken aloud. "Captain Fairbourne—Zach—is special."

That was all, and between them, that was enough. In return Juliette nodded, strangely serious and sad, but that, too, was enough, and hurriedly Amelie set the bowl with the bloodied water aside.

"I'll need your help now, Julie," she said. "We must work together to get him up the stairs, so we can put him to rest on the daybed."

It sounded well enough, a brisk sort of plan, but as soon as Amelie tried to lift Zach from the chair she realized how difficult such a briskly described task was going to be. Even with one of his arms across her shoulders and the other across Juliette's, he was a heavy, awkward, dragging weight between them that would have been hard enough to maneuver up an ordinary staircase. But the stairs from their shop to the upper chambers were Boston stairs, narrow and winding to conserve space instead of making a grand show, and the effort and strain of hauling him upward left both sisters at the final landing gasping and panting from exertion, the thin linen of their night-rails clinging damply to their backs.

The effort had taught them both something else as well, apparent as soon as they reached the doorway to the small front parlor.

"The daybed," gasped Juliette. "He—he's so—he won't fit."

Amelie couldn't argue. The rush-seated mahogany daybed with the carved claw feet had been their mother's final indulgence as an invalid, her way of pretending she wasn't truly as ill as she was. But while the daybed had been more than sturdy enough to support their frail, dying mother, the piece seemed to shrink when confronted with a man of Zach's size.

"Ours, then," she said as firmly as she could. There was no other choice, since in their small living quarters there was only the single bedchamber, and only the one bed. "He'll have to have ours."

Yet to see him there, unconscious though he was, sprawled across their own rumpled sheets, was enough to make Amelie blush. Whatever would Maman have said to this? He was too large, too masculine, his scale all wrong for the bed that she'd shared only with her sister. Before she lost her nerve, she worked his coat free from his arms as she would from a doll, and straightened his legs on the bed, arranging him into a more respectable symmetry, and next she unbuckled and tugged off his shoes and the stockings.

She told herself she was only trying to make him feel at ease, yet still she found herself appallingly aware of how muscular his calves were as she slid the knitted stockings down, how the dark hair curled thickly over the skin of his calves, how wonderfully, fascinatingly different he was from herself.

"You're undressing him?" whispered Juliette with horrified interest, hanging back as she rested one hand on the tall, straight posts of their bed. "All the way?"

"Of course not," said Amelie with a primness she didn't feel as she eased him more to the center of the bed. "I'm only taking off his shoes for the sake of the coverlet."

With one knee on the edge of the mattress, she leaned across to pull the sheets over him, and, almost tenderly, settled his battered head on the bolster, plumping the feathers before she smoothed the linen pillow-bier. In the moonlight—the same moonlight that had been her magical friend before—that streamed in through the windows, his face was relaxed, as if he truly were sleeping, and if it were not for the bruise that distorted his temple, she'd scarcely have believed he wasn't.

Yet knowing he wouldn't respond in a way freed her, too, and with a familiarity she never would have dared otherwise, she stroked the dark waves of his hair away from his forehead, letting her fingers trace along the side of his face to the the dimpled cleft in his chin. His jaw was unexpectedly smooth, the slight rough bristle of whiskers she'd remembered from kissing him this morning gone. Clearly he'd shaved before he'd come here this night, shaved with the hope of seeing her. How much she might stand to lose tonight that wasn't even yet hers to claim!

"Oh, Zach," she whispered as she bent over him, the words swept nearly to silence by the sea of her emotion. "Oh, Zach, please, please, forgive me!"

"He'll be fine, Amelie," murmured Juliette. "I know it."

Amelie shook her head as she pushed back to stand beside the bed, not nearly as sure as her sister. If only he would groan or turn his head, if only he'd show some sign that he'd come back, instead of this awful, deadly stillness.

She felt Juliette's arms loop around her shoulders, and blindly she slipped her own arms around her sister's waist, seeking the comfort they'd always found in each other.

"You'll see, Amelie," said Juliette softly as she leaned her head against her sister's shoulder. "There's nothing we can do for him now but let him rest. Most likely he'll be well enough by morning, and then, *la,* the mischief he'll cause us!"

Amelie knew she was supposed to smile then, to reassure Juliette that everything was and would be as fine as they both wished, but if she tried now she'd cry instead, and if she let herself begin she'd never stop. She had to be strong, or she'd be no use to anyone, not to Zach or Julie or even herself. She'd always believed that the only thing that could happen with a man was what Maman had told her: disgrace, shame, ruin. And oh, dear Lord, because she'd believed, how little she'd known, and how wrong she'd been!

She sighed, a great, deep, shuddering sigh that was nearly a sob, and this time, through sheer will alone, she was able to make herself twist her mouth into something approaching a smile.

"He *will* be fine, Julie," she said, wishing she had the power to make these words come true. "He *will.*"

* * *

Sitting beside the open window to catch the light of the afternoon sun, Amelie struggled to concentrate on the yellow rose taking shape in her fingers. She'd made such flowers, to decorate a fancy stomacher or broad-brimmed straw hat, more times than she could count, twisting and folding the narrow silk ribbon to form each petal between her fingers, catching the ends with a deft stitch or two to bind the petals into a blossom. But today her fingers had turned clumsy with the same fatigue and strain that hung over the rest of her body, and with a mutter of frustration she dropped the half-finished rose into her work basket and once again left her chair to go stand beside the tall-post bed.

Once again, and once again she was forced to admit that Zach looked no different than he had when she and Juliette had first brought him here during the night. His seagoing tan still lay over his pallor, his breathing still frighteningly shallow and soft for so large a man. He remained lost in whatever secret world the blow on his head had cast him, and well beyond her reach or care.

While Juliette had slept on the daybed, she'd been too much on edge to even try, and instead had sat here, near his bed, through the night and into this day so she could be ready for the change that had yet to come. Oh, he'd groaned once or twice, and she thought this morning she'd seen his eyelids flutter, but if she were truthful there'd been no improvement in his condition at all.

The longer Zach slept—for that was how she preferred to think of it, a sleep that would eventually end with him waking—the more worried she became. Not only did it mean he'd been more grievously injured than she'd first thought, but the longer he stayed here, in her bed, the more his presence complicated her life and Juliette's, too. He wasn't some stray, like Luna had been, that they could indefinitely keep for their own. It was one thing to wish to help when he'd been hurt, but quite another to keep him from his other life and responsibilities.

And, too, the question of who had struck him remained unanswered as well. With daylight Amelie had dared to go into the yard, and had discovered the footprints and scattered shells that marked some sort of scuffle or fight. No wonder Luna had fair flown through the door when she'd opened it! Though the rake had been tossed to one side and bloody handprints marked the railing, at least this time there'd been no threatening note. Perhaps, she thought sadly, because this time there'd been no need to explain the danger. She'd only to look at Zach himself to see it.

Gently she stroked his cheek with her fingertips, hoping that, in some way, he'd sense that he wasn't alone and that she was here. If their places had been reversed, she'd have wanted that same small comfort for herself.

Oh, Zach, oh, Zach, I am so sorry . . .

She heard the bell to the door of the shop downstairs ring as it opened, followed by the familiar cheerfulness of her sister's greeting. While she sat here with Zach, Juliette had tended the shop, continuing the routine of their lives in the only sure way that remained. The voices rose and fell, the pattern more audible than the words.

But that pattern seemed different somehow, without the usual easy rhythm of a sale, and curiously Amelie turned her head to listen. A man's voice: that was not usual for their shop, nor was the brusqueness of his tone.

"Amelie?" called Juliette, her voice pitched uncharacteristically higher with nervousness. "Amelie, could you please come here directly?"

In an instant Amelie untied her apron and smoothed her hair beneath the ruffles of her cap. She took one final look at Zach, touching his cheek lightly to reassure him—and herself—that she'd be back as soon as she could, closed the door to the bedchamber and hurried down the stairs.

"Good day, sir," she said as she entered the shop, her serene trade-smile firmly in place. "What do you buy this fine afternoon?"

One glance at the man standing at the counter before her sister, and Amelie knew the answer to her shopkeeper's traditional greeting: this man would buy nothing from her, not on this fine summer afternoon nor the coldest January morning. Barrel-chested and bowlegged, he could have been one of the men who'd bothered her when she'd walked along Ann Street. He wore no hat and his own hair, braided in a sailor's queue that balanced his balding crown, a checkered shirt and leather breeches, and such a determinedly righteous look on his pock-marked features that Amelie automatically widened her smile and prepared for a fight.

"This is Master Goodling, Amelie," said Juliette, her cheeks flushed with misery and her hands fluttering like a pair of newly caged birds. Clearly she'd been attending another customer, the neatly dressed young woman trying on hats before the mirror whom Amelie didn't recognize, when the man had come. "He says he wishes to make inquiries regarding Captain Fairbourne."

"Nay, I'm no master, but plain John Goodling," said the man without bothering with the nicety of a greeting. "First mate on the Fairbourne sloop *Diana,* and I've come a-looking for my cap'n."

Amelie nodded seriously, as if this were all grave news to her, while in her chest her heart was pounding so loudly she felt sure he'd hear it. "You have spoken with the watch regarding your captain?"

"Aye, 'course I have," he scoffed, with as much indignation as if she'd outright called him an idiot. "Do you think I'm daft? But they've seen none of him, no more than any other of his friends. Which be why I've come here for him."

"Here?" She forced another smile, sweeping her hand gracefully to one side. "*Grâce à Dieu!* This is a milliner's shop, Mr. Goodling, not a chandler's!"

But Goodling was not about to be distracted. "I came here to find Cap'n Fairbourne, not to buy him. He's not been in his lodgings, not since last night's supper, and I—"

"Pray, Mr. Goodling," interrupted Amelie hastily, already aware of how the other customer's face was glowing with fascinated interest beneath the hat she was considering. "Since your business seems to be of a private nature, why don't you step back to my desk with me so we might speak alone?"

"Nay, mistress, there's nothing I have to say needs be hidden away," he said, doggedly shaking his head so the queue flopped across his broad back. "My cap'n's gone missing, and it's not his nature, and I'm thinking you know where he be."

"I?" She hoped she looked properly bemused by such a suggestion. "To be sure, Captain Fairbourne is well known to this shop, having made purchases on behalf of his cousin's wife, Mrs. Anabelle Fairbourne. Because of her, your captain has become one of our better gentleman customers."

"I've heard different, mistress." Goodling lowered his

head like a stubborn bull, "I heard he's more 'n that. Mrs. Isham, a fair, God-fearing woman if ever there was one, *she* says when the cap'n left the Crescent he told her he was a-coming here. And now all I'm asking you is when he called here, and where he was bound when he left."

She met his gaze as evenly as she could, her half-smile of elegant composure still pasted in place on her face. This was the moment she'd dreaded, and her mind raced ahead as she considered what to say next. She wasn't about to give Zach up—how did she know Goodling was who he claimed, and not the man who'd struck Zach last night, come back to finish the job?—but she didn't want to trap herself by lying to protect him, either. No. Instead she must manage to be both truthful, and clever.

"I share your concern for Captain Fairbourne's welfare, Mr. Goodling," she said, clasping her hands at her waist. "Yes, I do. But I must tell you that your captain never called here last night, nor could he have left to be 'bound' anywhere else."

The man screwed his face up with doubt, clearly unwilling to believe her. "You're certain, mistress? I've known the cap'n a good long time, and disappearing like this isn't like him, not at all."

"Our shop was shuttered by eight of the clock," she said firmly. "No one could have called after that."

"Ah," said Goodling unhappily, shaking his head again. "There can be nothing more to that, can there? Boston can be a villainous place, mistress. I only pray the cap'n hasn't come to harm. But I won't trouble you more, and I wish you good day."

"Good day to you, Mr. Goodling, and my prayers shall be with your captain." There, that was true, too, and no one could say otherwise. But as Amelie watched the man go, his shoulders hunched with disappointment, she knew this sort of truth was so close in spirit to falsehood that she felt the same as if she'd lied, deceitful and low. The crestfallen look on Goodling's face hadn't helped, either. Just like her, he, too, was acting out of loyalty to Zach, and part of her wanted to run after him now in the street to tell him his captain was safe and asleep in her bed.

In her bed: that was the part that stopped her, and with her smile more forced than ever, she turned toward the woman trying on hats with Juliette.

"Have you found all you wish, ma'am?" she asked. "A rosette for the crown, perhaps, or a ribbon in a different shade?"

"Oh, no, Miss Lacroix, I am quite pleased," said the woman, untying the hat for Juliette to place it in its box to purchase and carry home. "I shall be sure to recommend you to all my acquaintance."

"Thank you ma'am," murmured Amelie with a bow. "You are too kind."

Yet from the woman's simpering smirk, Amelie was sure what she truly couldn't wait to share with her friends was the scene she'd just witnessed. Every word of what she and John Goodling had said linking her with Captain Fairbourne would be repeated with a raised eyebrow here, a suggestive emphasis there, until even the most honest truth would have been as damning as the boldest lie. And there was nothing, not one blessed thing, that she could do to stop it.

She could barely contain her temper as she ran up the stairs, purposefully thumping each step like a willful child. She had tried to be fair, tried to be good and honest, tried to protect the man fate had dropped into her care, and nothing but ill had come from it. Perhaps Maman had been right after all.

She was still fuming as she opened the door to the bedchamber, where Zach lay in such blissful ignorance of all the trouble he was churning around her. Juliette had been quite right about him causing mischief, but who would have guessed he'd do it without so much as raising his little finger?

"Damnation, Zach," she muttered crossly, borrowing his dubious vocabulary for her own as she returned to her flower-making at the window. "Why don't you come back and help me like you promised?"

"Amelie?"

She turned sharply back toward the bed, not sure she hadn't imagined the croaking sound of her name. "Zach?"

"Amelie?" He shifted restlessly in the bed. "You there, lass?"

She hurried to the bed. "Oh God, Zach, you're awake! How do you feel?"

"Like hell." He tried to crack open his eyes, only to squeeze them shut with a grimace. "Jesus, that sun."

With guilty haste she rushed to unloop the heavy checked curtains from the posts and draw them closed around the bed like a little tent.

"It's so warm here I thought you'd wish the air," she chattered, feeling oddly self-conscious to have him awake. "That's why I kept the curtains tied and the window open, too, and—"

"Amelie, sweet," he said, his voice gravelly. "Hush."

Contritely she sank to her knees beside the bed, resting her chin on her folded arms as she studied him, her ill humor forgotten. He was back, he'd be well again, and the sweet feeling of relief swept over her.

But he certainly wasn't sleeping: his face was too twisted with unmistakable pain for that. Shyly she dared to take his hand, and at once he linked his fingers into hers, holding tight.

"Amelie," he said groggily. "You're . . . well?"

"Of course *I* am," she whispered. "But you're not, not at all."

"No." His fingers moved restlessly along hers. "Head hurts, Amelie. Hurts like . . . hell."

"Don't try to talk, Zach," she urged. "There'll be plenty of time for that later. Now you need to rest."

"Aye, sleep." She could tell by the way his features were relaxing again that he was already drifting back.

"That's good, *mon cher*," she whispered, feathering a kiss on the unbruised side of his forehead. "You sleep."

To her surprise, he managed to smile. "In your bed, Amelie," he rasped. "In your bed."

The dream was the same one that haunted all sailors, with a few special twists to make it Zach's own.

The night was black as boiling pitch, with neither moon nor stars to guide the foundering ship. The wind shrieked like a wild creature, driving the waves as high as a meeting house spire, churning black water with white foam and the souls of all the others who'd been swallowed up and damned in their depths. Long, ragged strips of canvas whipped out from the yards like tattered cobwebs, all that remained of the ship's sails, and helplessly she plunged in and out of the waves, hanging high on one crest only to plunge down with sickening force into the valley of the next.

Yet still Zach fought, his hands clutching tight to the wheel's spokes to keep from being washed over the side. Like the others, he thought, like all the rest of his crew, for as he stood on the heaving quarterdeck he was alone,

*the one man the storm and sea had let live to torment.
Though he reeled with exhaustion, every bone and muscle
in his body crying out for some sort of respite, he still
refused to give in, and as another wave towered before
him, he threw his body against the wheel to try to swing
the ship clear.*

*But the wave crashed down upon him with such force
that he was torn free of the wheel and the ship, thrown
through the air and into the icy grasp of the water. He
struggled to rise free to the surface and his cold-stiffened
arms would not obey; he gasped for air and could not
find it.*

*He was going to drown, going to die, or maybe he
already had. Spinning like a Catherine wheel in the grip of
the wave, he saw a school of silvery codfish and the center-
board of his own ship, Diana picked out in gold, and his
own father watching and beckoning, the father lost before
he'd been born, the father he recognized now only because
they had the same face, the watery, terrified face of a
drowning man.*

*"No," cried Zach as the salty water filled and gurgled
in his open mouth. "Not yet, not this way!"*

*But still the water pressed down on him, swirling into a
solid, unyielding weight on his chest, his heart, an incubus
with sea-green staring eyes that would steal his very soul.*

"No!" he cried again with his last breath. "No!"

And with a jerk that tremored his limbs, he woke.

No banshee wind, or crashing waves, or water cold
enough to freeze a man's blood solid in his veins. Instead he heard the jingle of a horse's harness, the creak
of the wooden wheels of the cart the horse was pulling,
mewing gulls and chirping robins, and the pleasant,
distant murmurs of female conversation and children
playing. He was warm and he was dry, almost cozy,

lying on a surpassingly soft featherbed, in sheets that smelled wonderfully of lavender and women's skin.

Only two things intruded upon all this dreamlike bliss. The first was a head that throbbed and ached so badly he must have drunk a sea of bad rum the night before. At least that was a plausible explanation. The second intrusion didn't have one. For the weight that had pressed on his chest in the nightmare remained, squeezing down upon his lungs to make breathing an effort.

Perhaps, he thought fearfully, he'd suffered some sort of apoplexy or attack that had left him this way. Perhaps that was why he was lying in this unfamiliar bed, why his head ached, why he'd no memory of how or why he'd come to be here. Perhaps he'd somehow been reduced to the life of a dependent, ineffectual invalid.

His heart pounding with unknown dread, he slowly, cautiously opened his eyes, and faced the green-eyed incubus of his nightmare.

Luna.

The cat lay centered high upon his chest, her front paws turned neatly inward and her tail curled around her plushly rounded body and hindquarters. Her face was only inches away from Zach's, her chins fluffed out and her eyes glowing green as she watched him, daring him to make her move.

He would have laughed out loud with relief if he hadn't remembered the sabre-sharp claws tucked inside those plush little toes. He didn't have a good relationship with this cat as it was, and his position was far too vulnerable for him to risk upsetting her.

"Luna," he croaked, for his throat and mouth were dry as sand. "Luna, you vile beast, you have to shove off."

Still the cat stared at him, unblinking and unmoving, though Zach was sure the wretched creature understood every word he said. With the same caution he'd use in any life-threatening situation, he slowly moved one hand to the cat's head and began to scratch her ears. To his surprise Luna lifted her head against his hand, let her eyes close with pleasure, and began to purr, the same as any ordinary cat. He shifted his hand to one side and she arched her head to follow, and as she did she tumbled off his chest to the bed with a disappointed wheeze.

"There now, that wasn't so hard, was it?" asked Zach as he rubbed the cat's velvety ears once again, figuring it was better to have friends than enemies, even fur-covered ones. He sighed, squinting at the cherry-colored checked hangings, lit from behind by the sun, that surrounded the bed and trying to figure out how the hell he'd come to be here in Amelie Lacroix's bed with the worst headache of his life.

At least that was where he guessed he was. Though Luna had been his first clue, he now recognized the scent of the sheets belonged to her. He wasn't in hell, the way he'd dreamed: he was in heaven. But what a damnable pity that he couldn't remember the details!

With a groan he sat upright and shoved aside the curtains, swearing as the sunlight burned the pain in his head. It was Amelie's bedchamber, all right, for hanging on one of the wall pegs was the straw hat she'd worn to the shipyard with him. Everywhere he looked were tiny intimate signs of her: the bottle of scent and the silver-backed hairbrush, the neatly paired shoes with the balled stockings tucked inside, a delicate night-rail, folded over the back of a chair, of such fine linen it was nearly sheer. Now why the devil couldn't he remember her wearing *that*?

He muttered an oath to himself and swung his legs over the side of the bed, leaving the dozing cat behind. Strange that he was still dressed, and he wondered wistfully if, her bed or no, there really hadn't been that much to forget. How long had he been lying here, anyway? How long since he'd stood outside in the street in the dark, gazing up at her window? He touched his jaw, trying to gauge the time by the stubble of his beard. The better part of a day, at least, a day he didn't have to waste. He thought of everything at the shipyard that needed his attention, the delays that could be happening even now without him there to sort them out. Definitely high time to find Amelie.

He tried to stand, and the room careened so wildly around him that he had to cling, sweating and weak, to the bedpost to keep from falling. He felt disoriented inside his own body, edgy and off-balance. The pain seemed concentrated on one side of his head now, and gingerly he touched a rough lump the size of a goose egg on his temple.

Had he behaved so knavishly with Amelie that she'd clouted him? He smiled, enjoying the unlikely image, but as he did he recalled other, more genuine memories of her leaning over him to stroke his forehead, whispering tenderly to him, even a kiss or two that he'd been powerless to return.

He reached for the glass and the water pitcher on the table beside the bed, and drank deeply. That helped; his head still throbbed, but at least he didn't feel like he had half a beach upon his tongue.

He heard a woman laugh from somewhere below. There, he reasoned, would be the millinery shop, and there, too, at this time of day he would most likely find Amelie herself, and the explanations he needed. It was enough of a reward to make him try standing again, then walking, then to make his way down the narrow, winding staircase. The workroom was empty, but from the shop he could hear Amelie's voice, clear and true as she extolled the stylish virtue of some sort of newly arrived Italian lace, and already smiling, he followed the sound down the short hallway to the shop.

At first all he saw was Amelie, dressed in the same pale blue-green of a robin's egg, her arms gracefully spread to display the strip of ecru lace, and, more innocently, the narrow span of her waist and the double swell of her breasts above the tight-laced bodice. Her face was animated, her eyes bright with the challenge of making the lace irresistable, and, decided Zach, herself as well.

Then he realized there were two other women in the shop, too, standing on either side of Amelie. Juliette saw him first, her hand rising up to her mouth to cover her genteel gasp of horror at his unexpected appearance, while beside her on a chair sat a tiny, birdish old woman in a monstrously oversized wig who twisted about to meet his eyes with instant, unsettling recognition.

"Hah," proclaimed Mrs. Murray, tapping her walking stick against the floor with a dramatic flourish. "So the dogcatcher returns!"

❧ 8 ❧

$\mathcal{I}$t was, quite simply, worse than anything Amelie could have imagined.

Here she stood, in the center of her shop with a ridiculously costly piece of Venetian needlepoint-lace across her wrists like a banner, convincing one of the handful of ladies in Boston who could both afford the lace's cost and appreciate its beauty that she could not, must not continue to live without owning it. Mrs. Murray, the wealthy and appreciative customer, was enjoying every word of Amelie's persuasive attention, eagerly leaning forward on her walking stick to make sure she could admire the lace—the delicacy, the artistry of convent-bred fingers!—as it deserved. Behind the counter, alert to increasing the sale, Juliette was displaying a length of Lyon silk brocade that was assuredly the perfect foil and complement to the Venetian lace. On the step outside the door, propped open for the warm day, stood Mrs. Murray's liveried manservant, pretending to be able to hear her summons and nothing else.

And then, quite suddenly, in the middle of this elegant transaction, was Zach.

He appeared without warning, swaying unsteadily in the hallway arch as if blown back and forth by some gentle breeze, and there was absolutely nothing elegant about him. His black hair was untied and disheveled about his face and only partly covered the livid bruise, his jaw darkened by his unshaven beard, his eyes oddly unfocused above a lopsided grin. He was barefoot, which explained why Amelie hadn't heard him come down the stairs, and he still wore the same clothes as when she'd found him, clothes that were blood-stained and now rumpled beyond decency.

He looked like either a lunatic straight from Bedlam or a pirate from battle, or perhaps a lunatic pirate. But most of all, he did not in any way look as if he'd business being in the respectable shop of the Mademoiselles Lacroix.

Except, that is, to Mrs. Murray.

"So you've had to bring the man back to finish the job, missy, haven't you?" she continued, the stiff curls of her wig quivering with grim excitement. "I could have told you that before, the first time. Those little curs are the worst. As soon as one has found his way to mingo and mischief on your property and in your garden, why, then you can wager twenty guineas his friends will soon follow. Isn't that so, Master Dogcatcher?"

Mrs. Murray turned expectantly toward Zach, who was listening with a certain dazed concentration. Amelie remembered how confused he'd been when he'd wakened before, and she couldn't imagine what his poor battered head was making of Mrs. Murray's dogcatcher.

"I would not expect much of an answer, ma'am," she whispered as she leaned over the older woman. "He does not have his full share of wits, you know."

"Ah, yes." Mrs. Murray sat back in her chair and nodded sagely. "Of course. 'Tis far better to give such folk the odious tasks that would distress more sensible people, and keep them from burdening the almshouse, too."

Amelie didn't dare look at Juliette as she turned to smile patiently towards Zach. "You know you don't really belong here, Zach. Would you like me to show you back to where you, ah, were before?"

But Zach didn't answer, his smile spreading more exuberantly across his face, enough to make Amelie's heart flutter with a mixture of dread and excitement.

Mrs. Murray clucked her tongue as she openly ogled Zach from his bare toes to his wild-man's hair.

"What a pity he is not altogether as he should be," she whispered loudly to Amelie. "He is in other ways a perfect figure of a man."

"Aye, aye, ma'am," said Zach suddenly, his voice rough from disuse. "You meant the whelp that's torn up the ladies' garden?"

"Yes, yes!" exclaimed Mrs. Murray. "Have you caught the rascal, then?"

Zach winked broadly, in best maniacal style. "I have caught the very rascal in a hamper outside," he said with relish, "and his bitch as well."

Juliette made a strangled sound in her throat that she garbled into a cough, and Amelie glared at her sharply. She wasn't mistaken: her sister was *laughing*.

"Oh, mercy and thanks!" cried Mrs. Murray. "You cannot know how I loathe the vile dogs that plague this city! Come, come, man, you shall have a bounty from me for your good work this day!"

"That isn't necessary, Mrs. Murray," said Amelie hastily, wondering how another of her dubious truths had gone so far, and so disastrously, astray. "I shall pay his fee myself, and that—"

"Oh, be still, missy, and let me give the fellow my little bounty," said the older woman as she dug her gnarled fingers deep into her pocket for her coins. "I'm already decided upon that lace, if that is what's making you fuss about. Go along, wrap it for me and add it to my accounting, as if I'd have to tell you that."

"*Avec plaisir, madame.*" Automatically she dipped a curtsey as she handed Juliette the length of lace. "My sister and I thank you for your custom. But I'm not sure it's proper to, ah, reward Zach twice."

" 'Tis proper enough," he said gruffly as he came to bow low over Mrs. Murray's offered shilling. He stayed low, too, his hair flopping forward, long enough to force Juliette to swallow another mangled laugh. But when he stood upright again, Amelie saw at once that Zach's color had drained from his face, and his madman's wickedness had vanished. Instead he had the greenish, unhappy look of an ordinary man about to be sick to his stomach.

"Come along, Zach," she said, seizing his arm to guide him from the shop. "Your time here is done."

He was leaning against her again, relying on her for support.

"My head," he said, the thickness she'd heard before returning to his voice almost before they were beyond the others' hearing. "Should—must lie down."

"Not before you get up these stairs, you don't," she

said, drawing him forward. "I'm not about to carry you again."

But by the time they'd reached the top he was relying on her for support as he stumbled his way to the bed, collapsing onto the mattress with a groan.

"Shouldn't have done that," he murmured, covering his eyes with his forearm. "Head's still not right."

"*Certainement*, you shouldn't have done that," she said, striving to sound disapproving, as if the sight of him in such obvious pain didn't affect her. "Teasing Mrs. Murray like that, and taking money from her, too! Whatever possessed you to do such things?"

"Must have been that same bad little dog in your garden." He smiled, then winced. His color was already improving, though she'd still taken care to place the chamberpot on the floor within his reach. "But I couldn't help it. You beguiled me."

"I'll beguile you to the devil if you don't promise to behave." But her words had no fire, and with a sigh she soaked a cloth in the water in the washbowl. Gently she lifted his arm from his forehead and in its place lay the damp cloth over his eyes. "How do you feel, then?"

"I've been better, but I've been worse, too," he said, purposefully keeping his voice low. He wasn't moving at all, his arms and legs flopped out over the bed, but he was speaking in whole sentences again, which Amelie took to be a favorable sign.

Luna jumped onto the bed, landing with the hefty thump that always announced her arrivals. To Amelie's great surprise, the cat then lumbered across the coverlet to Zach and thrust her head against his hand. And more marvelous still, Zach obliged Luna, rubbing his fingers deep into the purring cat's skull behind her ears.

"She likes you!" exclaimed Amelie with delight. "You can't know how rare that is, Zach. Luna is most particular."

"She doesn't like me," said Zach flatly. "Like most females, she tolerates me for the pleasure I can give her. If I stopped it, I'll wager fifty guineas she'd leave."

He lifted his hand to prove his point. The cat sniffed his fingers, twitched her tail with scornful disdain, then jumped from the bed.

Amelie flushed, thankful she hadn't accepted his wager, and swiftly returned to discussing Zach's head. "You shouldn't have lurched head over heels before Mrs. Murray. That was enough to make anyone ill."

"True enough," he admitted, "and I've no great wish to do it again. But if I can remember to make more stately progress, I warrant I can get back to the Crescent by nightfall, before Sarah Isham calls out the militia. She must have been ready to spit when I didn't come back last night."

"It wasn't last night, Zach," said Amelie slowly. "It was two days ago."

"Two *days?*" He whipped the cloth from his eyes and shoved himself upright to stare, or rather squint, at her, openly aghast. "How the hell did that happen?"

"I'd hoped you could tell me," she said. "But do it lying down, if you please. You're looking green again."

He dropped his head back down on the bolster with a disconcerted groan. "I'm feeling green again. Two whole blasted *days,* gone, lost! Have you any notion of what that's going to do to the *Diana*'s schedule? My cousin's going to have my head, and for good reason, too!"

"It's hardly your fault." She sat on the edge of the bed to retrieve the damp cloth from where he'd tossed it on the coverlet. Downstairs she heard the shop bell ring with another customer, and her conscience told her she should go help Juliette. But she was also reluctant to leave Zach now, before he told her what he knew.

"I'd gone to let Luna in at the back door," she began, "and you tumbled in after her with that ugly knot on your head, though whoever struck you seemed long gone."

"You are never to unbolt your door at night again," he ordered sharply. "I don't care if that infernal cat yowls all night. You stay inside where you'll be safe."

"I could say the same of you, Zach," she said reproachfully. "In the morning my yard was full of footprints and my rake was tossed aside next to your hat, all the signs of a righteous row. But I didn't see anything that could tell me who'd been there besides you."

"I couldn't, either." He sighed deeply, and this time when she bent to smooth the cool cloth back over his forehead, he let her. "Though I wish to hell I did. You know as well as I that it's the same bastard that broke your window and trampled your garden, and I don't want to think what more he'd been planning when he ran afoul of me."

Involuntarily Amelie shivered. She'd told herself all along that Zach must have seen his attacker, that at last she'd learn who their tormentor was. Now, instead, she knew worse than nothing, for not only did the man's identity remain a mystery, but by striking Zach, he'd also escalated the violence of the attacks far beyond a few broken flowers.

With a frustrated sigh he reached for her hand, covering it lightly with his own. "I came here to watch over you, lass, and instead you end up having to play nursemaid to me."

"It hasn't been so dreadful," she said wistfully, and she meant it. Though being unconscious hadn't made him the best company, she was still going to miss him when he left. Besides, having him unconscious had made his presence excusable, almost respectable. Not even Maman could have objected to looking after a man who'd been injured in their defense. And in a way Amelie had never expected, she'd enjoyed the intimacy of having him here, too, of caring for him, and even the wicked, secret pleasure of imagining herself in the bed with him. "But you must go, Zach, right now. You must leave as soon as you're able."

"Aye," he said heavily. "True enough, and for a whole wealth of reasons."

"You must." She wished she could know if she'd truly heard that tinge of regret in his voice or only wished it there to match her own. "Before Mrs. Murray comes back looking for the handsome dogcatcher again."

"That was your doing, sweetheart, not mine." In spite of the seriousness of their discussion, he chuckled, his smile rakish against the dark shadow of his beard. "But I promise I'll leave this evening, once your neighbors aren't peeking and the sun's not so bright. The blasted light cuts through my skull like the devil."

"At least the lump isn't so bad as it was." She pulled her hand free of his, troubled by what she now had to confess. "And Zach. In a way Mrs. Isham did call out the militia for your sake. On the first day, she sent a man here looking for you."

"A man?" asked Zach warily. "Here? Did the rascal give his name?"

"John Goodling. A pock-marked man with reddish hair. He said he was your first mate."

"And so he is." Zach relaxed visibly. "Honest John. Ugly as a bulldog, but loyal as they come, and the best navigator on the coast. I'm surprised he didn't insist on sleeping here on the floor."

"I—I didn't tell him you were here," she admitted in a quick, desperate rush. "He asked if you'd called and I said no, since you hadn't, really. Oh, Zach, I didn't know if he was a true friend of yours or not, or only some bad man who wanted to harm you more, and I—I didn't want to give you up to him. I wanted to keep you safe, the same as you wanted for me."

He didn't answer, his face giving away nothing below the makeshift blindfold of the damp cloth. Despite her best intentions, she knew she'd made a mistake by turning Goodling away, but she hadn't realized until now how much her choice could upset Zach. He'd called Goodling "Honest John"; he couldn't say the same of her.

Too agitated to sit, she left the edge of the bed and went to stand by the open window. A fat bumblebee, lured to the window by the sweet-smelling honeysuckle vine that climbed along the shutter, drifted lazily inside, his rumbling buzz the only sound in the room between them.

"I would always rather tell the truth than not, Zach," she said softly as she brushed the bee back out the window. "But sometimes it seems that my truths cause naught but more trouble, and I am sorry for it. Honestly, Zach, I am most sorry."

"You should never have to apologize for telling the truth, sweet," he said. "Nor should you have to run away from me for doing it."

"I didn't," she said defensively, coming back to the side of the bed. "I don't believe in running away anymore than I do in lying."

"Bravery and truth, too," he said, musing in a way that made her think he didn't believe in either one. "A rare combination in anyone, especially a woman."

She dropped back on the edge of the bed, his smugness irritating her into taking his bait. "A woman can be every bit as brave, and as truthful, as any man. Even as any dogcatcher."

"Woof." He smiled, pulling the cloth from his eyes as he crooked one arm behind his head. "But you do sound as if you're challenging me, mademoiselle."

"I thought your head hurt," she said suspiciously.

"Like blazes," he admitted, "but you're making me forget it."

She narrowed her eyes at him, and thought again of that mad pirate. It was one thing to have him senseless in her bed, and quite another to have him propped up against the bolster with that half-smile on his face. Her instincts sensed the danger, and she began to rise.

"Wait." Gently he caught her wrist, holding her, and subtly everything between them seemed to shift. "If you're as brave as you say, you won't leave me. And if you're honest with yourself, you'll realize you don't want to."

"Ridiculous," she muttered, though her heart was racing so fast she was sure he must hear it. She felt as if all the warmth of the summer afternoon had somehow been instantly concentrated in that one room, swirling hot between them. "You don't know what I want."

"I don't, but you do." His eyes were heavy-lidded, whether to avoid the light or to watch her, she couldn't tell. "Be honest, Amelie. Tell me what you're thinking, and then I'll do the same."

"Very well." She gave a defiant little twitch to her chin, nervously smoothing a stray lock of her hair back behind her ear. Being honest was a good thing, wasn't it? "I'm thinking I'm thankful you're better, better enough to want to play this fool's game."

He chuckled, deep and low in his chest. He'd begun rubbing his thumb across the inside of her wrist, where the skin was so fine her pulse showed in the pale blue veins, racing quick to her heart.

"A good beginning, aye," he said, watching her with the same single-minded intensity that Luna could display stalking a robin. "But it's my turn now, and I'm not playing games, you see, but only telling the truth. I'm thinking how lucky I've been to have you watching over me, Amelie Lacroix, keeping me safe when I didn't deserve it."

"You were lucky that you weren't grievously hurt." She shrugged self-consciously, not an easy feat with him still teasing the skin inside her wrist. "I know next to nothing about physicking."

"Ah, but you knew the other things that I needed more, lass," he said. "And I'm thinking how bravely you risked your good name to do them."

His smile had faded and his expression turned serious, and she realized he was drawing her closer, or maybe she was the one leaning into him, curling her legs behind her onto the mattress. In perfect honesty, she couldn't tell for certain. At this point, she wasn't sure of her own name.

"Your turn, Amelie," he said, a rough whisper. "Be brave, and tell me what you're thinking now, tell me true."

She swallowed, flicking her tongue across her lips to moisten them. Three days ago, none of this would, or could, have happened, but the time they had spent together, when each had taken risks for the other, had strengthened the connection between them, more than either one quite understood. Carefully she dared to touch his face, as he'd touched hers before, her fingertips another way of knowing him.

"I'm thinking what a beautiful man you are," she whispered back, her cheeks growing hot at such a confession. "I'm thinking how all the time these last days, and nights, too, that I sat in this bedchamber with you, I never once was as tempted to wickedness as I am now."

"And I'm thinking it's not wrong to want, sweetheart, nor wicked, not like this," he said as she felt his fingers spread over the small of her back, guiding her body closer against his. "Haven't I told you that before? Be as brave as you claim you are, Amelie, and take what you want for your own."

She'd never believed a woman could kiss a man outright, or that she'd even wish it. But when she kissed Zach now, she could think of nothing in the world that she wanted more. She kissed him shyly at first, her lips barely brushing against his as she threaded her fingers into his wild-man's hair. Though he kissed her back, with unexpected gentleness, he was clearly waiting for her to take the lead, to be as brave as he'd said.

And she *would* be brave, but she was also taking this precious time to explore him with, all her senses, in ways she hadn't before. She'd meant it when she'd called him beautiful, for she had the rare gift to find the beauty wherever she looked. In her trade she'd relished the silky plush of a cut velvet, or the musky scent of Russian ambergris, and now she savored Zach with the same sensual curiosity. She twisted her body and settled over him, onto him, her pale blue skirts settling around them with a *shush* of pale blue linen and the creak of the rope springs beneath the mattress.

With her fingertips she discovered how his skin was stretched tight at his cheekbones and lined at the corners of his eyes, etched and polished by a life in the harshest weathers, and she felt the difference between the short, stiff bristles of his new beard and the softer, finer hairs of his brows, feathered black like a raven's wing. Their gazes met, and this close she could lose herself in the colors of his eyes, a thousand blues as varied as the ocean he loved. She feathered her lips from his mouth to his chin and tasted the faint tang of sea salt that would always cling to him, and as as she moved lower, to the place on the side of his throat where even the strongest man was vulnerable, she heard him groan with restless pleasure, felt the vibration of it where they touched.

She smiled, and brought her mouth to his again, boldly teasing him the way he'd done before to her. Bravery had its rewards, and as his lips parted she slipped gladly into the simmering cauldron she'd created. All the heat that had been swirling between them seemed to coalesce in this kiss, and her whole body sparked and caught flame.

She stretched, eagerly deepening the kiss, and at the same time welcomed the way his body moved beneath hers, his hands tight at her waist. Without remembering how, her legs now had fallen on either side of his, and through the layers of her petticoats she could feel the hard muscles of his thighs pressing against hers, easing them farther apart. The heat of their kiss was spreading through the rest of her, gathering in an odd, insistent heaviness low in her belly, a sensation that his movements, and now her own in answer, seemed to only increase.

She thrust her hands higher, digging deep into his hair, and felt his hand travel along her side to the front of her bodice. Lying as she was, her breasts nearly spilled from the tight lacing of her stays, and it took him no great effort to ease the neckline down another inch. She wriggled with surprise and gasped into his mouth as she felt her nipple slip indelicately free of her shift and her bodice, and gasped again as his fingers closed over the sensitive peak and the pleasure raced through her blood.

"My brave lass," said Zach, his voice reduced to a rasping whisper as she whimpered and arched against his hand. "My own brave, true—"

"*Amelie!*" cried Juliette. "God, what are you doing, what are you—oh, *oh!*"

Instantly Amelie rolled away from Zach, and in that same instant she saw an image of her sister that would haunt her forever: Juliette standing in the doorway of the bedchamber with a shaft of sunlight from the window slashing across her face, Juliette with one hand curled over her mouth as if to smother her own horror, her blue eyes round and filled with a heartbreaking mixture of shock, pain, and betrayal.

And then, in another fraction of a second, she was gone, her footsteps clattering down the stairs as a single lonely sob trailed after her.

"I have to go to her," she said to Zach, her words falling together in a miserable, shameful rush as she slid from the bed. "I have to go now."

He sat upright, reaching for her. "Give her a moment alone to gather herself, Amelie. It's kinder than—"

"How could it be kinder to leave her alone?" she asked, twisting away from him as she tugged her bodice back in place. "I must go to her now."

"Then let me come with you, Amelie," he offered, undeterred. "I made this mess with you, and I should help you make your apologies."

"No," said Amelie, not letting herself look back to him, any more than she'd let herself accept the offered comfort of his hand. Her whole body felt edgy, unfulfilled, in a way she didn't understand. "She's my sister. I'll go alone."

She found Juliette at the worktable in the back room, determinedly rewrapping the Lyon brocade that Mrs. Murray had decided not to buy. Furiously she thumped the bolt on the table with every turn, as if the silk could hammer away at her unhappiness.

"Julie," she began, striving to keep her voice even, calm. "Please, Julie, please, please, you must listen to me."

Juliette stared steadfastly down at the silk instead of Amelie, reaching to flick away some nonexistent bit of lint from the pattern. "You can say whatever you please, but I'm not going to listen to you now. I may never listen to you again."

"But Julie—"

"All my life you've told me how I must obey what Maman said and what Maman wished us to do, because you remember her and I don't," she said, shaking her head so hard that her hair began to slip free of its neat knot and drift in wispy pieces around her face. "And I've tried, Amelie, I tried to do it, because I thought maybe that way I could remember her, too, even a little."

"Oh, but you do," said Amelie with a little catch in her throat. "You're so much more like Maman than I'll ever be."

At once Juliette looked up at her over the fabric, her eyes both wounded and resentful. "Don't say anything else you don't mean, Amelie. Don't begin telling me again about how we must depend on each other for the sake of Maman's memory, how it's always been the two of us together and always will be. You wouldn't mean it now. Maybe you never did."

God in heaven, she was unknowingly so much like Maman now, not only with their mother's pale beauty but with the sharpness of her words, so sharp they could flick and slice and wound with a knife's keenness. She bowed her head in contrition, her hands folded. She deserved all that Juliette said for what she'd done, every cutting, hurtful word in return for how she'd wounded her sister by being with Zach.

But as Amelie's conscience writhed, she heard another voice speaking to her, this one deep and low, telling her to be brave, to be honest, to listen to what she wanted for herself. It was a daring idea, fresh and full of hope, and free of the darkness and secrets of the past, of Papa's sudden death and Maman's lingering final illness and all the other smaller sorrows that she'd shared with Juliette and no one else.

Bravery and truth, a rare combination . . .

And when she bravely raised her gaze to meet Juliette's, she now saw not the guilt and fear that had made her sister speak so harshly, but instead the small things that belied Juliette's true feelings, that proved the love they'd always shared was still what bound them the most tightly: those stray wisps of hair, say, that any other time Juliette would have immediately smoothed and tucked away, or the way her hands kept stroking the same patch of the brocade, sleeking and tidying the fabric without need or reason.

"Juliette, please, you must—no, no." Amelie frowned, took a deep breath, and began again. No more orders, no more "musts." She wasn't Maman; she was Juliette's sister. "I can't make you listen to me, Julie, and I can't make you believe me if you don't wish to. But I am sorry for—for what you just saw."

"But not for what you did, Amelie? What you were *doing?*" Now it was Juliette's voice that trembled, and swiftly she looked back down at the silk on the table. "What if Mrs. Murray had tarried five minutes longer, and what if I'd waited ten to come ask you the cost of the new thread? What shameful sight would I have found in our bedchamber—in our *bed*—then?"

Amelie's face grew hot, for there was no easy, truthful answer to such a question. "I know I was wrong, Julie, I know I—"

But she broke off at the sound of Zach's footsteps on the stairs. She could not imagine a worse time for him to appear, yet still her wicked heart beat faster as soon as he stepped into the room, and the ache of longing returned worse than before. In those few minutes, he'd made himself look as presentable as possible. Since he'd had no razor or soap for shaving, he still wasn't terribly presentable to anyone but Amelie, who, to her own surprise, had come to appreciate his piratical dress.

But in addition to buttoning his shirt at the collar and donning his shoes, socks, and coat, Zach now wore an expression so grimly serious that he seemed to have aged five years in as many minutes. He looked drawn and sad, far from his usual teasing, boisterous self, and Amelie hated to think that she'd been the cause of the change.

He bowed gravely, including both sisters. "Amelie," he said, "you'll agree that it's better I leave now."

"Oh, Zach, you shouldn't!" She felt herself torn, her loyalty pushed and pulled as she fluttered between him and her sister. "You told me yourself that the bright sun hurt your head more, that if you moved too quickly you'll get dizzy again!"

"I'll survive," he said, though from the strained, tight look around his eyes Amelie wasn't as sure. "I've lasted twenty-seven years on my own before this, haven't I?"

Flustered, she lowered her eyes, wondering how much he was including in that vague *this*. Did he mean simply this moment, this day, or did his definition expand to include her as well? Or was the mention of those twenty-seven years intended to remind her of his own independence?

"Are you sure you're well enough?" she asked uncertainly. As inexperienced with men as she was, she doubted that a kiss or two gave her the right to be proprietary, but she still could imagine all manner of disasters befalling him near the docks, of pickpockets and other thieves taking advantage of him if he grew light-headed again, or even the same unknown man who'd hit him before coming back to finish what he'd begun. "I could come with you if you wish."

"Oh, aye, then who would watch over you when you returned?" He smiled wryly, a smile that wasn't reflected in his eyes, especially since he was already looking somewhere in the distance—at least as far as the distance in the small room could be—over her head. "You're better off here at home, lass."

He didn't want her with him.

He wanted her here instead, away from his life.

Once she'd chosen to follow Juliette—chosen to go after her sister instead of staying with him—he'd decided in turn that he'd do better leaving her behind.

Amelie swallowed hard, doubting he could make his wishes any clearer. If this was how it was to be between them, it was better she learned it now, or so at least she tried to tell herself. But oh, how much it still could hurt!

He bowed again, gingerly settling his hat on head, but still winced as the inside of the crown brushed against the bruise.

"I thank you, ladies," he said formally, "thank you for all your help and hospitality. Thank you, and good day."

All Amelie could do was nod, not trusting her voice to speak, and watch as he left through the same door where she'd found him—two nights ago, was it, or three? She'd lost all sense of time, and all sense of herself, but what more she would have given, freely, to hear him laugh and pretend again to be the dogcatcher!

She heard Juliette come to stand behind her. "He's gone, then."

"For now, yes." Amelie sighed forlornly. Sometimes the truth shone bright and golden, but now it only seemed bleak and cold. "I cannot say if he'll be back or not. But remember, Julie: if he hadn't come here to look after us, he never would have been hurt himself. Like it or not, he's tangled in the middle of our troubles now, too."

"Oh, *la*," said Juliette flippantly. "In the middle, is he? Is that why you decided to reward him like a slattern and take him to our bed?"

"Please, Julie, I don't want to quarrel," said Amelie wearily. "Not about Zach, not about anything. I don't think I've the power even if I did wish to."

Amelie dropped heavily into their father's old armchair, and leaned her head into her hands. Without the anxious excitement of Zach's presence, she began to feel the sleeplessness of these last nights and days pressing down upon her like a weight.

"You say I'm just like Maman," she continued, "that because of her, I always know what to do and say. But God help me, I don't now. I feel as if my head's stuffed with cotton wool, there're so few clear thoughts in it. And it scares me, Julie, scares me nigh to death."

With a self-conscious sigh, Julie sat in the smaller chair beside her and picked up the sleeve to a gown that she'd begun stitching this morning. "He—Captain Fairbourne—could he tell you who hit him?"

Amelie shook her head. "He said it was too dark. But he believes as we do, that it must have been the same person as before. And that we must take better care with our locks after dark."

"Meaning you must stop letting Luna in and out all night long as if you were her servant." The only sound was the pop-poke of Juliette's needle through the glazed linen. "Do you love him, then?"

"I don't know," said Amelie miserably. "I don't *know!*"

"Well, you should." Juliette thrust the needle into the cloth. "I could understand all of this so much more if you did. If you love him, then what—what you were doing upstairs wouldn't be shameful or strumpety."

"But Maman always said that love didn't really exist, not for women."

"Perhaps because it didn't exist for *her*." The bell in the shop jangled to announce a customer, and Juliette rose to get it, quickly setting aside her sewing but pausing to shake out her skirts. "Mind, she didn't approve of cats, either. If it had been Maman's decision, you never could have kept Luna. Perhaps you should think of Captain Fairbourne as another, larger cat."

Amelie sighed again, wishing life really were as briskly and easily explained as Juliette wanted to make it. And yet hadn't she herself pondered exactly the same disloyal questions about Maman and love?

"Is that how you see Oliver Richardson, then?" she asked, trying to smile. "As a great purring cat who wishes to be only your friend?"

But this time it was Juliette whose smile vanished. "A tomcat, yes," she said carefully. "But as for purring—no, Oliver never purrs."

Juliette crouched beside the slanting, slate headstone and lifted the vine that curled over the carved winged death's-head. " 'Abigail Postlethwaite, A.E. Above 99 years,' " she read. "What a pity the poor lady could not live to see an even century!"

"The real pity's us being here along with her." Uneasily Oliver glanced around the churchyard, hunching his shoulders as if to protect himself from any errant spirits on this gray afternoon. "This is a damned queer spot for a tryst, Juliette."

Juliette let the vine fall back over the stone and rose, dusting her hands together. "That's precisely why I chose it, Oliver. Who would question any meeting in such a solemn place?"

"Anyone with half a wit, that's who," grumbled Oliver, taking her arm. "Now for once oblige me, sweet, and come with me to a coffeehouse I know in the next street."

"Not today, Oliver." Pointedly Juliette slipped free of his hand. "In fact, I fear I cannot keep meeting you like this at all."

Oliver's jaw dropped open with the sort of broad surprise that proved how seldom he was refused anything. "Why in thunder not, Juliette?"

"We've had certain . . . troubles in the shop," she explained. "Until they are resolved, I think it unwise for me to be abroad, especially in your company."

"Troubles?" He drew his snuffbox from his coat pocket, tipped the ground flakes onto the back of his hand for inhaling, and indulged in a large, noisy sneeze. "What manner of troubles? I thought you kept a decent shop."

"I do," said Juliette tersely. "We do. Which is why I believe it wise for us to end this, ah, arrangement between us."

"But see here, dear Juliette, I'm not ready for that!" He lay his hand over his heart, striving for a picture of lovelorn devotion. "You've been my angel, my most loyal friend, my agent of grace, my very goddess of truest love! Another fortnight, dearest, dearest Juliette, to settle the last details of the journey. Another two weeks only, sweet, I vow!"

Juliette sighed unhappily. She'd resolved on her way here to end her part in this romantic misadventure—how, really, could she advise poor Amelie on love and men when her only experience had come from observing Oliver?—but when he pleaded like this, his handsomely sorrowful features forming the very picture of heroic longing, how could she refuse?

"One more fortnight, then, Oliver," she said finally, already regretting her weakness. "Two more weeks to set your affairs in order and arrange the passage to New York, one more chance to prove to me the seriousness of your love. But two weeks, Oliver, and that will be all."

❧ 9 ❧

*W*ith an ostentatious clatter, Sarah Isham dropped Zach's supper tray onto the table beside his open account book and waited, thumbs tucked into her apron strings, until he finally, balefully, looked up from his calculations to her.

"I cannot believe you'd ever be so pigheaded wrong about a woman," she proclaimed, loud enough for anyone in the street beyond the open window to hear and snigger over. "You, Zachariah Fairbourne, that's had the females nibbling at your fingertips since you fair could walk!"

Zach grumbled with cross-tempered incoherence. How could he find enough mere words to explain everything that was currently wrong with this evening?

He'd just lost his place in tallying a long row of figures—in ink—and he would have to begin again. The ropes and lines he'd ordered three months ago for the *Diana*'s rigging still had not been delivered to the yard. He'd received a letter from his cousin Joshua announcing he was coming for the *Diana*'s launching next week, a letter resplendent with the hilariously misguided assumption that the sloop's building was on schedule and without delays. His headache had grown increasingly worse since he'd risen before dawn, so that now, at the end of the long day, he felt as if a tiny smith stood working inside his skull, relentlessly striking away at his minuscule anvil.

He sincerely wished his landlady wasn't his mother's oldest friend, therefore believing herself entitled to offer precise critical comments on his personal life.

He hated boiled halibut, and he hated boiled peas, both of which were swimming about together on the same pewter plate for his supper.

But worst of all was missing Amelie.

"I wasn't being pigheaded, Mrs. I.," he said, trying to sound reasonable and not defensive. "Just the opposite. She'd made it clear as day that she'd had enough of me, and I wasn't about to stay there on her doorstep, all pitiful with my hat in my hands, until she had to shovel me out into the street along with the ashes."

"Ha, I don't believe it!" scoffed Mrs. Isham with an emphatic twitch of her apron. "Not that fine young lady, not to you!"

He looked at her suspiciously. "All along you've been calling her the worst sort of names and now she's become a 'fine young lady.' What's changed your mind, eh?"

"Maybe you did," she said promptly. "Staggering in here two days ago like something foul left behind with the tide, telling me that cautelous tale of hitting your head on a fence post. On a *fence*."

Her scorn was so withering he nearly writhed beneath it. Oh, aye, there were definite skills his mother must have taught her outright.

"I thought then it made no sense," she continued, "but you being Sally's boy and hurting and all, I was willing to let you be. Men can have their secrets, same as women."

Just not in Mrs. Isham's company, added Zach mentally. At least she didn't seem to be noticing that he hadn't touched the halibut or the peas. He'd have to give her credit there. She did find only one fault at a time.

She lifted her head, raising her tall ruffled cap so high it brushed the ceiling beams. "I was willing, that is, until I learned what mischief you'd truly been about. Making those two poor sisters fuss and worry over you, then hauling one of the little trollops into the bed with you for wicked amusement—there's no overlooking such, Zachariah."

"Now where in blazes did you hear a lie like that?" he demanded sharply. "Amelie Lacroix is a good, decent woman, and I won't have you carrying tales to ruin her!"

The older woman's mouth curved into a proud half-smile. "I knew you'd speak for her, Zachariah, like the gentleman your mama raised you to be."

"You're damned right I'll speak for Amelie," he fumed. "I kissed her, aye, but that was all, and all my doing, too. She's no trollop, and you'll do well to remember it."

Mrs. Isham beamed. "I told the lass this morning you'd say that, too, though I'm not certain she believed me."

"This morning?" he repeated, dumbfounded. "You're saying Amelie was here at the Crescent?"

"The same. Here and asking after you, not that she wanted you to know it. Made me promise not to tell, too. Strange how I forgot that part." She winked broadly, not in the least repentant. "But after you left the lass so sudden, she feared you'd come to some harm. And here *you* are, thinking she's the one who doesn't give a fig!"

For a long moment, all Zach could do was stare at that plate of halibut. Not that he was so intent on the fish—he wasn't even seeing it—but learning that Amelie might still care for him.

"But why didn't she tell me herself?" he asked, shaking his head, then wishing he hadn't. "Damnation, Mrs. I, if you could have seen how fast she ran down those stairs, trying to get away from me after I'd kissed her—"

She stared at him with undisguised pity. "Don't be a dunderhead, Zachariah. If you'd caught your sister dallying, wouldn't you have wanted to talk to her first?"

"No," he said firmly. "I know because I did catch Miriam with that infernal Jack Wilder, and after I'd thumped Jack about a bit, the only talking I did to either him or Miriam was to make sure he wed her."

But Mrs. Isham didn't seem particularly interested in the trials of having a sister like Miriam. "It's early days for that, of course, but you could do worse, aye, you could. She knows her own mind, and she has her own trade, just like that fisher-girl you was so fond of."

Zach frowned. He *had* been fond of Polly Bray, the "fisher-girl," and he was still, for she'd married his cousin Samson. He'd even fancied himself in love with her for a while. Polly was one of the most sensible women he'd ever met, and the only one with the right to call herself a sailor, and her trim little figure climbing up a ship's rigging, wearing the boy's breeches she favored, was a sight no red-blooded man would ever forget.

But comparing Polly to Amelie was purest folly. Amelie was a lush, lovely beauty, dressed and displayed to perfection and with an eye for what pleased men. But she was also clever and quick-witted, worldly in the special way that all Frenchmen and -women seemed naturally to be, and, he suspected, better at keeping her books and writing an elegant hand than he'd ever be. Not that he objected to that, either. He liked her independence, how she had dreams of her own. And each time he'd kissed her—no, there was no comparison with Polly, or any other woman, for that matter.

"There's no other woman like Amelie," he declared soundly, and, he realized suddenly, he'd never meant anything more. "None."

"Oh, aye, you'd know, for you've certainly done your share of looking." The older woman smiled, fondness and indulgence mingled. "But you're two of a kind, you and your Amelie, and I never thought I'd live to say that about some dark little Frenchwoman. I only pray you won't both be too stubborn for your own good."

He thought of how Amelie still hadn't confided to him the details of the threats against her and Juliette. She refused to even mention it, and she'd likely have fits if she knew he'd posted one of his sailors to watch her shop while he was here. With luck, the man would be discreet enough that she wouldn't notice, so Zach wouldn't have to explain how it was for her own good. She wasn't like other women that way, either, refusing to be looked after by a man. In that way, Mrs. Isham was right: Amelie *was* stubborn. But stubbornness was something she could be taught to outgrow, and in time she'd learn to trust him. Aye, trust, and he thought of how sweetly brave and agreeable she'd been up in her bedchamber.

He'd like to kiss her again like that, and there was plenty of moonlight tonight. . . .

"I'm going to call on her now," he said as he thrust the cork back into the ink bottle and closed the cover on his ledger. He wasn't naive enough to believe that all their problems could be solved in an instant, but the fact that she'd come to ask after him was encouraging, encouraging indeed. "We can talk then, and she can—"

"Zachariah," interrupted Mrs. Isham gently. "It's half past ten. She'll be in bed, if not asleep."

"You're right, of course." He slumped back into his chair with frustration. After he'd told Amelie to lock her home and shop tight against intruders for the night, he could hardly appear himself, and he hadn't forgotten the threat of scandal and gossip she'd always been so careful to avoid. "But tomorrow I must spend at the yard and with the men from the rope works, or the sloop will never be done."

"Somehow I expect she'll be willing to wait, Zachariah," said Mrs. Isham as she reached out to pat his arm. "Now eat your halibut."

This was the part of her trade that Amelie liked best.

She was making a wrapping-gown of yellow and green silk brocade, pomegranates and twisting vines, and she now stood before the form of a lady's figure that had on a borrowed pair of her customer's stays so as to mimic the woman's shape precisely. The plain inner lining had already been cut and fitted, and with that as a guide she could now work with the brocade itself. Most mantua-makers made strict paper patterns at the start, planning out every snip and stitch, but Amelie preferred to design as she went, trusting her eye and her instincts as she twisted and pleated the shimmering silk.

She'd been told it was dangerous to work this way—a gown like this could take as much as thirteen ells of imported fabric, which would represent three-quarters of the cost of the final garment—when a single impulsive cut could ruin the gown, but she also believed that this was what made her gowns and mantuas so special and so popular, too, with each one uniquely flattering to the wearer.

She squinted critically at the fabric as she held it in place. The pattern of the brocade was large and grand, an indulgent gift brought from London by a prospering sea captain husband, while the woman who'd wear it was small and slight. A sea captain: her thoughts snagged sadly on that insignificant fact as she tried to shove aside the memory of a certain other sea captain. With each day that passed without a visit from Zach, the fainter her hopes of seeing him again grew. She knew he'd returned safely to the Crescent, and she knew he'd been well enough to go to the shipyard the following day. If he'd wished to, he could certainly have come back here to Marlborough Street.

If only he'd wished it. . . .

Resolutely she turned her thoughts back to the green and yellow silk, trying to lose herself in her work. She'd have to keep the gown simple, the bodice close to the body and the sleeves plain, or all those tumbling silk pomegranates would overwhelm the wearer. Perhaps if she cut the back *en fourreau*, in one piece with the skirt, then the whole wouldn't—

The bell on the shop door began to jangle, and with a sigh of impatience at being interrupted Amelie left the half-made gown. With Juliette spending the day at another customer's home, remodeling gowns made too small by the recent birth of a baby, Amelie was alone in the shop. Briskly she hurried down the hall, the silver chains with her scissors, thimbles, and needle-cases hanging from the chatelaine at her waist jingling in counterpoint to the shop bell.

"Good day," she called, composing her hands neatly at her waist and a smile on her face. "And what do you buy this fair morning?"

But instead of a genteel customer, she found an untidy boy standing in her doorway, kicking the door back and forth so that the bell would continue ringing. He wore a knit cap pulled down nearly to his eyes, a faded striped shirt, and flapping canvas trousers that came to the middle of his bare shins: a ship's boy, she decided, with manners from the docks to match his ill-kept appearance.

But those were things she noticed later. All she saw now was the enormous bundle of cut flowers he held cradled self-consciously in his arms.

"These be for Miss Lah-croy," he said, mangling her name the way so many Bostonians did before he sniffed to show his disdain for the French. "Do you be her?"

"I be," she said, "and I am."

She took the flowers from him, ignoring the water that dripped from their fresh-cut stems as she held the bundle to her face to breathe deeply of their scent. Red roses from a sheltered garden, pale clusters of spring cress on their nodding stems gathered from alongside a stream, and bright yellow blossoms of Saint-John's-wort from some sunny meadow, all mingled together in a heady, sweet fragrance that spoke of summer itself.

"They be from Cap'n Fairbourne," said the boy, shifting restlessly from one foot to the other. "They be for you, ma'am, wit' his compliments."

Belatedly he drew a small, crumpled note from the waistband of his breeches and handed it to her. Amelie shifted the flowers to the crook of her arm and cracked the seal—only a hasty blob of dried wax, without any crest or mark pressed into it—with her thumb to open the folded paper. She realized this was the first time she'd seen Zach's handwriting: straightforward and plainly direct, like the sealing wax and like himself, without any gentlemanly flourishes.

> For dear Amelie,
> Though not so Sweet as your own dear self, these Flowers will I trust make you Think of Me and my Regards until next we meet.
> > with Affectionate Respect and Regards,
> > Yr. Obedient Dogcatcher,
> > Z. Fairbourne

She grinned stupidly, unable to help herself. She'd never been given flowers by a man before, not even the tiniest nosegay, and she was amazed at what a perfectly wonderful gift they could be. She'd heard from ladies that some gentlemen gave flowers as a cowardly way of saying farewell, but Zach's note promised a future, and as for signing it "Yr. Obedient Dogcatcher"—he certainly wouldn't have done that if he'd meant to disappear from her life, would he? Her grin grew wider as she lightly touched the flowers again. What other woman in Boston could boast of having red roses *and* her own private dogcatcher?

"Do there be an answer then, ma'am?" asked the boy, obviously eager to be gone. "Cap'n said to wait to see if you'd give one."

"Tell Captain Fairbourne—no, wait one moment, please." Carefully she lay the flowers on the counter, and reached beneath it for a pencil and a sheet of the paper used for orders in the shop. If she'd never received flowers from a gentleman, she'd never written a correct note in reply, either, but somehow she suspected the acceptable manner of address wouldn't necessarily apply with Zach. Relief made her playful, almost giddy.

With quick strokes she drew a picture of a small, ugly dog, with sharply pointed ears, a curling tail, and dots for eyes that were too close together. She gave the dog a wide, naughty grin that wasn't particularly doglike, but she thought Zach would like it anyway. Her message, written between the dog's paws, was short: "I'm waiting." She didn't make it clear whether she was supposed to be the dog herself, waiting to be caught, or whether the dog represented a nuisance she hoped her dogcatcher could contain, but that was an ambiguity she thought Zach would also appreciate.

"Here," she said, quickly folding the drawing for the boy. "It's most important that you give this to your captain at once. Do you understand that? At once!"

The boy nodded, though his expression remained so willfully blank that she pressed a shilling into his hand for good measure. That, at least, made him tug on the front of his knitted cap before he ran down the steps and into the street.

Merrily humming a song to herself, Amelie searched for something to hold the flowers. Cut flowers such as these were a costly indulgence for wealthy folk alone, and as a result their modest household included no vases specifically for the purpose. But a large creamware water pitcher would serve well enough, and as she arranged the flowers in it she realized she was still grinning with pleasure, while an hour ago she'd been feeling so sad and sorry for herself she would have wept at the slightest provocation. Now, however, thanks to the flowers and the note, she was humming and grinning like the happiest creature in paradise. She hoped the drawing of the naughty dog would do the same for Zach.

She set the pitcher with the flowers proudly on the counter, though she slipped the note into her pocket for safekeeping. Then, still humming, she twirled on her toes so her skirts belled out around her. Once, when she'd been very young, when Juliette had been but a swaddled baby, Maman had arranged for a dancing-master, another transplanted Frenchman, to come to the shop after hours to teach them fashionable steps by candle-light. As Amelie remembered it now, it seemed a strange thing for Maman to have done, considering how closely her newly widowed mother watched her coins. But Amelie could still recall a few of the steps, back and forth, with the hands gracefully outstretched and arched and the toes turned out, *précisément*!

"Miss Lacroix."

Amelie lurched to a lopsided halt to confront the grimly disapproving gaze of Esther Drummer in the doorway.

"Mrs. Drummer, ma'am, good day to you," she said breathlessly. "What will you buy this morning?"

"You amaze me, Miss Lacroix," said Mrs. Drummer as she entered the store at the same awe-inspiring pace as a ship o' war drawing into enemy waters. "I wonder that you believe I've any interest in your goods after such a display."

Swiftly Amelie collected herself, wondering what demon had made her behave so ridiculously in the store, and whether the same demon had been responsible for luring Mrs. Drummer, of all the worst luck, in as a witness.

"I regret any, ah, dismay that I might have caused you, ma'am," she said, adding a curtsey for good deferential measure. Mrs. Drummer was far too regular a customer to offend. "It shall not happen again. I hope that Miss Drummer is not ill today? We've newly received a selection of polished shoe-buckles, engraved most cunningly, that are exactly what she was seeking when last she visited us."

"Miss Betsey is in perfect health," said Mrs. Drummer as she stalked toward the pitcher with the flowers. "It was my decision that she stay away today. Since when has it become your custom to keep such lavish flowers, Miss Lacroix? Or is that another of your *French* indulgences?"

"The flowers are a gift, ma'am," murmured Amelie. The emphasis on "French indulgences" made her uneasy, as did the possibility of any further questioning about the flowers by Mrs. Drummer. "I know we had originally spoken of next week for your gown for the governor's house, but I believe it is finished now, if you would wish to have a final fitting before—"

"I do not wish it," said Mrs. Drummer as grandly as

the duchess she imagined herself to be. "Nor do I wish the gown at all."

Amelie frowned uneasily. "You confuse me, ma'am. I speak of the bronze satin with the bowed stomacher, that was bespoke by you last month."

"My memory does not falter, Miss Lacroix. I recall the gown perfectly." She bent to sniff one of the roses, her bulbous red nose hovering over the flower like some dreadful insect that Amelie longed to swat away. "But I find it will no longer suit my taste."

"Very well, ma'am," said Amelie as she swallowed her surprise. She was a good judge of her ladies' tastes, and Mrs. Drummer had dearly loved that bronze silk. "But such problems are easily remedied. With a different cuff, perhaps, or another flounce on the—"

"You misunderstand me, Miss Lacroix. I do not wish the gown, in any form or style. I am refusing it, and I am also refusing any other small trifles my daughter may have ordered as well."

Her small eyes glittered in her fleshy face. God, but the horrid woman was enjoying herself!

"With all apologies, ma'am, you cannot do that," said Amelie firmly, fighting the first wave of panic. "Your gown and the others were bespoke, with the assurance that the reckoning would be paid within the agreed time. If you will but step back to my desk, I'll show you my ledger, with the amounts and when they will fall due."

"For the sake of my mortal soul, I will not step anywhere further with you, Miss Lacroix," said Mrs. Drummer. "Because of your traitorous sympathies to King Louis, my husband has long urged me to patronize another milliner. But because I favored your accomplishments, I chose to ignore Mr. Drummer's wise counsel, and came to your shop with my daughter. You are French by birth. You cannot help being as you are."

"But Mrs. Drummer—"

"*You* shall not interrupt," ordered Mrs. Drummer severely. "You have betrayed our trust, Miss Lacroix. You have shamed us with your behavior until, as respectable ladies, my daughter and I cannot continue to be seen in the sordid company of you or your sister, or even in this shop."

Amelie felt the flush begin low, creeping up her throat to stain her cheeks. Could Mrs. Murray and her dogcatcher story have traveled this far, this fast? And she faulted Juliette, too—Lord, Lord, had some gossip seen her with Oliver Richardson? Or worse, had Oliver himself bragged of a conquest? She knew that Mrs. Drummer couldn't possibly have any proof of her own, but in her world a falsehood whispered behind a fan could be better, and infinitely more fascinating, than cold, dull truth.

She swallowed hard, striving to control her emotions. For years she'd tried to be so careful, so cautious, for the sake of keeping a respectable shop, just the way that Maman had preached. Yet the first time she'd strayed from Maman's warnings and dared to find a bit of happiness for herself, she'd been caught, and her gaze wandered toward the damning bouquet of flowers.

"I have done nothing to deserve this from you, ma'am," she said urgently. "I've always done my best to dress both you and Betsey in the best taste and style. Haven't I always accommodated all your wishes, and obliged you in every way possible? Have I ever once given you any article that was unsatisfactory?"

Mrs. Drummer flicked her hand, dismissing all of

Amelie's claims. "No more than any reputable trades-man would be expected to do."

"Then why have you always praised me for it in the past?" demanded Amelie, her temper barely under control. "Why were you so willing to go against your husband's wishes, if I have not treated you in the very best way possible? What else should matter?"

"Do not make me repeat the filthy scandal I've heard, Miss Lacroix," said Mrs. Drummer with the sort of relish that proved she'd like nothing better. "I am not a lady given to low gossip. But I have heard the stories, heard them all. It would be impossible to frequent the better houses in Boston, as I do, and not hear them. At last it seems you have given in to the wicked impulses in your filthy French blood."

"Very well," said Amelie tartly. "I shall have my bill sent to Mr. Drummer directly so your account may be settled."

"You can send all the paper you wish," said Mrs. Drummer airily. "But since you are the one who has failed us, do not expect to receive anything in return."

"Then you are no better than thieves." Amelie was so furious that she struck her fist on the counter. "Decent folk pay what they owe."

"Do you think I would care for the opinion of such as you?" Mrs. Drummer sniffed loudly. "This will be the last you see of me, Miss Lacroix, and my daughter as well. I've no doubt that once I have acquainted other ladies with your iniquity, that they, too, will choose to follow me, away from you. Good day, Miss Lacroix, and may God have mercy on your heathen soul."

She swept down the steps, thoroughly pleased with herself, and without bothering to close the door behind her. But Amelie was, this last time, happy to oblige her, and slammed the door so hard that the glass panes of the window rattled.

"Mean, ugly, old, meddlesome *biddy!*" she muttered, longing for stronger words, in English or French, than any she knew. "Nasty, interfering, wicked, pious daughter of a *sow!*"

She thumped her fists on the counter again, so hard that she made them hurt, and still it wasn't enough. It wasn't fair: none of it was. Still muttering, she pulled the small copy of her account book from her pocket and opened it flat on the counter. Running her finger down the entries, she made a rough tally of how much the Drummer women owed her, and swore.

Not only was there the bronze satin gown for Mrs. Drummer—the silk alone for that had cost the shop nearly fourteen pounds before the labor—but the "trifles" for her daughter included a mantua, two petticoats, and two dressed hats, adding nearly another twenty pounds. Then there was the account for other goods already received, for Amelie, like every other merchant who dealt with the gentry, was expected to extend credit to her customers. In the sixty days since the last bill had been sent to and paid by Mr. Drummer, his ladies had accumulated over two hundred pounds more in purchases.

Two hundred and forty *pounds.*

Amelie sank her head in her hands on the counter. The hats and petticoats that Betsey had ordered could be remade and sold, but the mantua and the gown for Mrs. Drummer could well be taken as an out-and-out loss; any lady who could afford to have such clothing made expected something fresh and new, made just for her, and not cut down from the unclaimed leavings of someone else.

Nor could Amelie reasonably expect to see any of that back account paid, either. It had been satisfying to call Mrs. Drummer a thief, and true, too, but the sorry fact was that if Amelie dared to take the Drummers to court to collect their debts, she was almost certain to lose, and possibly be charged for slander by them for her trouble. As a woman, as a tradesperson, as someone with a French surname, her case would be decided before she placed one foot inside the courthouse.

It was the vindictiveness of Mrs. Drummer's action that made the least sense now that her temper had cooled. Perhaps there was another, deeper reason for the woman's outburst. Though she hadn't heard any rumors, perhaps Mr. Drummer was suffering a setback or two himself. Merchant-adventurers and speculators like Mr. Drummer often foundered. Perhaps he'd found it easier to default on his wife's bills than to pay them.

For one moment, Amelie even let herself wonder if Simon Drummer could have been behind the threats to her and Juliette. But if he were in financial difficulties, he certainly wouldn't be throwing gold guineas through windows, and with a sigh of frustration she flipped the ledger shut.

It wouldn't be agreeable or easy, but she and Juliette could absorb a loss of a hundred pounds. They didn't have much choice, anyway. But if Mrs. Drummer could persuade enough of her friends to shun them as well, then they'd be ruined. It was as simple, and as simply unfair, as that.

She heard a muffled meow from the other side of the door, and with another sigh went to let Luna in.

"Foolish kitten," she scolded gently as she cat squeezed past her with a chirrup of thanks. "You never can decide what you want, can you?"

Yet today she felt the same. Her mood had gone down and up and down so many times this morning that she'd lost count. The half-finished gown on the mannequin held little appeal for her now with her thoughts in such confusion. She felt restless, unsettled, and unhappy.

Maybe, like Luna, a walk would be the answer, a chance to stretch her legs and clear her head and figure out what to do next. Except for the boy with the flowers and Mrs. Drummer, she'd had no customers this morning. Surely she could spare the time for herself, and before she could change her mind she reached for her hat and, on impulse, pulled one of the rosebuds from the pitcher and tucked it into the front of her bodice.

Yet as she paused on the steps to lock the door and tie her hat ribbons, she noticed a man in a dark knitted cap and a green waistcoat leaning against the fence across the street as he read a sheet with the latest news. There was nothing remarkable about the man or the news, except that she could have sworn he'd been there this morning, too, when she'd said farewell to Juliette.

She shook her head as she began down the street, resolving not to look for more trouble than she already had. The morning was warm but not unpleasant, with little torn tufts of white clouds drifting overhead in the breeze that always came from the water. But Amelie decided to go west instead, away from the harbor and up the hill toward the town beacon instead. Though the great trees that had once graced the hillside had long ago been cut for firewood or building, the meadows of the common were green with grass and wildflowers and darting yellow butterflies, a place where June in summer still meant more than it did along the cobblestone streets.

But the peace that Amelie sought eluded her, and with each step her thoughts only grew more confused. If she wished to save whatever remained of her shop's reputation and her own with it, she must give up Zach and insist that Juliette do the same with Oliver, if, of course, there was anything there for Juliette to give up. But to do that would also mean giving up the first real taste of new happiness she'd known. Zach made her laugh, he made her think, and he made her feel like a beautiful, desirable woman. She liked those things, and she liked him, too, both as a man and a friend, and that was where the trouble lay.

It had been wonderfully easy to follow Maman's warnings when men were only hazy villians bringing sin and ruin. But it was much, much more difficult when *men* became *a man*, one with blue eyes and broad shoulders and a sunburned nose, one who could impersonate a mad dogcatcher as readily as he could kiss her until she thought she'd found Heaven. And what would happen when his *Diana* was finished? There'd never been any promises of a shared future. His livelihood would take him away from Boston, just as surely as hers must keep her here, and so, for her, would come the end of roses and kisses and wishing on stars.

She climbed upon one of the lopsided stone fences that marked the common to sit across the broad crown, the stones beneath her warmed by the sun. Before her russet-red cows grazed, the brass pegs on their horns glinting in the sun and the bells around their necks chiming gently in off-kilter harmony as they moved. Amelie had never envied cows before, but as she watched them now, standing knee-deep in the grass as they ate, there was a certain predictable placidity to their existence that, today, seemed downright appealing.

"Moooo," she said softly, trying to see if she could speak—no, low—their language. After all, she already jingled like them, her chatelaine her own silver bell. "Moo-mooooo."

"Amelie?"

Chagrined that she'd been caught mooing, she quickly twisted about on the wall to see who'd called her name, squinting into the sun from beneath the straw brim of her hat.

"Zach?" she asked, not quite believing her eyes. "Zach, what are you doing here?"

"I could well ask the same of you, lass," he said as he joined her. His grin was so wide with delight that it lit her day like another sun, his eyes as blue as the summer sky above them. He swept his hat grandly, bowing over his knee with a cow-pasture courtier's elegance, and she was glad to see that he could do it now without keeling over in the dust at her feet.

"Your head is better," she said, feeling strangely self-conscious. Here she'd been thinking of him night and day, and now that he'd actually appeared she could think of nothing sensible to say. "The bruise looks ghastly, all green and yellow, which I know means it's better, too."

"I am mending," he said as he resettled his hat, clearing his throat with such uncomfortable emphasis that Amelie wondered if he, too, wasn't quite sure what would happen next between them.

She could think of nothing, nothing to say, and then worst of all, she said the first dreadful words to rise up in her consciousness. "You left so suddenly before."

He let out his breath with an odd little whistle that showed how much she'd taken him by surprise. "I thought that was what you wanted. With your sister and all, I mean."

"No, not at all." Oh, dear Lord, what had made her say such a thing? He would think she *was* the strumpet she'd behaved like. "That is, when you left I was worried that you were still unwell."

"And so you came to ask after me?"

"How embarrassing," she murmured, wrinkling her nose with chagrin. "Your Mrs. Isham promised not to tell you!"

"And I'm damned grateful she did." His gaze wandered down to the rosebud nestled cozily between her breasts, lingering there with an interest that had nothing to do with the flower and everything with how Amelie now blushed. "So that young rascal Sam found you with the posy, did he?"

"Most generous for a posy!"

"Ah, well," he said, his expression turning serious. "I suppose you've gotten many to judge in comparison."

"Never one," she said shyly. So he hadn't received her drawing of the dog yet; just as well, considering. "Yours this morning was the first."

He brightened. "You liked it, then? I'm sorry I couldn't have brought it myself, but I did choose the flowers at the market."

"They were—are—lovely." She smiled again, but this time with wobbling conviction. "They were the single best part of my morning."

He sat on the wall beside her. He didn't ask permission first, but she didn't mind. "How many gloomy parts could there be on a morning as sunny as this?"

"Only one, but she was large enough." Her sigh wobbled as much as her smile had, making her look down at her lap. "One of my customers called in the shop to tell me she wasn't going to accept the gown she'd bespoke, and she wasn't going to pay me for the things she'd already taken on credit, all because I am impudent French chit, given to scandal."

Zach swore, using all the words Amelie had wished for herself earlier. "She said that to your face?"

"In so many words," said Amelie, trying to pretend it hadn't hurt as much as it did. "More, actually. But, oh, Zach, it wasn't just her refusing to pay. She made me so angry, implying so many hateful things about me and Juliette and Maman, too, that I didn't know if I wanted to jump at her throat or cry."

"I'd have chosen her throat," said Zach. "With a knife."

"Oh, Zach." She tried to smile, but now the tears of frustration and shame she'd fought back this morning came back instead, hot tears that spilled from her eyes and down her cheeks. "I came here to—to cheer myself, and now—now I'm crying. Oh, I'm such a fool!"

"Not foolish," he said. He handed her his own handkerchief, an oversized white square of plain-hemmed linen that seemed big enough to be a sail on his sloop. "Not foolish at all. And now, it seems, it will be up to me to cheer you instead."

"I can't," she said miserably, shaking her head as she balled the handkerchief in her fingers. "I shouldn't. All the hateful things that Mrs. Drummer said—I shouldn't."

"And I say you shouldn't let her rule your life," he said firmly. "But I can guarantee that the place I'm headed will cheer you immeasurably, and with absolutely no chance that Mrs. Drummer will see you."

"Truly?" She thought of all the places she and Juliette went for cheering in Boston: the parlor of a genteel lodging-house for a dish of Chinese tea, or the square where the traveling balance-masters would sling their rope between two windows and dance upon it, marvelously high in the air, or the house of the famous Mrs. Hiller, at the head of Clark's Wharf, to view her waxwork display of great kings and queens.

"Truly," said Zach as he slid from the wall, offering his hand to her for assistance. "I'm bound for Lynde's ropewalk for new hempen lines for my *Diana*, out near Barton's Point. I promise you there's no more cheerful place than a good ropewalk."

Skeptical, she looked at him sideways beneath her hatbrim, sure he was teasing again. A *ropewalk?*

She told herself she shouldn't leave the shop closed, that she should return to finish the wrapping-gown she'd begun, that to spend more time with Zach Fairbourne could only lead to worse, not better. All this she knew to be true, and yet with no more than a moment's hesitation she took his hand and hopped off the wall.

And at Lynde's ropewalk, she'd be absolutely sure not to meet Mrs. Drummer.

"You see how it works, Amelie," said Zach as he leaned over her shoulder to point. "The yarns are laid out along the walk, across the skirders—those are the flat-topped posts with the teeth, there—with one set of ends bound to the farthest point of the traveler—that's the part that moves—and the other looped through the hooks on the rope jack, here down where we are. Oh, and that funny chunk of wood strung in the middle is called the top. It keeps the yarns from tangling. Now, with everything in place, all Lynde must do is turn the crank on the jack to twist the yarns, and there you are with your rope!"

Because he'd visited ropewalks since he'd been a boy, the process seemed clear as day, and perfectly sensible, too. But from the slightly bored look on Amelie's face as she watched the workers trudging along the walk to lay out the yarns, he doubted he'd made it understandable.

"Very well," he began again. "You see it's all a matter of twisting the hemp yarns in order, and then—"

"I do understand, Zach," she interrupted. "I'd be rather a ninny if I didn't, wouldn't I?"

She was smiling, so he guessed he was spared from answering such a difficult question. He'd always thought he understood women, but Amelie could trip him up short if he wasn't careful. She was a challenge that way.

"It's exactly like making a length of silk cording," she continued. "My silk thread behaves just the same. If I twist it over and over with my fingers—my fingers behaving like your rope jack—then it shall eventually curl back upon itself and stay that way into a cord, without ever coming undone or raveling. Like so."

"I suppose it's the same idea, aye," he said uneasily, not really sure that there should be such similarity between such a fine manly craft like ropemaking and her making dainty little milliner's cords with her fingers. She'd already caused enough disturbance today in the ropewalk, making men practically fall on their faces gawking at her yellow stockings and ruffled petticoats and that infernal teasing rosebud between her breasts, without her speaking such heresy in anyone else's hearing. "But there's a real skill to making a first-rate rope. I'll have to stake my life on Lynde's work in a gale, and I don't want to be praying that it won't give way."

"I daresay not." She tipped her head to one side, raising her forefinger for emphasis. Tiny bits of hemp from the yarns, almost motes, floated and danced in the beams of sunlight around her as if she were standing in a shower of golden flecks. "But my skills are not so very different, you know. Your sailmakers and painters and ropemakers and goodness knows how many others—aren't they all making your *Diana* beautiful and seaworthy?"

"Aye," he admitted, fearing what was coming next. "But I don't see what that has to do with you selling shifts and gowns."

She laughed merrily. "Why, it has everything to do with it, Zach, as I know I have told you before! All that these men are doing is dressing your ship. When a lady comes to me, I can can lace her stays more tightly to make her waist smaller, or fit her with hoops to make her hips wider, just as your shipbuilder did with your sloop in the yard. I can offer her paint to deepen the color of her cheeks, or powder to lighten them. And the gown I make is every bit as important as your sails, for the right one will make my lady dance as gracefully as your *Diana* will upon the waves. It is exactly the same."

It wasn't the same, not at all, and he stared at her, unable to think of a suitable reply. When he'd thought about Amelie these last days, he'd always imagined her sweetly, bravely yielding, the way she'd been in her bedchamber, or gazing up at him wide-eyed in the moonlight, as she had when they'd been on the *Diana*'s hull and in the Richardsons' garden, or even as he'd come across her so unexpectedly earlier this morning, perched on the stone wall like a china shepherdess on a mantelpiece. In short, he liked to remember her needing him, just as he'd told Mrs. Isham.

But this nonsense about dressing his sloop—*his* sloop!—like some furbelowed lady was part of the other, more independent side of Amelie, the side that Mrs. Isham must have meant when she'd called her "stubborn." Zach had to admit that while this part of Amelie had always been there, too, from the first night, he found it a great deal more, well, disconcerting. She had never once asked for any single thing from him, no favors or little gifts or indulgences, the way that every other woman he'd known had done. Hell, even Polly Bray had asked him for advice! But for a fact Amelie had seemed irked, even irate, when he'd so much as offered to help or watch over her, which had struck him as odd indeed, and a little insulting in the bargain.

Yet when he finally had been able to make her a gift, a common bundle of flowers from the market, she'd obviously been touched far out of proportion to the flowers' value, charmingly flushed and pleased. He'd been pleased, too, of course, but also puzzled by the incongruity.

And he couldn't wait to give her something, anything, so he could see it happen again.

She was looking impishly at him now, peeking up from beneath the curving brim of her hat. Nearly every woman, old and young, in Boston wore a wide-brimmed straw hat in summer, but only Amelie's managed to look quite so engaging, almost rakish. "You look as if you fear I'm going to tie silk ribbons on the front of your precious sloop, ah, *très belle*!"

"I'm not sure what you're going to do," he declared. At least he'd managed to cheer her, though not exactly the way he'd planned. "I never am."

She laughed again, but before she could reply Mr. Lynde returned with the papers for Zach's order.

"There you are, Cap'n," he said. "The bulk shall be delivered to Heward's on Monday, as you required, ready for your rigging to commence after the launching. That's a pretty little sloop you'll have there, Cap'n, as pretty as they come. But then it's always an honor doing business with the Fairbournes, and you be sure to tell your cousin I said so."

He nodded seriously as he shook Zach's hand, then glanced at Amelie.

"Does the lady like pretty sights?" he asked as if Amelie were either deaf, or not standing at Zach's side. "The lilies have come, you know."

"The lilies?" repeated Zach, mystified.

"Oh, aye, aye, the lilies on the pond," said Lynde gravely. " 'Tis their time to flower, and ladies do admire them. You take the path away from the west door, wind down the hill a bit beyond the shed, until you come to the pond. There's an old pinnace tied up there if you wish to go out. Ladies like that, too."

Though Zach listened, he'd already made up his mind to refuse the man's offer. It must be the middle of the afternoon by now, and though he'd certainly enjoyed this unexpected time with Amelie, he still had a mountain of details to supervise at the shipyard. The *Diana*'s launching was only a few days away, and he couldn't believe how much more remained to be done.

"Pond lilies?" asked Amelie excitedly. "The ones that float like saucers on the water?"

Lynde nodded. "The same. The flowers be about big as the saucers, but the leaves, now, they're about big as platters." He held his hands in an oversized circle to demonstrate the size. "Something to see, all right."

Amelie turned and impulsively grabbed Zach's arm. "Oh, Zach, could we? I've never seen real water lilies before, only pictures. Please?"

Her dark eyes gazed up at him, beseeching with all their considerable power. Damnation, the first favor she'd asked, and it came on a day when he already had ten thousand tasks to cram into a space meant for far less.

"Please, Zach," she said softly. "Oh, I know I

shouldn't take any more time away from my shop, especially not today with Juliette away, too, but who knows when I'll have the chance to see water lilies again?"

Shyly she shrugged her shoulders, as if shaking off some sort of last hesitation. "Or when to see them with you?"

Zach nearly groaned aloud, knowing he'd been beaten as squarely as a man could. If she could spare time from her shop to gawk at these wretched water lilies, and to do it so she'd be with *him*, then what choice did he have, really?

"Very well, then, Lynde," he said, striving to sound much more captainly and in control than he felt. "Because Miss Lacroix wishes to see your pond lilies, I believe we shall take a short walk down your path."

Soon after, he and Amelie were on their way on the path winding down the hill and a bit beyond the shed, as Lynde had described. The path was sandy and rough with loose stones, and if Amelie in her delicate heeled shoes needed to cling to Zach's arm for balance, then he considered it well-deserved compensation.

"You know Lynde only suggested this in the hope I'll keep all the Fairbourne business here," he grumbled. "As if his damned flowers are going to influence me or my cousins one way or the other."

"If the quality of his rope and his prices are even with those of another walk owner," said Amelie, "why, then him being hospitable about his lilies might make the difference in your returning another time. Though I would think taking you off to his counting room to share a tumbler of rum might have had more effect."

Zach looked at her suspiciously. "What do you know of such things, eh? Do you take toddle your ladies off to your desk for a snip of ribbon and a sip of rum?"

She grinned. "No, though I rather like that: a snip and a sip. Ha! There are more than a few fine ladies in this town who'd welcome an offered bottle, too."

Zach snorted. "I won't ask for names."

"And I won't tell them," said Amelie promptly. "No, no! But if these lilies are all that Mr. Lynde promises, then I mean to remember them. I have several ladies from other colonies who travel with their husbands to Boston, and who look for genteel entertainment while the men arrange their business affairs. A visit to a pond full of rare lilies might be exactly right to offer, and to make them remember me as pleasantly as I'll remember your Mr. Lynde."

"You're too clever for your own good," admitted Zach with admiration that he wished he could make sound more grudging. No wonder she thought she didn't need help from anyone else, he thought glumly. In most ways, she didn't, especially not from him. "And I'm damned glad I'm not competing with you in the same trade."

"You would have much company." Proudly she raised her head high, the straw hat worn with the imperious air of a crown, though, to Zach's relief, the extra sparkle in her eye showed she wasn't being entirely serious. "In Boston, among milliners and mantua-makers, the Mademoiselles Lacroix have no rivals."

She'd have no rival anywhere, as far as Zach was concerned. Whether she was standing in the middle of a ropewalk on Barton's Point or in King George's court at St. James Palace (or even King Louis' at Versailles), she'd still be the one woman that every man would see at first. He opened his mouth to tell her so, but she opened hers first and faster, with a gasp of delighted wonder.

"Look, Zach, just *look!*" she cried and the shrewd, regal lady of business vanished, replaced by a wide-eyed young woman squeezing his arm with excitement. "It's beautiful! *C'est très, très belle!*"

Lynde had called his pond a "pretty sight," but that didn't begin to describe the scene before them now. On the far side of the hill the land dipped and flattened out into an open meadow, bright green as the grass always was so near to the sea, and dotted with white and yellow wildflowers. A rambling stone wall haphazardly divided the meadow, and a small shed or storage house with lobster traps stacked beside it, unpainted and silvered by the wind and sun, were the only marks left by man. Surrounded by taller grass and a few scrubby trees, the pond shimmered in the summer sun, dancing back the blue to the sky overhead.

But that was the water that lay open; a good third of the pond's surface was covered with the lilies, scores of them jostling cheerfully together for sun and water. As Lynde had said, the leaves were round, shiny green circles rimmed with deep red, as big as dinner plates, while the flowers floated between them, exuberant clusters of white spiked petals and centered with bright yellow stamens that rose up like flames.

The lush beauty of the pond and its lilies would have been a marvel anywhere, but to find it here, so close to the stern, gray-clapboarding town of Boston, made it seem unimaginably exotic.

"No wonder Lynde's so proud of this," said Zach. "Looks more like Martinique than Massachusetts, doesn't it?"

"I want to see closer," said Amelie, and before he could stop her she was running, skipping, down the path with her arms outstretched for balance, the rib-

bons on her hat trailing out behind and the chains on
her chatelaine jingling. Yet when she reached the
pond's edge, the lilies were still tantalizingly out of
reach and view, hidden by the tall grass and rushes
along the water's edge.

"Oh, fah, I thought I'd be able to see more," she
said with frustration, craning her neck. "How irritating,
to know they're so near!"

"Would you like to go out in the pinnace?" he heard
himself asking, and realized his business at the shipyard
had just been postponed again. "We could go right out
in the middle of them if you wish."

She frowned, uncertain. "The pinnace?"

"It's a boat, sweetheart," he explained. "Remember
Lynde offered it to us to use."

"I'd like that," said Amelie. "I've never been to sea,
you know."

"You won't have been after today, either," he said
as he pulled and shoved the small boat from the reeds
where it had been partially hidden for safekeeping.
Only Lynde would know why: the boat was old and
battered, likely scavenged from some long-ago wreck.
But from the damp waterline on its sides and on the
oars laid neatly inside, Zach figured it had been recently used with no ill effects. "Lynde's pond's not
exactly the sea. Now hop aboard before I launch her
off the bank."

Gingerly she climbed into the boat, bunching her
skirts clear, and when she sat on one of the boat's two
seats, her skirts seemed to fill the narrow hull with a
froth of incongruous petticoats. "Very well, then, I'll
grant you it's not the sea. But it *is* the first time I'll
ever have been on water of any sort."

"No," scoffed Zach as he pulled off his shoes and

stockings. He couldn't remember a time when he *hadn't* been in a boat. "I can't believe that. You've lived all your life half a mile from the harbor and never once gone out in a boat?"

"Never," she declared. "I'm a seamstress, not a sailor. You must be my captain, for my first voyage."

At least that was a pleasing idea, being the first anything in her life. "I can't promise you—what in blazes are you doing?"

He didn't really need to ask, for it was apparent enough. She'd unbuckled her shoes, reached up beneath her skirts to untie her garters and now was rolling her yellow stockings down over her ankles and feet. Her toes were small and pink, and she didn't seem to care that he could see a good deal more of her bare ankles and shins, the skin gleaming pale and smooth. And if she didn't care, then he shouldn't either.

Like hell he didn't.

She looked up at him innocently, tying her stockings together with her garters. "I'm just doing what you did," she said. "I thought that's what one must do in a boat."

"That's why I had you get in first, while we were still aground," he said, his voice oddly strangled. He kept thinking of her bare feet and ankles and knees and thighs and all the rest of her, not two feet away. "I'll be the one to shove off so you can stay dry."

"Oh." She shrugged, and tucked the stockings into her pocket. "No use putting them back on now, I suppose. I'll just be barefoot like you, a real sailor, until we're done."

A real sailor: he couldn't think of a polite reply to that one, either, not with his head still so muddled by her bare legs. Instead he resolutely pushed the boat and her in it forward, down the bank and into the water, jumping in as soon as it was afloat and sitting on the bench opposite hers. She gasped and giggled in wordless delight at the unfamiliar sensation, and as he rowed them towards the lilies, he had to admit that being a captain, even of so tiny a vessel, had never before held such out-and-out appeal.

"Hold tight, now," he warned, though she was already hanging to the sides with both hands. "Don't want to lose you overboard."

Cautiously she peered over the side, into the water. "How deep do you suppose it is?"

"Oh, at least a hundred feet," he answered blithely. "This is a freshwater pond, you know. Perhaps two hundred at the deepest part."

She smiled sweetly. "Liar."

"I could have you put in irons for that," he growled, making his voice deep and grim. "Don't you know the captain's word is law?"

"Not for me, it isn't." The boat was just beginning to reach the first of the lilies, and she twisted back to look over her shoulder. "How beautiful they are, Zach!"

"Not as beautiful as you," he said, and he meant it. The sun was reflecting upward from the water, lighting her face beneath the hat to make her whole face radiant.

But Amelia wouldn't hear of it. "I've told you before, Zach, I'm not beautiful, and having to hear you say it again won't change my mind, or my bumpy nose, either. But these—these *are* beautiful."

She was wrong, of course, but he wasn't going to waste this moment arguing with her. Carefully he nudged the boat in among the clusters of white flowers until they were surrounded by blossoms and the dark green leaves. Iridescent dragonflies darted over the water's surface as they moved from flower to flower, their wings no more than a blur of speed in the bright sunlight.

"Don't want to go in too deep or we'll be mired here in the middle of your pond lilies," he said as he poked aside one of the thick underwater roots with the oar. "Wouldn't that be a pretty way to spend the day?"

"I wouldn't mind," said Amelie wistfully, trailing her fingers through the water, the cut-garnet ring she always wore catching the light like a little red flame. "It's so quiet here, without any of the racket of the wagons and streets. I—I wouldn't mind at all."

Neither would he, really. He shipped the oars in the boat, trusting the combination of still waters of the pond and the vegetable embrace of the lilies to hold them steady. It was an oddly intimate place, just the two of them rocking gently in a pond full of white flowers, and oddly companionable, too, sitting across from each other, face to face on their own narrow benches.

"When I was a little lad, scarce more than a baby," he said as he rested his hands on his knees, "my mother would take me out in a boat like this on our river. Just the two of us, bobbing about in the water much like this."

Amelie's eyes widened. "She rowed herself? With a baby?"

"Oh, aye," he said, smiling at the memory. "She'd grown up on the river—her father was a sailor and so was my father—so she thought nothing of it. No one else in Westham did, either; it's not that sort of place. We might have fished, too, or pretended to, as an excuse, but mainly I think it was her way of mourning my pa. If she was near the water he'd loved so dearly, then she was near to him as well. And, of course, it was a grand way to keep a wild small boy like me occupied and out of mischief for an afternoon."

He shifted his shoulders sheepishly, embarrassed that he'd spoken so personally. He didn't know why he'd done it; he'd never said any of this to anyone else, not that he could remember, not even to his half-sister Miriam, who might actually have been interested in old stories about their mother.

But to his surprise, Amelie seemed interested, too. No, more properly, enthralled, leaning forward to listen, and he could have sworn that there were tears of sympathy glistening in her dark eyes.

"Did your father drown, *mon cher?*" she asked softly.

"Lost in a nor'easter off Halfway Rock," he said evenly, "two months before I was born. My poor mother only had him to herself for a year before he drowned."

"Oh, Zach," murmured Amelie, resting her hand over his, on his knee. "That was the same way with Juliette, for she was born after Papa died. How dreadful for your mother, but how fortunate that she had you."

"Aye, that's what people said." He stared down into the bottom of the boat, remembering. Perhaps it was the rocking of the boat that brought it all back; they'd had good times then, he and Mam. "As I grew, everyone in Westham said how much I favored my father, how now I was the man of the family, the one who must watch after my mother. I did, too, as much as a boy that age can."

He could still recall every detail of that little house by the river, the one room that served them for everything.

There'd been only two windows with tiny diamond-shaped panes of watery glass that distorted the world when he pressed his nose to them, a half-loft with a ladder that he'd pretend was his ship on snowy days, and wild ducks with bright green heads that Mama had tamed to waddle right to their doorstep for bits of cornbread. It had been just the two of them in that little house, and sometimes it seemed he'd never been that blissfully happy again.

"What happened to your mother, Zach?" asked Amelie, the gentle pressure of her fingers on his bringing him back. "Or do you not wish to speak of it?"

"Oh, nothing bad," he said quickly, wanting to reassure her. "Not by any means. She married again, married Henry Rowe, who owned the ordinary by the ferry. A big step up for her, I suppose—a house with plaster walls and a parlor!—and she's always seemed happy enough. And I wouldn't have my sister Miriam or my little brother Henry without Mr. Rowe to father them. But it wasn't the same between my mother and me after that. How could it be?"

He smiled, trying to lighten the gravity of his story. "Do you know that it took nearly a year after my mother had wed Rowe before I'd speak to him? Guess I couldn't forgive him for stealing Mama away."

But Amelie didn't laugh, or even smile. "Is that why you're so protective now?"

"Now?" He looked at her strangely. "I can shake Rowe's hand now, if that's what you mean."

She didn't answer, but even without one he could tell she'd meant something else. She turned his hand over and slipped her fingers into his, as neatly as if they'd always belonged there.

"You're not an easy man, Zachariah Fairbourne," she

said softly, leaning forward to look down at their joined hands. "You want the world to smile at that handsome face of yours and look no further, but there's a great deal more to you than that, isn't there?"

He couldn't quite tell if she wished him to kiss her or not. Her eyes were dark and inviting, her lips slightly parted and ready, her body leaning across the slight space between them toward him. Yet damnation, he still wasn't sure. The last time, in her bedchamber, it had been obvious that she'd wanted him to kiss her as much as he did, and though for Amelie's sake he'd worried about what she'd had to say to her sister afterward, he hadn't regretted it one bit.

But this felt different. Somehow, when he hadn't noticed, things had shifted between him and Amelie, and he couldn't begin to figure out how or why. It was simply different. Maybe it was knowing that he'd been the cause of her trouble with that mean old bitch of a customer this morning, or maybe it was realizing how much he'd missed her for the days they'd been apart. Maybe it was the more complex realization that, despite her independence and age, she was still an inexperienced innocent where men were concerned; he'd only to recall how she'd gasped with surprise and trembled when he'd caressed her bare breast. Knowledge like that was a responsibility.

And maybe, worst of all, this was what came of talking too much of his mother.

Troubled and tempted at the same time, he looked down from Amelie's mouth, down past their linked hands, down to their bare feet in the worn wooden bottom of the boat. His were big-boned and nothing pretty, his toes marked with the same squared knuckles that were on his fingers. But hers—hers were as elegant as the rest of her, the toes neat and small, her ankles as fine-boned as a racehorse's. Feet like hers were made to be adored, to be tickled and teased with kisses all the way up the inside of her thighs to the honey-sweet place at the top; feet like hers were made to curl around his waist and over his back, linking together to hold him there as he buried himself deep into her, again and again and—

"We're heading back to shore," he announced abruptly, easing his hand free of hers to reach for the oars. "High time we returned to town, anyway."

He fussed with fitting the oars back into their locks, as clumsy as any landsman, but he didn't dare look her in the face, not with the lewd, lascivious thoughts he'd had about her still surely showing plain on his. It wasn't as if he were going to toss her on her back here in the boat—logistically, certain actions weren't advisable in a small boat—but those toes of hers had done him in.

Her *toes*, for all love.

"When next you see Mr. Lynde," said Amelie, looking back over her shoulder as they pulled into the open water, "please tell him how much I enjoyed his lilies."

"Aye," he said, sure that saying more would be unwise.

"Though perhaps I should let him know myself, in some small way," she continued.

"Aye." He was beginning to sound like a schooled parrot, but he didn't want to err again.

"If he has a wife, then I might send her a tiny gift from the shop, a handkerchief or somesuch."

"Aye."

"And does this wife of his have green hair and a

long purple nose?" she asked. "I would wish to choose a gift to flatter her, you know."

He looked at her then, and she smiled a small smile that gleamed with triumph. "Aye, and aye, and *aye*, Zach Fairbourne, until *I* declare that *I* have had enough."

She didn't wait for him to pull the boat up onto the bank, but clambered out herself, splashing unsteadily through the shallows with her skirts hiked high with one hand and her shoes and stockings in the other. He settled the boat before he followed, finding her beside the shed.

She'd pulled off her hat, and was leaning with her backside against the wall, struggling to pull her cotton stocking up over one damp foot as she tried to balance on the other. She muttered in French frustration, the stocking becoming more and more misshapen the more she tugged and twisted it up her calf. Belatedly she realized he was standing there, and let her skirts drop as she stood upright, her face flushed from bending over.

"Yes," she said with an imperious twitch of her head. "Or should I say 'aye'?"

"Damnation, Amelie, I didn't mean it like that!"

"Then how did you mean it?" she demanded. "How did you mean any of it, or did you mean nothing at all?"

"Amelie, please." He reached out his hand to her, hoping for reconciliation that way.

"No!" She swatted at his hand with her other stocking. "Whenever you start worrying that you've told me more than you intended about yourself, Zach, enough that I might actually begin to *care* about you, you go and hide everything away again like a squirrel burying his favorite acorn. You don't want to share with anyone, except when you can decide how much or how little."

"That's not true," he answered automatically, without even pausing to consider if it was or not.

"Yes it is. You're doing it again right now." She hit him again with the stocking for emphasis. "All I wanted to do was to thank you, and say I'd never forget this day, and the roses and the lilies, and everything else you've given me that I thought I'd never have, and—and—oh, why must you be so *difficult?*"

Before he could answer she'd flung her arms around his neck and shoulders and kissed him, her mouth fierce and hot and demanding. She'd caught him off balance, and together they rocked backward, thumping hard against the shed. Her bare foot brushed blindly against his leg, then worse, returned to run tickling along it. In his present state, that roving leg was the proverbial spark to his all-too-dry tinder, and he forgot that his imagined reluctance had ever existed. His whole world seemed to narrow to Amelie, and giving her the same pleasure she seemed intent on giving him.

He was already devouring her, their kiss so deep and potent that his blood was racing hot through his whole body, then, strangely, turning cool on his back. But it wasn't his blood: it was Amelie, greedily yanking his shirt free from the waistband of his breeches to slide her hands up inside, across the bare skin of his back, pulling him as close as they'd been when they'd kissed on her bed. Holding each other up like this against the wall, the thick ridge of his arousal pressing against her belly, she couldn't miss feeling how much she'd affected him, even with the layers of clothing between them.

Layers that, for now, he'd just as soon do without. He grabbed a fistful of her skirt and shift, hauling up the acres and acres of linen that were keeping him from the sleek, smooth skin of her legs, wonderfully bare above that single, drooping stocking. His hand spread to caress the long sweep of her thigh, then impatiently traveled higher, to the softest place of all.

She gasped when his fingers touched her there, shuddering as she turned her face against the front of his chest. Gently he stroked her, feeling the unmistakable moisture of her gathering need. She shifted her legs instinctively to ease his way, arching toward the pleasure he was giving her while her breath broke into ragged, keening cries against his shirt.

"Oh, no, no," she moaned. "Oh, Zach, no!"

"Yes, sweetheart," he said, his voice harsh from the effort of controlling himself. "Don't try to stop it."

But the sound that came from her now was a broken, heartbroken sob, more an animal sound than any words as she tried to muffle it against the front of his chest. Startled and concerned, he pushed back from her, letting her skirts drop as she slumped against the wall. Smudged tears blotched her cheeks, and misery twisted her flushed face as she hid her eyes with her hands.

"Amelie?" he gasped, bracing himself above her. He had to remember that she'd never gone so far before, and he cursed his own lack of control for moving so fast. He couldn't deny he'd wanted her badly, desired her more than he'd ever wanted a woman before, but he also wanted her to desire him in return. He wasn't going to take her by force; she had to be there with him, too. But his arms were shaking from the abruptness of his denial, his body still hard and aching, his breathing harsh and ragged. "Amelie, lass, it's all right.

There's nothing to be frightened of. You're fine, sweet, you're fine."

"Don't—don't excuse me," she said, her words muffled as she kept her face hidden in her shame. "I—I do not deserve it."

"You—we—did nothing wrong," he said firmly as he brushed his fingers along her cheek. "I tell you, you're fine."

"No, I'm not." Finally she lowered her hands to meet his gaze, her eyes red-rimmed from tears and misery. "Oh, Zach, look at me. I'm not fine at all. I'm exactly the sluttish, low harlot that Mrs. Drummer says I am. Maman warned me and I did not listen, I never did, and now—"

"Hush," he said, gently covering her mouth with his hand. "I don't want to hear you talk like that about yourself, Amelie. It's not true, none of it."

She took his hand in hers, turning it so she could kiss his palm before she shook his head. "It is true, Zach," she said sorrowfully. "You can't make it otherwise, though I bless you for trying. But, mon Dieu, the worst is knowing I don't want to change. I don't want to be a good woman any more, and I don't want to give you up the way I should. The way I must, if I wish to keep my shop and my trade."

He frowned at her uneasily, not understanding. "You're making no sense now, lass."

"Oh, Zach, you've given me so many reasons!" The tears welled up fresh again in her eyes as she searched his face. "I could tell you how you make me laugh and bring me roses and show me pond lilies and dragonflies and stars to wish on. I could tell you how when you kiss me and—and touch me like you just were doing, I feel alive and happy and—and joyful. Yes, joyful!"

"Where's the harm in that, now?" he said softly. He'd never wanted to hurt her, and joyfulness proved he hadn't. "Where's the wrong?"

She sniffed back her tears and looked down, her words rushing on as if somehow, now that she'd begun, she'd no choice but to finish.

"You told me to be brave, and you told me to be truthful," she said. "But when I kiss you, Zach, and touch you, I feel like it's the only time you're honest with me, the only time you're not hiding yourself away, and oh, Zach, I'd face a hundred Mrs. Drummers not to lose that!"

He'd never thought he'd hidden from anyone. He'd always been called a brave man, a courageous sailor, a leader who wasn't afraid of hurricanes or pirates, and one, too, who'd used his strength to help others, not hurt them. That was why he'd sought to protect her in the first place, wasn't it? She'd needed him, and he'd been there, and he'd tried his hardest to be there for her again.

So where had he gone wrong? Why was she saying this now? He'd tried to make a sanctuary for her, but the only place she wanted to go was the one locked deep inside himself. He liked Amelie, he liked her fine. More than fine, if he were being honest, the way she wanted.

But he didn't love her. No. He was quite sure of that. Being brave and strong meant he wasn't vulnerable to that sort of gentle-hearted sentiment. He was twenty-seven years old, and though there'd been several times with several other women when he'd thought he might be in love, it had never lasted. Oh, he'd seen it happen to other men, his friends and his cousins, and he respected the change love seemed to bring to them. But since he'd gone this long in his life without experiencing it himself, odds were that love, like measles, simply wasn't something he was susceptible to.

But when he looked down at Amelie's trusting, tear-stained face, he knew he wasn't cruel enough to tell her that now. He liked her fine, and he liked her far too much to hurt her with that kind of honesty. Instead he plucked her hat from the grass and handed it to her.

"I pray you'll never have to face Mrs. Drummer again," he said tenderly as he bent to kiss her forehead. "Not for my sake, or anyone else's. Now come, I'll see you home."

She hesitated for a moment, her eyes still sad and troubled, before she finally sighed, and nodded, and sat down on the grass to put on her second stocking and her shoes. As they began back up the path, Zach curled his arm around her shoulders and she rested her head against him, peacefully, and he marveled at how well they understood each other.

Oh, aye, he liked her very fine indeed.

❧ 11 ❧

"You can leave me here," said Amelie as she and
Zach came to the corner nearest the shop. "I'll be well
enough on my own."

"Are you sure?" asked Zach, his gaze sweeping across
the quiet street for whatever villains he felt sure must
be lurking. "If you give me your key, I'll go open up
the shop and make sure all's clear."

"Oh, yes, and be sure to chase the dust from beneath
the beds, too." She sighed, and rubbed her hand over
her forehead. "I'm sorry, Zach, but it has been a long,
difficult day. Better to say our farewells and good nights
and thank yous now and have them done, eh?"

She hadn't meant to sound so testy, nor so flippant,
but she was tired and unhappy, and the day could not
end soon enough to please her. He looked unhappy,
too, though she doubted for the same reasons. The
balance, the *rightness*, she'd felt with him earlier at the
pond had disappeared so completely that they'd both
stopped trying on the way home, instead walking side
by side in awkward, lonely silence. She'd slipped free

of his arm as soon as they'd reached the first houses, where they might be seen, and he hadn't tried to put it back, and now that it was time to part, she wasn't sure he'd even make the effort to kiss her.

"Do you think your sister will be home yet?" he asked, ignoring both her apology and her testiness to look past her toward the shop. "I like knowing you're both home snug together."

"She'll be home when her work is done," said Amelie, relieved not to have to speak any more of herself. "Most likely the Connellys will give her supper, too, before they bring her home. But she'll be safe with them. I wouldn't have let her go otherwise."

"Are you reassuring me, or yourself?" He smiled. She'd come to recognize how the lines around his eyes deepened when he was tired or in pain; they made him look older, but they also somehow made his eyes seem bluer in contrast, and she caught herself wondering if his head was bothering him again.

"You wish to protect the whole world," she said, though the bite had left her words now. "I prefer to concentrate on my sister."

"And a handsome job you do of it, too."

"Not always." A stray gust of uneasy wind swept through the street, swirling dry leaves past their feet, followed by the first distant rumblings of thunder. "The winter I was eight, I was supposed to be watching her in our bedchamber while Maman was fitting a gown to a lady downstairs. I was angry at having to stay with a baby, and played with my doll Loulou in the middle of the big bed, where Juliette couldn't follow. And she didn't. She went to find Maman instead, and fell all the way down the stairs. It took three women to hold her while the apothecary set her leg with the splint, but it still didn't heal straight, which is why she limps to this day. Because I wasn't watching her."

She looked at Zach evenly, waiting for his reaction. She didn't know why she'd told him now, nor why she'd even told him at all. Not that it was a great secret; any one of their neighbors could have told him the same, likely with more lurid details added by time and gossip. Perhaps since he'd told her about his own childhood, she'd needed to tell him something of hers in return.

Or perhaps, given everything else, she'd only wished to shock him. For most people, the part about the misaligned splint on Juliette's tiny, broken baby leg was more than enough.

But not for Zach. He met her eye with the same unflinching evenness with which as she was regarding him.

"Then neither of us were much good as watchdogs, were we?" he said levelly. "I failed my father's memory, and let my mother marry another man, while you failed Juliette, and made her a cripple."

She flushed. "That's putting a rather bald face on it," she said defensively, realizing too late that he'd called her bluff.

"Guilt does that, doesn't it, Amelie?" he said, his half-smile burdened with long-ago sadness. "Especially to sorry little children like us. We're more alike than either one of us wants to admit."

She certainly didn't want to, not after this afternoon. Another errant gust grabbed at her skirts, made her hold tight to her hat, while the sky darkened with the coming storm.

"I must go now, Zach," she said, though she didn't move. "Now. Before it rains."

"Aye, you do," he said, glancing past her. "So do I."

She turned, following his gaze. The man she'd seen earlier, the one in the green waistcoat and knitted cap, was still lounging beside the goldsmith's mulberry bush, fighting to hold his news sheet steady against the growing wind.

"Do you know that man?" she asked. "He's been there all day, fussing with that paper. I've half a mind to call the watch on him."

"Don't." Zach shook his head with dismay as the man waved. "His name's Curwen, and he's one of my people. I guarantee he's much a better seaman than he is a watchdog, and he'd be the very devil to replace if you have him carted off to gaol."

Curwen waved again, clearly delighted to recognize his captain, and Amelie whipped around to face Zach.

"A watchdog, is he? And who, pray, is he supposed to be watching?"

He shifted so the wind would blow his hair back from his face, not into it. "You said I was bent on protecting the whole world. I'd say I've focussed my attention more on this part of it, right here on this part of Marlborough Street."

"You *didn't.*" Of course he had, but she hated to believe it of him. "Oh, Zach, you didn't! You ordered one of your sailors to guard my shop, my home, without even thinking to tell me?"

"I thought of it," he said, wincing a bit in anticipation. "I thought you'd say no, even if it was for your own good."

"My own good?" She stared at him, too angry to know where to begin. "C'est incroyable! You made me a prisoner in my own home, and you wonder why I'd say no? Did you have him make reports back to you, too, so you could know when I left and returned and whom I saw?"

"I wanted to know you were safe, lass," he began. "I can't see that—"

"You order him to leave, Zach, and you do it now, or else I *will* call the watch!"

He shook his head, incredulous. "You won't call the watch when your window is broken and your garden destroyed, but you will do so when a friend wishes to help you?"

"*Adieu, monsieur le capitaine.*" She turned and marched away toward her shop, steadfastly refusing to look back at either Zach or his sailor-guard.

"*Au revoir*, Amelie!" Zach called after her. "Damnation, lass, not *adieu*, but *au revoir!*"

For a second she hesitated, torn. She hadn't thought he'd know the difference: *adieu* was good-bye, with all its finality, while *au revoir* was more promising, more open-ended, a wish toward a safe return. She'd used the first word intentionally, but so, apparently, had he chosen the other.

The thunder rumbled, closer now. The leaves of the mulberry bush that had shaded Curwen rustled, flickered their silvery undersides.

"*Au revoir*, Amelie Lacroix!"

She wouldn't turn back. He'd been the one who'd presumed too much, and now he could shout himself hoarse. She only prayed the rest of the street wouldn't hear him.

She quickened her steps, holding her skirts, practically running by the time she reached her own door. The first rain was beginning to fall around her, fat, splattering drops so heavy they might have been thrown instead.

She would *not* turn back. . . .

She threw open the door and cried out as the first flash of lightning lit the inside of the shop. The cream-ware pitcher with the flowers still stood where she'd proudly placed it on the counter. The roses still arched gracefully from the pitcher's mouth, surrounded by the long-stemmed clusters of the fluffy spring cress.

But with deliberate, destructive care, every last one of the stems of bright yellow Saint-John's-wort had been plucked from the pitcher and scattered across the length of the shop's floor. With the same appalling thoroughness that she'd seen in her destroyed garden, the petals had been torn apart and scattered, the stems mangled.

"Oh, no, not these flowers, too!" she cried softly as she knelt to touch the crushed yellow petals. "Not Zach's flowers!"

But this time *was* different. This time, she knew the culprit, because, her heart pounding, she realized the culprit was still in the shop with her.

"*Luna!*" she shrieked. "You are so *bad!*"

The cat was lying sprawled among the tattered flowers and leaves, languidly nibbling on the remains of a stem as she blinked at Amelie.

But Amelie was in no mood for blinking. "Luna, you wicked, wicked beast! The one, the only, time someone gives me flowers and you *eat* them! Bad, bad cat!"

Luna's gray ears flattened, more with offense at the volume of Amelie's voice than with any real sense of feline shame. But when Amelie snatched the broom from behind the counter, the cat understood that perhaps she'd do better to leave and, with her tail down, she galloped from the shop with a skidding of claws on the floorboards and up the stairs as fast as she could to hide until her mistress' humor improved.

Thunder rattled the glass in the shop windows as the rain began in earnest. Luna, who hated thunderstorms, was being doubly punished.

"Wretched cat," muttered Amelie as she began to sweep away the mangled flowers. "Wretched, horrid cat, to do such a thing."

She'd barely begun her sweeping when the knock came at the door behind her, anxious and rapid enough to make her jump. Her first thought was Zach, come to escape the storm, and she couldn't decide whether she should let him in or not. But when she peered through the water-streaked glass, she saw her caller was smaller and female.

"Betsey!" she exclaimed as she held open the door for the Drummer girl, bracing it against the wind. "Whatever are you doing out in this rain?"

The girl darted inside, shaking the raindrops from her skirts and slipping her shawl off her head. "I'd almost given up waiting, Miss Lacroix, hoping and hoping I could see you and Julie. She is here, too, isn't she?"

"I'm afraid not, Betsey. She's gone to do some sewing for Mrs. Connelly today, and I don't know when exactly to expect her back." Putting aside the broom, Amelie held a chair out to the girl. "But you're welcome to wait, of course. Here, rest yourself, and I'll put on a kettle for tea."

"No, no, I can't stay any longer than I have to!" cried Betsey, wringing her plump hands together with agitation. "If Mother knew I'd come here at all, she'd have my head, she would!"

Amelie couldn't argue there. "Then pray, tell me how I can help you."

"Oh, Miss Lacroix, it should be the other way round!" She swept around the shop in a tight circle, a little dance of anxiety. As Juliette had said, without her mother's presence Betsey lost her automaton's blankness, and when her round face was animated, she was, if not beautiful, certainly appealingly pretty. "I cannot believe what Mother has done to you! After everything you have done for her, the way you have dressed her—dressed us both—why, it is unforgivable, and if ever I've any money of my own, I vow I'll see that our account is paid."

"That is most kind, Betsey," said Amelie gently. "Most generous, too. But as good a customer as your mother has been, it shall take more than your mother's account to ruin us."

"Ooh, but it isn't just us!" cried Betsey unhappily. "This day alone Mother has been calling on as many of her acquaintance as would receive her, telling them vile lies about you and making them promise to take away their custom."

Amelie stood very still, trying to absorb this. Though she knew it must be true—Mrs. Drummer had promised to do exactly this, and Betsey herself would have no reason for repeating it if it weren't so—she didn't want to accept it, or the consequences, either "Have you any idea why she is doing this to us, Betsey?"

"She says it's because you're French, and she and Father have always hated the French. But I think—I fear—it is because of me." Now Betsey sank into the chair, pulling a lace-trimmed handkerchief from her pocket to dab at her face. She looked fearfully at Amelie, lowering her voice to a hushed whisper of confidence. "Has your sister told you of—of our great secret?"

Amelie tipped her head to one side, striving to recall any "secret" that Juliette might have shared regarding Betsey. "She must have kept it as your secret alone."

"Oh, oh, dear." In confusion Betsey began twisting her handkerchief into a tight ring around her finger. "Then I must—are you very certain she is with Mrs. Connelly and not elsewhere?"

"As certain as seeing her put into Mrs. Connelly's chariot this morning," said Amelie uneasily. The girl's anxiety was catching. "Betsey, if you are in some sort of trouble that I might help you—"

"No!" Betsey scrambled back to her feet. "That is, thank you, there is nothing that you can do for me, nothing at all. Except, that is—oh, I know I must trust you!"

She reached into her pocket for an unaddressed letter, so fat with folded sheets that the seal barely held it closed, and with obvious reluctance she handed it to Amelie. "Please, please, give this to your sister. She'll understand, I know, because she is so good to me, but please tell her again how very sorry I am for all that has happened. And you, too, Miss Lacroix. Thank you for—for oh, everything!"

Impulsively Betsey flung her arms around Amelie and hugged her, nearly knocking her over with her exuberance. Then just as suddenly she grabbed her shawl, opened the door, and ran into the rain, the shawl flying out behind her like a sail.

Quickly Amelie shut the door after her, pausing for only a moment to make sure that Curwen had left his post beside the mulberry bush. He had; on account of the rain, the street was as empty as if it were midnight, and about as hospitable, too. She hoped that Juliette was still snug and dry at the Connellys, and wouldn't try to return until the storm had passed. The lightning and thunder had already swept on to the west. Now all that remained was a steady summer shower, enough to fill cisterns and troughs and make farmers glad.

With a sigh Amelie returned to her sweeping, gathering her thoughts, as well as the broken flowers. She couldn't tell exactly how much influence Mrs. Drummer had. Among the older families, like the Richardsons and the Clarkes, she suspected very little, but with the women like herself who'd risen quickly along with their husbands, overbearing Esther Drummer could have as much influence as a parliamentary politician. And unfortunately for Amelie and Juliette, these were the women who made the best customers, for these were the ones most eager to display their husband's success through costly, luxurious clothes. She would simply have to wait and see, and keep her fingers crossed for good measure.

But what, wondered Amelie, was Betsey Drummer's great secret? Had she bought more, with Juliette's help, than her mother had known? Amelie shook her head, remembering how at least half of the Drummers' entries in the ledger had been in her sister's handwriting. She'd have to have another talk with Julie about granting credit, especially to impulsive young daughters. For now she'd put the letter for her sister propped on a shelf behind the counter, where Juliette would be sure to see it as soon as she returned. Juliette was a genuine friend to Betsey, and most likely the letter was no more than a girlishly effusive apology for her mother's actions.

Carefully she dumped the last of the yellow petals

into the rubbish bucket. She looked at them mournfully, remembering how beautiful they'd been this morning, and then pulled the rosebud from the front of her bodice. That, too, had suffered, wilted and dry from the heat and crushed by Zach's embrace. There was little use in keeping the rosebud now, and with a sigh of regret she tossed it on top of the yellow petals. The flowers had been the first she'd ever been given by a man, and after the way she'd parted with Zach, they could be the last as well.

She could not begin to figure out what was happening between them. One minute she felt closer to him than any person she'd ever known, and she knew from how he acted that he felt the same. When he'd spoken of his mother on the pond today and when she'd told him about Juliette; when he'd teased her about the imaginary little dog in her yard; when he'd shown her his beloved *Diana* in the shipyard—all of these were moments of rare intimacy that she'd never forget.

But then abruptly he'd draw back into himself, using his pleasant Captain Fairbourne face as completely as if it were a mask carved from wood, and there seemed to be no way at all to make him put it aside. She should never have told him he had let the mask slip when they kissed, for at once he'd clearly decided that even kissing her wasn't worth the risk. If he'd grown angry or shouted at her, then she could at least have fought back, but there was no fighting his eternal, infernal good nature.

Perhaps, she thought glumly, this was the way he coped with a sailor's rootlessness, never being in one place long enough for lasting ties. If he didn't let himself care deeply for anyone, then he wouldn't be hurt when they parted. He could talk all he wanted about protecting those he cared for, but it seemed to her what he was best at was protecting himself.

She'd overheard Mr. Lynde say that he'd deliver the cording for the *Diana* this Monday. That must mean the sloop was nearly ready for launching and would be completed and ready for sailing soon after that. How much longer would Zach be in Boston, before he cleared for his homeport of Appledore? Another week or two, she guessed, maybe three if there was some problem with the rigging. Another week or two for her to try to be as cheerfully uninvolved as Zach himself, to save whatever was left of her heart and her business as well? Or should she refuse to see him at all again, and make the break now?

It was not much of a choice, considering how hard a decision it would be to make. But one thing she'd already decided: she would not let herself be alone with him again. She'd discovered she'd absolutely no virtuous resolve, no willpower, where he was concerned. She was every bit as weak and bad as Maman had feared and Mrs. Drummer had declared, and she shuddered now to realize how close to real ruin she'd been this afternoon, there against the shed with her skirts rucked up like some common dockside slattern. Her livelihood was precarious enough now without adding the disgrace and responsibility of a bastard child on top of it.

And yet all she had to do was think of Zach's smile, his laugh, the way his black hair flopped down over his forehead and how he gestured with his big-knuckled hands when he talked, and before she realized it she was imagining a baby, their baby, with all those same qualities, a tiny version of Zach that would always love her without question or restraint and never sail away. . . .

With a muttered oath at her own miserable weakness she went back to the workroom where the half-finished dressing-gown still sat on the stand. The rain was nearly gone now, little more than drips from the eaves, and she propped open the back door to let in what little light remained with the fading day and a breath of evening air as well. She set a tin lantern with a high-polished flashback for reflecting on the table beside her, more light to guide her finer work. Pulling her work stool up close to the gown on the stand, she kicked off her shoes, rubbing her heel where she was sure she'd have a blister from walking so far in damp stockings, and concentrated on shaping the silk before her.

She was so lost in her work that she didn't hear Juliette's return, or even realize she was back until she was standing directly before her.

"The way you've set that sleeve with the pleat and the tucks is most cunning," said Juliette, stepping back and folding her arms to study the gown. "You'll have every other woman in town clamoring for the same."

"I will if they deign to come to our shop," said Amelie, and rapidly she told her of Mrs. Drummer's visit that morning.

"But she cannot *do* that!" cried Juliette furiously. "To go about telling lies like that about us!"

Amelie jabbed a pin into the stiff silk, imagining Mrs. Drummer's meaty, freckled shoulder was inside. "She can, and apparently she has, if Betsey's to be believed. She came here, too, to apologize for her mother. She was most distraught that you were out, you being her special favorite and all, but she did leave a letter. It's on the second shelf, in the shop."

"Dreadful old woman." Juliette disappeared into the shop long enough to retrieve the letter. "Where did the flowers in the pitcher come from?"

"The roses and spring cress?" As if there were so many pitchers of flowers in the store to cause confusion! Amelie heard how her voice squeaked guiltily higher. "Those were a gift from Captain Fairbourne, by way of thanking us for our hospitality when he was hurt."

Juliette snorted as she turned the letter over in her fingers. "Not 'our' hospitality, Amelie, but 'yours.' You were likely the most hospitable hostess he'd ever, ah, met. Though I know I rather liked having him here as a guest, especially when he pretended to be the dogcatcher for Mrs. Murray."

Amelie blushed, wishing she, too, wouldn't remember the dogcatcher quite so charmingly. "You won't think so well of him when I tell you how he'd posted one of his sailors as a guard outside the shop. Can you imagine what our ladies would say to that?"

Juliette looked up at her over the letter, one brow slyly cocked. "Captain Fairbourne is taking care of you, Amelie. He wants to be sure nothing happens to you," she said, teasing. "I think it's rather sweet."

"Sweet?" repeated Amelie indignantly. "It was a *guard*, Julie, as if we were prisoners who needed watching!"

"And I still think it's sweet," said Juliette, more seriously. "He's a capable man, Amelie, besides being a handsome one. If he says we need a guard, then perhaps we do. And if it were up to me, we would have already told Captain Fairbourne all about those awful notes and the bag of money. *He* would have known what to do."

"So do you, from the sound of it!"

"Which is nothing remarkable, that I can see." Juliette held Betsey's letter up to the light. "There's no name or address written on this. Are you certain Betsey meant it for me?"

"She said you'd understand, so it must be for you," answered Amelie, relieved to be done discussing Zach. "She said another odd thing, though. She said that what her mother had done was all her fault, that it had to do with some 'great secret' that she shared with you. And whatever it was, she certainly wasn't about to tell it to me."

"Her secret?" Now it was Juliette's turn to look strangely guilty. "It's nothing for you to worry over, Amelie, I promise."

"You haven't granted her too much credit, have you?" asked Amelie. "We have to be careful that way, especially now."

"Oh, no, that's not it," said Juliette quickly. "It has absolutely nothing to do with money, or with the shop, either."

"Then what could—"

"I promised Betsey I wouldn't tell, Amelie," said Juliette reluctantly. "If you really need to know, I will tell you, but I'd rather not."

"Then I won't ask," said Amelie, but her uneasiness remained. Juliette was not by nature a secretive person, and for her to keep a "grand secret" now for Betsey Drummer was a serious matter. "Aren't you going to read her letter?"

"The letter?" Juliette looked down at the letter in

her hand as if she'd forgotten it completely. "Ah, no. I'll read it later."

She stuffed the letter into her pocket and yawned dramatically. "Lord, I'm weary," she said, though to Amelie her sister hadn't seemed tired at all before now. "I can't begin to tell you how much ripping and stitching and piecing of skimpy seams I did this day. I do believe I'll take myself to bed now, before I fall asleep here at your feet."

"If that's what you wish." What Juliette really wished, thought Amelie wryly, was to be able to read Betsey's letter in private in their bedchamber. "But beware of Luna cowering beneath the coverlet. She was very bad this afternoon, and I wouldn't be surprised if she's still hiding from my scolding as well as from the thunder."

"I'll look for lumps beneath the covers." Dusk had fallen early on account of the storm and the clouds that still hid the moon and stars, and she lit a candlestick from the lantern on the table to take up the stairs with her. "Don't work too late, Amelie."

Amelie watched Juliette go, up the same twisting staircase she'd bumped and crashed down so long ago. She must be tired after all, for she was limping more noticeably than usual. That, or Amelie's conscience, made it seem worse than it was.

While a day didn't pass that she failed to remember the accident, telling Zach about it this afternoon had brought it back more vividly than usual: Juliette's shrill, agonized screams, the smell of the spilled rum they'd tried to make her drink to sleep, the crush of too many neighbors in their house, all too eager to help and to watch. And she remembered how she'd crouched by the fire, forgotten by everyone, and wept and wept as she'd watched her poor doll Loulou twist and crumple in the flames where Maman had thrown her as swift and horrible punishment.

No wonder she'd never forgotten. No wonder, too, that ever since she'd always put Juliette first.

Wearily she rubbed her temples. It had been a long day for her as well, and if she—

"*Amelie!*" cried Juliette, her fear palpable. "Oh, dear God, Amelie, come quickly!"

But Amelie was already racing up the stairs two at a time, her skirts held high in her hands.

"Julie, sweet, what is it?" she said breathlessly as her sister flew to her arms outside their bedchamber. "What's happened?"

With her fingers linked tightly in her sister's, Juliette pointed toward the room. "In there," she said in a voice hushed with dread. "On our bed. Look."

Amelie inched to the doorway and peered inside. At first glance, the room seemed peaceful enough. The white curtains fluttered inward at the open windows with the evening breeze, and from the chest the candle's flame flickered and danced where Juliette had set it down. The bed's hangings were still neatly tied back and looped for day, the coverlet smoothed, the bolsters plumped, with an uncontrite Luna curled and wheezing gently in the valley in between.

But in the center of the coverlet lay another leather bag of coins, a twin to the one that had broken their window. This time the bag had been thrown in the open window, not through a closed one, though the force had buried the bag in a deep hollow in the featherbed. Two of the coins had spilled out, more guineas, the gold glinting in the candlelight.

"What shall we do?" asked Juliette in a tentative whisper, as if the bag and the guineas could hear.

"We'll shut that window to begin with," said Amelie, quickly slamming it closed. Someone had come into their garden, either taking the time to unlatch the gate or boldly climbing through their neighbors' fences, and had known that this window would belong to their bedchamber.

She didn't want to touch the bag. She didn't want even that much connection to whoever had thrown it. But she didn't want to leave it there on their bed, either, and with a show of being brave for Juliette's sake, she snatched it from the bed in one hand, sweeping up the two stray guineas with the other.

"Is there another note?" asked Juliette. "Oh, I wish this wasn't happening!"

"Well, it *is*," said Amelie impatiently. Yet her heart was pounding, too, as she eased open the leather drawstring and slipped out the folded scrap of torn paper, the same grimy-gray that the others had been. The rough letters drawn inside were the same, too, but this time their message was as crude as the note itself:

French whore. Here is your price.
Now leave Boston.

"Oh, Amelie," whispered Juliette as she clung to her sister. "Who would hate us this much?"

"I don't know," said Amelie, her fingers trembling. The same someone who'd thrown this note must have seen her this afternoon with Zach, must have watched them together. She thought of how she'd sent Zach's guard away, and how later she'd been working downstairs, all alone and lost in her work with her back to the open door. She felt sick, threatened, and in more danger than she'd ever dreamed possible. "I don't know."

Juliette put her arms around her sister's shoulders, and they clung to each other, afraid to let go.

"Tomorrow, Amelie," she whispered fiercely, "you must show this to Captain Fairbourne. You *must*. And if you don't, I will."

❦ 12 ❦

"*I* don't even have to ask," said Mrs. Isham as she
set the pewter plate with the fried eggs and ham before
Zach with a clatter. "You spent the whole night and
that thunderstorm, too, sitting on a fence like some
old tomcat, yowling after your lady-love."

"Not the whole night," admitted Zach cheerfully.
"Only until Ben Tallman could come take my place."

"Look at your poor hat," scolded Mrs. Isham, picking
it up from the table. The dark gray felt was still damp,
its round crown and cocked sides sadly misshapen.
"You're a gentleman now, Zachariah. You have to take
more care with yourself. This hat would shame a tinker now."

"At sea I'd consider that hat too fine by half," he
teased, loading his fork full of breakfast. He was in too
good a mood this morning for even Mrs. Isham to
spoil it. He'd managed to do exactly what Amelie had
wanted, sending Curwen away, but he'd also done exactly what *he* wanted, which was to stand outside her
shop himself to make sure no one came to cause her

trouble. "At sea I'd just tie an old kettle on my head with a length of stout rope, and thank the tinker who'd mended it."

Not amused, Mrs. Isham jabbed her forefinger into his shoulder. "You're wicked, you are," she said sternly. "And your dear Mam didn't teach you to talk smart like that, either. Do you believe that that pretty Miss Lacroix is going to take you wearing a kettle on your head like some half-witted dunderhead? Why'd she want to be the lady-love to a fool like that?"

"She's not my lady-love, Mrs. I," he said, drinking deep of his coffee. "She's more a lady-friend. A good friend, mind, a most excellent and agreeable friend, but a friend rather than a love."

Irritably Mrs. Isham jabbed at him again. "That's more dunderheaded talk, Zachariah. Men don't stand outside in the pouring rain because a woman's *agreeable*, and they don't have their cousin's new sloops painted all gaudy on her say-so. And if Miss Lacroix's only *agreeable*, then you wouldn't get all moony and soft in the face whenever her name's brought up. You'd be out chasing a least a half-dozen other *agreeable* lasses, the way you always have before."

Zach took his time to swallow before he answered, not wanting to seem too interested in such a discussion. "That's a pretty tale, Mrs. I, and it's a blessed shame there's no truth to it."

"Oh, aye, there is," she said triumphantly. "If you didn't fancy that lass special over others, you wouldn't be trying so hard now to pretend otherwise. I know you, Zachariah, and I've known you since you was still in leading-strings, and you've never once behaved like this about any other woman. Miss Lacroix's the one you're fixed to have as your wife. I'll wager ten shillings you'll be promised to her before this summer's done."

"Done," said Zach in a confident instant. He couldn't imagine a surer bet. He meant to spend the rest of this summer on his first trading voyage in the *Diana*, not making wedding plans. "Ordinarily I hate to take money from a poor widow-woman, Mrs. I, but I'll be glad to claim that stake from you."

"And I'll be more than glad to see you pay up to me, there with your new bride cooing beside you." She jabbed him one last time. "You're asking her to the launching, are you?"

"Of course I am. Amelie and her sister Juliette, too." He couldn't wait to show off his sloop to Amelie, and to show her off in turn to all his friends. He could already picture her there in the sun with the water dancing behind her, the most ravishing young woman in the entire city, smiling up at him from beneath the brim of one of those broad-brimmed hats she favored so. If he could figure a way, he'd have even asked her to break the bottle over the prow before the sloop went down the ways, but by rights that honor had to go to a Fairbourne lady. "Can't have too many fair lasses at a launching, can we?"

"Nay, you cannot," agreed Mrs. Isham, heartily enough to make Zach suspicious. "Especially not with all your family gathered there. How much your Mam will enjoy meeting Miss Lacroix!"

Damnation. Why hadn't he thought of that?

When he'd pictured the launching, he realized he'd been seeing two different versions of the same day. Both versions had their share of bright flags and ribbons, cheering shipyard workers and honored guests, plenty of rum and excellent food, and a small band playing celebratory music.

In the first, he had Amelie on his arm, gazing up at him with unabashed admiration as he shared his glory with her, while he in turn was the envy of every other young seafaring man in Boston, graced with such a first-rate sloop and such a delectable lass.

But in the other version, he was surrounded by his family, from his mother and Mr. Rowe and little Henry, Miriam and her husband, Jack, from Westham, to all the Cape Cod Fairbournes, Polly and Samson, Joshua and Anabelle, Serena and Gerald, and however many dozens of children they'd sired among them. It was an immense amount of family to have gathered in his honor. He'd be the son made good, the youngest cousin proving himself worthy at last of being called a Fairbourne captain, and, lastly, he'd make real the dream his own father hadn't lived long enough to fulfill.

Both possibilities had their obvious appeals, and each would have been the sort of day Zach had anticipated all his life, and would remember ever after. But somehow, in the middle of that pleasant wallow of anticipating and remembering, he'd forgotten he'd have to reconcile the two versions into one single day.

"What a grand time it will be for your Mam," Mrs. Isham was saying, or more accurately, gloating. "Her boy made master and captain of a fine new vessel like that! And I know she'll like Miss Lacroix every bit as well as I. Oh, don't you worry now, Zachariah, I won't carry any but the best tales to your Mam's ears. I'll tell her how much that lass cares for you, tending to you proper when you'd hit your head on that, ah, fence post. I'll tell her how prosperous she is in her own right, how her trade will bring a pretty penny to a thrifty husband."

"Mrs. I, don't," said Zach, desperation creeping into his tone. "Don't tell her a word."

With a smile that chilled him to the bone, she gathered up his empty breakfast dishes onto a battered tray.

"All I'll do is tell her what matters most," she whispered, bending over his shoulder. "I'll tell her how much you love the lass."

He whipped around to answer, but she was already heading toward the kitchen, chortling to herself as she passed other curious guests.

Wishing all manner of evil on the shoulders of the Crescent's landlady, Zach snatched up his much-maligned hat and headed for the door. He'd already planned a quick trip to Marlborough Street, to see if Tallman was more discreet than Curwen had been, but now he decided to offer his formal invitation to the Diana's launching to the sisters Lacroix as well.

As he walked quickly through the winding streets, he told himself he was asking them now so they'd have plenty of time to decide what to wear, ladies being like that. He told himself it had nothing to do with what Mrs. Isham had said. He wanted Amelie there with him at the launching. After all the time they'd spent together while he'd been here in Boston, she belonged there to share the day with him as she already had so much else, and he certainly wasn't ashamed to have his family meet her.

Far from it. She wasn't like some of the women he'd dallied with in the past. It didn't matter that she was a milliner, a seamstress. In her manners and graces, she was more of a lady than most who were wealthier or better bred. Yet she wasn't priggish or prim, either.

He'd only to remember how fervently she returned his kisses and caresses to know that. When they finally did lie together—and he didn't doubt they would, eventually—they'd probably scorch the very sheets. And despite what she claimed about her nose or her mouth, she was hands down one of the most deliciously attractive women he'd ever seen.

So why, then, was he feeling so oddly reluctant about having her meet his family, most specifically his mother? He kept his head down and his hands thrust into his pockets as he walked, considering this question so deeply he nearly plowed into the middle of a flock of honking geese being herded to market.

It wasn't that he feared his mother *wouldn't* like Amelie, he slowly realized. He was afraid that his mother would like her too much.

While he hadn't seen the resemblances between them at first—his mother was short and inclined to plumpness, blond and fair and blue-eyed, and though she was always tidy in her dress, no one would ever mistake her for a lady of fashion—Amelie and his mother were alarmingly alike in the ways that mattered. They both toiled hard at work they enjoyed, work that combined their interests and talents with a shrewdness for business and handling their customers. They were both clever and quick-witted, but kind, too, in a way that made them pleasurable company. They could, he suspected, become the fastest of friends in next to no time.

But where, he wondered, did that place him?

His mother had been badgering him for years to wed, to marry the nice girl in the next house and begin the mysterious business of "raising" a family, as if children, like peas, needed no more than water and plenty of sunlight. Miriam had already given her grandchildren, so she had another generation of babies to kiss and coo over, and she was still so young herself that she wasn't looking for a chimney-corner and a patient daughter-in-law to watch over her in her dotage.

But she did believe in love, and, worse, she held the firm, feminine conviction that without love life held little real happiness. He supposed what followed was inevitable. His mother loved him dearly as her first son, and wanted him to be happy, and thus she wished, longed, hoped, begged, cajoled, and pleaded with him each time he came home between voyages to find a wife to love and to love him. That he hadn't was his single failing as a son, and she seldom let him forget it.

All Mrs. Isham would have to do was *think* the word love in connection with him and Amelie Lacroix, the vaguest thought drifting somewhere near the ceiling beams over her head, and his mother would be in ecstasy.

And he would be—well, somewhere else, preferably surrounded by a great deal of deep blue saltwater.

Right now he was standing before Amelie's shop, and that was enough to make him shove all his other concerns to the back corners of his mind, where they could wait until the launching itself. He glanced up and down the street, and was glad to see no visible sign of Tallman. That was as it should be; that bull-head Curwen had practically hung a lantern around his neck, he'd been so easy to notice. Everything else looked as it should, too, from the fresh nosegay on the door to the small gray bear masquerading as a cat while she slept amid the silks in the window.

The bell over the jamb jangled merrily as he opened

the door, and he smiled to see the place of honor, there on the counter, that had been given to his flowers, with Amelie's effortless art evident in every stalk of the blossoms' arrangement in the pitcher. The simple pleasure she'd so obviously found made him want to give her flowers every day they were in season.

"Good day," called Amelie breathlessly as she hurried forward. "And what will you buy this—oh, Zach, it's you."

"Don't sound so cheerful about it, lass," he said, mightily cheerful himself to see her. He felt like it had been weeks since they'd parted, not hours, and though he felt himself grinning like an idiot merely from being in the same room with her, he couldn't help it and he didn't care.

But her own mood seemed joyless and worried, and as she held out her hand to greet him he noticed the blue circles of sleeplessness beneath her eyes.

"I am happy you're here, Zach," she said softly, almost sadly. She'd been working, sewing, for on her third finger was a well-worn silver thimble, topped with a berry of red carnelian. "I didn't expect to see you this morning, but it's been so quiet that I'm doubly glad you've come."

"Then so am I." After last night, he was surprised that she'd kept hold of his hand, but pleasantly so. He could feel the round, hard callus on her thumb, the finger that worked in opposition to the thimble, as unconsciously she traced around the leathery places of his own palms. Working hands, hands that weren't afraid to be useful; he liked that about her, too. "Is Juliette here?"

Amelie shook her head, smoothing a stray wisp of dark hair back behind her ear. "She's off upon an errand."

Her eyes narrowed, the familiar spark returning. "But just because we're alone together now, Zach, doesn't mean I'm going to be weak and wanton with you again."

"Then don't put such notions into my mind again, sweetheart," he teased, running his fingers up the inside of her wrist, across the tracery of pale blue veins, and he felt her shiver. "But I asked about your sister because I wished her here, not otherwise. I have something to ask you both."

"Both of us?" she repeated, curious.

"Aye, both," he said firmly. "The *Diana*'s set for launching on Wednesday, the luckiest day there is, and in the morning, at ten, to be doubly sure. I'd be honored if you and Juliette would be my guests, to watch Anabelle break the Madeira over the bow as well as for the entertainment afterward. My special guests, Amelie, and you know you can't refuse the captain."

"Oh, Zach." She slipped her hand free, her eyes shining so brightly that he feared she'd weep. "That is most kind of you, but you needn't—"

"Aye, I do," he said. "I want you with me. It's more than just sliding the hull into the water, you know. We'll have music and food and a great deal of drink. I expect most of Boston to be there, too, so wear your prettiest gown since they'll all be watching."

She smiled half-heartedly, with only a hint of her usual confidence. "They're all very pretty. I made them, didn't I?"

"Then make something new," he said with a grand sweep of his hand to encompass all the finery the store had to offer, "something to astonish that old bitch Mrs. Drummer."

"*Chut*, Zach," scolded Amelie uneasily. "Hush. Someone might hear you."

"Do you think I care?" he declared, and he didn't. "Amelie, this is your chance to show them you don't give a damn what they think! They'll all be there, you know, the Richardsons and Quinceys and Clarkes and God knows who else."

"The Richardsons?" she repeated faintly, and too late he remembered the unsavory sight of Oliver Richardson skulking away from her sister.

"I'm not sure I can invite old John without his son," he admitted, "but if you feel it will be impossible for Juliette otherwise if he's there, why, then—"

"Don't even consider offending John Richardson," she said swiftly, "not on our account. Besides, Juliette has told me that she and Oliver were but friends, and that even that is ending."

"Ah." He hadn't wanted to know that, and it embarrassed him. Oliver Richardson had never been mere friends with a woman in his life, and Zach hated to think of sweet little Juliette being one more in Oliver's endless parade, almost as much as he hated Amelie having to accept, and repeat, such a preposterous explanation. "Well then, the Richardsons can join all the other worthies, ready to drink my cousin Joshua's liquor and guess at how much more money he's made this year."

"But not us, Zach," she said. "It's kind of you, but we don't belong."

"The hell you don't!" he said soundly. "I'm asking you, same as I'm asking them. Show them your spirit, lass, show them you won't be broken by a few wagging tongues!"

"Well, it's too late for that," she said, and what little remained of her smile wobbled forlornly.

"Ah, Amelie, don't say that," he said, reaching for her hand again. "What about being brave, eh?"

But she shook her head, instead pulling three crumpled, folded scraps of paper from her pocket.

"This is what comes of being brave, Zach," she said as she began unfolding them one by one and handing the first to him. "This is all I've gotten for showing spirit."

He frowned at the rough notes. "How did you come by these?"

She took a deep breath, steadying herself for confession. "The first came with a bag of twenty guineas, thrown through our window. We—Juliette and I—put the coins in the poor box and resolved to pay it no heed."

"The broken window?" he asked sharply. "Damnation, Amelie, why didn't you tell me then?"

She didn't answer except to hand him the second note. "This one was stuck on a branch when they ruined my garden."

He took it, his concern deepening by the moment. The tone of the note was disturbing, the warning not exactly a threat nor blackmail but an odd, menacing combination of both.

"You should have shown these to me before. This is serious, Amelie. Have you any idea which 'friend' would threaten you?"

She shook her head. "None. We thought at first it might be a jest, apprentices out to give us a fright, but what apprentice would have twenty guineas to throw away?"

"That Drummer woman, or one of her cronies?"

Again she shook her head. "This started long before she became unhappy with me. Besides, it doesn't have the feel of something one woman might do to another, and most women wouldn't have that kind of coin to waste any more than apprentices would."

She looked down at the last paper, still in her hands. "He, or they, or whoever it is, didn't leave a note when they struck you, but I'm sure it was the same man. It had to be. Maybe he thought your head was warning enough. He left us alone for a while after that, and I dared to hope that he'd gone for good. Until I found this last night, inside another bag of guineas."

Reluctantly she handed him the last note. "He'd thrown it into our bedchamber, through the open window and onto the bed. It could have been any time during the day or evening; I don't know exactly when."

But Zach did. Those five or ten minutes after he'd left her and made a great show for her benefit of taking Curwen away with him, before he'd crept back to watch himself for most of the night. He thought he'd been so damned clever, he thought with disgust, and look what had happened.

Yet as soon as he read the note, all he felt was anger, white-hot and raging. He was furious at whoever was doing this to her, who'd dare call her such a foul and undeserved name, and he was furious at himself for believing her when she'd assured him nothing was wrong, for not persisting to make sure she was safe.

"Get your keys," he said sharply. "We're taking this to the constable now."

"No!" she cried, snatching the note back away from him. "That's exactly why I didn't tell you before now!"

"Amelie, this man is dangerous," he said as patiently as his temper would let him. "You and Juliette are *in danger*. You must do what you can to stop him. Can I make it any simpler than that?"

"You take this to the constable," she said, her agitation now matching his, "and all of Boston will know of it by nightfall, and by tomorrow morning I will be ruined! What lady will come to a shop where there might be danger? What husband would want his wife or daughter to be helped by a woman called a—called a—"

"But that's my point, Amelie!" He struck his fist hard on the counter. "This bastard is already telling lies about you! That damned Drummer woman may be only the first one to listen, but you can be sure that others will, too. You have to fight back, Amelie, or else they'll destroy you for certain!"

"But I *can't!*" she cried, her voice wavering with anguish. "Maman would never have wanted a constable here, not in her shop! She would have hated it all, the scandal, the shame of what I've—"

Abruptly she broke off, turning away from him, her little hand with the thimble curled in a tight fist at her side. He remembered how beautiful she'd looked when he'd kissed her beside the shed, her face and body so open and generous and loving, aye, loving, and he realized of how much that one ugly, hateful word in the last note had hurt her.

"Amelie," he said, resting his hands on her shoulders. "Amelie, listen to me. You've done nothing wrong, understand? I want to help you, lass, not hurt you. Trust me that none of this is your fault. The constable isn't going to punish you."

"But I will be the one who suffers," she cried, more to herself than to him. "Maman was right. She was right about everything."

He could feel how rigid she was, her shoulders as tight as if they'd been carved from wood, and gently he began to work his thumbs into the tense muscles.

"How the devil could your mother be right about something she didn't live to see?"

"She knew about scandal," she said unhappily, though he could feel her begin to relax, just a little, beneath his hands. "Enough to warn me of, oh, so many things!"

"If your mother lived here on her own with two young daughters that she loved," said Zach, striving to calm her with reason, too, "then she also knew how to watch after herself. She would have gone to the constable, lass."

She shrugged off his hands and twisted around to face him. "Not yet, Zach," she pleaded. "Don't make me go yet. Maybe this man will stop, or confess, or— or just go away and leave Juliette and me alone."

"Amelie, I don't think—"

"*You* didn't go," she said, gently touching the fading yellow-green bruise on his temple as a reminder. "When they struck you, in my garden, you didn't go to the constable."

"That was different," he said quickly. He hadn't gone because his pride hadn't even let him consider it. He would have felt like an impotent, careless fool, confessing that he'd let himself be jumped like that, nothing he was going to admit to Amelie. "After two days, I had too much business waiting at the shipyard to go waste my time swearing before some bench."

"And so it is with me," she said quietly. "I care for my trade, too, and I can't afford to do what you want, not yet, not now."

It had been her rare independence that had attracted him first that night at Richardsons', and it was that same independence now that he knew he must respect, even as it went against his best judgment.

He hesitated only a moment. "Then you will do exactly what I say. Keep the notes and the guineas in a safe place, in case you need them later for evidence, but don't tell anyone else about them. Not a soul. Neither you nor your sister is to leave here after you have closed your shop for the day, and you'll open your door to no one. No one, mind? I'll have one of my men posted across the street day and night, and if anything ever strikes you as strange, you're to scream as loud as you can so he can hear you to come."

She nodded solemnly. "And these men of yours— they will be, ah, ready?"

"They'll be armed, aye." He'd be breaking the law by making sure his men carried pistols as well as knives hidden beneath their coats, but Zach didn't care. He had never walked away from trouble, and he believed in fighting his own fights, and he certainly believed in watching over Amelie.

But this wasn't some lawless, cutthroat island in the Caribbean. This was Boston, a town ruled by order and judges, where even the night watch carried only a wooden rattle for alarms and a short cudgel against stray dogs, and a town where those same judges would look undeniably askance at the idea of his sailors armed and patrolling the streets. He, and his sailors, would have to be careful indeed.

"They'll be armed," he said again, for emphasis, "and they'll do whatever's necessary for your safety. And, of course, I'll come here myself as often as I can."

"How wonderful," she said faintly. "To think I shall have my own little army of defenders."

He reached for her hand, the one that still wore the thimble, finding he wanted that connection even more than he wished to comfort her. "I'm a fool not to have done it for you long before this."

"Never a fool, *mon cher*," she said softly, twining her fingers into his. "More like a man who never doubts what to do next."

But he did doubt, doubted so much he wondered that she'd any confidence in him at all. Not about the guard, of course, for as a ship's officer he'd been making such arrangements in dangerous ports for years, but about her, and where exactly he fit into her life and she into his.

For the first time since he'd become a sailor, he didn't want to clear land for the open sea, because for the first time he'd found someone he didn't want to leave behind.

Because, for the first time, he'd fallen in love.

He wasn't sure why it had happened, let alone how, but when he looked down into Amelie's eyes, he realized he'd never been more certain of anything. He loved her. He *loved* her.

Now all he had to do was find the words to tell her.

She'd laugh out loud if she knew how much that little French endearment made his heart jump.

"Isn't that why you told me?" he asked instead. "Because you needed someone who could help you?"

She shrugged elaborately. "I suppose I must have."

With unexpected grace, Luna jumped on the counter beside them, coyly nosing first at the flowers before gliding next to Amelie, the cat butting her head against her mistress's shoulder in demanding adoration while she glared green-eyed hatred at Zach.

"She's jealous," said Zach balefully. "Look at her. I tell you, that animal hates me."

Amelie laughed softly, giving the cat the caress she

sought. "Poor darling Luna. She is so faithful, so loyal to me, yet she has never sent me flowers, has she?"

She glanced up at Zach, her head tipped beguilingly, every bit as coy as Luna. Then, to his surprise, she left the cat and came to him, resting her cheek against his chest with a sigh as she curled her hands around his waist.

"I'm so scared, Zach," she whispered as he slipped his arms around her. "I wake in the night and think of all that has happened these last weeks and it scares me so much I can't breathe."

Now, you stupid bastard, he told himself, *tell her now!* To have her there against his chest, whispering to him, confiding in him the way he'd dreamed of from the first. Yet everything he wanted to say fled from his brain, the words vanishing into the air before he could seize them.

"I'm doing my best, lass," he said finally, words so wrong he winced inside.

"I know that," she said swiftly, her voice muffled by his coat. "I do. Honestly. I *know* that. But what will I do when your pretty sloop is launched and her sails are set, and you have sailed away from me? Oh, Zach, what will I do?"

She didn't mean the sailor-guards, or the threats or the notes or the thrown bags of guineas. He knew she meant *him*, and he didn't know the answer, any more than he knew what he was going to do without her. He wished to hell he did, but he wouldn't pretend otherwise, not to her.

Then tell her you love her, cried his heart, ignoring the hard facts of his leaving, her shop, the responsibilites that weighed down upon them both. *Tell her now!*

"We'll have to figure that as we go, Amelie," he

said instead, holding her as if he never wanted to let her go. "Day by day, sweetheart. Day by day."

And he wouldn't think of how few days there were left.

In the next four days, six more ladies notified the Lacroix sisters that they would no longer be requiring the services of French milliners. One made the announcement herself, nervous and gloating, while the others were more cowardly, and sent tersely worded notes by way of servants.

And only one offered to pay for goods already bespoke.

The new issue of the *New-England Courant* contained several stories of note.

The sloop *Diana*, built to the most current designs and at considerable expense by Captain Joshua Fairbourne and Brothers of Appledore, Barnstable County, would be launched from Heward's yard on Wednesday next. Able-bodied seamen desirous of a berth for the first voyage of so fortuitous a vessel should attend Captain Zachariah Fairbourne, master, at the sign of the Crescent in Ann Street.

The felicitous weather was expected to continue, a boon to mariners and farmers. The most aged woman in the almshouse recalled only once before a June so fine, and it had been followed by an unnatural snowfall in July.

And on the second page, masquerading as a letter from Lady A****th, Duchess of B*****ham, London, was a plea to all her sisters in the colonies to support the Crown and Britannia herself, and shun the goods and designs of traitorous French-speaking persons who seek to corrupt, cheat, and deceive the honest English lady and housewife.

But as Maman had warned and Amelie had learned to her sorrow, gossip traveled more swiftly and efficiently than the printed admonitions of Lady A****th.

Neighbors who had lived on Marlborough Street long enough to remember the sisters as girls seemed now to forget they'd ever been introduced. Amelie and Juliette became strangely invisible: their greetings were ignored, their queries as to health and weather went unanswered, their thank yous at the water pump ceased to receive you're welcomes in return.

Fewer and fewer women, whether fine ladies in need of a gown for dining with the governor or serving-girls with a few spare pence to lavish on new thread stockings, came to the shop.

On Friday, for the first time the bell over the door was silent from morning until dusk.

On Saturday, the shop bell rang twice, both times to announce the arrival of silk merchants desiring immediate payment of all open accounts in the name of Miss Amelie Lacroix, for Spitalfields' goods received.

On Sunday night, after Zach had finished his supper with them and left, Amelie tallied her books three separate times to make sure she'd ciphered correctly. There was the value of their stock and fixtures, of course, and the building itself, but those could, and would, be discounted by creditors if it came to an auction. For now the money in the strongbox was all that really mattered.

One hundred twenty-three pounds, ten shillings, and eight pence. That was the sum, and all that stood between the shop of the sisters Lacroix, and ruin.

*　　*　　*

The woman who stood in the center of the shop was short and round, of a middling age and unashamed of it. Her eyes were still a clear, keen blue and beneath her plain white cap her sandy brown hair showed only the first threads of gray. But though the woman was plainly dressed and without any style—in an instant Amelie could mark her country clothing as homespun and home-stitched, too—from her self-assurance she was clearly her own mistress, nobody's servant.

"Good day, mistress," said Amelie, eagerly grateful for any customer. "And what will you buy this morning?"

The woman's ruddy cheeks pinked deeper with pleasure and, thought Amelie, a certain shyness. "Good day to you, too. Are you, ah, Miss Lacroix? Miss Amelie Lacroix?"

Amelie nodded, praying that wouldn't be enough to send the woman fleeing from the shop. "What might I show you, then?"

"A hat," said the woman. "I need a hat for a grand occasion, and I was told you had them."

"We most certainly do," said Amelie, "of every sort and for every pocketbook. And when you have made your choice, we can dress it for you in the latest fashion, with ribbons or rosettes or Italian paper flowers, as you please."

The woman nodded. "Red ribbons," she said, "and a big brim, like the grand ladies wear. I've always wanted a bonnet like that, and I've never in my life had one."

"Then I'm doubly honored you've come here to me." Amelie held the chair out for her, before the counter with the short lookingglass on a stand. "Here, mistress, pray, be seated, and I'll fetch a selection for you."

"Thank 'ee." The woman sat on the edge of the chair, her eyes as wide as a child's in a confectionery.

Her excitement pleased Amelie, who'd seen too many ladies who'd reject everything on a whim, believing that bored disinterest was the mark of true gentility. She'd rather make the most beautiful hat she could with red ribbons, possibly the only such hat this woman might ever possess, than a score of others for a jaded merchant's wife.

With an extra flourish Amelie brought out a half-dozen hats, lifting them one by one from their fancy-papered boxes while the woman gasped with unfeigned delight. The untrimmed hats in fashion were much the same, stitched from blond Milano straw, with the only variety coming in the exact width of the sweeping round brim or the height of the crown. The trimmings were what made each one distinctive and special, and as soon as the woman chose the hat she wished, Amelie spread out an assortment of ribbons and laces on their neat wooden spools, explaining the merits of each one. When the final choices were made, Amelie came to stand behind the woman's chair, her hands full of scarlet silk ribbons.

"Because your eyes are so fine," she began, deftly twisting the flexible brim around the woman's face in the lookingglass, "the hat should frame them, not hide them. Now if you could dress your hair with the knot a bit higher in back—only a bit, like this—then we could tie the ribbons behind your nape instead of beneath your chin, which is much more graceful. *Vraiment!* And some more twists of scarlet here on the crown, for height, don't you think?"

"Oh, aye," breathed the woman, her face transfixed

as she stared at her reflection. "Oh, how comely that looks!"

Carefully Amelie lifted the hat from her head. "If you wish to wait, mistress, I can stitch it now," she said, already pinning the ribbons in temporary place. "Unless you'd rather I had it sent?"

"I'll wait," said the woman, her gaze so intent on the hat that clearly she'd no wish to leave it behind. "If you do not mind, that is."

"Not at all." She took the hat to sit at the low table and chair in the window where the light was best for sewing. She was glad the woman had chosen to wait. Not only was she enjoying the chance to create the special hat, but after so many grim days in the empty store, Amelie relished the company of a customer. "You say you will be wearing the hat for a special occasion, mistress?"

"It's a party for my son, given to honor him by them he works for," she said, her face beaming with pride. "My oldest boy, you know. He's worked so hard to make something of himself, and now he's near to being a gentleman himself."

Amelie smiled, biting off a length of thread. "You must take some of the credit for his success, mistress. Not even the finest boy can raise himself."

The woman grinned happily. "Ah, he's such a good, clever lad, I expect he could have. But that's a mother's way, isn't it? Now your own mother, she must be proud of what you've done here, isn't she?"

"She would have been, yes," said Amelie wistfully, trying not to think of what Maman would say of how precariously close to closing they were now. Maman had bought this shop soon after Papa had died and Juliette had been born, and they'd lived here ever since. "Alas, she died long ago, but I've made her shop grow and prosper since she left it to me."

"I am sorry for your loss, miss," said the woman gravely. "But how fortunate that you've been able to keep beneath the same roof. I had to move about when my first boy was little, and it made him a wanderer, always roaming and restless for what's over the next hillside."

"But isn't that the way of all men, mistress?" said Amelie absently, frowning over the precise place for a silk rose. "Never content with what they have, or where they are, eager to better themselves like your son has done?"

The woman sighed. "I warrant you're right. But I do wish he'd pause long enough to wed. No man's happiness is complete until he takes a wife to share it with him and to love all his days."

"The trick will be in convincing your son it's true, won't it?" said Amelie, inevitably thinking of Zach.

These last days they'd fallen into the pattern of eating their cook-shop supper together with Juliette, then retreating to the back steps to sit and talk or simply look at the stars, her head resting on his shoulder. Everything between them was pleasant, enjoyable, even amusing, but not once did either of them again mention the time he would leave and she would be left. Though they kissed in parting each night, the kisses were oddly chaste, as if each feared to raise the passion that was always simmering between them. Day by day, he'd said, day by day by day, and day by day their time together was slipping away as relentlessly as sand in an hourglass.

She clipped the last thread and held the finished hat up on her hand. But the woman was watching her closely, her expression thoughtful, and uneasily Amelie wondered if she'd let her own thoughts wander on so long that she hadn't heard something she'd said.

"It's very beautiful, don't you think, mistress?" she said as she came to settle the hat on the woman's head, tying the ribbons in a bow at her nape. "The red was exactly right. Your son will be the proud one when he sees his elegant mother now!"

The woman gasped, speechless, staring in such wonder that Amelie felt her own eyes fill briefly with tears. With all her worries over the shop, she'd nearly forgotten how much she enjoyed creating the hats and clothes that gave other women this kind of pleasure, and how dreadfully much she'd miss it.

"The hat is very beautiful, very, very beautiful!" the woman finally managed to say. "Everything they tell of you is true, Miss Lacroix!"

Amelie smiled wryly. "Not exactly all, *Dieu merci*. Shall I fetch you a box, or do you wish to wear it?"

"A box, if you please." Reluctantly the woman untied the bows and lifted it from her head, gazing at it with genuine awe. "I must save it for the party, to surprise my son. What is the reckoning that I owe?"

Quickly Amelie calculated the bill in her head for the hat as they stepped back to her desk. In her enthusiasm, she'd gone against the wisdom of long experience and let the woman choose ribbons that were surely beyond her means, and the Bolognese flowers she'd added on impulse had made it more costly still. It was bad business, true, and the shop was scarcely in the position for her to be charitable, yet the pleasure she'd taken in creating the hat, combined with the woman's once-in-a-lifetime joy and excitement, were worth far more than a few shillings.

"That will be six shillings, mistress," she said, under-valuing her expenses and her labor by at least two-thirds as she copied out a receipt. "And your name, if you please, for my books?"

"Mrs. Rowe," said the woman with a warm smile as she fished the coins from her old-fashioned knitted purse. "Mrs. Henry Rowe."

She paused as she handed the coins to Amelie, con-sidering her shrewdly. "Your prices are most fair, Miss Lacroix. Some might say unfair to you."

"I think not. But I do thank you for your custom, Mrs. Rowe." Dutifully Amelie wrote the name, striving to remember where she'd heard it before, and handed her the hat box. "Good day to you, and I pray you'll enjoy your son's party."

Yet the woman lingered, holding the oval box before her in both hands like the prize it was. "You truly don't know who I am, do you?"

Amelie paused; it was poor business to admit to for-getting a customer's name. "I'm sure I'll recall in a moment, Mrs. Rowe, if only I—"

"I'm Zachariah's mother," she said softly. "Down from Westham for the launching."

Amelie gasped, horrified that she'd forgotten so important a name. "Oh, forgive me, I'd no notion!"

"I know," said Mrs. Rowe, her warm smile so much like Zach's Amelie wondered how she'd missed the resemblance. "And I can't tell you how glad I am you didn't. I'll tell you another thing, too, Miss Lacroix, and I mean every word: if Zach doesn't ask you to marry him, then he's the greatest fool-man in creation. And so, Miss Lacroix, I mean to tell him."

❧13❧

"*L*ook at you, Amelie," said Juliette, clapping her hands together with gleeful excitement. "Oh, dear Lord, what people will say! *Look* at you!"

Amelie did look, and winked back at her reflection in the tall looking-glass. "Zach told me I must show my spirit to Mrs. Drummer and the rest of them, and I cannot think of a better way to do it."

"Mrs. Drummer," said Juliette with relish, "will be *sick.*"

Amelie only smiled, plucking a final bit of fullness into her lace ruffled cuffs. No, her *engageántes*. She could call them by their proper name now, just as she could fervently hope, with all her heart, that at the sight of her this morning Mrs. Drummer *would* be horribly, hideously sick.

Zach could call it spirit, but she'd settle for revenge.

She'd taken the gown that Mrs. Drummer had refused and completely remade it to fit herself. In the process she'd also made it infinitely more stylish, more daring, to suit her own much younger and slimmer figure—differences she hoped Mrs. Drummer would notice, too.

The sharply angled seams accentuated her tight-laced waist just as the shorter petticoats, over full hoops, showed off her ankles and red-heeled slippers and, countering the fashion for melting pastels, she'd trimmed the bronze silk and her wide-brimmed hat with shocking slashes of black velvet ribbon. The contrast of colors not only suited her own dark hair and deep-toned skin, but her mood today as well.

Dressed as boldly as this, not even a blind man would miss her, and as for Zach—well, she'd enjoyed that time they'd spent together on her back steps, but enough was enough. She was bored, and she was restless, without enough work in the shop to keep her busy, which in turn had given her far too much time to think. Though she knew he'd been so busy with all the last-minute details of the launching that by the time he came to her in the evening he was exhausted, *she* was tired of simply sitting and waiting for something to happen between them.

In her trade she'd recognized the power of clothing to change people's perceptions, just like an actor could change costumes to suit his roles, and if tight-laced stays and bronze silk and black velvet didn't give her the confidence to speak her mind to Zach, then nothing would. That she wasn't yet sure what that mind of hers wanted to say so badly didn't bother her; it was the chance that mattered more. She winked again at her image as she tweaked the curling white plume on her hat over the brim and towards her face.

She was almost ready to face whatever the day would offer. But there still remained one small task before they left.

"Julie, wait," she said, watching her sister, behind her, reflected in the glass. Though not dressed as dramatically, Juliette in pale blue would still be among the most stylish women at the launching, as Amelie had insisted. Just because they were on the edge of ruin didn't mean that they had to dress like it. "Zach told me that Oliver Richardson may be there today."

Juliette shrugged, seemingly not in the least concerned. "I would expect him to, yes. Oliver never can refuse a party of any sort."

"And you are not—not concerned that you might see him?"

"Why should I be?" said Juliette as she tugged on her gloves. "I told you before, Amelie, that Oliver was only a friend, an acquaintance, and not a close one at that. Now we should be going if we don't want to be late. Zach said they'd begin at ten sharp, and to remind you that sailors are always prompt."

She certainly looked as if she were telling the truth, and Amelie knew from experience that dissembling did not, fortunately, come easily to her sister. She wanted to believe Juliette, too, wanted to very much, for she'd trouble enough right now without adding Oliver Richardson to her worries.

"Then I suppose we should be on our way, if we're to—oh, no, that can't be the bell!" said Amelie impatiently as they both turned toward the stairs, listening. "Days go by with not a soul, and now *this* morning someone comes calling. And I know I put the sign saying we were closed in the window."

The sign was still there, but Amelie hadn't yet locked the front door, and as she hurried down the stairs she could hear voices in the shop. She didn't want to be late at the shipyard, not for Zach, yet a customer was a customer, and with an effort she made herself smile as she swept into the shop.

"Good day to you, and what will you—Mrs. Fairbourne!"

"*La,* you didn't expect to see me here now, did you?" exclaimed the black-haired young woman as she rushed toward her. "It's my little surprise, Amelie, my little indulgence to spoil you. How vastly happy I am to see you!"

She flung her arms around Amelie with a gust of expensive scent and a dusting of face-powder before she disentangled herself with a throaty chuckle. Everything about Anabelle Crosbie Fairbourne was like that chuckle, lush and extravagant and full of voluptuous life, sparkling with her own spicy good humor and the royal ransom of jewels she wore even at this time of day, and all of it the complete opposite of her stern-faced but adoring husband, Zach's cousin Joshua.

"Now no more of this Mrs. nonsense," scolded Anabelle merrily, "else you'll put me to mind of those ogling servants at the inn who keep calling me their 'ladyship.' *Their* ladyship, ha, as if they'd any more right to me with a title! But Anabelle it must be from you, dear Amelie, and to keep me clear of all the other Mrs. Fairbournes about us today. And, of course, this other little Fairbourne-lady. Yes, yes, come here, my sweet girl, I haven't forgotten you, either."

But the little girl beside the counter didn't budge, one chubby hand pointing upward to Luna, staring down at her with all the arrogance of being comfortably out of reach.

"Diana want that kitty," proclaimed the little girl. "Want kitty *now.*"

From her black hair and blue eyes, the child was

definitely a Fairbourne, but from her imperious two-year-old manner, her high-bred blood was asserting itself, too. Anabelle was the highest-born lady in New England, the granddaughter of a duke and the sister to an earl, and while her elopement with Joshua Fairbourne nearly six years before had caused a great scandal in the London she'd left behind, it had also made her the closest thing to royalty most of Massachusetts had ever seen.

And, as Anabelle wryly noted herself, foolish Massachusetts was generally willing to throw itself down to kiss the toes of her favorite silk-covered mules. But in Amelie, Anabelle had discovered a mantua-maker rivaling the ones she'd left behind in London, as well as a friend who wasn't overwhelmed or intimidated by her position and past. Though the ever-growing Fairbourne family had made Anabelle's visits to Boston infrequent, their friendship had held firm despite the separation.

Now Anabelle stood tapping one of those silk-covered mules with impatience as she frowned down at her daughter.

"Yes, sweetmeat, I am sure you do want the kitty," she said, "but the kitty belongs to Miss Lacroix here, and just because you want it doesn't mean she's going to give it to you. Amelie, this is my daughter Diana. Diana, dearest, say good day to Mama's friend Miss Lacroix."

Diana stared at her in rebellious silence, her hand still raised toward the cat she coveted. She was dressed in exact miniature of a fine lady, in a yellow silk gown over the same kind of laced whalebone stays and hoops that shaped her mother, her fine black hair pinned into a knot and covered with a lace-trimmed linen cap, a strand of coral beads around her neck.

"Diana," said Anabelle, maternal warning implicit in her voice. "It is not too late for me to send you back to the inn to stay with Baby Edmund. If you're not old enough to greet Mama's friend, then you're surely not old enough to launch a ship."

And that, clearly, was warning enough, as Diana bobbed up and down in a jerky little curtsey, her skirts held out to either side in her chubby fists.

"*Bonjour, mademoiselle*," she rattled off, obviously speaking the sounds by rote and without any understanding of what she said. "*Comment allez-vous?*"

"*Très bien, merci*," answered Amelie, trying hard not to laugh at the deliberate seriousness of the child before her. "Your French is beautiful, *ma petite*, but you don't have to speak it upon my account. Now would you like to see Luna? You have to be gentle with her, for she's not accustomed to little girls, and I don't want to see her scratch you."

Diana nodded, and carefully Amelie lifted Luna from the counter to the floor beside the little girl. The cat gave a low, moaning meow of long-suffering protest, then gathered herself into a tight, protective ball as she eyed Diana warily. To say Luna wasn't accustomed to little girls was something of an understatement; the reason she wasn't was that the neighborhood girls (and boys) had long ago discovered her uncharitable nature, and now crossed the street to avoid her. But to Amelie's surprise, when Diana reached out to stroke the soft gray fur on the cat's back, Luna only blinked, then arched her back against the girl's hand with a wheezing purr of pleasure.

"Just for a moment now, Diana," cautioned Anabelle. "We can't keep your father and uncles waiting."

"She's a beautiful child," murmured Amelie, still watching Luna with the little girl. The resemblance among the Fairbourne cousins was so strong that when she looked at Diana she could easily imagine Zach's children as well, with a sharp pain of longing for what would never happen. "What a joy she must be to you!"

"What a trial she *is*," said Anabelle with an exasperated sigh. "She may look sweet enough now, but she spends entirely too much time with her older brother Alexander and the other boys around the docks and in the marshes, bringing home dead crabs and filthy petticoats and stockings covered with cockleburs."

"Just the way you've said you were, then?"

"Oh, vastly like me," agreed Anabelle. "How can I not be distraught? But she might still be salvageable, as was I. You do see that today I am entirely dressed by the wondrous Mademoiselle Lacroix?"

She turned to be admired in her bright green brocade, holding out her right hand with the white swan's-down muff over her wrist, and laughed when she saw Amelie blush.

"Ha, I could not forget that, could I?" she teased. "I knew Zach would be perfect for you, exactly perfect. You only needed to meet, and that order for a muff performed admirably. And wasn't I wicked to make it a muff? *La!* Poor Zach, to have to ask for such a thing from a lady like you!"

"But you couldn't have planned this," protested Amelie with dismay. For most of her life she'd only had Juliette to fuss over her, and the idea of so many concerned Fairbournes was overwhelming. It was bad enough to have Zach's mother threatening to order him to marry her without having Anabelle, too, taking credit for matchmaking. *Mon Dieu*, was the entire family plotting around her? "I met him somewhere else, before he came to the shop with your note."

Anabelle wiggled the muff on her wrist. "Then that only proves how perfectly right I was, if you managed to find one another on your own, too. Ah, here's your sweet sister so we can be on our way. The hired carriage will be a tight fit for all our hoops, but I do believe we can squeeze together if I take Diana on my lap."

"A *carriage?*" Amelie hurried to the window, and there indeed was a hired carriage complete with hired footmen in livery, and a good assortment of neighbors, too, come to gawk at such a grand conveyance on their street.

"Well, yes, of course," said Anabelle, unperturbed as she patted at the plume-shaped brooch of diamonds in her hair. "We can't be expected to walk to the shipyard, can we?"

"But Mrs. Fairbourne—Anabelle—this is too much," said Amelie, already envisioning the kind of entry a carriage like this would make into Ann Street, and the shipyard. "There'll be talk about how we're aping our betters, reaching beyond our station!"

"Oh, *la*," scoffed Anabelle. "From what Zach has told me, there's so much ill-natured talk about you in Boston already that a bit more is certainly not going to make a difference."

"But that doesn't—"

"Yes, it *does*," said Anabelle severely. "I understand that you have run afoul—that's lovely mariner-talk that I've claimed from Joshua, because it sounds so much like what it is—that you have run afoul of cer-

tain mean-spirited old crows who think themselves too
fine to come to you. I'm here to show them how vastly
wrong they are. It will not be difficult, considering how
handsomely you've turned yourself out today. You must
come with me and stay at my side while I tell everyone
what an incomparable mantua-maker you are, and
those old crows will simply have to find someone else
to peck. Now come, come, we can't keep the coach-
man waiting any longer!"

But Amelie was too stunned to move. She'd been
anticipating this day for the last week, before Anabelle
Fairbourne had swept into the shop and turned all her
careful plans inside out. She liked Anabelle, and she
did appreciate what she was offering to do. But she
hadn't asked for a protectress to defend her. That was
what the bronze silk gown was for, all the magic armor
she was going to need today. She'd wanted to challenge and win on her own terms, by herself, and gently
she took Anabelle by the arm. "Anabelle, please, I
would rather—"

"Pray don't thank me, Amelie," said Anabelle absently, beckoning to Diana. "It was my husband's notion, after he'd heard of your troubles. Sometimes, once
in a great while, even men can have clever ideas.
Hurry now, sweetmeat, leave the kitty and come
along!"

But it wasn't clever, not to Amelie, and as she sat
crowded between Juliette and Anabelle in the open
carriage, the hooped petticoats of the three women and
one little girl ruffling into each other, she felt crowded,
too, by the overzealous attentions of Zach and his family. When she'd come to him for help after the last
note, she'd done it because she'd had no other choice

left to her. He'd helped her, maybe even saved her life and Juliette's, and she'd never regret turning to him.

But now she felt smothered, as if her whole lifetime of hard-won independence was being taken away in one well-meaning sweep. They all meant well, yes, but they never stopped to ask her if what they did was agreeable to *her* before they went ahead and did it. Did Zach, too, feel this way, or was it just her?

By the time the carriage had neared Heward's, the shipyard and the street before it were already clogged with crowds of well-wishers. A launching was grand entertainment, a spectacle not to be missed, especially not in a town where theaters were still outlawed.

Not only was a launching the reward for all the various crews who'd worked together to raise the hull of the new vessel to this stage—the plankers and caulkers and painters and general carpenters as well as the ship's architect and master builder—but the day was also an excuse for all of seafaring Boston to celebrate one more ship sailing from her docks to the rest of the world, one more shining mark that she'd make on the sea.

For Joshua Fairbourne, the launching was an opportunity to extend lavish hospitality to friends and competitors alike, a chance for braggery and boasting on a grand scale, not only about the new vessel but about the commercial success of the Fairbourne brothers in general.

But the most important reason of all for celebrating a launching was to give the vessel itself an auspicious start on what everyone hoped to be a long, fruitful, and safe career. Sailors and shipowners alike recognized this, and the *Diana*, with the Fairbourne name on her registry, was to be given every advantage of a spectacular ceremony.

With a pair of footmen to forge a path through the crowds, Amelie, Juliette, Anabelle, and Diana threaded their way from the carriage into the shipyard. Their progress was slow, not so much from the crowds alone but from how many times Anabelle stopped to greet a friend or wave to another.

"Could you ever have imagined such a scene?" shouted Juliette excitedly over the din into Amelie's ear. "No wonder poor Zach has been so weary, having to arrange all this!"

"All this" truly was an astounding amount. Yet as Amelie gazed over the long tables ready for food and drink, the rows of planks for spectators, the red and white flags that snapped and cracked in the breeze from the water, she couldn't help but think of the last time she'd been here, when she and Zach had been alone together on the Diana's empty deck, watching the sun set over Beacon Hill. Wistfully she knew she would have traded this entire gaudy spectacle today to be back there alone with him again, and she scanned the bobbing sea of people, searching for him among all the others.

"Miss Lacroix!" She turned toward the man who called her name, the red-faced man with too much gold lace on his coat and his pink-cheeked daughter clinging to his arm: Simon Drummer and Betsey.

"Miss Lacroix," said Drummer again, clearing his throat while his watery gaze slid past her and Juliette to Anabelle. Of course he'd know who Anabelle was, and for someone as determined as he and his wife were to rise in the social world, her aristocratic connections must be irresistible. "Miss Lacroix, and, ah, Miss La-croix, you're both of you looking most fine today."

"Thank you, sir," answered Amelie. He wouldn't recognize the bronze silk, but from the shock in Bet-sey's eyes she most certainly did. "Miss Drummer, how good to see you as well. I trust your mother's not ill?"

Drummer shook his head, his own face suddenly queasy. Good, thought Amelie; he might not remem-ber the gown, but by now he'd recalled how his wife had refused to pay her account. "A minor indisposi-tion, that's all. A pity she missed this, eh?"

Betsey smiled sweetly enough at Amelie, but her expression was so full of wicked amusement she seemed barely able to contain it. "Perhaps Mother needed something new to wear, Father. Perhaps, when she's better, she should call on Miss Lacroix again."

Juliette was right about Betsey: there was far more to the girl than Amelie had ever realized. This time it would be Betsey, and not her mother, who'd make use of Mrs. Drummer's well-honed circle of gossip and innuendo, and Amelie would wager the story of the bronze-colored silk would be tittered over for weeks.

So why, then, wondered Amelie, did it feel like such a hollow victory?

"Indeed, indeed, she should," blustered Drummer, far too heartily. "She must! My ladies can't have too many gowns, and Miss Lacroix's the best at making em in Boston, isn't she? Ah, ahem, isn't that Her Ladyship Anabelle Crosbie Fairbourne, there?"

"Oh, la, my dearest Amelie, here you are," purred Anabelle mischievously as she came to tuck her hand in Amelie's arm so the Drummers couldn't help but understand they were together. "There's someone *important* I'd like you to meet, someone who—"

"Amelie," said Zach, suddenly there in front of her, and just as suddenly everyone else in the shipyard vanished for her as he took her hand. He was for once dressed like a gentleman, and she'd never seen him look more handsome, or more happy. "Come with me, lass. I've been waiting to find you all morning."

"Oh, no, you don't, Zach," protested Anabelle. "I still have scores of people for her to meet. Where could you take her that would be more important?"

He grinned at Amelie, a conspirator's grin, a dogcatcher's grin, a grin she hadn't seen since he'd rowed her among the pond lilies. "On board the *Diana*, of course. I know she'll want to ride out the launching with me."

Anabelle gasped indignantly. "You can't do that, Zach! It's not right for a lady, and it's not safe!"

"And since when has that ever stopped you, Anabelle?" His grin swung around to include her, warm enough that Anabelle chuckled and poked him in the arm with her fan as he took Amelie by the hand.

"Go ahead, Amelie," urged Juliette, giving her sister her own little shove of encouragement. "I'll be well enough with Mrs. Fairbourne."

"Where *are* we going, Zach?" asked Amelie breathlessly as he guided her, nearly running, through the crowd. "I thought we couldn't go on board until the sloop was launched."

"You can if you're with the captain," he said as they reached the sloop. Her sides were now beautifully painted exactly as Amelie had suggested, the whole hull finished and ready for the masts and rigging to be added once she was afloat. The ungainly forest of supports that Amelie had remembered were gone, replaced now by a narrow, slanting track of timbers that led into the water. The wide plank walkway with the hand-railings to the deck was gone, too, and in its place was propped a single, wobbling board.

"Up you go, then, mademoiselle," he said, gallantly bowing before the plank. "I'll be right behind you to steady you if you need it."

Amelie looked at him with amused disbelief. "Zach, I can no more balance upon that than I could on a ropedancer's line, and I'm not about to fall off trying before all this people."

"It's not that narrow," he said, "and I promise I won't let you fall."

"Zach, I'm wearing hoops! I won't even see my own feet!"

"Then keep your eyes straight ahead," he said. "You should, anyway. You'll only get dizzy looking down. Handsomely, now, lass. We haven't much time."

She realized then that the two men waiting near the planks were there to take them away as soon as she and Zach had climbed aboard. She didn't want to do this, not even for Zach, not with so many people watching.

"Be brave," he said, leaning close to her ear. "For me."

With a deep breath she pulled her skirts to one side and took one tentative step on the blank. The plank bounced and shimmied beneath her weight and automatically she tensed, fighting her panic. She hated this, she hated this, and already she'd begun to inch backward to return to Juliette when she felt Zach's hands at her waist to hold her steady.

"You'll be all right, lass," he said. "Just do it for me."

Trust Zach, she told herself fiercely, *trust him and you can do this. For him, and for yourself.*

He wouldn't let her fall; he'd never make her do anything where she'd be hurt. She took another step, feeling her way with her toe and not looking down, then another, until with a final little hop, she'd reached the deck.

"I *did* do it, Zach!" she crowed with excitement as she squeezed her hoops through the narrow gangway. "I didn't look down, just like you said!"

But to her surprise there were even more guests here on the deck, twenty or more gentlemen who crowded around them to congratulate Zach yet again, all of them so boisterous that Amelie was sure they'd already been celebrating since dawn. Though by their clothes they were all gentlemen, their revelry was as crude as any pack of sailors at a rumshop, enough to make Amelie uncomfortably aware of being the only woman among them.

"Come aft with me, Amelie," he said to her as two more men thumped him on the back and called him a right fortunate fellow. "This way."

His hand on her waist as he guided her through them toward the stern reassured her now the same way it had on the plank, and with a certain tender possessiveness that, uncharacteristically, she liked even more. They came to the ship's wheel, looking oddly exposed where it jutted up through the mastless deck, and suddenly they were as alone as if they'd come through a gate that had locked behind them.

"Welcome to my quarterdeck, Amelie," said Zach, lifting his hat to her. "My own private captain's sanctuary, even today, and open to lowly mortals by invitation only. Which, of course, I've granted to you."

"*Merci beaucoup.*" Amelie laughed, relieved to be free of the noisy crush toward the stern. Without the masts or any rigging, the deck seemed as open as a ballroom floor, the new pine planks holystoned to a satiny perfection. "I'm honored, Captain."

"You should be." His expression softened as he looked at her, his eyes squinting into the sun making his smile even more brilliant. He was dressed all in midnight blue, twin rows of brass buttons down the front of his coat, and a red and white striped flag snapping in the wind behind him, and with a little lurch of her heart she realized that this was how she'd remember him once he'd left.

"I'm glad you came, Amelie. More than glad. I can't tell you how many times I've imagined you here with me," he said as his gaze lowered and lingered on her body with unmistakable approval, "but I never did get the gown right in my head."

More nervously she laughed again, conscious of how more than the breeze was swirling between them now. When he looked at her like this her skin felt as warm as if he were touching her. "Do you like it?"

"Oh, aye, how could I not?" His gaze wandered lazily across the tight front of her bodice, to where the black lace scarf she'd tucked over the tops of her breasts served more to entice than conceal. She'd been pleased with the effect—part of the plan to build her courage—but she wasn't prepared for him to react this strongly. "Silk satin, black velvet, and lace: I'm only a man, Amelie."

Only a man, she thought with a shiver, but more than enough to make her heart beat wildly beneath her stays. This wasn't helping her speak, that was certain. The last time she'd felt this way with him, she'd nearly lost her maidenhead against the wall of a fishing shed. But what could possibly happen on the deck of sloop before so many witnesses?

But she took a single skittish step away from him, ostensibly to show the gown. "It's the one that Mrs. Drummer refused to pay for. Or at least it was, before I changed it over to suit me." She raised her chin defiantly. "I wished to make a point."

"Jesus, you did that!" He laughed, and shook his head. "The same gown, you say? I told Joshua he didn't need to have Anabelle look after you. You're the most independent female I've ever met, and that's the truth."

She looked at him sideways. "But is it a compliment, Captain?"

"Oh, aye, 'course it is," he said easily. "You being on your own was what caught my eye that first night at Richardsons'. That, and the moonlight. You remember that, too, don't you?"

"Of course." But she didn't want to remember now. Soon enough all she'd have were memories. Instead she purposefully turned to the railing, gazing out at all the people gathered in the yard and on the beach below them. They weren't so high that she couldn't make out faces here and there that she recognized: the Drummers again, Mrs. Isham with Zach's mother in her new hat with the red ribbons and her younger son, Henry, a stone-faced John Richardson with Oliver standing sullenly beside him, even Mrs. Murray.

Oh, *mon Dieu*, Mrs. Murray: if the elderly lady looked up at the sloop now, she'd see her with the half-witted dogcatcher himself. But instead of worrying her, the way it would have in the past, now Amelie simply smiled to herself. Maman would have been appalled by the sight of her here on such open display with Zach, but if Amelie were honest with her heart, there was no place on earth she'd rather be.

Maybe that was what she should tell Zach. Maybe that was what she'd been trying to find the courage to say for, oh, all her life . . .

"My cousin Joshua must be in heaven to have so many come to pay him homage," said Zach as he leaned his elbows on the railing beside her. "How many people do you guess that is?"

Amelie looked at him doubtfully from under her hat-brim. She never been good at such guessing-games. "Dozens?"

"Oh, scores, I'd say," he teased. "At the very least. It's a fine day, and there's always the hope of seeing some grievous disaster at a launching—workmen crushed, spectators drowned—that brings out the bloodthirsty masses."

"Hundreds, then!"

"A thousand," he said with mock solemnity. "Maybe as many as a thousand and one."

"Stop!" She laughed, jabbing at his arm with her elbow. "Call it a sufficiency, and be done."

"Oh, aye, it's that. A sufficiency." He slid his hand along the polished rail until he found hers, covering it. "A sufficiency to have taught me so much that I know, to have helped make me who I am. A sufficiency of people to build this sloop and give me the chance to be worthy of their trust."

She hadn't expected such candor from him, and it touched her. She curled her fingers into his, sliding along the railing to be closer to him. "You *are* worthy, *mon cher*," she said softly. "Don't ever doubt it."

He smiled wryly. "That's the other side of being

independent, isn't it? Even a captain has to learn he can't do everything himself, and if—"

But what else a captain must learn was drowned out by the rolling flourish of three drummers, announcing the start of the launching ceremony. In an instant the crowd fell quiet, with hats pulled off in respect as the balding minister, his face framed by the swooping white linen wings of his clerical collar and the long powdered curls of his wig, intoned a prayer for the safety of the sloop and all men who would serve in her.

It was a grim, solemn reminder of how dangerous a calling the sea could be, and silently Amelie added a second prayer of her own for Zach alone. She could not imagine him lost, drowned in the horrible way his father had been, or her life continuing after his had ended. Was that, too, something she should tell him, or keep to herself as he sailed away?

Next Joshua Fairbourne stepped forward, to the prow of the sloop, and Amelie expected him, as owner, to make some sort of grand speech. In his way he was even more imposing than the minister had been, standing there in the sunlight dressed in somber dark gray, his black hair now streaked with white at the temples. He was known as a hard, fair, fearless captain, and it was still the whispered marvel that such a stern man could find happiness with a woman as lighthearted as Anabelle.

Yet all Joshua's severity melted away as soon as his daughter Diana joined him. His smile for her glowed with love as he carefully lifted her onto the enormous hogshead that had been draped festively with bunting for her use. She stood poised like a tiny yellow fairy on the barrel, using both hands to take the bottle of

Madeira, tied with a long ribbon to the sloop's bow-sprit, that her father offered her.

"I name thee *Diana*," she shouted shrilly, "because that's my name, too!"

Then she swung the bottle as hard as she could at the side of the sloop with such practiced force—how many empty bottles had she broken with her brother Alexander for practice?—that the glass smashed on the first try, showering her skirts as well as the sloop with the wine. She hopped and grinned with delight as the crowd roared its approval.

"Have you every seen anything more enchanting?" said Amelie, once again wistfully thinking of how Diana could just as well be Zach's daughter as Joshua's. "If she were—oh, Zach, what's happening? What's that noise?"

"They're knocking away the braces," shouted Zach over the mallets' thumping and the shouting of a thousand and one people. His whole face glowed with anticipation, as excited as any boy in the crowd. "There's a hundred pounds of tallow greasing the ways, so any second now, Amelie, any second and— hold on, lass, hold on tight!"

With a rumble like thunder beneath them, the sloop shuddered and lurched to life, its weight forcing it down the sloping, greased ways, faster and faster as it lumbered toward the water. With a shriek Amelie grabbed the nearest stable thing at hand, which was, of course, Zach, and held on as tightly as he'd ordered. Gulls were squawking and diving overhead with terror, the river was coming closer and closer, the tons of oak and pine slipping faster, and Amelie shrieked again as the sloop plunged into the river with a huge, crashing spray of water, drenching them as surely as if they'd fallen stern-first into a wave.

"Oh, Zach!" cried Amelie, blinking the water from her eyes to look down in horror at the soaked silk now hanging lankly from her hoops. Of course he'd known this would happen, and she understood now why there were no other women on board for the launching. "Oh, no!"

But while the same water was dripping from his hat and his nose and even his chin, Zach was laughing like a joyful idiot as he pulled her closer.

"How can you *laugh*, you great fool?" she sputtered, squirming against him. "How *can* you, when—"

"Because I love you, Amelie Lacroix!" he roared at the top of his lungs. He yanked off his sodden hat and sailed it across the deck, then tore off hers, too, for good measure. "Because I love you!"

"But—but you can't!" she stammered, realizing just now why he couldn't. "You can't because I was going to say it first to *you!*"

"But you didn't," he said, pulling her back into his arms, "and I did."

And then, to make sure she understood, he kissed her.

❧ 14 ❧

It had been, decided Zach, the happiest day of his life to date.

He'd qualify it like that to himself not because he wished to belittle the happiness he felt now, glowing away inside him like his own personal source of contentment, but because with Amelie at his side he was sure that that same happiness was going to continue to glow brighter and burn hotter in the future. Today was the happiest for today, but next Tuesday, say, could be the happiest for then, and then the Thursday after that could—well, he didn't want to consider it too much or too far into the future. But he was definitely happy tonight, and that, for now, was enough.

"Is the feather ruined for good?" he asked, following Amelie's glance down to the misshapen hat that she was carrying in her hand as they walked. It was late now, well after dark, for after the launch and the long, long celebration at Heward's yard, Joshua had brought the entire family back to their lodging-house for supper and more celebrating. Through some convoluted maneuvering, Anabelle had arranged to return Juliette home later, allowing Zach to walk Amelie back to Marlborough Street alone. He was sure he'd find Anabelle's maneuvering difficult to accept on a daily basis, but he was heartily grateful for it tonight.

Amelie sighed as she held the bedraggled white feather briefly up before letting it flop forlornly down again. "For good, and for bad, too, I'd say. Fine plumes do not survive water."

"I'm sorry," he said contritely. "I'll buy you another. I'll buy you a dozen."

"Or a thousand and one?" They were walking slowly, in no hurry to reach the shop. "But I believe the plume gave its life for a grand cause."

She smiled up at him shyly, the moonlight that filtered down into the street both hiding and revealing her face. "Do you know, Zachariah Fairbourne, that you are the first man who has ever told me he loved me?"

"Hah," he said, feigning a scowl worthy of his cousin. "I'll wager I'm not the first to kiss you."

"No," she admitted. "But the only other time was with a cheesemaker's apprentice, a nasty boy named Giles with moist hands that always smelled of whey. He told me he was most skilled in lovemaking and because I was only eleven, I believed him. Both of us, I fear, were wrong. For me it was rather like kissing a dog, wet and sloppy."

"Poor Giles," said Zach sympathetically. It was easy to be sympathetic with a rival who stank of whey and was so far behind in the past. "It's just as well he didn't meet with the dogcatcher."

She giggled, an unexpectedly girlish sound from her that charmed him. "Mrs. Murray was there today, you know. You'll have to account to her sooner or later. She's one of my best customers."

"Then I'll simply have to be the most successful rising dogcatcher in history." He let his arm slip from around her shoulders to her waist. "You know you're the first woman I've ever told I've loved, too."

"Only ever *told* you loved, or loved outright?" she teased.

"Both," he declared, and truthfully, too. "I'm far too honest to be a rake."

She'd slipped her arm around his waist, too, inside his coat and under his waistcoat to rest comfortably at the band of his breeches. Though she specialized in women's sewing, she also seemed to have an easy familiarity with men's clothing that he found strangely, wildly exciting in such an inexperienced woman.

"You might not have been a true rake, *mon bien-aimé*," she scoffed, "but I can't believe you've never been in love before this. You have so much to make a woman love you!"

"Well, then, I cannot believe it of you, either." Though most of his French had to do with trade, he recognized that "*bien-aimé*" for the "beloved" it was, and that warm glow of happiness grew brighter again. "Perhaps we've been waiting for each other all this time, eh?"

She made a purely Gallic noise of disgust. "More likely no one else would have us." She glanced up, past his face to the square of velvety open sky behind the tower of Old South Meeting House. "There's a star. Do you dare make a wish on it?"

"If you will, too," he said, staring into the sky as he tried to think of something wish-worthy. He didn't really have anything left to wish for tonight, not without feeling greedy, and settled on good health and long life for those he loved, which, now, included Amelie. "But mind, no telling this time, and no wasting wishes upon farmers and crops."

She grinned, and silently mouthed her wish toward the tiny pinprick of light overhead, adding a kiss cast upward on her fingertips for good measure. "No telling at all."

"No." He bent to kiss her while her face was still upturned, a kiss that lingered with promise. "I can't tell you how much it meant having you there with me today, sweetheart. To have you there to share it with—that made it doubly fine, Amelie."

She glanced at him oddly, her dark brows drawn together as they began to walk again. "Your mother said almost exactly the same thing to me."

"Oh, Mam says a great many things." He shrugged sheepishly, unwilling to venture more against his mother. Mam had spoken to him, too, after she'd gone to spy on Amelie with the eager assistance of Sarah Isham. He still couldn't believe Mam had done that, but what he didn't *want* to believe was that she'd told Amelie what a fine wife she'd make for him, the way she'd claimed. Sometimes Mam exaggerated, and he prayed that this was one of those times. What woman—particularly a woman as independent as Amelie—wanted to hear the first words of a marriage from her sweetheart's *mother?*

"She said it about your father," she said softly. "About the two of them together."

"Ah, well, I expect my pa's been on her mind as much as my own." He sighed restlessly. "You couldn't know it, of course, but so much of what happened today had to do with him. Or because of him, really.

The Appledore Fairbournes, Joshua, Sam, Serena, and Danny, their father was my father's older brother. When their father drowned, my own pa wasn't much more than a boy himself, fifteen or sixteen. But Joshua never forgave him for not helping out with his brother's widow and children, especially when the county broke the children up and set them out with different families. I don't know what Joshua thought my pa could do, not at that age, and then before he could amount to anything, he'd drowned himself. Seventeen, he was, same as Mam."

He shook his head sorrowfully for his dead father's bad luck and the short life that had come with it. "Me being made captain of the *Diana*, showing Joshua I could do it no matter whose son I am—that's all for my pa, Amelie. He didn't leave much to show for his life, so I guess I'm trying to do it for him."

"But he did, Zach," said Amelie gently. "He left your mother with you, and the memory of all the love they'd shared. What better gift to leave behind?"

Zach frowned uneasily. He'd said too much himself, babbling on about things that had happened so long ago that Amelie couldn't possibly be interested. "Did Mam tell you that?"

"In different words, perhaps." Amelie smiled, a smile that managed to ease the aching vacuum he'd always felt where his father should have been. "But not everything your mother says is foolish."

"No," he said, desperately wondering again what else Mam had told Amelie. All he could do now was plunge on ahead as best he could on his own and pray that she hadn't muddied the waters too badly for him. "No, whatever else she is, Mam's not foolish."

"No," agreed Amelie. She glanced up at him again, curiously, waiting for him to say something more.

And God help him, he did. "With the *Diana* launched, we'll step her masts tomorrow, then begin the rigging. With any luck she'll be ready to take cargo and sail in a fortnight."

"Oh, Zach, don't talk about the future!" she pleaded anxiously. "I don't want to think about anything else beyond this day, and how happy we are now!"

"But we should talk about it, Amelie," he said. "We don't have that much time to squander before I sail, and I don't want to leave you without knowing you're settled!"

"No!" she cried, almost frantic. "Don't spoil this, Zach, I beg you! I love you, Zach, and you love me. Isn't that enough for now?"

"It wasn't enough for my father," he insisted. "Amelie, I—"

"*No!*" she cried again, pulling away from him and putting her hands over her ears. "Your mother, Anabelle, the rest of your family—they all want us to marry, Zach. It's true. I know because they've told me, and I'm sure they've told you, too, and I—I don't want it to happen, not like that."

He stared at her, stunned that not only his mother but Anabelle, too, had dared to meddle in something so private and important. This was all new enough to him that he'd just decided to ask for an understanding from her before he sailed, that she'd receive no other men before he returned. On his own he hadn't thought of asking her to marry him, but as soon as she said she wouldn't, the more he instantly, perversely, wanted it so.

To know she would always belong to him alone, to

free her from the scandal and gossip that plagued spinsters, to be able to lie with her in that big curtained bed and make long, endless love to her with every husbandly right, to love her completely the way she deserved, the way he wanted—the more he considered it, the more a swift wedding before he sailed would be the best thing imaginable for them both.

"Then I'll ask you proper." He dropped down to his knees there in the middle of the empty street, blocking her path. "Marry me, Amelie. Please. I haven't much to offer you yet except my heart and the rest of me, but I promise you'll never want for anything. Especially not love. Say yes, sweetheart, and be my wife."

But instead of the sweet acquiescence he'd hoped for, she frowned. "Get up, Zach. Get up *now*." She flicked her skirts to one side and began to edge away from him. "*Vraiment*, this is the most preposterous thing I've ever heard!"

"No, it's not," said Zach, scrambling back to his feet to follow her. "You love me, and I love you. Getting married is what most people choose to do in that situation."

"No, Zach, no," she said, shaking her head furiously. "You've been listening too much to your mother, or Anabelle, or maybe even little Diana, though likely she has more sense than you do right now."

"All right, then, I'll be sensible, if that's what you want," he countered, his thoughts racing ahead with all sorts of possibilities. "Damned sensible, and practical, too. We can get married now, this week, while all my family's still here in Boston. Then you can come south with me, as a sort of wedding trip. Martinique, Bermuda, Barbados—you tell me where you'd like to go and I'll make it so."

She didn't stop walking, almost marching, and she didn't look at him either. "And what about *my* family? What about Juliette? I can't abandon her to run the shop on her own while I go paddle about your precious islands with you."

"Juliette will manage better than you think," said Zach, lengthening his stride to keep up with her. They were nearly to her shop, and he wanted this settled between them before she had a door to slam in his face. "Your business isn't as brisk as it has been, anyway. And I'd wager your sister might even welcome the chance to step away from your shadow a bit."

"My *shadow!*" cried Amelie indignantly. "And I suppose you'd wish me to move to Appledore with all the rest of the good little Fairbourne wives?"

"It's not such a bad spot, Amelie," he said. "It's a pretty little town, right on the bay, and it's a sight safer place for children than Boston."

She stopped so abruptly he nearly ran over her. "So you have it all decided, then? You and your family?"

"Amelie, lass," he said softly. "My dearest Amelie. Don't you love me?"

Her lips were pinched tightly together as she struggled with herself. "I love you," she whispered, her voice strangled with emotion. "I love you now, and I always will. But loving you doesn't mean I own you, or you own me, which is what this—this *marriage* you are proposing would be. I love you, Zachariah Fairbourne, with every bit of my heart. But I'm not going to marry you."

"Amelie, please, I—"

"*Fire!*"

They turned in unison, toward the man's shout. Boston hadn't had a large fire for over ten years, but in a close-packed city built largely of wood and heated by fire, with so many distilleries for the rum trade and flammable marine goods—tar, pitch, turpentine, gunpowder—in the stores and warehouses, a wayward spark from a hearth could burn down an entire neighborhood in an hour. Down Marlborough Street they could see a faint glow between buildings, an unnatural brightness that shouldn't be there.

"Fire, fire!" shouted the man again. "This way!"

A woman screamed, and farther down came the urgent clattering alarm of the watchman's rattle and running feet, the creak and thump of windows being hurriedly thrown open for news.

"*Mon dieu*, it's near the shop," said Amelie, already beginning to run. "Oh, *non, mon dieu, non!*"

Zach followed. He didn't bother praying, because with sickening certainty he already knew where they'd find the fire. The notes, the threats, the destroyed garden: what could follow next but arson?

People were already gathering before the millinery shop, aimlessly gawking in their nightcaps with their clothes tossed half on. The walls of the shop was built of brick, but inside, with wooden beams, floors, and the entire stock of fancy goods, was much that would burn. To Zach's relief, the front shutters and windows upstairs were still dark, unharmed, but beyond the fence, from the yard in the back, came the unmistakable crack of flames and the scent of burning wood, and the bright patches of firelight dancing along the neighboring walls. He wondered what had become of the man he'd had guarding the shop; he prayed they'd still find him alive.

"*Aidez-moi, aidez-moi!*" cried Amelie, sobbing in

French as she tried frantically to push past the others. "*Mon dieu, ma boutique, oh, au feu, au feu!*"

Yet the others merely stared at her, unable to understand her and unwilling to yield their view of the fire to her.

"Do you know the pair o' French hussies what own the shop, miss?" asked one woman in a ruffled mobcap. "Too fine for their own good, I've heard, and preachin' treason against good King George behind their counter, too. 'Tis a pity to see them burned out, but sometimes there's justice in suffering."

But Zach saw no justice in suffering, or inactivity, either. "You there, in the front, open that gate," he ordered, his voice unconsciously assuming his captain's authority. "You three, take those buckets and any others you can find to the well. Go, now! Your houses could be next if we don't stop this now!"

Immediately the men grabbed the buckets and ran to fill them, while others scattered for buckets of their own from home. Zach grabbed Amelie's hand and pulled her with him, through the gate to the yard. The acrid smoke stung his eyes and filled the narrow space as he squinted at the flames.

"Oh, Zach, look," said Amelie, coughing as the smoke filled her lungs. The wooden back steps were outlined by the fire, the flames licking at the door itself and the window frames. "Hold this over your mouth," he said, giving her his his still-damp handkerchief. The first man had returned with his bucket filled, and Zach grabbed it from him, throwing the water to hiss on the flames. While he waited for the next he seized the long-handled garden shovel and began digging and dumping shovelfuls of dirt onto the flames to smother them. The next man with a water bucket came, followed by the woman with the ruffled cap, and the next, and the next, a steady procession from the well at the end of the street.

"Oh, Zach, it's Luna!" gasped Amelie, lowering the handkerchief from her mouth at his sleeve as she pointed with horror. "My poor, sweet cat."

Zach dragged his sleeve across his eyes and squinted up to where she pointed. No matter what Amelie claimed, there was nothing little nor poor about Luna, but even he couldn't deny the cat *was* terrified, crouched on the sill of the open upstairs window, her eyes wild and her tail puffed fat as a raccoon's with fear. Smoke curled from the window behind her, though Zach couldn't tell if it had been drawn up the staircase from below or from another fire inside, and as soon as the cat saw Amelie she yowled piteously.

"I can't leave her there, Zach, I can't!" Tears marked pale tracks through the soot on her cheeks. "I can't leave her there to die!"

She bunched her skirts in one hand and began to rush towards the still-burning steps.

"Are you out of your wits?" demanded Zach hoarsely as he grabbed her arm to jerk her back. "You can't go in there now!"

"But I can't leave Luna there, either! She's my baby cat, Zach, *ma chère Luna,* my—"

"I'll go," he said, stripping off his coat, "even though the infernal animal hates me. Let me have the keys to the front door."

"Thank you, Zach," whispered Amelie, her tears welling up again. "Be careful, *mon bien-aimé!*"

She pulled his face down to kiss him quickly, before he dunked his neckcloth in a bucket of water and wrapped it over his mouth and nose. He tried to hold on to the memory of that kiss as he fumbled his way through the darkened shop, back towards the muffled sounds of voices and the fire outside. As far as he could tell, they'd caught the flames in time, and there wasn't any damage inside, and there wasn't even much smoke, though he'd no real wish to linger. His main enemy now was the darkness. He barked his shins against a chair, stumbled forward and nearly fell, swearing. Who'd have thought he'd have needed a candle to rescue that damned cat from a fire?

"Luna?" he called up the winding staircase, hoping against hope that the cat would come down and spare him the task of going up. "Here, here, Luna, come to old Zach."

Of course the cat didn't, and with another disgusted oath he began to feel his way up the stairs to the bedchamber. There was more smoke here because of the open window, but not nearly as much as he'd thought from outside. Amelie was lucky as hell, especially when he thought of what could have happened if the two sisters had been here asleep.

"Here, Luna, you wretched excuse for a cat," he called, and this time he spotted her, still crouched in the window. "Time to shove off, Luna, and back to Amelie."

Cautiously he approached the window, reaching out one hand towards the cat. Luna, however, was in no mood for rescuing, hissing at him with her ears flattened back against her head.

"Enough of your charm, you vile hell-cat," he muttered, but as he drew closer the cat lunged at him, raking her claws down the length of his arm as she jumped. Now Zach yowled, clutching at his arm and the four tidy tracks of dripping blood.

"Zach!" he heard Amelie cry with concern—though not, he thought, as much as she'd shown for Luna—"Zach, are you all right?"

He thrust his head out the window. "Right as rain, lass," he said gallantly, a ragged cheer rising up from the people below. "Luna and I will be down directly."

Luna was unconvinced. She sat in the center of the bed, glaring at him with green-eyed venom.

"I told Amelie we'd be down directly, you fur-covered she-devil," he said, slowly circling the bed, "and you're not going to make me a liar, not to Amelie."

He pulled one of the long bolsters from the bed and shook out the pillow inside. He folded the case three times, a long, flat strip of linen across the coverlet. Then, as fast as he could, he grabbed the cat and pressed it down on one end of the linen, and rapidly wrapped her around and around in the linen so that only her head stuck out one end and her tail the other. The cat growled and hissed again, but this time her claws were ineffectually tucked inside the linen.

"Who's the master now, eh?" said Zach as he gathered up the swaddled cat in his arms. "Captain Fairbourne, that's who, and don't you forget it."

There was more cheering when he appeared with the cat, and Amelie raced to meet him, with a man he guessed was a constable trailing behind her. The fire was out, the steps and railing reduced to a few charred outlines, the smoke thinning to a few grey wisps, and most of the bystanders had already drifted back home to bed.

"Oh, Luna, poor little baby," she crooned, cradling the cat in her arms against the sorry remains of the bronze-colored gown. *"Ma chère petite chatte!"*

"There's nothing poor about that beast," said Zach,

wishing Amelie would lavish the same sort of attention on him. "Look, she tried to slaughter me outright."

Amelie glanced briefly at his shredded shirt and blood-covered arm. "What do you expect, Zach? She was terrified, that was all."

"Well, so was I," he said with disgust. "You can take her with us back to the Crescent, but you and your sister will have to keep her locked in your room and clear of Mrs. Isham and her kitchen."

Amelie looked up at him with surprise. "Whyever would we be going back to the Crescent?"

"Why?" repeated Zach incredulously. "Why? Because you can't stay here, that's why."

"Of course I'm staying," she said evenly. "This is my home, Zach. Our home, Juliette and me together. You know that. The constable says there will be some smoke in the house, but as long as I don't try to use this door it should be safe enough."

"Safe enough? Amelie, someone tried to burn down your house and you want to go back inside to give him another chance while you sleep? Did you tell the constable that as well?"

She raised her chin, as imperious as she could be with half her hairpins gone and her hair trailing down in uneven pieces around her soot-smudged face, her eyes red from weeping and smoke, her gown in shambles and an immense, furious, ridiculous cat bundled in swaddling-clothes in her arms.

And damnation, she looked so beautiful she could have broken his heart in one blink of her red-rimmed eye.

"This is my home," she said again, "and I am staying. Besides, whoever it is never comes back the same night."

"There's a precious fine line between being independent and plain bullheaded stubborn," he said, fuming, "and you've crossed it now, Amelie. Can't you hear what you're saying?"

She glared at him, as mutinous as the cat. "There is nothing wrong with my hearing, Zach. Now would you please return my keys?"

He bent down and snatched his coat from the grass where he'd left it, pulling the ring of keys from his pocket to hand them back to her. "If it matters at all to you any longer, Amelie, I still do love you."

"And I still love you, Zach," she said, awkwardly shifting Luna to the crook of one arm to take the keys back. "I told you before that I always will, too. But I'm not your wife, and I don't have to obey you."

And without another word, she turned and walked away.

❦ 15 ❧

Carefully Amelie spread the blue-flowered damask over the last clothesline, making sure the selvages didn't trail into the dirt. By stringing rope back and forth from one fence to the other across the yard, she'd finally been able to hang all the cloth out to air, an exotic silk tent-city in the middle of Boston. While nothing in the shop itself had been damaged in the fire, the scent of smoke still clung to all the fabric that had been stored upstairs. No lady wished to dress herself in silk damask or brocade that made her smell like a holiday ham, but Amelie hoped that the sun and breeze would take away the worst of it.

Wearily she sat on the chair she'd brought out from the workroom, granting herself a quick rest in the sunshine. Next she meant to scrub at the smudges of black smoke ringing the whitewashed plaster around the windows in their bedchamber, and though the marks weren't dangerous, she wanted all signs of the fire removed. Already she'd had a carpenter come this morning and clear away the blackened remains of her back steps, and she expected him to return soon with fresh timbers to rebuild them. It was an expense she couldn't afford, not now, but she hated having any reminders of what had happened the night before.

The night before, the night before . . .

Unbidden, the rest of what had happened last night came racing back to haunt her, and with a groan she buried her face in her hands. How had she gone from such happiness to such despair in one evening? Zach hadn't come back this morning, and though she'd let Juliette go to sew for Anabelle in the secret hopes that he would, deep down she was miserably sure he wouldn't.

Why should he? He'd proposed marriage to her and she'd refused, refused as clumsily and insensitively as a woman possibly could. When he'd asked her reasons she hadn't even been coherent enough to offer any, and had simply fallen back on criticizing his family instead. She didn't *deserve* for him to return, not after that. He'd told her he loved her, offered her his hand and his heart and knelt—actually *knelt!*—in the middle of Cornhill Street to prove it, and while the tiny voice in her own heart was practically weeping with joy, the wicked, louder voice in her mouth couldn't say enough bad things to send him away. No wonder she'd insisted on staying here in the smoke-blackened shambles of her home, instead of following him wherever he went, the way she so desperately wanted; here she could cry her shame alone, without anyone to see her, curled in her misery in the center of the bed he'd laid in, too.

She loved him, she loved him more dearly and deeply than she'd ever dreamed possible. When the wave had splashed over them at the launching, she'd felt she'd somehow been granted a new life to match the sloop's, a fresh, giddy life with Zach beside her. There on the deck in his arms, everything had seemed possible and promising.

But the closer they'd come to the shop last night, the more that delightful future had been darkened by Maman, her long-ago voice once again sounding warning after warning in Amelie's ears.

Men will tempt you with love, Amelie, and ruin you for amusement.

Trust in yourself, not in love, and never in a man.

Love is a danger, a peril always to be avoided.

Marry for love, suffer in sorrow.

There is no such thing as true love . . .

For twenty-five years she had tried to obey, to listen, to live the way that Maman had wanted, and until she'd met Zach Fairbourne it had been easy.

But Zach had changed all the rules. Zach had taught her other, sweeter lessons that were free of dark bitterness, lessons that had made her laugh with joy.

No man's happiness is complete until he takes a wife to share it with him, and to love for life.

That was the sort of lessons he'd grown up hearing from his mother, so different from hers. He had made Amelie question Maman's word, and he had made her fall in love.

No, he hadn't "made" her do anything. She'd fallen gloriously on her own, into such rare companionship and contentment and passion and blissful happiness that she'd been willing to risk everything else for more of it.

For more of *him.*

Until he'd asked her to be his wife, and Maman had spoken for her instead.

"Miss Lacroix?"

She jerked her head up at the sound of the man's voice, immediately wiping away her tears.

"I hope I didn't disturb you," he said from somewhere on the other side of the bright lengths of silk shifting and trembling in the breeze. "No one answered at the shop door, but when I saw the gate was open I thought you might be within here instead."

The voice was deep, worn with years, a gentleman's voice that she didn't recognize. Yet the gentleman knew her, and quickly she staightened her cap and rose to greet him.

He was older, as she'd guessed, though the years sat light enough on his shoulders that he still stood straight and tall. He was dressed with a cleric's severity, there among the gay-patterned silks, a black suit and stockings, a tall white curled wig, an ebony walking stick topped with silver, and his features, too, had the same Old Testament grimness of the first colonists, a face that would welcome the tests of Judgment Day.

A face once seen and never forgotten.

"Master Richardson, sir," said Amelie swiftly, dipping low, as he'd expect and to cover her discomfiture. He had never come to her shop before, leaving such frivolity to his daughters, but of course she'd recognize him. "Good day, sir, and pray forgive my delay in receiving you."

"There is nothing to forgive, young woman," he said solemnly. He glanced past her to the blackened bricks that marked where her back steps had been. "You have had trouble enough of your own."

"Yes, sir," she said. Why was he here, she wondered uneasily, and why did he care about her troubles? "A small fire, sir, nothing of real import."

"No one was hurt?"

Amelie shook her head, wishing, too, that she were wearing something better than worn old homespun for housecleaning. The Richardsons were gentry. "We were frightened, to be sure, but as you can see the damage isn't lasting."

"You are fortunate." He nodded gravely. "We live in restless, godless times, Miss Lacroix, when such mischief can befall even the most respectable. May I trouble you for that chair? I have a weakness in my chest that worsens when I stand, one of the burdens of age."

"Of course," murmured Amelie, quickly bringing him the workshop chair. She wished it were grander, her father's armchair, for instance, but she didn't wish to inconvenience him further. "My mother suffered from that, too, and on days as warm as this the pain seemed often worse."

"Your mother." He looked up at her beneath a bristle of white brows, one eye narrowed, appraising. "You favor her, you know."

Amelie flushed, startled by the compliment. "Thank you, sir. I didn't know you were, ah, acquainted."

"We were," he said slowly. "We were. But I've come to you on a troubling matter, a matter requiring discretion and caution."

He waited, and she nodded, not sure what else he expected.

It was apparently enough, for he nodded in return. "As all this town knows, Miss Lacroix, my son Oliver is a severe disappointment to me. He is frivolous and willfully ignorant, and given only to his own amusement. I sorrow for his soul, Miss Lacroix, for I can see no peace, no salvation for a son who so denies the counsel and wisdom of his elders."

"He is still young, sir," said Amelie hesitantly. "He could still come around."

"Not on the course he has chosen for himself now," said Richardson with gloomy certainty, "nor with the companions he prefers to make his ruin complete. But that is where I ask your help, Miss Lacroix. It is bad enough that he destroys himself, but I will not sit by idly and let him take an innocent with him on his path to hell."

"An innocent, sir?" asked Amelie, though with dreadful foreboding she'd already guessed what was coming.

"Your sister, Miss Lacroix, that pretty young creature called Juliette," he said, poking his walking stick impatiently into the ground. "I have much reason to believe that Oliver is conducting an intrigue with your sister, Miss Lacroix, and that he is even now plotting to elope with her to the West Indies."

Amelie gasped, shaking her head in furious denial. "No, sir, that's not possible, that's not true! I've already suspected such an—an attachment between Juliette and Oliver, but Juliette has assured me that your son is an acquaintance only. I have her word that she has given him up as even that."

"The word of a girl!"

"The word of my sister!"

"Then you have been deluded, Miss Lacroix, as blind as I to the truth," he said, shrewdly gauging her reaction. "Yesterday, at the launching ceremony for Captain Fairbourne's new vessel, I saw them myself, familiarly together, and I have learned that he has, through another, been making inquiries about a passage to the Indies for two persons."

"But not Juliette," said Amelie, refusing to doubt

her sister again. Juliette had promised her there was nothing between her and Oliver, and her word was enough. If Richardson had heard differently, then there had to be some other explanation. "She wouldn't lie to me, not about something like this."

"Then you agree that this is an unsuitable match?"

"*Mais oui!*" said Amelie indignantly. "I do not wish to insult you, sir, but your son's flaws are widely known in this colony, and I'd hardly wish them on any respectable woman, especially not my sister!"

"Honestly put, young woman," he said grudgingly, "if not with grace. And it is well you believe that, for she'd not have a penny of mine because of Oliver."

"She wouldn't want it," said Amelie firmly, "and she wouldn't take it. I would make sure of that."

He laughed then, a wheezing, rattling laugh dry from disuse. "You *are* much like your mother, Miss Lacroix, but I wonder if I can trust you any more than I could her. She, too, knew the power of her beauty and its value as well. And ah, she was a grand beauty, a rare Venus, wasn't she?"

"Maman?" She'd never heard her mother spoken of quite like this, especially not from a gentleman like Mr. Richardson.

"Aye." He nodded, his eyes looking inward to a remembered past. "Your mother—your 'Maman'—and I were good friends, fine friends. I wonder that she never mentioned it."

"She didn't." John Richardson might be one of the most respectable gentlemen in Boston, but Amelie still hated the disturbing tone of these questions where her mother was concerned. "After Papa died, she was too busy running this shop and tending to us to have many friends, especially once she became so ill herself."

"Ha, your father," said Richardson with a contemptuous sneer. "He was nothing to your mother."

"That isn't true!" she cried. "He was my *father*."

"And little more, young woman. He was a fearful, shrinking little tailor too stupid to learn the king's English. Do you think your mother would have done so well for herself if she'd relied only on him?"

"The reason Papa couldn't help her was because he was ill," said Amelie defensively, repeating the well-learned version of the past that she'd never had reason to question before. "Otherwise Papa would have helped her more—he would have! He left her the money to buy this shop when he died, didn't he? And after that she succeeded because she worked hard. I remember that. She worked harder than anyone I've ever seen."

"Oh, yes, she knew how to *work*," agreed Richardson with withering emphasis. "But how could the tailor have left such an estate? She earned this building all by herself, I think. All that hard work."

She remembered the two dark, damp rooms they'd shared behind Papa's shop, the best he could afford for his family, and she remembered, too, the awful quarrels between Maman and Papa where "disappointment" had been the only word she'd understood. And then Papa had died, killed by his cough, and she and Maman had moved to this pretty shop with the rooms upstairs, and Juliette was born.

Your father's last blessing to us, Maman had said, dabbing the handkerchief to her eyes that shed no tears. Such a good husband, such a devoted father!

Yet how could a failed, sickly tailor have left such a gift?

All that hard work, said John Richardson, and he would be the one who knew.

Oh, Maman, the lie you lived! How you could have done this, and with such a man! Was there no other way to feed your daughters, no other way to find us shelter? The shop I've kept so proudly in your memory, bought like this? Was your dream worth the price you paid? No wonder you mistrusted love, no wonder you tried so hard to keep us from following you!

Oh, Maman!

"You doubt me," he was saying. "The ring that you wear, the garnet. That belonged to your mother, did it not? Inside there is a sweet little inscription, 'Love Never Dies,' I think. Not that your mother believed in such callow sentiments. Oh, no."

The ring had been the one memento Maman had left to her, the single thing she'd cherished most for the inscription that had given her such comfort when Maman had died.

Oh, Maman . . .

"Slip it off, if you wish," he said, "and read it for yourself."

"And I think, Master Richardson," said Amelie, her voice shaking and her hands in tight fists at her sides, "that it is time for you to leave."

"You would send me away, then?" he asked, bemused. "You believe that I would care for your pride?"

"I believe that you care for nothing but yourself," she said. "If I might ever have considered a match between my sister and your son, you can be sure that now I can think of nothing—*nothing*—I would wish less. Good day, sir. Forgive me if I don't show you out, but then you know the way, don't you?"

"You're bold as polished brass, young woman," said Richardson as he rose unsteadily to his feet, but as he studied her Amelie sensed a grudging sense of admiration, too. "But you are Jeanne's daughter, no mistake."

"I am," said Amelie, her chin high, "and my father's as well."

That much he couldn't take from her. She was dark like her father, and she had inherited his unmistakable hands, short-fingered and strong with little fingers that crooked inwards as if they'd been broken and healed, clever hands with a thread and needle.

But Juliette had always been different, with her golden hair and fair skin. Maman had explained it away by claiming she favored her family, but now, when Amelie thought of all the golden-haired Richardsons, she began to wonder to her horror if it was another family entirely that Juliette favored. What, now, if Julie and Oliver were more than the friends her sister claimed?

Oh, Maman, had you really strayed so far?

"More honor than the tailor deserves." He made a cursory bow in Amelie's direction before finding a path through the waving lengths of bright silk. Yet at the gate he stopped and turned, his eyes as hard as flint and his hand like an eagle's claw as he grasped the post. "One last question, Miss Lacroix, and I tell you to answer me as Jeanne's daughter would."

She waited, dreading, though she knew she owed him nothing.

"Tell me, Miss Lacroix," he persisted, his voice laced with the most bitter irony. "Do you still believe there's no such thing as true love?"

His dry, empty laugh echoed in her ears long after he'd left, nearly as long as the words she'd spoken herself at Deborah Richardson's wedding celebration. When at last she bowed her head to weep, her sorrow was no longer for herself and Zach, but for her mother, and for the girl she'd always called sister.

And for this last, and hardest, lesson of love.

* * *

The coverlet was brushed wool, a brilliant red against the pale green paneling, and the new mattress beneath it was stuffed with the softest wool, the pillows fat with goosedown. Oh, aye, he'd sleep well here, thought Zach with satisfaction as he patted the coverlet on his bunk. How could he not?

Yet as he admired his first captain's quarters, the satisfaction he told himself he must feel had an odd, empty quality to it. Oh, the *Diana* was still his dream of perfection made real, a fast, lovely sloop that every other shipmaster in New England would covet, and these quarters, the first place he could call exclusively his home, would be the envy of a good many housewives, too. Though he still wouldn't put to sea for another two weeks, his mother and Mrs. Isham had seen that his cupboards were well-stocked with indulgences, from raspberry jam to Rhode Island rum, and they'd polished the pewter on his table until it shown like silver. His chart table and desk were rich mahogany, the lantern overhead gleaming brass, and the long sweep of the stern windows near his bunk offered a view of Boston harbor that not even the governor could claim.

He'd worked most of his life to reach this place, worked hard, and he'd still done it in fewer years than most. He'd earned the respect of his peers, made his mother ecstatically proud, and honored his father's memory. In two years, if his voyages lived up to this splendid beginning, he could be a prosperous man, and still not thirty. Three years after that, and he could be wealthy enough to leave the sea altogether, like his cousin Joshua, to build a grand gentleman's house and sip tea poured from a silver pot. Few in Boston could rival his prospects as he stood here at the stern window with his hands clasped behind his back.

He had everything a man could hope to have, and more.

But he still didn't have the one thing he wanted most, and that was Amelie Lacroix.

Though the cabin door was open, John Goodling still knocked on it, respectfully, as if it were closed, and waited until Zach acknowledged him.

"We're done for the day, sir," he said, "and the harbor watch is already aboard. Should we lock up tight now, sir, or will you be staying here a bit longer before you come ashore, too?"

"I'll lock up here when I'm done, Goodling," said Zach without turning. From his window he could see the fiery ball of the sun slipping behind the hills to the west, and because he remembered watching such a sunset with Amelie, he wanted to stay. "But you go home to Mrs. Goodling now, mind?"

"Thank you, sir, I will." Goodling shut the door, and the sound of the mate's booted feet retreated down the companionway, across the deck, and, Zach supposed, down the gangplank and the wharf and the streets until he reached the warm, welcoming arms of Mrs. Goodling and their tumbling mass of small children.

Zach frowned, determined not to waste his time envying his first mate. He should be thinking of other things, more noble thoughts, worthy of a deep-water captain.

Amelie should be sitting down to supper now with Juliette, at that old cherrywood table with the uneven leg with a prop of cork to keep it level. He'd promised them that once the *Diana* was launched he'd fix that leg so their coffee wouldn't slosh and spill from their cups if they'd leaned the wrong way. Now that leg was going to have to stay uneven, with coffee spilling. If Amelie didn't want a husband, he thought moodily, then she wasn't going to get a free carpenter, either.

How the hell could she love him as much as she claimed—as much as he *knew* she did—and still refuse to marry him?

The sun was nearly gone now, the sky above it rosy red and pink. He should be gone himself, too. He'd have plenty of nights alone in this cabin ahead of him, and there wasn't much point in hanging about now, feeling sorry for himself, when he had so many friends and family members still in town to dine and drink with.

Another knock sounded at the door, likely one of the men from the harbor watch come into see if the new captain really was sitting alone in the dark, watching his beard grow for excitement like some gloomy old hermit.

"Enter," he barked, determined to discourage any more interruptions.

Behind him the door opened tentatively, the hinges still new and stiff.

"Well?" said Zach impatiently. "What is it, man?"

"Good heavens, Zach," said Amelie. "Is there some sort of law against candles at sea?"

"Amelie!" He whipped around, fearful he'd only imagined her voice. But even in the twilight her shape was unmistakable, even her scent familiar. "You're here?"

"So it seems," she said, taking one step toward him. "Though I can't see well enough to be sure."

"Here, here, I'll find a light directly." He took her

hand—why the devil were her fingers so cold, anyway?—and guided her across the cabin to the cushioned bench beneath the long windows. He couldn't remember where the flint was kept, opening and shutting the cupboards, until he remembered he'd one in his pocket, too.

"There," he said as he finally lit the candle in the lantern that hung from the beams overhead. "That's better, isn't it?"

"Much. I came to see you, Zach," she said softly, "and now at least I can."

"Yes," he said, clearing his throat self-consciously as he came to sit on the cushion beside her. "And now I can see you, too."

She smiled shyly, twisting to look out the window. She was simply dressed in pale pink linen with her dark hair in a simple knot, more like a country lass than the fashionable milliner now, and he didn't want to think of how many lovelorn sailors she'd left swaying in her wake as she'd come here to him.

"You shouldn't have come here alone, sweetheart," he chided gently. "Not down here any time, but especially not so close to nightfall. You know it's not safe."

"I know," she said, "but I wanted to see you."

The artlessness of her answer stunned him, and the courage of it did, too. While he'd chosen to spend the day alone nursing his wounded pride, she'd been the one who'd come to gamble her heart.

Lightly she touched her fingertips to the glass. "Do you think I can wish on another star now?"

"Why not?" he asked. "Every night brings a new first star, doesn't it? I'd say that entitles you to a new wish, too."

"Good." Solemnly she whispered her wish, her lips

barely moving, then added the kiss on her fingertips the same way as she had the night before. "I hope that one comes true."

"Then so do I." He didn't care what her wish was as long as it made her happy.

"You should." She turned back toward him, her smile turning wistful. "Because I wished that you'd love me."

"Oh, Amelie." He reached out to cup her cheek against his palm. Something had changed about her since last night, something he couldn't quite define. But he also knew her well enough by now not to ask; if she wanted him to know, she'd tell him when she was ready. "You know if you tell the wish it won't come true. But since that's already a fact, not a wish, I suppose it won't make a difference to the star. I love you, sweetheart, and I do believe I always will."

"I don't deserve it," she said, her eyes serious. "Not after what I said to you last night."

"You were upset," he said quickly, eager to give her any excuse that would keep her here with him. "Frightened on account of the fire."

"That was Luna," she teased, before her expression grew serious again. "No, no, Zach, it was more than that. When you asked me to marry you, I was so happy—oh, you can't know!—but I was also scared. To give away half of myself that way, even to you—I didn't think I could do it."

"It's not all bad," said Zach. "You get half of me in return."

She tried to smile. "It's not that easy, dearest. Nothing is. I thought I knew who I was, what I believed, but everything seems so different now that I don't know where to turn next."

"You could try me," he suggested, gently slanting her face so their lips could meet. "You won't have to turn very far."

She slipped her hand up into his hair, drawing him closer.

"Oh, Zach, I already love you," she whispered. "But now you're all I have left to trust."

"Then trust me, love," he said, his voice raw with longing as he bent to kiss her. "Trust me."

But in her heart, Amelie already did. All afternoon, since John Richardson had left, her thoughts and heart had been twisting with confusion, denial and loss and pain all tangled together. For the first time in her life she'd felt rootless, helpless, terrified, without any of the familiar bearings that had always guided her before.

Yet even as John Richardson had torn apart her long-ago past, he'd also unwittingly handed her the key to her future with it. True love, he'd taunted scornfully, daring her to believe in such foolishness. How could she believe in true love?

But as she'd sat there mired in her sorrow, she'd realized she *did*. She believed in true love because that was what she'd found with Zach Fairbourne, love that was infinitely rare and precious. All at once she'd realized she wanted to spend her life with him, wherever that life would carry them together, whether Martinique or Appledore. She wanted him as her husband and lover and best friend. She wanted to bear his children, lots of children, and she wanted to spoil them with the warm, generous mother's devotion that she'd never known. That was true love, and oh, yes, how she did believe in it.

And now, with Zach, she meant to prove it as well. She slipped her arms around his shoulders, leaning into him as they kissed so that the soft tops of her breasts above her stays pressed against his chest, as bold an invitation as she shyly knew how to offer.

But it was more than enough for Zach. At once he deepened the kiss, hungrily moving his mouth across hers as if he could never taste her enough. His tongue pressed deep inside her mouth, seeking hers, and as they touched she felt the first little curls of pleasure spiraling through her body. Her fingers spread wide over his jaw to hold him there, his day's growth of beard in rough contrast to the wet heat of his kiss, until suddenly with a frustrated groan, he pulled away.

"What have I done?" she murmured in confusion. "Oh, *mon cher*, forgive me if I've—"

"It's I who should be asking forgiveness," he said wryly, taking both her hands in his as he rose from the bench. "Unless you wish to provide a spectacle to make Boston forget yesterday's launching."

She followed his gaze to the wide sweep of uncurtained window and blushed. At sea privacy would not be an issue, but with the sloop tied here to Heward's wharf, they'd be giving a splendid view of everything to every vessel, from Navy coasters to fishermen's dories, that happened to glide by.

He laughed ruefully at the expression on her face. "I know we've made something of a practice of, ah, sharing our pleasures, but this time I'd rather it was between us alone."

She laughed, too, but more from nervousness than amusement, and it faded as he led her to the red-covered bunk. A bunk was a bed, and a bed seemed infinitely more serious somehow than the bench had been.

Gently he turned her face to his. "You don't have

to stay. It will nigh kill me, but I'll take you home instead if you wish it."

She shook her head, not trusting her voice, and he kissed her.

"Good lass," he whispered. "My brave, clever Amelie."

But as he he unlaced the back of her dress she didn't feel clever, and as he eased the sleeves from her shoulders to slip the gown from her she felt instead like the carved wooden doll they had in the shop for showing new fashions. Except that instead of showing fashionable dress, she was displaying undress, as one by one he untied her petticoats and let them drop over her hips and to the deck.

"You—you have done this before, haven't you?" she asked, wishing her voice wasn't quavering as he tugged the lacings of her stays through the eyelets. She could feel her body relaxing as the whalebone fell away, returning to its own womanly shape and not the stiff, conical one that respectability dictated. Her shift was such fine linen that once he'd pulled off her stays her nipples were visible, and self-consciously she covered her breasts with her hands. "Else you've been a mantua-maker yourself, to know how to undress a woman so."

"Then we shall make it even," he said, holding his arms over his head. "Come, your turn. Take off my shirt."

She hesitated only a moment before she grasped the hem with both hands and pulled the billowing shirt over his head. But unlike the slow teasing revelations, bit by bit, of her own clothes, he now stood before her in the lantern light in complete and unabashed glory, all hard muscles and curling black hair that stole her breath away. His worn linen breeches concealed little more, hanging on his lean hip bones, the fabric so soft that the extent of his arousal was glaringly evident.

He followed her glance downward and grinned wickedly. "I'm glad you're staying," he said. "But if you wish, we can leave the breeches on a bit longer, and you can keep your shift."

She nodded, both relieved and disappointed.

"Then come with me now, lass," he whispered, drawing her into his arms. "Trust me, and let me love you."

Gently he pulled her down on top of him, the way they'd been on the bench, with her knees on either side of his thighs. She leaned forward again to kiss him, her breasts swaying freely against him now without her stays, and she gasped as he filled his hand with her soft flesh. He rubbed his thumb across her nipple and the rosy nub instantly puckered as sensation burned through her body.

She braced herself against him, her palms flat against his chest as she restlessly shifted over him, seeking more of what instinct told her she needed. Instinct, and Zach, too, for soon she could feel his other arm against her hip as his hand began possessively rubbing back and forth over her linen-covered bottom even as he held her steady. With a low moan that was lost in his mouth, she arched against his hand, rocking back and forth into his caress.

He broke the kiss long enough to trail a damp path of sensation along her throat. "Brazen little cat," he whispered hoarsely. "You like to be petted as much as Luna."

She sighed, loving his touch. "I told you she liked you. Now I know why."

"Umm," he said, finding the hem of her shift so he

could slide his hand along her bare leg, above her garters. "But I much prefer your skin to her fur."

She wanted to laugh at that, but the anticipation of his caress rising higher on her thigh made it impossible. She remembered what had happened by the lily pond, how she'd thought she'd lost her wits when he'd touched her that way, and skittishly she tried to draw her knees together. But she'd forgotten how his own legs were already between hers, a block she couldn't overcome, and she shuddered helplessly as he found that soft, secret place between her legs, and found, too, how shamelessly open and damp she was for him there.

"Oh, *mon Dieu*," she murmured helplessly as he eased a finger inside, teasing and readying her at the same time as the pleasure swirled faster through her body. "Oh, Zach, what are you doing to me?"

"Loving you, sweetheart," he said, his voice sounding raw and strained. "The way I promised I would. It's what you want, isn't it?"

She was gasping, crying, her body shaking and so tight she feared she'd explode, and then in an instant she did, the pleasure sweeping over her with such force that she collapsed on his chest, dazed with joy. He shifted beneath her, and in some distant way she realize he'd pulled off his breeches.

"We've only just started, sweetheart," he said, his voice ragged with restraint as he moved her down, lifting her, easing her legs apart as he moved himself in place. But it wasn't his fingers now, and too late she remembered what she'd only glimpsed before, and then he was inside of her, hard and hot and stretching her so wide she cried out with startled pain.

"There now, Amelie, it's done," he said, holding her

close as he let her grow accustomed to the feel of him. "My own brave lass, it's done."

But it wasn't done, not by half. The pain was already easing, and tentatively she began to move, raising herself to let him slide almost free, then easing back down to bury him deep. It felt different then when he'd caressed her, different but better, too, and when he groaned she realized that he liked it as well.

"Am I doing this right?" she asked breathlessly, taking him deeper.

"Damned right you are," he said through clenched teeth as he bucked his hips up to meet hers.

She found his rhythm then, his fingers digging deep into her hips to guide her, and she felt the pleasure building again, deeper and stronger because she shared it with him, until she tensed and cried out his name and the whole world shattered around her, the stars and moon falling free with her joy.

They lay still together for a long time afterward, her cheek on his chest where she could hear the steady rhythm of his heartbeat, neither wishing to break the magic of the moment.

At last she pushed herself up to kiss him, her lips barely grazing across his. *"Je t'aime,"* she murmured. "Oh, how I love you."

"I love you, too." Tenderly he reached up to brush away a damp wisp of her hair from her forehead. "And I'm glad you came here tonight."

She smiled crookedly, wishing the moment would last forever. "I had to help you launch your bunk."

He smiled back, tracing the outline of her lips with his finger. "Then marry me, Amelie," he whispered. "And soon, before I'm too old for any more of these launchings."

She chuckled deep in her throat, and kissed him again. "You make it sound as if I don't have a choice."

"That's because you don't," he said. "Not after this."

"No?" she asked, chuckling again so he could feel the vibration deep inside her where they still were joined.

"No, you won't marry me?"

"No, I didn't say no," she answered. "But yes, I will. Marry you, that is. *Mon Dieu*, but English makes everything so complicated!"

In one easy move he rolled her over onto her back, taking her shrieking with him.

"Then perhaps," he said as he began to move with her again, "before you're plain English Mrs. Fairbourne, you'd better show me how you'd do this in French."

She obliged, happily. And afterward he thanked the heavens that she was so wonderfully fluent in both.

❧ 16 ❧

$\mathscr{S}$he was surprised to find the house dark and empty.

True, Juliette had spent the day with Anabelle and little Diana, but Amelie had expected her back soon after supper. Yet once she lit the candlestick, she could see the note she'd left about going to the *Diana* was still on the table, the plate with the slice of cherry pie still covered by the checkered napkin.

"Julie?" she called up the staircase. It was possible that her sister had already gone to bed. "Julie, are you home?"

"I'll wager she's still with Anabelle," said Zach, coming up behind her to slip his hands around her waist and kiss the nape of her neck. "Anabelle does make people forgetful. And if she is, then that means we're here alone, doesn't it?"

Amelie giggled, letting herself savor his touch for a second before she pulled away. "I have to be sure, Zach," she said, curling her hair behind her ear. "I don't want her to have to find us like she did before."

He grinned wolfishly, and before she was tempted she ran up the stairs to the bedchamber.

"Juliette, are you here?" she called. Luna trotted out to meet her with a chirp of hello, and Amelie bent to rub the cat's head. "Juliette?"

She'd already begun to turn to go back downstairs when she caught sight of the dark shadow on her sister's pillow. Amelie raised the candlestick so the light would fall across the bed, and the shadow became another of the leather bags, lumpy with coins. But this one couldn't have been tossed in the window, for the window was shut and latched and unbroken.

Someone had been in the house, in this room, standing over their bed. Someone who hadn't had to force his way in.

"Zach!" she called frantically as she set down the candlestick to tear open the leather pouch to find the note she knew must be inside. "Zach, oh, Zach, come quick!"

Your sister is mine now, you foolish whore.
Why didn't you leave when you could?

But Zach didn't answer, and as soon as she raced down the stairs, her heart pounding with fear for her sister, she saw the reason why.

He was standing in the middle of the back room, the door thrown open behind him, the raw pine of the new steps pale in the moonlight. In his hand was a pistol she'd never known he'd owned, the hammer cocked and the long barrel gleaming as it thrust into the back of another man, bent over their worktable with his arms spread. She gasped, and the man looked up.

"Amelie," rasped Oliver Richardson. "What the hell has happened?"

"That's an excellent question, Richardson," said Zach, his expression set and hard as he gave the other man a shove for good measure. "What the hell were you doing out there, anyway?"

"I could ask the same of you, Fairbourne!" protested Oliver indignantly, twisting around as far as he could to glare at Zach. "Since when do I have to account to you for anything, considering that—"

"Juliette's gone," interrupted Amelie, holding the note out for Zach to read. "They say they have her, Zach, and oh—oh, I know it's my fault!"

"It's not your fault at all, sweetheart," muttered Zach as he concentrated on the note. "But damnation, how did they get to her? The door hasn't been forced, the windows are shuttered, and I know Anabelle would have had one of her footmen search the house before she left your sister here."

Amelie knew she must not cry—tears wouldn't help them find Juliette—but she was so frightened for her sister's sake that it took all her willpower not to give in. Seeing how comfortable Zach was with a gun in his hand didn't help, either. How could the world have toppled so completely in so short a time?

"It must have been someone Juliette knows, Zach," she said, struggling to think straight, "someone she knew well enough that she'd open the door."

Zach stared pointedly down at Oliver. "What about you, Richardson? Would Miss Lacroix have unlocked her door for you?"

"Zach, please, put the pistol down," said Amelie. "You can't expect him to answer your questions when you've got a gun jabbed in his ribs like that."

"Here, here," said Oliver weakly. "Listen to the lady, Fairbourne."

With a sigh Zach uncocked the gun and raised it, resting the barrel back against his own shoulder. "Only because Amelie wishes it, Richardson. Now tell me what you know about Miss Lacroix."

Oliver straightened and faced them, pausing briefly to smooth both his cuffs and his dignity. "Juliette— Miss Lacroix—is a special friend of mine. Beyond that I'm sworn to say no more."

"Oliver, please," begged Amelie. "Can your secret be worth more than Juliette's life?"

"No. Juliette's been too good a friend to me for that." He frowned, considering his words. "These last weeks she's helped me arrange a, ah, certain complicated personal matter, and now that it's, ah, nearly resolved, I'd come here tonight to thank her. I certainly pray she's unharmed, for she's been an angel to me."

Zach listened suspiciously. "What kind of personal matter?"

"Because it involves another, I'd rather not—"

"For Julie's sake, Oliver," said Amelie. "Please."

Oliver sighed deeply. "On the early morning tide tomorrow, I will have the honor of sailing from Boston with the one woman in the world that I love with all my heart, Miss Elisabeth Drummer, who has agreed to be my wife."

"*Betsey?*" repeated Amelie, stunned. There might be more unlikely couples in Boston, but she'd have difficulty naming them. Ruddy-faced, quiet Betsey with Oliver, the extrovert peacock: who would have thought it?

Yet even Oliver Richardson might have been changed by love, and as Amelie watched him she realized his clothing was less garishly extreme, that he stood straighter and that his manner and speech seemed less affected. In other words, he'd finally begun to grow up, and his beloved Betsey must be the reason.

"Yes, Betsey," said Oliver, clearly wounded by Amelie's response. "She's the sweetest, dearest girl I've ever known, but because her father was a butcher in Old England, Father would never agree to the match, and neither, therefore, would her father, for he won't be able to squeeze a farthing from my father. So with dear Juliette's help, my Betsey and I will be sailing together for Nassau."

He shook his head sadly. "Poor Juliette. After all she's done for us, I'll do whatever I can to help her."

In an instant, a half-dozen little mysteries resolved themselves for Amelie: the whispered meetings between her sister and Oliver, the furtive conversations in the fitting room with Betsey, the notes and letters hastily squirreled away. There could even be reason for Mrs. Drummer's behavior here, if she'd suspected Juliette of helping her daughter. But what touched Amelie was how eagerly Juliette, endlessly kind and hopelessly romantic, would have agreed to help such forbidden lovers, Juliette who believed so fervently in true love in the face of all of Maman's teachings.

And the other irony, of course, involved John Richardson. He'd worried that his son was involved in an dalliance with an unsuitable seamstress, when in reality what Oliver was doing would be far, far worse in his father's eyes: marrying for love, not for profit. For that alone Amelie felt they deserved a long and happy life together.

"Of course I wish you joy with your lady-love, Oliver," said Zach impatiently. "But none of this is helping us find Juliette."

Rubbing her temples, Amelie began to reconsider the few facts they had. "It had to be someone she knew because of the doors, and it had to be someone who knows *us* because they put the note and the pouch of coins on Juliette's pillow."

"The same number of guineas as before?" asked Zach.

Amelie held the pouch in her hand, judging its weight. "I haven't counted, but I'd say that—"

"Let me see that, Amelie," said Oliver suddenly, reaching for the bag, "if you please, of course."

Unceremoniously Oliver dumped the guineas out into a glinting pile on the table, ignoring them in favor of the pouch. Quickly he turned the rough bag inside out, running his fingers along the seams and the thong that had laced the top shut.

"I know this will sound odd," he said, "but I can almost guarantee that this bag is connected to my father. Among his ventures, he once ran a gristmill, until he suspected the miller of cheating him and sent the man away. He never bothered replacing him—not enough money to be made in milling, I suppose—so the whole place is tumbled-down, or was last I heard."

"And the pouch, Oliver?" asked Amelie. His story of the mill was interesting enough, but again she failed to see the connection with Amelie, and they didn't have time to waste.

"They were one of my father's special inventions to prevent cheats," said Oliver with the scorn he seemed to reserve for his father, and which, realized Amelie, his father had used when mentioning *him*. "The miller had taken one of his milling tricks stitching the meal and flour bags a half-inch narrower all around so they looked fat and full, even if they're not and tried to apply it to the cloth bags of coins he sent back to my father's counting house. Father had special leather pouches made so he'd have to be honest.

Zach leaned closer with excitement. "And you're sure these are the same pouches?"

"I should be," said Oliver. "I was always trying to steal an empty one from the mill myself when I was a boy, to put marbles in. And can you see these backward stitches? Father hired an old one-eyed Wampanoug to make the pouches, and this is the sort of seam he made. But how this came from Father's old mill to here—"

"Because your father sent it," said Amelie, her voice taut with guilt and grief. "Because he kidnapped Juliette. He thought you were running away with her, Oliver, not Betsey. He came here to me to ask me to help today, and instead I sent him away. And now he's taken Juliette."

Everything made sense now, hideous, wrongheaded sense. The notes John Richardson had sent damning her as a whore were not aimed so much at her, but at her mother, the anger shifting from one generation to the next, the way it had with him this afternoon. Because he'd been unable to control her mother as much as he'd wanted, he was trying again now with her and Juliette. Even the gold guineas made sense, coming as they did from one of the few men in town who could afford to throw such sums away.

It made sense, yes. But when Amelie thought of her sister in Richardson's hands, her blood turned to ice.

Furious, Zach struck his fist down hard on table. "Damnation, Richardson can't do this! Kidnapping, threats, destroying your property, even setting that fire! He cannot do it!"

"Lud, my father does them all the time," said Oliver with long-practiced resignation. "Or rather he hires the men who will. If he did kidnap Juliette, then I'd wager these same guineas that he's keeping her at the mill, too. Father likes his symmetry nearly as much as he likes getting his own way. If you wish, I'll take you there."

"Then hurry, Richardson," said Zach as he slipped his arm around Amelie's shoulders, holding her close. "We've wasted enough time here already."

"Well enough." Oliver looked at the pistol still in Zach's hand. "And if I were you, Fairbourne, I'd bring that as well."

The windmill stood high on a hill overlooking the water, facing to the east and the sea where the wind would blow the hardest. But even by the light of the half moon, Amelie could see that many years had passed since any wind had caught these blades to turn the grinding stones within. Most of the shingles had been torn from the six sloping sides of the mill, and the ones that remained were split or sloping, with the bare battens of the frame left exposed to weather.

The mill's four long blades, their spokes as thick as the tree trunks they once had been, still stood at their four-cornered places, but the thinner slats along the blade that had supported the sails were snapped off and jagged, like broken rungs on a ladder, and the white canvas sails that once had spun so briskly in the ocean breezes had long since torn away and disintegrated. Not even the ropes that once had lashed the blades to the ground-posts for safety in a gale or at night remained.

Brambles and tall beach grasses grew all around the

foundation, and the path that had once been wide enough for a farmer's cart of grain was now a barely noticeable trace. Once the mill would have bustled with activity, a center for gossip and gathering as well as grinding corn, rye, and wheat, but now the only sounds on the lonely hillside came from the countless crickets in the grasses, the distant rush of the waves, and the faint, low-pitched groan of the old wooden machinery as it shifted with the wind.

"I don't like this place," whispered Amelie, her hand tight in Zach's as they crouched down behind the cluster of large rocks at the base of the hill. "It scares me!"

"That's the point of a good hiding place, lass," he whispered in return. "You want a spot that everyone else will avoid like the plague."

Amelie shivered, more with dread than with any chill. "Poor Juliette, to be trapped in such a place!"

"Better to hope that she *is* in there," said Zach, checking the powder and flint in his pistol. "Because if she's not, we don't have the slightest notion where to look next."

"Someone's been here," said Oliver to Zach, pointing up the hill, "and they didn't particularly care who knew it, either. A team of oxen couldn't have trampled that grass more thoroughly."

"Ready, then, Richardson?"

Oliver nodded, and the two of them headed up the path, keeping low and taking care to make as little sound as they could moving though the sweeping grasses.

"Wait," hissed Amelie as she bounded up after them. "I'm coming too!"

Zach stopped. "You can't come, sweetheart. It's too

dangerous. I want you back there, where I'll know you'll be safe."

"And I want to be with you to know that *you're* safe, too," she pleaded. "Please, Zach. She's my sister."

He groaned, but held his hand out to her, and together the three of them hurried toward the mill. The front door was windowless and likely barred from within, but to the left was one high, small casement, the plank shutter faintly outlined by a tiny line of lantern light from inside. Silently Zach pointed up at the casement, and Oliver nodded.

"Lift me up," whispered Amelie. "If I stand on your shoulders, I'll be able to look in."

The two men exchanged such exasperated glances that she felt sure they'd refuse, but instead Zach shoved the pistol in the back of his belt and bent with his hands linked together like a step for her. She'd never been particularly good at climbing, but for Juliette's sake and with considerable help from Zach, she managed finally to stand, wobbling like a third-rate acrobat, on his shoulders and at the perfect level to peer inside.

Three bored men, sailors from the look of them, sat on the floor in the light of a single lantern, throwing dice. And off to one side, perched on the bottom step of the ladder to the millstones with her hands tied at the wrist and her head bowed in misery, sat Juliette.

Frantically Amelie waved her hand, motioning Zach to let her down. "Julie's in there," she hissed. "With three men to guard her."

Zach looked up, shoving her skirts away from his face, where they'd been blown by the wind. It was not a ladylike position for Amelie to be in, but after all they'd done together on the *Diana*'s bunk earlier that evening, she supposed she and Zach were well past such considerations. "What?" he mouthed silently.

"Juliette," she whispered again, pointing to the window. "In there."

He shook his head, still unable to make out her words, and Amelie leaned forward a fraction to try to make him understand. But that was a fraction too much for their tenuous balance, and abruptly Amelie felt herself begin to pitch forward, toward the mill. She shrieked with fear, grabbing the windowsill to catch herself, and realized that her feet were no longer resting to Zach's shoulders, but instead were flailing against the cracked shingles.

"Zach!" she cried wildly as she clung desperately to the window sill. "Zach, where are you?"

But when she looked down over her shoulder, it wasn't Zach's face she found peering up at her, or even Oliver's, but instead one of the sailors she'd seen inside. And worst of all, he was obviously enjoying the view from below.

"Well now, missy," he said heartily as he grabbed her by the ankles. "Lookin' for a bit o' company, are you?"

"Let me go!" she shouted, trying to kick him away, but he'd already too firm a grasp on her leg, neatly peeling her from the wall to tumble into his arms. What, she wondered desperately, had become of Zach and Oliver?

"Let me *go!*" she shouted again, fighting to free herself. But instead the man calmly pinned her hands together and pushed her before him into the mill, kicking the door shut behind him.

"Look 'ee what I found outside, mates," he said as

he bound her hands together. "Now we got us a pair, don't we? Pretty little things, too."

"Amelie!" cried Juliette, shifting into French so that the men wouldn't understand. "What are you doing here? How did they catch you, too?"

"I was supposed to be rescuing you," answered Amelie in French as well as the first man led her to the same ladder, tying her rope to Juliette's and looping the end around one of the rungs to tether her there. "Get away from me, you ugly goat!"

"I think she fancies you, Tom," said the man, with a coarse laugh. He was younger than the other two, scarce more than a boy, and eager to impress them with his bluster. "We're not being paid to keep her, you know, so maybe we can see if you fancy her, too."

Tom's grin, framed by his beard, was missing an eyetooth. "Mayhap we will at that, Timothy," he said as he reached out to squeeze Amelie's thigh. "You wait here, dolly. I've got to make sure there's no more of you outside, but then we can try some tricks together, eh?"

He reached for one of the two muskets propped by the door and ambled outside, leaving the other men behind with the dice.

"If Tom don't come back," said Timothy, puffing out his thin chest, "then the dark chit's mine."

"Why are we here, Amelie?" whispered Juliette, again in frantic French. "Why would these men want us?"

"It's not them, but Mr. Richardson," she whispered back. "He's been responsible for it all."

"Mr. Richardson!" Juliette gasped. "But that was why I opened the door! The man said they'd a special message from Mr. Richardson, but I thought they meant Oliver!"

"His father," said Amelie grimly. "He thinks you meant to elope with Oliver, and this is his way of stopping it."

She paused, listening for signs of a fight from outside. She hated the thought of Zach outside somewhere in the dark, his pistol facing Tom's musket. "Oliver came here with Zach and me. He told us all about what you've done for him and Betsey, and he blames himself for what has happened tonight. He insisted he come help. Not, of course, that any good's coming from it."

The single gunshot echoed across the fields, and Amelie gasped as Juliette reached out to squeeze her hand.

Not Zach, please, please, dear God, let it not be Zach, not the only man I'll ever love!

The third man sighed, stacking the dice in his palm before he handed them to Timothy. "Wasn't supposed to be no shooting tonight," he said wearily. "Not enough brass in it for that. But I best go see what kind of coney Tom's caught, or if he just managed to shoot his own fool head off instead."

He took the other musket, slamming the door after him. Timothy rose and stretched his arms over his head as he leered at the two women.

"Now, isn't this snug?" he said. "Two o' you, and one o' me. Agreeable odds, I'd say."

Amelie glared at him as ferociously as she could, refusing to be intimidated no matter how much she feared for Zach. She hated being here with this man, and hated more not knowing what was happening outside. Beside her Juliette huddled close, and for her sake, too, Amelie was determined to be brave.

Be brave, lass, Zach had told her. Be brave for me.

Oh, Zach, my one true love . . .

She jumped at the next gunshot, followed by a man's muffled cry of pain and surprise, then one more shot after that.

"Amelie?" said Juliette, and from her voice alone Amelie could tell she was crying. She didn't want to look, for if she did, she knew she'd cry, too.

Please God, not Zach . . .

But at that second shot, Timothy decided that he'd heard enough, his own fear plain on his thin freckled face.

"Up you go, you stupid chits," he ordered, twisting the rope that bound them around his wrist as he jerked Amelie and Juliette to their feet. "Up, I say, or I'll beat you until you do."

In his hand the man held a crude cudgel as thick as Amelie's wrist, and from the bullying look in his eyes as well as the knife in a sheath at his waist she decided not to test him.

"Come along, Julie," she said, clumsily gathering her skirts to climb the ladder. "Better to do as he says for now."

"I hate him," sobbed Juliette as she awkwardly followed. "I hate them all!"

Slowly they climbed the zigzagging ladder inside the mill, Timothy jabbing the stick at their legs when he felt they'd slowed. But though Amelie strained her ears to listen to what was happening outside, she heard no more cries, no more gunshots, nothing beyond the creaks and groans of the old mill itself.

Finally they reached the top of the ladders, to the small upper floor where the massive windshaft that held the blades entered the mill. Timothy set the lantern on the floor and, using the cudgel as a lever, he pried the long door beside the windshaft open, swinging it outward with a shuddering creak. One of the blades stood poised directly outside, swaying gently back and forth, and beyond it Amelie could just make out the moon. She guessed they must be at least twenty feet high, maybe thirty, though the hillside made it seem higher still.

"Almost like bein' in the foretop, isn't it?" said Timothy as he leaned from the window with a sailor's fearlessness of heights. "You two should come closer, to see the moon."

Roughly he jerked their rope, hard enough to make Juliette stumble and fall forward with a plaintive cry to the plank floor.

"Look what you've done!" cried Amelie furiously as she knelt beside her sister. "She never hurt you, did she?"

"Shut your mouth," warned Timothy, "or when Tom and Parker get back I'll learn you what really hurts."

Deftly he flung the end of the rope over the top of the windshaft, then wrapped it around one of the posts supporting the roof. He threw his weight behind the rope to drag the two women closer to the open door, their hands over their heads while their heels scrabbled vainly across the floor.

"Don't look down," ordered Amelie as she tried to shield Juliette's eyes. Zach had told her that, too, and he'd been right. But, oh, they'd come so dangerously near to the open door, and the yawning drop beyond! If Zach looked up from outside—if Zach *could* look up—he'd see them framed there in the opening like some macabre millinery display.

Timothy cackled as he tied the rope tight. "That should keep you two for—"

But all three of them jerked around at the sound of

the door opening downstairs, thrown back with a violent thud that made Amelie gasp.

"That you, Tom?" called Timothy anxiously as he began inching down the stairs into the dark, the cudgel raised in his hands. "Tom, that you?"

But though the silence stretched longer, and longer still, none of them doubted that someone was waiting down in the dark. The only question was who.

"Tom?" asked Timothy, taking another step as he searched through the gloom. "You there, Tom?"

But as he craned his neck to peer below the rail, a large black shadow lunged up from below, driving him backward up the steps. Timothy landed hard on his back, the cudgel flying from his hand as he skidded across the floor. The other man scrambled up the steps to follow and into the light of the lantern, a spent pistol held with the clublike butt backward as a weapon in his hand.

"Zach!" cried Amelie, her joy at seeing him alive tempered by the terrible danger he was in now. At the sound of her voice Zach glanced up swiftly and grinned, and in that instant Timothy pulled his knife and crouched down low, poised to strike.

Zach tossed the pistol thumping down the stairs behind him and drew his own knife. Slowly the two men circled the narrow room, their long-bladed seaman's knives ready in their hands. With an animal growl, Timothy was the first to jump forward, slashing wildly in Zach's direction. But Zach had the advantages of size and experience. Again and again he dodged Timothy's knife, letting the smaller man tire himself before at last Zach flew forward and struck the other man's wrist, his knife skittering away, behind Zach.

"Let it go, boy," said Zach as he carefully approached

Timothy, his hand outstretched. "This wasn't your quarrel. Don't pay for it."

Timothy was panting from fear and exertion, his freckled face glistening with sweat and his eyes bulging with the terror of a cornered animal. But just as Zach had nearly reached him, Timothy suddenly twisted around and grabbed Juliette by the waist and held her close. As she whimpered, he balanced on the very edge of the window, one foot on the windshaft itself.

"Your choice, mate," he shouted wildly at Zach. "You let me go free, with a fair start, or I'll take the lass with me, too!"

Amelie froze, her heart constricting with terror as the rope that tied her to her sister tightened. If Timothy lost his balance and fell, then he would take all of them to their deaths.

"Mon Dieu, no," she whispered against the wickedness of fate, and sought Zach's gaze for what could be the last time. He looked at her helplessly, striving to put into that single look a lifetime of things they might never get to say.

"Your choice," said Timothy again, his voice crazily triumphant. "You decide, mate."

"For the love of God!" wailed an anguished voice from the ground below. "For mercy's sake, let my daughter go free!"

Startled, Timothy turned to look down. As he did, he began to slip, and let Juliette go to seize the big blade before him for support. But instead of holding firm, the blade began slowly to spin beneath Timothy's weight, stretching him farther and farther from his perch on the windshaft, until at last he dropped. His scream as he fell echoed through the night, to end with a horrifying abruptness.

"Juliette!" cried Amelie as she and Zach together pulled her sister back inside to safety and into her arms. "Oh, Juliette!"

"Oh, Amelie," murmured Zach as he cut the cords at her wrists to hug her close. "If I'd lost you then—oh, Jesus, love!"

"Juliette!" came the same ragged, anguished voice from the ground, more a plea than a shout. "Juliette!"

Over Zach's shoulder, past the slowly spinning blade, Amelie saw two men standing together, their faces turned towards the mill, one young and straight, the other bent and dressed in black, son and father. As John Richardson glimpsed her, he gave an oddly strangled cry and sank backward, his hand pressed over his heart.

"*Mon Dieu,*" she murmured, pulling away from Juliette and Zach. "Not like this, please, not even for him."

"What is it, love?" asked Zach, fresh concern on his face.

"I must go to him," she said. She knew she owed him nothing, nothing by blood or right or law, yet still she ran down the steps and out the door, through the swaying tall grass to where Oliver was sitting with his father's head in his lap.

With his wig fallen back to the grass, John Richardson's skull-like face was ashen in the moonlight, his breath coming in tight, tortured wheezes, his features so contorted by pain that Amelie knew, just as Oliver did, that the only release would come with death.

Amelie knelt beside him, taking his icy, gnarled hand in hers. His eyes had already begun to glaze, but when he realized she was there with a great effort he managed to fight back.

"You and your sister," he whispered, his lips barely forming the words. "You were not supposed to suffer."

"We didn't," said Amelie gently, for compared to what he was suffering now, they hadn't. "We're fine."

He clutched convulsively at her hand. "I had to do it. I could not let such—such a terrible sin happen to those I love."

"Don't vex yourself, Father," said Oliver, his voice breaking as he awkwardly patted his dying father's hand. "Everything is well enough now."

The old man tried to smile. "Now, yes. But if you had laid with her, no, no. She is my daughter, too, my blood, my flesh, as are you. Pretty Jeannne Lacroix. I loved her, you know, but she wouldn't love me back, not the way I wanted. She would never let me forget I'd already a wife and children, no matter how much I loved her."

Stunned, Oliver looked to Amelie for explanation, but Amelie only shook her head. She felt Zach come to kneel beside her, and Juliette, too, her face full of confusion as she huddled beside Oliver.

"What is he saying, Amelie?" she asked, her voice quavering with uncertainty and panic. "What about our Papa? How can I be *his* daughter?"

Amelie felt Zach's arm slip across her shoulders giving her the strength she needed to face this. Love was like that, she marvelled as she sadly looked down into the dying man's face. But then she'd been lucky enough to find her true love in Zach, lucky and blessed in a way that too many others never would be, in a way she must never forget.

"I loved her," whispered John Richardson, his voice fading further away, his eyes flickering with the last desperate need to tell, to confess. "I loved her . . ."

Swiftly Amelie pulled off the ring that her mother had always worn, the garnet ring that John Richardson had given her so long ago, and pressed it into his palm, folding his fingers closed over it.

"Love never dies," she whispered fiercely, her tears falling on the hands holding the ring that carried the same message. "True love never dies."

She felt the circle of Zach's arms tighten around her as the old man's eyes closed, felt the matchless warmth and promise of Zach's love for her.

"Never, Amelie," he said softly. "As long as I live and after, I will never stop loving you."

And as she twisted around to bury her face against his chest, to seek the comfort only he could give, her heart knew the meaning of eternity.

❦ Epilogue ❦

Martinique
Windward Islands

*T*he sun had finally dropped below the horizon and into the shimmering calm of the Caribbean, and the breeze that filled the sails of the *Diana* was as gentle and sure as a lover's caress. At the helm stood handsome Captain Zachariah Fairbourne, at his side his beautiful wife, Amelie, and cradled in her arms, with her head resting on Amelie's shoulder, slept an enormous gray cat.

It was, thought Zach, as pretty a picture of blissful love and contentment as he'd ever imagined. Except, perhaps, for the cat.

"I think, love, that Luna needs to go below," he said as he gazed out across the water.

Amelie looked down at the cat in her arms. "She seems content enough."

"Very well, then," said Zach. "I think she needs to go below."

"Ah, that is a difference, *mon cher*, isn't it?" Amelie bent to set the cat on the deck, where she arched her back to wake and stretch and then trotted off toward the companionway.

"I think Luna does quite well with her sea legs," said Amelie as she slipped her arm affectionately around Zach's waist, the curve of her hip pressing gently against him. "She's made quite an excellent ship's cat, don't you think?"

"She made an excellent shopcat, too," said Zach with a sigh of resignation. "I'm sure she would be of even greater use to Juliette in Boston."

Amelie twisted around to face him. "You've grown fond enough of Luna. Truly. You can pretend otherwise, but I've seen how she curls next to you on the bunk, and how you can't resist petting her in return, as if you two were the oldest of friends."

"Once in a great while," he said unapologetically, though they both knew what she said was true. He and Luna had reached a kind of truce, for Amelie's sake, and he'd have to admit that the cat hadn't drawn his blood for the entire time that they'd been at sea. "She is, I suppose, agreeable enough for a cat. And she does keep the rats at bay, doesn't she?"

"I told you she was useful. More useful, certainly, than to Juliette." Her thoughts turned inward, her eyes sad, and Zach knew she was thinking again of her sister. The days after John Richardson's death had been hard ones for all of them, but particularly for Juliette, who'd known nothing of Richardson's involvement with her mother. They'd never know for sure if John Richardson was truly her father, but no one doubted now that it had been love, both for Juliette and her mother, that had driven him to act as desperately as he had.

And to Oliver Richardson's credit, he had proved as good a friend to Juliette as she had been to him and Betsey Drummer, including her as much as he could in plans for the wedding. Having Amelie leave the shop in Juliette's hands had helped, too, and by the time Amelie and Zach had sailed, Juliette was already busy making grand improvements to *her* shop, proudly promising it would be even better than the one that Amelie was planning to open in Appledore.

"Juliette will be fine, lass," he said gently, pulling Amelie closer. "She's just as strong as you are, which is powerfully strong indeed."

"*Mais oui*, because we *are* sisters," said Amelie firmly, "and nothing can change that."

"Nothing should," he agreed, glad that she was finding her own peace, too. He leaned forward to kiss her, catching her charmingly by surprise. "I do love you, Mrs. Fairbourne."

"And I love you, Captain." She smiled, leaning back into the circle of his arms. "Look, there's the first star. Are you ready to make your wish?"

He followed her gaze to the first bright pinprick of light in the velvety twilight sky. "Nay, lass, I'll leave it to you."

She turned in surprise. "No wish?"

"No," he said, bending to kiss her again. "Because now that I have you, lass, I've nothing more left in this world to wish for."

❧ *Sunrise* ❧

Miranda Jarrett

*Coming soon from
Sonnet Books
Turn the page for a preview
of the wonderful sequel to
Moonlight*

❦ 1 ❧

Nantucket Island
September 1726

He could not keep away.

It was the season for hurricanes and nor'easters, cruel winds and devil-driven seas, for weather so wicked that any sane man would huddle close to his fire and thank the good Lord that he'd no need to move. But Daniel Fairbourne had long ago lost the blessing of an easy, reasonable mind, and on this black and howling night he once again bent his shoulders into the wind and walked the beach with all the grim purpose of a man driven by desperation.

Desperation—and guilt. He would never forget what had happened five years ago. Five years, three months, seventeen days, a handful of uncounted hours and minutes, yet still the pain of his loss was as keen and sharp as it should be. As it *must* be.

No, he thought with every step, he would never forget.

He walked close to the water, his boots leaving deep prints in the wet, packed sand until the next wave curled and hissed his marks away, bits of foam clinging to the worn leather toes. He'd come this way so many times before that his feet knew the way, and his gaze stayed focused on the sea, searching the waves and moonless horizon with the glass-sided lantern in his hand.

He was a large man, in his prime, a blacksmith whose trade had made him the strongest man on the island. He realized that if he must labor so against this storm, then any poor unfortunate cast into the sea on such a night would surely perish before he could help. No one else would fault him if he turned back now. The wind sliced through his heavy coat, the cold cutting deep down to his bones, and the driven spray peppered his face like shards of salty ice, yet still he walked, still he searched.

Curving to the west, the beach grew rougher now, the waves breaking over the great granite rocks that marked Siasconnset. It was here that ships and sailors most often came to grief, confounded by the twisting currents of the shoals, and as Daniel climbed to the crest of the rocks, he held his lantern high, sweeping the flickering light over the shallow pebbled beach before him. Rocks, more rocks, a shattered cask, a limp mass of wrack-weed, and a tangled knot of tarred rope.

And the lifeless body of a woman.

As Daniel clambered down the rocks, he wondered if he'd imagined it, his grief playing cruel, false games with his conscience, but the closer he came the more he could see, and the heavier his own heart became in his chest.

The woman lay on her side on the stony beach where the waves had left her, her face turned away from him and her long, tangled hair streaming out behind. She was wrapped in a cloak of sodden red wool that clung to her like the shroud it had become, covering her, hiding her, except for one leg that lay bent at the knee, curled behind her. One small, pretty leg in a white stocking with three hearts embroidered in pink over the ankle and a half-tied striped garter trailing forlornly down the calf, a red-heeled shoe buckled high with a pinchbeck buckle that glittered in the lantern light.

A brave, saucy show for one small, still leg to make, thought Daniel sorrowfully, and far too brave to find death on a rocky Nantucket beach. Gently he pulled the cloak over the woman's leg, giving her back her decency as he murmured a little prayer for her soul.

He'd found sailors before, men like himself, but never had he come across a woman, and he hesitated before he turned her over. A woman was different, her suffering worse. No woman should have to know the terrors of drowning like this, and he dreaded seeing the face of one who had. He struggled to remind himself how he'd be sure that this lady would have a Christian burial, that her friends and family would know what had happened to her, that she wouldn't vanish into nothingness as if she'd never lived, the way his own wife had done.

His wife: his fair angel, his dearest love, his sweet, lovely Catherine, who had gone away forever and would never return from her sister's house in Bridgetown, not to him, not to anyone.

With a strangled sound deep in his throat, Daniel gently eased the woman onto her back. Her hands were bruised, her fingers scratched, and her nails torn; clearly she'd fought to save herself, and he wondered what had become of the others on her ship.

He set the lantern beside her head and, pulling off

his glove, he carefully, almost tenderly, swept the tangle of wet hair from her face. Her skin was icy beneath his fingertips, bluish pale except for the angry bruises left from the stones, and he swore softly when he saw how young she was. Nineteen, he guessed, twenty-two at most, and far, far too young to die. Her face belonged with that fancy stocking and striped garter, a merry face fashioned for beguiling rather than pure beauty, with full cheeks that he'd wager would have dimpled when she'd smiled and a generous mouth with a tiny mole near one corner, as if pointing the way for a kiss, a kiss that, now, would never come.

"Poor little lady," said Daniel softly, bending close to shield her from the wind. "What was your name, I wonder?"

He thought it was a trick of the lantern's flicker across her face, the way she seemed to shudder, her brows twitching as if she were waking from a dream. Then suddenly her eyes fluttered open, blue eyes that were large and bright and very much alive, and very much startled to find him to close.

"Juliette," she gasped, her voice raw and rasping. "My name is Juliette. But oh, *mon Dieu*, who are you?"

**Look for *Sunrise*
by Miranda Jarrett
Coming in 2000 from Sonnet Books**

Read all of the thrilling romances from Sonnet Books

Linda Lael Miller

SPRINGWATER SEASONS

- ○ **Rachel** 02684-4/$3.99
- ○ **Savannah** 02685-2/$3.99
- ○ **Miranda** 02686-0/$3.99
- ○ **Jessica** 02687-9/$3.99

MIRANDA JARRET

- ❑ **Wishing** 00341-0/$6.50
- ❑ **Moonlight** 03261-5/$6.50

Victoria Malvey

- ○ **Enchanted** 02071-4/$6.50

Geralyn Dawson

- ❑ **The Kissing Stars** 01518-4/$6.50

Stef Ann Holm

- ○ **Hooked** 01941-4/$6.50

JO-ANN POWER

- ❑ **Never Say Never** 02422-1/$6.50

UNDER THE BOARDWALK

Linda Howard, Geralyn Dawson,
Jillian Hunter, Mariah Stewart,
and Miranda Jarrett

**A DAZZLING COLLECTION OF ALL-NEW
SUMMERTIME LOVE STORIES**

○ **Under the Boardwalk**
Coming in July 1999

Kimberly Cates

❑ **Briar Rose** (now available) 01495-1/$6.50

Laura Lee Guhrke

○ **Breathless** Coming in July 1999

Andrea Kane

❑ **The Gold Coin** Coming in August 1999

Tracy Fobes

○ **Heart of the Dove** Coming in August 1999